IRON GARLAND

ALSO BY JEFF WHEELER

The Harbinger Series

Storm Glass

Mirror Gate

The Kingfountain Series

The Poisoner's Enemy (prequel)

The Maid's War (prequel)

The Queen's Poisoner

The Thief's Daughter

The King's Traitor

The Hollow Crown

The Silent Shield

The Forsaken Throne

The Legends of Muirwood Trilogy

The Wretched of Muirwood

The Blight of Muirwood

The Scourge of Muirwood

The Covenant of Muirwood Trilogy

The Banished of Muirwood

The Ciphers of Muirwood

The Void of Muirwood

The Lost Abbey (novella)

Whispers from Mirrowen Trilogy

Fireblood

Dryad-Born

Poisonwell

Landmoor Series

Landmoor

Silverkin

the HARBINGER SERIES

JEFF WHEELER

Published by 47North, Seattle

www.apub.com

ISBN-13: 9781503903975
ISBN-10: 1503903974

Cover design by Mike Heath | Magnus Creative

Printed in the United States of America

To the real Raj Sarin

I was born in Averanche, a border town between Occitania, Ceredigion, and Leoneyis. Although my brother Jorganon was older, he lacked the imagination and ambition to lead the family. When Father died, that role fell on me. I knew I was Fountain-blessed by the time I was twelve. Always a voracious reader, I studied all the battles and strategies of the heroes of old: Owen Kiskaddon, the Maid of Donremy, and Tryneowy Llewellyn. But it was the rise of Gahalatine that stirred my soul the most. I volunteered to join every war I could find, for that is where honor and glory can be made.

When I was twenty-five, I was chosen to lead the army of the duchy of Occitania. I won back the duchy from the grip of Kingfountain and helped restore it to its former glory. It became a kingdom once again. As a reward, my king made me Duke of La Marche, the ancient title tied to Averanche. My further ambitions were thwarted by the hollow crown. I lacked the strength to topple their throne as well. But as the adage goes, the enemy of my enemy is my friend. There are more worlds to conquer than this one. So I staged a war between the worlds.

Glory may be fleeting. But obscurity . . . it lasts forever. I am determined that will not be my fate.

—Leon Montpensier, Duke of La Marche

PROLOGUE

Pavenham Sky

Mr. Clarence Skrelling worked as an advocate for the firm of Sloan and Teitelbaum in the disease-ridden slums of the Fells. He was an ambitious young man from humble origins and, not content with letting others be his master, had worked evenings to bolster his own private interests. Though the Fells became dangerous after dark, he knew the ways of the street gangs and had learned which neighborhoods to avoid. Clarence had taken upon himself a mission, a solemn duty, to unmask the identity of his true love's mother. His true love, Miss Cettie, had been educated with him at Muirwood Abbey, and she was now the keeper of the manor Fog Willows. Her guardians, the Fitzroys, hoped to adopt her, but no one at Sloan and Teitelbaum had managed to locate her mother, and her father refused to relinquish his claims to her without a sizable bribe. Clarence had visited Fog Willows at Whitsunday to apprise his ladylove of his progress. Or lack thereof. His heart churned with emotion when he thought of her, when he imagined how grateful she'd be upon learning he had at last discovered the truth of her illustrious parentage.

The zephyr he'd hired bobbed on an air current, causing him to grip the wooden bench more tightly. The weather was poor, and rain lashed at his cloak and dripped down his face. Unpleasant indeed, but he would not let a little storm prevent him from reaching his destination. His hat was tucked under his arm, or else it would have blown off the zephyr to be found by a peasant somewhere in the gloom below.

"Are we almost there?" he shouted to the zephyr's pilot. With the war going on, it had cost a small fortune to pay the fare. Of course, he'd haggled on the price, but every sky ship was a rare commodity now. Three years of war had changed the world. Well, *worlds* was a more accurate way of putting it. Their enemy, after all, lived on another world, accessible only through the mirror gates. Three years since passing the Test at Muirwood. Three years that had flown by faster than a zephyr.

"Eh?" the pilot shouted back.

"Are we almost there?"

"Are we not going fast enough for you, Mr. Skrelling? You did notice the storm, did you not?"

"My clothes are soaked through. No need to get cheeky." His impatience flared up, and he vowed to dock the man's pay a little for his impertinence.

"This is a fool's errand, if you don't mind me saying so," the pilot shouted.

"I'm not paying you for your wisdom," Clarence shot back. "How far are we from Pavenham Sky?"

"If that's what you wanted to know, you should have asked that from the start!"

"I did—oh, just answer me!" He realized the pilot was toying with him. Cheeky sod.

"We would have been there an hour ago were it not for this storm. I wish I could afford the storm warnings out of Fog Willows. Wouldn't have come if I'd known. Or I would have charged you more!"

I'm sure you would have tried, Skrelling thought darkly. "Well? How far off are we?"

"Eh?"

"How far off are we?" he shouted back more firmly. The wind was truly a monster. "I didn't ask what time we *would* have arrived. I want to know when we will."

The pilot was silent. Had he even heard the question? Wiping the rain from his face, Clarence shivered and waited for a response. Confound it, would he have to repeat himself again?

"See those lights up yonder?" the pilot called back to him.

Squinting, Clarence looked and shook his head. "I see nothing."

"Of course you don't, cuz you're sitting down there. If you were to stand, you'd see it. That's Pavenham Sky up ahead."

Clarence rose unsteadily to his feet, gripping the side railing to balance himself. He trembled with cold and the misery of sodden clothes, but he saw a glimpse of the floating manor. Another jolt from the zephyr, and his heart jumped as he lurched against the side of the sky ship. The pilot practically cackled with mirth as Clarence slunk back down onto the seat, an angry scowl on his face.

Within a quarter hour, they rose to the grand estate. Clarence had never been there before. No, someone of his station would never have merited an invitation from Lady Corinne of Pavenham Sky. She hosted only the most glamorous guests.

The stinging rain in his face made it difficult to see the details of the main building itself, but he squinted and tried to make it out. Yes, the manor was more opulent than any he had seen. It was an impressive display of wealth and power. Lady Corinne's husband, he knew, was off fighting in the war. The lady herself had another manor in Lockhaven, of course, but his sources had all indicated he'd find her here in Pavenham.

The pilot came to the landing yard, where at least two tempests were moored below. There was enough space to land a dozen more. The squall had veiled the sun and brought an early dusk, but a few Leerings glowed on the grounds, the eyes of the stone faces casting enough light for him to make out the well-sculpted greenery.

"Here we are, an hour or more late, but we made it in one piece." The pilot sniffed and gazed longingly at the tempests, which were much larger and had more shelter from the elements for passenger and pilot.

"I will see if we can stay for the night," Clarence said, rising from his seat. He removed his hat from beneath his arm and brushed the droplets from it, but it was a hopeless task. His things were soaked.

The pilot gave him a mocking look. "You think you're even going to make it past the front door, man?" He snorted.

"I do indeed. I have news that Her Ladyship will want to know." Oh yes, he would get a room and a warm fire and perhaps even a change of clothes. Especially after risking his life to fly here on a zephyr.

The pilot didn't look convinced by Clarence's assurance. "Would you care to wager on that, sir? Three crowns says that they won't let you in."

Clarence bridled at the affront. He was not in the habit of taking idle bets like most of the young men in his station, who thought their chances were better in winning a fortune by luck. Not him. He meticulously saved as much of his income as he could. Some even called him a miser. He gave the pilot a nasty look and then went to the rope ladder and started to climb down. In a trice, he had walked the long landing platform and entered a courtyard leading to a set of double stairs that zigzagged up to the huge main doors. He hastily mounted the steps, aware of his shoes splashing in puddles along the way. The air had that delicious smell of fresh rain.

He arrived at the doorway, feeling it loom over him. The doors were massive. Rather than knock, he triggered the Leering set into the wall beside the doors. He delicately adjusted the hat on his head and waited. And waited.

Eventually the door opened, and a handsome man stood in the gap, peering at him in the gloom. He wore the livery of a servant, but it likely cost more than Clarence's expensive suit.

"Who the devil are you?" the man asked as if Clarence were the strangest sight he'd ever seen.

"I'm-I'm Mr. Skrelling of Sloan and Teitelbaum," he stammered, trying to steel himself. He gave the man a practiced air of disdain, standing with his hands clasped behind his back, trying to look formal and impressive despite his disheveled appearance.

The man, probably a butler, looked behind him. "Was your zephyr blown off course? Are you seeking shelter?"

"No, I am here deliberately. I seek an interview with Lady Corinne."

The man arched his eyebrows. He looked surprised by the audacity of the request. "She doesn't give *interviews*, sir. Are you with the gazette?"

"No, I said I was part of Sloan and Teitelbaum."

"I know you said it. But that doesn't make it true."

"My news is important enough to brave a storm on a zephyr," Clarence said. "Her Ladyship will want to hear what I have to say." He pursed his lips, then nodded at him. "Am I to stand here all night? I'm prepared to."

"No doubt you deserve to," replied the man. Then he opened the door wider and motioned for him to enter. A welcome invitation. Clarence stepped into the warmth of the inside corridor and closed the door behind him.

"Stay here," said the butler firmly. He then slipped through another door, leaving Clarence alone in the front entrance, gazing up at the high ceiling and the impressive decor. Clarence rocked on his heels a bit and then saw a woman in a gown appear at the balustrade. He recognized her instantly, and judging from the way she immediately started down the staircase, she recognized him too. It was the emperor's daughter, Sera Fitzempress.

"Mr. Skrelling?" she asked while still at a distance.

He had gone to school with her at Muirwood, and, indeed, she had been Miss Cettie's particular friend, but she'd left abruptly before the final Test. Soon afterward, she'd gotten caught up in a scandal that had tarnished her reputation. He hadn't made many inquiries, but he knew it had something to do with a young officer in the Ministry of War who had perished during one of the first skirmishes in the war with Kingfountain. Something about letters. She'd been sent here to Pavenham Sky to rehabilitate herself under Lady Corinne's tutelage.

As she approached, he noted that she had not grown any taller since the last time he'd seen her. Her face was rounder now, and she'd bloomed into a great beauty—albeit a short one.

"Greetings, Miss Fitzempress," he said with a bow.

She approached him and bowed her head, and he nodded back stiffly.

"What brings you, of all people, to Pavenham Sky?" she asked with genuine interest.

"A private matter," he replied enigmatically. In the past, he had volunteered much of what he learned through his sources. He'd since become more circumspect—information was power, after all. "It's good to see you again."

"I'm starving for news," Miss Fitzempress said eagerly. She glanced around. "Have you seen Cettie recently?"

"A few months ago, ma'am, but I hope to see her again shortly." Indeed, he *hoped* very much. How grateful would she be when she learned that Clarence, and Clarence alone, had discovered her true parentage? The giddiness inside of him wrenched his emotions like rope. *Say nothing. Reveal nothing.*

"Well, please tell her that I miss her very much. If there were any way that I could come to Fog Willows to see her, I would. I'd—"

The side door opened, and the butler reappeared. A wary look crossed his face when he saw Sera talking to Clarence.

"Hello, Master Sewell. This is just an old friend from Muirwood. You needn't be nervous. We've only spoken for a moment."

"Alone?" he said with a tone of remonstrance in his voice.

Miss Fitzempress took a step backward. "I see your point." Her eyes flashed with anger, but her tone was submissive. Clarence could tell she didn't like her prison very much, no matter how gilded.

"She will see you now," said Master Sewell, gesturing for Clarence to follow him. He obeyed and gave a curt nod to Sera.

"I'll pass along your regards," he said to her, and Miss Fitzempress flashed him a pretty smile.

He followed Master Sewell through a twisting series of corridors, probably reserved for the servant set, before arriving at a door. The butler knocked on it. Clarence heard no response, but Master Sewell turned the handle and pushed it open. It was the library. Bookshelves full of volumes lined the walls, and ladders were scattered around so visitors could reach the upper shelves. It was an impressive collection. Clarence followed the butler in and glanced at the stuffed chairs and the hearth shining with flames. A glass door at the far side of the room led to a veranda. Rain dripped down the transparent surface, reminding him of his own sorry condition. Clarence had been so deluged with rain he was still dripping on the carpets.

Master Sewell shut the door behind him, leaving him alone in the room. He took off his hat and held it in the crook of his arm. He tried to smooth the dripping hair from his forehead. Then a side door opened, and Lady Corinne entered.

Of course he recognized her instantly. He'd never met her before, but her face was famous throughout the empire. He'd seen its depiction in the gazettes. She was dressed in a beautiful teal gown with a fancy vest and a ruff of lace at her throat. The outfit wasn't adorned with any jewelry, but he shouldn't have expected to see any; this wasn't a ball or a party. She wore gloves that matched her gown, and her dark hair was done up elegantly. A stately woman in her early thirties in appearance, she had little expression or animation in her face, implying that her emotions were carefully guarded. He could still discern from her body language as she approached him that she felt a bit of wariness but no true concern. That would soon change.

"It must be important news to bring you here on a day like this, Mr. Skrelling," she said simply.

"Indeed, ma'am," he replied and then coughed into his fist.

She went to a small sofa and sat down, her hands folded primly on her lap. Her slightly inquisitive look conveyed a clear message. She would not have a conversation with him. She expected him to say his piece and depart.

"Thank you for agreeing to see me, ma'am. I'll dispense with idle chatter. I do not wish to waste your time." There was a flash of lightning from the storm outside, followed by a boom of thunder. The cloud cover swallowed any light, making it look like the middle of the night.

She didn't respond to his statement. Instead, she tilted her head patiently and waited.

"I'm here, ma'am, on behalf of a young woman I regard highly." He assumed the posture of his profession and began to pace slowly in the room, as if she were a judge he was arguing his case for. "My masters have for many years labored to discover the identity of Lord Fitzroy's ward so that he might adopt her legally. Her father's identity is one Mr. Pratt of the Fells. The mother's identity has been hidden for many years. Until now."

She revealed no expression of alarm or concern. He had carefully prepared his little speech in the hopes that she might betray something. She did not.

"You must discern, madame, that I would not be here if there was not incontrovertible proof that this child's mother is, in fact, Your Ladyship."

He inhaled deeply, searching her face. She had yet to reveal any emotion, but there was something in her eyes. Just a slight narrowing, an interest sparked. She was a master of self-control. Not even the stage performers in the City could have been so poised.

"And by what evidence do you make such a claim, Mr. Skrelling?"

Ah, she wished for him to play his cards first. She was keeping her secrets close, then. "I have made this search the focus of the last several years of my life, Lady Corinne. You know, as well as I do, how the Mysteries of Thought work. I have been relentless in my pursuit. I have eschewed failure and spurned setbacks. There are no birth records because she was never born in a hospital. She was born in secret. In shame. And so only the mother would know where or when. You were never a suspect because you appear to be so young. You would have needed to be at least twelve or thirteen years old nineteen years ago—unlikely but not impossible—and since you have no heir with Lord

Lawton, it would be logical to deduce that you are barren. But I did not solve this riddle through conjecture, Your Ladyship. Proof, as I said."

He paused, trying to see what effect his words had on her. She gazed at him with earnestness, hands still placid on her lap.

"In order to free my lady of her state of uncertainty, I needed proof," he continued. "Three years ago, while I was at school, there was an intruder at the abbey who attempted to kidnap Miss Cettie. Lord Fitzroy's youngest daughter was then abducted by the same man. One Caulton Forshee was sent for, from Billerbeck Abbey. He possesses a priceless device called the Cruciger orb, which has the power to find anything. Mr. Forshee used it to find both the girl and the attacker. All of this started the war we have now been fighting for three years. I visited Billerbeck Abbey, ma'am. I . . . used the Cruciger orb myself to answer the question that has tormented me for these many years. I know it's forbidden to use without the permission of the privy council, but Mr. Forshee was unaware that I used it." He swallowed. "It revealed your name to me, Lady Corinne. The rest I have pieced together myself. Young, but not impossibly so. A scandal of such proportion would undoubtedly rock the world. I've come to offer terms so that Miss Cettie can be legally adopted and your reputation preserved. As you no doubt know, even though she is legally an adult, the adoption can still be made official, provided an agreement is reached with one of the parents, the mother's side being the stronger. I will submit to a binding sigil that will forever prevent me from speaking of what I know. Not even Miss Cettie needs to learn the truth. Just you. And I." He gave her a slight nod. "She will be wealthy enough as one of Fitzroy's heiresses. I do not seek a claim to any of your property." He gestured to the grand library and, indirectly, to Pavenham Sky itself.

"What say you, my lady? Can we reach an agreement?"

Lady Corinne rose from the sofa. Her expression was still guarded, still calm. There was not a flush to her cheeks, no pout of regret. "Well, young man. Thank you for visiting me. You were very helpful indeed. My servant will escort you away."

Clarence flexed his brows. “M-ma’am?” he stuttered.

Then he felt an awareness, a plunging feeling of darkness and doubt. He saw Lady Corinne nod to someone else, and he whirled, expecting to see Master Sewell. He’d not heard the door open.

Another man approached him from behind, walking so quietly his steps couldn’t be heard. He looked more like a merchant than a servant, though the scar on his face gave him a rough appearance. Clarence recognized him instantly as the man he’d seen in Vicar’s Close. The one who had then kidnapped Miss Cettie and Anna Fitzroy. Panic and dread slithered down his spine. Clarence tried to bolt for the door, but the man seized him, twisting his arm behind his back, ignoring his flailing. His attacker then marched him to the veranda door.

Lady Corinne stared impassively at him as he gaped back at her. In a moment of clarity, he realized just how badly he had blundered. The man opened the veranda door wider and dragged Clarence out into the rear gardens. Rain lashed at them violently, and more thunder rippled in the sky. There were no groundskeepers out on a day like this. No witnesses.

“P-please, man!” Clarence wailed, trying to master his terror. “Let me go! I w-won’t . . . tell a soul!”

The man grunted and hauled him through the garden. Clarence’s shoes slipped on the grass, but the grip on his arm was merciless.

They reached the end of the gardens. There was a small wall, and Clarence could see the open sky beyond it.

“W-what are you d-doing?” he stammered.

They reached the edge of the wall. Clarence’s heart quailed. He couldn’t think. It was all happening too fast. He shouldn’t have come. He should have revealed the information to someone else to protect himself. In a misguided attempted to protect Lady Corinne’s honor, he’d duped himself into . . .

The scar-faced man hoisted him over the wall and shoved him off the side of the manor.

He couldn’t even scream as he fell.

CETTIE

CHAPTER ONE

Cettie of the Clouds

Of her many duties as keeper of Fog Willows, Cettie's least favorite was arguing with the admiralty. It meant a voyage to Lockhaven, where she was always put down in ways both subtle and direct for her ill breeding. They all knew her story, how her mentor and father had rescued her from a hand-to-mouth existence in the Fells, and she could see they despised her for it. It didn't matter that she was the coinventor of the storm glass, the invention that allowed them to track storms capable of waylaying their sky ships. She was roundly disparaged each time a new payment was transferred from the Ministry of War to the accounts of Dolcoath Mines and Sigils. Surely part of her mistreatment came because she was a woman, because she came from the Fells, and because she was immune to the attempts at bribery and extortion that were typical in the business dealings of the day. Fitzroy led the soldiers, but the Ministry of Law's edicts guaranteed he had as much right to perform business as anyone else. The government itself ran on contracts, on money exchanged for goods and services and speculation. Everyone knew there was money to be made in war. Or lost.

"Confound it, young lady!" said the aggravated Admiral Peckton, his cheeks puffing out. "Think of the rations that your scheme is depriving our brave men of on the front! Surely you would consider a discount, this month only, so that we may supply enough bread to our starving dragoons!"

Every month it was a different ploy. They'd attacked her patriotism, they'd tried to intimidate her, they'd even questioned her intelligence until she'd proven that Mrs. Romrell's teaching in mathematics quite eclipsed their own. Now they appealed to her compassion, to the waif she'd been in the Fells. Well, let them. The common people would be better off if she was paid. She and her guardian had agreed that a large portion of the profits from their endeavor would be donated to charities helping the families of the fallen—a cause that received little support from the government.

"Admiral Peckton," she responded in a firm, steady voice, "you should have considered the stores of bread when the Ministry of War bid for this report. Though perhaps it is best that you did not. There is a storm coming, I assure you." She tapped the rolled map on the heel of her hand. There was a seal closing it, affixed with Fitzroy's coat of arms. His key hung from her belt, the key to Fog Willows, granting her the authority to use the Mysteries on his behalf. Her own abilities, however, were more than sufficient. And the admiralty had learned *that* when they had tried to intimidate her with a Fear Leering.

The admiral had thick bronze whiskers and a seething countenance. He sat in his chair and muttered under his breath about her lack of feeling.

She stood at the head of the council table, facing four admirals at once. The prime minister, Lord Welles, was seated in an ornate chair at the other end, watching her shrewdly.

"Just pay her, Peckton," he snorted. "Be done with it."

Cettie nodded to him, still surprised that someone of her station was addressing the prime minister of the empire. She was only nineteen, and this was the third time she'd attended him in his office.

"Thank you, my lord," she said, "for honoring the terms of the deal."

He gestured at her, a small wave of annoyance. "Open the scroll, my dear."

She stood still, watching as Admiral Peckton consulted with his ministry's advocate before signing the order that would transfer the funds. After he signed it, the advocate signed it as well and then presented it to her. She quickly glanced the form over to ensure all was in order. One time they had left out the date of the transaction, which had delayed the transfer of funds. The next month, she'd spiked the price higher in return.

"All is in order, then," she said, taking the paper from them and handing over the huge rolled map. *Vociferous,* she thought. It was the command word to release the binding sigil on the seal. The map would burn to ash if someone tried to open it without knowing the password.

Admiral Peckton took it from her and broke the wax seal. The paper made a stiff crackling sound as it was unrolled. Weights were used to hold down the corners as the other admirals gathered around to view it. Lord Welles remained in his chair, watching her.

"As you can see, my lord admirals," Cettie said, "there is a new storm wall forming over Hautland. The storm glass predicts that it will move southwest to strike the shores of our lands by week's end."

"Are you certain it will follow the marked path, young lady?"

"Don't be daft, Peckton," said Admiral Clifton, pushing back his thick silver hair. "She draws the maps herself."

She did. And the Ministry of War learned the news days in advance of the other ministries. It was one of Fitzroy's strategies to force the four ministries to bid against one another for the knowledge. Since the war with Kingfountain had started three years ago, the Ministry of War refused to be outbid, even though the Ministry of Law often attempted it. In truth, Cettie would never withhold the information from her own father, who was, after all, at the front lines of the battle. No doubt they knew it, but they were not the trusting sort. If Fitzroy was to have the information, they wanted it too. Knowledge was power.

"This is valuable information," said Clifton, appraising her. "We were going to send transports that way to bolster Fitzroy's forces."

"He already knew about the storm," said Lord Welles shrewdly, bringing his fingers together. "Once again, you've proven the usefulness of your invention. Well done." He dipped his head to her, though some of the other admirals looked at her with undisguised scorn.

It was tempting to be flattered by his praise. But she knew Lord Welles was a politician above all. His kindnesses, when given, were given for a reason. She'd seen his temper before and felt it too. Just being in the room with him made her uneasy, especially knowing how he had contributed to her friend Sera's downfall. She gathered the contract and the leather tube case she'd brought to transport the map and turned toward the door. Welles stopped her again.

"Here is a bit of news for you, Miss Cettie. One that will not cost *you*. Lord High Admiral Fitzroy has gathered our forces to Hautland to prepare for a major engagement with General Montpensier. There will likely be a huge battle by week's end, regardless of the weather. If you would bear that news to Lady Maren, I would be indebted to you. But keep it secret otherwise. How he knows where our enemies will attack next . . . well, it's nothing short of a miracle." His eyes narrowed slightly as he said the words.

"He's a bloody harbinger," said Admiral Peckton angrily.

"It's a good thing he's on *our* side," Clifton countered.

Cettie knew Welles was watching her, gazing keenly at her face to judge her reaction. She knew Fitzroy was in Hautland. She was the one who'd told him to go there after her vision two days before.

"Do you think it will end the war?" she asked Lord Welles.

He entwined his fingers and shrugged. "Only the Knowing can say, my dear. We would have been defeated long ago if not for your guardian's efforts. But nothing is certain in war. Three years of fighting." He sighed. "So many dead. There will be a dearth of young men when this conflict is over. Mothers grieving for sons. Sisters for their brothers. Ghastly business. You do your guardian credit. He's trained you well."

"Thank you, Prime Minister," she said, her cheeks flushing.

"Go," he said with a little wave of his hand. Again, his politeness unnerved her.

As she headed for the door, she heard another admiral say, "Are you sure it's wise, my lord, to allow Fitzroy to draw all our forces there? In a storm, no less? The other garrisons have been stripped naked. If Montpensier attacks any of them, we'll crumble to dust. Why would he attack Hautland?"

"Because it's the biggest mirror gate," Lord Welles said with a sigh. "It's also on the coast and within easy striking distance of our shores. One would think he'd avoid it for being too obvious, especially since we've always kept it well guarded, but Montpensier always strikes where we'd least expect him to. He's a genius on the waters.

"If Fitzroy is right—and he *has* been, time after time—then our enemies are going to flood our realm with this one final push. We'll need every man jack ready to fight him. This storm may be the very thing that allows us to hinder his fleet. His greatest strength is the ships that pass unseen beneath the waters, but the storm will make it difficult for him. His usual strategy of sending the underwater ships first may not work."

"It could also ruin our sky fleet," said Peckton. "We'll face the same difficulties."

Cettie knew she was lingering too long at the door. The storm would strike when Montpensier's fleet arrived through the mirror gate. She'd seen it. Part of her longed to share the details of her vision with the prime minister. The visions had started after she took the Test at Muirwood three years ago, but she and Fitzroy had agreed to keep them a secret. She never knew when the visions would come, and she and her guardian feared she'd be exploited for political purposes if the privy council discovered the truth. This way, she was kept safe, and her visions were used to help protect her world from being overrun by another civilization seemingly intent on destroying it.

⁓

Cettie climbed up the rope ladder to her tempest to return to Fog Willows. Joses met her on deck, grinning broadly.

"Is that a victory smile, Cettie?" he asked, flashing a grin. Her childhood friend had been spared military duty because he was a servant in a wealthy household, *her* wealthy household. Had he still been living in the Fells, he would have ended up in a different kind of uniform. He was a year younger than her, which they had found out after Fitzroy had successfully hunted down his deed. No longer starving, Joses had grown into a broad-shouldered young man with a quick wit and an adventurous air. They had drifted apart during her years at Muirwood Abbey, but now that she was the keeper of the house, she saw him daily.

"They paid the price they promised to," she answered, handing him the empty map tube. "Let's get back home."

"Can we go shopping in the City first? The last time we came, we took a jaunt down there."

Cettie shook her head no. "Not this time, Joses."

"Please?" He gave her his most convincing forlorn look.

"I have a message for Lady Maren," Cettie answered. "Maybe next time."

"Very well," he grumbled, then winked at her. "I'll make ready to depart."

"Thank you."

As Cettie climbed the steps to the helm, she found herself thinking about the first time she had piloted a tempest. It had been with Aunt Juliana's sky ship, and she had practiced her piloting skills over the fenlands surrounding Muirwood Abbey. With the command of a private sky ship, she could have tried to visit Sera at Pavenham Sky. Of course, she had little doubt she would be turned away. All Cettie's letters to Sera had been returned unopened. Every single one.

Cettie invoked the Leerings, and soon the tempest made its way from Lockhaven. She never grew tired of looking down at the palatial manors glinting in the sunlight. A fog shrouded the City below, as it normally did, obscuring both the tenements and the larger homes that thronged beneath the massive floating mountain supporting Lockhaven. Cettie increased their speed and set the course.

They had not gone far when Joses cried out, "Cettie! I think we're being followed!"

She looked down and saw him leaning over the rails. The ship could practically fly itself, with or without someone at the helm, so she rushed down the planks to the lower deck and joined him at the railing.

"See there!" he shouted over the roar of the wind, pointing. "Two tempests just rose from the fog after we passed by. They're coming straight for us."

They were, and quickly too. Cettie felt her pulse start to race. She opened her mind to the Leerings on board and ordered them to track the incoming sky ships.

"Another one just popped up ahead!" Joses shouted. "That's three of them. Can you see the markings?"

Cettie couldn't see that far with her natural eyes, but the Leerings on the hull were specifically designed to enhance the vision of the person piloting the ship. Their pursuers were not from the Ministry of War. They were merchant ships from the Ministry of Law. They had almost outbid War for the information from the storm glasses this time. Were they seeking revenge?

"What do we do?" Joses asked as he walked up to a bound chest and unlatched it. It was where the arquebuses were stored.

Cettie could sense the three ships rising from the fog. She needed to be sure they were truly being followed. As she climbed back up to the helmsman's deck, she instantly changed course, increasing altitude promptly and veering away from the nearest tempest. All three sky ships responded to her maneuver and then increased their pace.

"They're definitely following us," Cettie cried out to Joses. She increased the speed and the rate of the ship's ascent.

Joses clung to the railing to hold his position. Neither of them were tied on, which would limit their maneuverability.

"Think they'll try to board us?" Joses asked.

"They'd better not," Cettie replied angrily. She had always been powerful in the Mysteries. Once they got close enough, she could try to overwhelm their command of the Leerings on board their ships. How would they respond to that?

"Are you going to try to outrun them?" he asked.

In her mind's eye, she remembered the storm map she'd drawn before leaving Fog Willows. There was a wall of clouds to the north, not enough to create a storm, but wide and deep enough to hide a sky ship.

"Get belowdecks," she ordered, taking hold of the helm and pouring her thoughts into increasing the ship's speed and height.

"What if they try to board us? I want to fight, Cettie. You can't send me down below."

"I'm the captain of this ship," she insisted. "Get belowdecks."

Joses scowled at her and went down below, slamming the door hard behind himself. Cettie felt the wind get colder as the ship rose higher. The other three tempests were coming hard in pursuit. The two from behind wouldn't catch her, but the one ahead was in a better position. In her mind, she thought of the different geometries she had studied with Mrs. Romrell at school. No matter how high she went or how quickly, the lead ship would intercept her.

Three tempests? The Ministry of Law must be desperate for information. Well, the next time she would not let them purchase the reports at all. Let them be blind to the weather for a fortnight.

She saw the clouds in the distance, at least a league away. Her mind filled with determination as she gripped the helm. She would not be caught by these other pilots. The wind buffeted her craft, but she kept the angle sharp, watching as the lead tempest drew closer. As it closed in, she suddenly swerved the tempest around, angling it sharply the other way. She heard the noise of Joses smashing into something belowdecks. Well, better that than falling off.

The tempest below reacted to her sudden erratic move and tried to adjust, but she had already righted her ship and lunged another way, going around his ship on one side. Her maneuvers bewildered the other captain, whose thoughts she could distantly sense now that their ships were near. These ships were hostile. They might not be operating under the Ministry of Law's official approval, but that didn't matter to her at the moment.

Cettie's affinity for Leerings made her piloting skills much more advanced, especially her ability to make them respond quickly and unpredictably to her demands. It gave her an edge that she had every intention to use. She wrestled with the other pilot's mind for control of his craft and then sent it plummeting without thrust, dropping like the massive weight it was. She pulled her tempest up and vaulted again toward the clouds, still being pursued by the other two. After several moments of sheer panic, the third pilot regained control of his ship and stopped the death dive. He didn't chase her after that.

Cettie kept her mind fixed on the clouds ahead as she raced the other two ships. They couldn't beat her on speed, so it was just a matter of time. Her tempest entered the clouds, bucking and rocking with the windy gusts. Just as she'd hoped, the view was totally obscured. Cettie then slowed and lowered farther. The other two tempests would overshoot her and chase her blindly into the cloud bank while she dropped straight down.

A smug smile stretched over her face. In the feathery whiteness, she remembered the nickname Raj Sarin, her guardian's bodyguard, had given her years before. Cettie Saeed.

"Cettie of the Clouds."

CHAPTER TWO

GIMMERTON SOUGH

When Cettie spied Fog Willows from a distance, her heart surged with a thrill. She never grew tired of its grounds, the jagged rock supporting it above the green pastureland stretching in every direction beneath it. Sunlight gleamed off the tower spikes.

"How different from the Fells," said Joses, standing near her on the helmsman's deck. "No dark things at night. Plenty of food. What fate or chance brought us both here, I'll never know." His voice changed at the end. "What's that? Is that another tempest in the landing yard?"

Cettie squinted, but he was right. There was another ship there. It wasn't the *Serpentine*, Aunt Juliana's vessel. She increased speed to get them there sooner. The manor was her responsibility, after all, and no guests were expected.

"I recognize it," Joses said, his vision sharper than hers. "It's the Gladdings' ship. Phinia is back."

A feeling of unease seeped into Cettie's gut. Again, she hadn't heard about an impending visit. Not that Phinia and her husband wouldn't be welcome; it was just unexpected—and the unexpected always put Cettie on her guard.

"Did you know they were coming?" Joses asked, glancing at her. He observed her face for a moment and nodded. "Why do you think they came?"

"I have no idea," Cettie answered. The manor loomed before them as their tempest raced toward it. How long had Phinia and Malcolm been there? Had they timed their visit purposefully so Cettie would be gone?

Cettie landed the tempest in a hurry. After securing the mooring ropes, she dropped the rope ladder and hastened down to the yard, leaving Joses to collect their things. Due to her position as keeper, she had unlimited access to the manor's Control Leering, kept behind locked doors, which meant she had the use of every Leering in Fog Willows—each of which could be used to directly connect to the Control Leering. As she walked, she invoked the Control Leering to determine where the visitors were. The Gladdings had brought Stephen, Fitzroy's eldest, who now managed the family mines in Dolcoath. And true to form, they were dancing to music in the study as if they were youngsters again.

Stephen's presence was highly unusual, as his duties at the mine required his near-constant presence. No doubt he was here to enact some scheme he'd concocted with his sister.

Servants opened the door, and the aging butler, Kinross, came shuffling down the corridor toward her. He'd been in service to the family for many years. Mrs. Pullman, the former keeper, had wrested much of the power of his office from him, but Cettie had come to rely on him over the years. They were friends who shared the burdens of household management equally. He was loyal to the Fitzroy family and had a soft spot in his heart for the youngest, Anna.

"Mistress Cettie," he said, shaking his head and trying to catch his breath. He put his hand on his lower back and winced. "I'm glad you are back. No doubt you saw the Gladdings' tempest in the yard?"

"How long have they been here?"

"They arrived shortly after you left for Lockhaven. They've been here three days. I assume you didn't know they were coming, because you didn't mention it before you left."

"I didn't know," Cettie said, a little flustered. "They're in the study?"

She started to walk that way, and he fell in beside her. "Oh yes. They've done a few jaunts and made a few visits, but they've mostly kept to the manor. All the neighborhood is abuzz. Gimmerton Sough has been leased. They came bearing the news."

"Leased? You mean the Hardings aren't returning?"

"No, ma'am. The Lawtons have leased it to a brother-and-sister pair, the Patchetts. Their father was an admiral who died at the battle of Dochte. He did not name either of his children heirs to his fortune but instead put them in wardship to his steward, Mr. Batewinch. The deed is in the steward's name."

"So they're children?" Cettie asked.

"Not at all, ma'am. The sister, Joanna, is twenty. The brother, Randall, is slightly older."

"Neither was chosen to inherit, even though they're both adults?"

"That is correct, ma'am. Seems unnatural, if you ask me."

"Thank you for the information, Mr. Kinross."

"One more thing before you go in," he said, touching her sleeve as she was about to open the door. She paused and looked quizzically at him. "They'll be ambushing you, Mistress Cettie. Their minds are fixed on having a ball here at Fog Willows to welcome the new pair. The master wouldn't approve, and though they've been working on her these last few days, neither does the mistress."

"Nor will I," she answered, giving him a reassuring smile. Then she steeled herself and opened the door to the sound of music.

It was the middle of "Genny's Market." Stephen was dancing with Phinia, and Anna danced with Phinia's husband, Malcolm. Lady Maren, who was watching them with an indulgent smile, was the first to notice Cettie. She rose from her couch to come greet her with a hug and kiss.

"Now *all* my children are home," she said, pleased, taking Cettie's hands. Though Cettie appreciated the sentiment, she had a notion the eldest children had only come to cause trouble. "How did the business go in Lockhaven?"

"The transaction went through. I had a little trouble trying to leave. Three merchant vessels threatened us."

Lady Maren's brow pinched in worry. "They wouldn't have dared if it were Brant," she said in an angry undertone.

"Well, they didn't succeed," Cettie answered. "We escaped into a cloud bank and lost them there." That reminded her. Reaching with her mind, she activated the manor's Control Leering, instructing it to alert her of any approaching sky ships and to forbid any visitors from landing without approval from her.

"I'm glad you're safe, dearest. I can sense you are already at work making us safer." She pulled up her sleeve and exposed the gooseflesh there. "Your abilities have only grown stronger."

Cettie didn't reply, for the music had ended, and Anna was rushing forward to give her a hug. Phinia, Malcolm, and Stephen all remained behind.

"You're back!" Anna said, squeezing her. "Have you heard the news? Gimmerton Sough is occupied again. It's a brother and sister . . . our age! Isn't that wonderful?"

"I've only just heard about it," Cettie said. She hugged Anna back. The youngest Fitzroy had passed the Test at Muirwood the previous year and returned home. Several young men had sought to court her, but she was waiting for Adam Creigh to return from the war and had rebuffed all the others. Cettie hadn't told her almost-sister that Adam had left a precious book with her—a notebook filled with his thoughts and observations—which she looked at every night. A bit of lavender was crushed in the pages, making it even more precious. If he had left such a token with Anna, Cettie was convinced her sweet sister would have told everyone straightaway. She kept silent to preserve Anna's feelings. And because she wanted to savor it for herself.

"You've returned," Phinia said with a haughty manner. She hooked arms with her husband, who hadn't cared in the least that she'd failed the final Test at Muirwood. Malcolm was a doughy young man who had an ample fortune of his own, which he'd gladly amplified with Phinia's dowry. He was a reckless young man in his business dealings, but kindhearted and immune to his wife's teasing. He had curly brown hair and an easy laugh and smile.

Stephen had grown much in the last three years. His shoulders were broader, and all the young ladies swooned over his handsome looks, but his gray eyes were flecked with anger. He resented his appointment to Dolcoath and never attempted to disguise how much he loathed working there.

"Welcome back, Cettie," Stephen said.

"What are you doing here?" Cettie asked him warily.

"This is my home," he said with a snort. "I have every right to be here."

"That's not what she meant, Stephen," Lady Maren said with a sigh.

Cettie knew how painful it was to Lord and Lady Fitzroy that their eldest child and only son had rebuffed their efforts to train him in the family business. She didn't want Lady Maren to feel forced to defend her.

"What I meant, Stephen," Cettie said firmly, "is that you're supposed to be running the mines."

"I left them in very capable hands, *Sister*," he said, with an edge to the endearment. "More experienced than my own at any rate. They are running well and producing on schedule. You needn't fret."

"Milk and I stopped by to see him and share the good news," Phinia said. Cettie hated the nickname Phinia had given her husband, which seemed intentionally demeaning. He didn't seem to mind it at all, however, and smiled whenever she used it. "I asked him to come back with me, so if you want to blame anyone, Cettie, blame me. It's lonely there in the mines." She rubbed her brother's shoulder sympathetically. "And we'll take him back after the ball. I know how much you hate to travel, but I adore it."

Cettie's brow furrowed.

"Yes, we're holding a ball," Stephen said, hands on his hips. "To welcome the Patchetts. Father used to invite the Hardings all the time.

How can we make friends with our new neighbors without being friendly? We have the finest manor in the area. We should be the first to send our goodwill. I think next midweek would be soon enough?" He looked at Phinia for her reaction.

"That would suit nicely. Next midweek it is."

So they were testing her. Testing her authority, testing her will. Cettie had never shied away from uncomfortable situations. She wasn't about to start now.

"That's out of the question," Cettie said firmly, shaking her head.

Stephen's cheeks flushed with heat. Cettie wondered if he might appeal to his mother, but that would make him seem weak, and he wouldn't lower himself in front of anyone. His fists clenched. "It's just one little party, *Sister.* How many times have we gone to them at the Hardings'? Why make a fuss about it?"

"Because Father never allowed balls to be held here *before* the war," Cettie answered firmly. "I shouldn't have to remind you of that, Stephen. It's a liberty, and he wouldn't approve."

His arms trembled with fury. His eyes flashed hot. "If I want to have a ball here, I shall have one." She could feel him pushing his will on hers, attempting to dominate her. Given the things she'd faced, it felt like a child pushing against a heavy door.

Cettie took a step toward him. "Not until you are lord of this house, Stephen Fitzroy. Father would be disappointed you're even demanding it."

"He is not . . . your . . . father!" Stephen snarled.

It was a deliberate thrust, meant to cause her pain. Her own anger was beginning to flare, but she ruled her emotions better than he did. She stood firm, even when she heard Anna stifle a sob.

"But he will be," Lady Maren said forcefully, coming up and putting her arm around Cettie's shoulder. "And she has as much right to use the title as you do, Stephen. Son, you are making a fool out of yourself. I don't approve of holding a ball either."

"You didn't resist it when we suggested it yesterday!"

"Silence does not mean consent," Lady Maren said, shaking her head. "If wishes were zephyrs, even beggars would fly."

"Am I a beggar, then?" Stephen railed. "I'm your son. I cannot believe you are taking her side over mine. How will I ever learn to rule a household unless I am given the opportunity to practice? To learn for myself? Even Gladding here has more authority than I do. His mother never prevents him from using what is his. Phinia has access to her inheritance, and no doubt Anna will get that privilege before I do. I'm the eldest!"

"Son," Lady Maren said, shaking her head.

"I'm an exile from my own family," Stephen barked. "Because of her." He stabbed his finger at Cettie. "I wish you'd never left the Fells."

His words hurt her. They were meant to, and he'd clearly longed to say them for some time. They also hurt others. Anna's sniffles had turned to sobs, and even Phinia looked shocked. Malcolm fidgeted, an embarrassed smile twitching on his mouth.

"That was beneath your dignity, Son," Lady Maren said, her voice throbbing with emotion. "And ungrateful. Without Cettie, we wouldn't have any of this."

"Spare me another lecture, Mother," Stephen said in a low, dead voice. "It's your fault she's here too. I think we've wasted enough treasure on trying to find her polluted parentage. She's a keeper of the house. What higher honor could be afforded to one of her station? But no, she'll not be satisfied until she's wrested it all away. Every last farthing." His lip twitched. "I just wanted a little ball. A chance to make merry with friends I've not seen since you made me a slave at the mines." He shook his head, his thoughts clearly jumbled. "Take it all away. My inheritance. I don't care. You don't think I'm fit to have it anyway."

Then he turned and stormed out of the room.

Cettie watched him go, her heart forming blisters. She'd known he didn't like her. But she hadn't realized how deep his seething feelings went.

CHAPTER THREE

Captain Francis

Cettie's room at Fog Willows was above the kitchen, and it overlooked the entire manor. It had belonged to her tormentor, Mrs. Pullman, years ago, and she'd worried bad memories would assail her. But Mrs. Harding, who had fulfilled the duties of keeper after Mrs. Pullman and before Cettie, had worked some sort of magic on the place. She had completely redecorated it and even turned the drafty, dusty garret above the room into a pleasant space with windows and rugs and end tables and small bookshelves. The space that had once belonged to Cettie's enemy, the woman who'd attempted to control and quiet her, was now her safe haven.

Stephen's words still stung her heart, but she refused to let them sink in deep. Cettie wouldn't grant him the power to control her. He was miserable because he hadn't tried to earn Fog Willows the way his father had hoped he would. Rather than focus on the fine points of running the estate, or even the mines, he preferred to enjoy himself. To covet more riches. That outlet had been taken from him, and his frustration was likely wreaking some havoc on his mind. Lady Maren had tried to apologize to her for her son's behavior, but Cettie refused to let her mother take responsibility for it. Cettie loved the Fitzroys.

Even Stephen. But she did not think his behavior was improving with age. She wasn't sure what would improve it.

She smoothed the quilt that covered the bed and arranged the pillows. She hadn't slept there in a few days. Joses had brought up her trunk, so she set out the dresses that needed laundering and arranged the shoes in a neat pile. There was quite a bit to do that day. She'd need to go to Lord Fitzroy's study and compile the latest measurements from the various storm-glass devices throughout the realm. He'd also entrusted her with the family ledgers, and she would need to update them with the latest payment from the Ministry of War. On top of her duties as keeper of the house, there were guests now to be aware of—Phinia and Malcolm and Stephen. They would make demands on the staff, which would require her approval and attention. Cettie rubbed her temples in anticipation. It would be difficult, yes, but she would face it.

A throb of warning came into her heart from the Control Leering. Three sky ships were quickly approaching Fog Willows. Cettie walked to the windows facing the direction from which she sensed their approach and parted the curtains. From her vantage point above the kitchen, she had an uninterrupted view of the black marks in the sky descending toward the manor. A twinge of misgiving went through her. She sent a thought command to the Leering to notify Kinross to come to her at once. Then she activated the manor's defenses and felt a thrum of power rising from the depths of the estate. Fog began to seep out of the stones.

As she watched the ships approach, the mist soon swirled around the grounds, turning the manor into a giant cloud. After a few minutes of this, she could no longer see the ships, but she could still sense their presence. Were these the same ships that had followed her exit from Lockhaven? Though she could not verify it by sight, her instincts warned her that they were. She stood there, watching, waiting, trying to judge their intentions. Surely they wouldn't attack Fog Willows? No one could be that brainless. Lord Fitzroy was the Lord High Admiral of the Ministry of War, the commander of the fleet. But it wasn't wise to underestimate some men's willingness to court self-harm.

The Leering informed her the three ships were slowing down as they made their final approach. The sudden fog shielding the manor would no doubt unnerve them. She heard the noise of footsteps coming up the stairs and saw, through the Leering's eyes, that Kinross and Lady Maren had both responded to her summons.

A tapping sound came from the door, and then the butler and the lady of the house entered.

"What is happening?" Maren asked with concern.

"The three tempests that tried to intercept me when I left Lockhaven may have followed me back here," Cettie answered, still gazing out the window.

Lady Maren frowned. "That's rather bold."

"Should we send word to the Ministry of War?" Kinross asked with a scowl.

"Even if we did, it would take them too long to get here," Cettie replied. "No, I think we must face this threat on our own."

The three tempests came back into view as they approached the landing yard. She could see the smudges of shadow as they began to lower. Then there was a small tremor in the floor as the manor's Leerings repulsed them.

"They're trying to land," Maren pointed out.

"I'm not letting them," Cettie said resolutely. The three tempests had been shoved off course by the magic, and all three began to loop around. She felt a collective push against the manor's defenses as the lead ship tried again to land and failed.

One of the captains reached out to her with a direct thought. It was the keeper of the manor who always received such messages.

This is Captain Francis of the Glennam, *requesting permission to dock at Fog Willows.*

"Now they're asking for permission," Cettie said with a smile.

"I'd like to speak to them," said Lady Maren angrily. Kinross nodded in approval.

"If you wish," Cettie replied. She invoked the Leering in the fireplace and connected it to the main Leering and then to the *Glennam*. Another throb of magic filled the air, and Cettie felt the gooseflesh go down her arms.

"This is Maren Fitzroy. State your business, please, and come no closer."

There was a pause. Had they expected to deal with the lady of the manor?

"Hello, Maren," said Captain Francis. There was a tone of familiarity. Maren's eyes shot wide with recognition, and her face paled instantly. She knew the voice. She knew the man.

"W-what are you doing here, Clive?" she demanded, her cheeks suddenly flushing.

Cettie was confused. She'd never heard of a Clive Francis before, but the name had an immediate and profound effect on Lady Maren. A suspicion began to form.

"Can we talk about this in person, please?" the captain said. "There's been a little misunderstanding. Your keeper ran away before we could announce our intentions. She threw one of my friend's ships down. That wasn't very kind. Please, Maren. My master wishes to purchase the latest weather map. Surely we can come to an arrangement."

A look of anger filled Lady Maren's eyes. The emotions battering her—surprise and dread and rage—seemed to verify Cettie's guess. She put her hand on Lady Maren's arm and gave her a warning look.

"No, I do not think that would be wise," Maren replied, her voice trembling just a bit.

"Maren," the captain said with a sigh. "Give me a chance to explain."

Maren screwed up her face and shook her head no, even though the captain would not be able to see her. "Explain it to our advocates,

Mr. Sloan and Mr. Teitelbaum, in the Fells. Do not come back here, Clive."

Another sigh traveled over the connection, but her tone must have convinced the captain it was a useless cause. All three tempests broke away and left.

Maren bowed her head, trying to master her emotions. She bit her lip and shook her head in regret. "I should have let you handle this on your own," she told Cettie with a smile. Then she glanced with sympathy at Kinross, who seemed beside himself. "You can tell her after I'm gone."

Cettie had rarely seen Lady Maren so distraught. After the door closed and they heard her footsteps retreating down to the kitchen, Cettie turned to Kinross in wonderment.

"The blackguard," Kinross muttered. He looked as if he didn't even know where to start. "I've been with the family for a long time." He sniffed and sighed deeply. "The master didn't marry for many years after inheriting the estate from his father. I thought he might be content to stay a bachelor. But then he met Maren, who is, of course, connected to the Hardings. She loved another man."

Cettie's eyes widened. She had heard this story before, of course, but now she finally knew the name of the final player. Perhaps that alone was indication of the pain the incident still caused. "Captain Francis?"

Kinross chuckled. "He was no captain *then*, Miss Cettie. A spendthrift. A wastrel. A rogue. He may have loved Maren . . . or he may have not. Either way, he used her to gratify his pride. Then he tossed her aside for a rich heiress in Lady Corinne's set." He said the last words as if they were bitter in his mouth. "Well, he took his wife's money, and he gambled it and spent it a hundred times over. He ruined them both. I wouldn't be surprised if there is a deed on him until he's eighty. He's a merchant mariner now, is he?" He clucked his tongue. "It's been many years since that travesty. But he stole part of Lady Maren's heart, and it hasn't quite healed all the way. Nearly killed her. And it's no coincidence that he was sent to wrangle a price. The villains."

Before noon the next day, Mr. Sloan arrived on a zephyr from the Fells. Cettie had summoned him the previous day after the mishap with the ships. She met him in the sitting room where Fitzroy kept all his documents and ledgers. Mr. Sloan was a kindly man, very patient, and she admired the dignity with which he performed his office. He was favoring his cane more and more these days, and his white hair was thinning rapidly.

"I hope you will stay for dinner," she said by way of invitation.

"I would be honored to, thank you," he said with an easygoing smile. She offered him the stuffed chair, and he sank down, wincing with pain. She sat across from him in her own chair. "My heart isn't getting any younger," he said with a groan. "I'll need to leave the practice eventually, but some days it seems sooner than others. It's good to see you again, Miss Cettie."

"Thank you, Mr. Sloan. I hope the journey wasn't much of a trouble for you." She didn't like to visit the Fells—too many memories haunted her there—and was grateful he was sympathetic to her feelings.

"None at all, none at all. So . . . Captain Francis. I was civil to him, but I wouldn't trust that man to hold a pencil for me. His employers knew they couldn't outbid the Ministry of War, and that to even try would only enrich your family further," he added with a wry smile, "so they opted to try and take the information by force—very foolish—and when that failed, they thought flattery and bribery might prevail."

"Did they admit as much?" Cettie asked in surprise.

"Of course not. They wouldn't have compromised themselves in such a way. But I'm summarizing the facts for you as I see them. This is a faction within the Ministry of Law, mind, not an action sanctioned by the minister himself. My advice as your advocate is that you refuse to sell this fortnight's information to the Ministry of Law at any price as punishment for the misdeeds of the few. While it will injure your revenues slightly this term, it will prevent such intrigues in the future, and I'm sure the minister will punish the rogues for their ill-conceived gamble."

His recommendation was completely unaffected by the fact that he himself was affiliated with the Ministry of Law. He served the interests of his client above his party, an attribute she highly valued.

"Thank you for the advice, Mr. Sloan. I think it would be wise to heed it. It's disgusting that they used a man like Captain Francis, who has a history with this family, to try and leverage the situation. They should be punished."

"I agree. It was low. But people will do unspeakable things to earn a profit. I nearly gave Captain Francis my opinion that neither you nor anyone else here at Fog Willows would take a bribe. But . . . I have to say, frankly, I'm not certain of that anymore." He gripped the head of the cane and leaned forward in his chair. His eyes were serious. "I've come to learn, Miss Cettie, that Stephen has taken on some debts against his future expectations. I was sorry to hear it."

Cettie's heart sank. "How *did* you hear about it?"

Mr. Sloan frowned, which was incongruous for his normally cheerful face. "Someone came to me seeking information about his future inheritance. Of course I gave him nothing, but I did make a few well-timed comments to insinuate doubt. He spilled the story to me out of worry that he wouldn't be paid back. I think Stephen has been approached by several creditors who have offered him money that exceeds whatever living he might feasibly get. They want him to be in bondage before he even inherits his dues. Better to sink their hooks into him now. I say this because he is here at the manor right now when he should be managing the affairs of the mines. That doesn't bode well, you see."

It certainly explained part of Stephen's outburst from the previous day. She thought of Fitzroy's study and the maps and data readings kept there . . . If Stephen was in debt, he'd feel the need for money more keenly. He might even stoop to betraying them.

"Thank you for telling me, Mr. Sloan. I will keep my eyes wide open."

A placid smile replaced the frown on Mr. Sloan's face. "I knew you would. You're a canny girl. I've always admired you. While you are keeping your eyes open, would you inform me if you hear word of Mr. Skrelling? You haven't heard from him recently, have you?"

He was a friend—of sorts—of hers from school. "Not for several months. Why do you ask?"

He shrugged and labored to rise from the chair. She hurried over to help him. "He went north to Billerbeck Abbey, and I haven't heard from him since. He's been missing for some time now. He's always been such a dutiful and pragmatic worker. He was one I was considering making a partner someday. Now he's disappeared. It's a little odd, but then he's always been just a little odd. I thought he might have stopped by here on the way, since he writes you all of those letters."

Cettie's cheeks flushed. "As I said, I've not heard from him."

"It's probably nothing," Mr. Sloan said, wrinkling his nose. "I'm sure he'll turn up."

Some say the conflict between our world and the empire of Comoros comes down to a conflict of religion. That is true to some extent, but truly, religion is what keeps the poor from murdering the rich. The true source of our enmity is envy—we want what they have. Cities floating in the air. Air ships. Base emotions are easily inflamed.

I am a great student of history and have learned these facts as taught through the ages. The reason my soldiers fight for me is because I take care of them. I fight for their needs, for food and proper boots. For equipment and pay. For cannons and black ash. They will obey me above all men because I suffer what they suffer and fight for them just as fiercely as they fight to win my battles.

Our conflict with Comoros began when they realized their riches had been plundered by Gahalatine to drive his war machine. Of course they were plundered! Their kingdoms had destroyed one another in a fit of pique. Why shouldn't we come to take the pickings?

The only way for them to get the wealth back is through trade or plunder. They alternate between each like a hammer and the forge. Even if many of our clashes have happened on in-between worlds we both trade with.

Envy. Greed. Malice. These are the forces that drive the proud in their flying cities. Not religion. They seek to enlighten our minds, but in truth they seek our knowledge and secrets just as surely as we seek theirs. I grow tired of playing their game. The time has come to defeat them once and for all and take what we want from their stores. Then we will rule the air and the sea. Only one of our civilizations can remain dominant. It will be ours.

—Leon Montpensier, Duke of La Marche

SERA

CHAPTER FOUR

A Dead Tree

Sera Fitzempress kept her true feelings locked away in her heart. If her father believed that her isolation and confinement at Pavenham Sky would break her, he was dead wrong. It was a gilded prison, to say the least. She'd not gone hungry for food, although she was starved for companionship. She wasn't allowed to interact with the guests invited to the Lawtons' luxurious manor. No, her torture was to see the social gatherings but not participate in them. This, she supposed, was intended to drive her into a frenzy of conformity. A willingness to do and say and be anything others wanted her to be. It had instead fostered the opposite effect. Sera was stubborn by nature, and her defeat three years ago hadn't broken her. If anything, it had emboldened her.

They could take everything from her. They could treat her like a doll—dress her in the latest fashions, surround her with exquisite food and music, and lecture her about comportment until they were blue in the face. They could shun her and sneer at her and play with her mind. But they could not break her. They could not control her.

So she waited, biding her time, keeping her heart a secret place she divulged to no one. She was more determined than ever that if—no, when—she was allowed her freedom, she would speak for the downtrodden, the people who had no choice but to fall in line with whatever the upper classes wanted.

But there were some advantages to being at Pavenham Sky, one of the largest being its situation on the coast. The floating manor and its hovering gardens were suspended over a series of sea cliffs that led to a private beach that was isolated on both sides. The weather shifted constantly, often going from fog to sunshine in a matter of hours. By patient observation, she had discovered that the tide came in and out at certain intervals depending on the cycles of the moon. She loved to visit the beach beneath the flying manor. Walking along the shore was her favorite pastime, and although she was never allowed to wander alone, she made regular journeys there until she knew every nook of it. Sometimes she'd climb the massive tree, the *Shui-sa*, which had fallen off an outcropping of rock nearby and been dragged by the waves to the shore, where it was stranded and eventually bleached. She loved walking up and down the trunk, careful not to fall. But her newest enjoyment was the tide pools.

In fact, she was crouching there when Master Sewell came walking up the beach to fetch her back to the manor. She had taken to drawing the varieties of sea life she found hidden in the shallows. The rocks were encrusted with different kinds of life, strange things that thrived under the constant pounding of the surf. She was particularly fascinated by the little sea stars that clung tenaciously to the rocks despite the unrelenting waves. Sometimes Sera could pry one off to study it. Sometimes their grip was too hard to break. She was like that.

Her focus at Muirwood Abbey had been Law, not the Mysteries of Wind, but her interest in the world around her had deepened and broadened in her captivity.

"Miss Fitzempress," Master Sewell sighed as he approached her on the treacherous rocks. Though she never went anywhere alone, the butler was the only servant who'd been given leave to talk with her. He was the only one who seemed to have fully earned the Lawtons' trust. "Your hem is soaked through."

Sera didn't straighten. Some of her hair had blown loose in the wind, although it had been braided tightly. Pencil in hand, she sketched the little crab she saw scuttling in the shallows. "We've had this conversation before, Master Sewell. You won't permit me to wear pants and boots, so I must do the best I can with what I have."

"It really wouldn't be proper, ma'am, to have a princess of the realm wandering around in servant's breeches, now would it?"

She glanced up at him. "I won't tell if you won't."

He arched his eyebrows at her and nearly broke into a smile. "I think not. It's time to go back to the zephyr."

"But I haven't been able to come out here for *days* because of the storms." She turned back to the pool and watched another crab-like creature emerge from its shell. It had blended in with the rocks so perfectly as to be invisible. What she wouldn't give to have a book of sea life from Muirwood Abbey . . .

Sewell sniffed and put his hands on his hips. "I don't know why you insist on coming here so often. The footing is treacherous. You could fall into the surf."

"I'm always careful, Master Sewell. I've not fallen in yet."

"Just because it hasn't happened yet doesn't mean it won't. The other day you were climbing that rock yonder and nearly broke your neck; I'm sure of it."

"It afforded a better view. The most colorful sort of life thrives on the other side of that rock, where the waves crash the hardest. Did you know that?"

"I don't believe I care to know it, even though you've just told me," he said with a hint of exasperation. "Next you'll be caring about the seagulls. Remember your fixation with the turtles?"

She smiled. They had charmed her immediately. "Perhaps you're right. There have been a lot of seagulls today picking through the weeds over there." She pointed toward the funny things.

"Can we go back up now, ma'am?"

"Give me a few more minutes," she said, turning back to her sketch.

He sighed long and profoundly. She could sense him wrestling with himself on whether to humor her or rebuke her. He'd never grabbed her arm to force her obedience, but she suspected he would if necessary.

Sera hurriedly finished her sketch and then closed the little book with the pencil trapped inside. She rose and brushed off the front of her dress. "See?"

Lady Corinne was the center of fashion in the empire, and as her ward, Sera was expected to model whatever looks she declared in vogue. The new style of gown that year had Sera feeling restricted. In addition to the corset, there was a stiff bodice like a breastplate that covered her bosom up to her collarbones. Lady Corinne thought it more modest and ladylike. It made bending over difficult, and Sera didn't like the stiffness of it or the pinch of the collar and the sleeves. Her waist, because of the corset, felt like it was constantly being squeezed. She wore it because she was expected to. But she silently resented it.

The hem of her dress was damp, but that couldn't be helped. Master Sewell offered his arm to guide her off the uneven ground of the tide pools. She didn't need his help but accepted it to be gracious. She noticed even more seagulls on the beach, gathered around a large pile of seaweed that had been stranded on the shore. The sound of the waves was music to her. Sometimes she could feel the Mysteries come through to her in little faint throbs on these walks by the shore.

She felt one of them strike her at that very moment.

It's a dead man.

The little whispers didn't come very often, but she always took notice of them. Like the time she had discerned Prince Trevon of

Kingfountain was disguised as one of Lady Corinne's servants at a gathering the lady had held at Pavenham Sky before the war.

Gazing at the pile of seaweed and the squawking birds, she began to pull Master Sewell's arm.

"This way, ma'am," he said, trying to steer her back to the cliffs. The zephyr was parked at the top of the wooden stairs leading up to the next tier of the property.

"There's something over there," Sera said, pulling her arm away. A strange buzzing feeling came alive in her heart.

"It's just seaweed, ma'am. The birds are pecking at it."

She was closer now—close enough to smell something decaying and to see a human hand sticking out from the pile of green weeds. It was covered in sand and, like the little crab she'd just seen, had blended in well with its surroundings.

"Master Sewell, look at this!" she said, striding faster. Her shoes sank deeper into the sand as she walked. The white birds squawked in more agitation as they saw her approach. The body was covered in seaweed like a death shroud. It lay face-first on the beach, the skin pale and waxy. The birds pecked at the hair, and her stomach began to twist with revulsion.

Sewell came up alongside her and immediately put out his arm to block her from walking any closer.

"It's a man!" he said in surprise.

"A dead one," Sera agreed, feeling a strange curiosity. Evidence of the sea's power littered the shore—the splintered bones of the trees it had killed and dragged far away. This time, the water had claimed a human life, as if it were some sacrifice from a heathen age.

Now that she was closer, she saw little sea insects crawling across the corpse. Seaweed obscured its hair, but she saw the dark locks and felt a shudder of recognition.

"Come, Miss Fitzempress," Sewell said, grabbing her arm as she was about to go nearer and stoop closer. "This is no place for a lady. I'll send some men down to fetch the body."

Mr. Skrelling had just come a few days before. Was that why the image was still fresh in her mind? The shape of the body reminded her of him. Normally she would have voiced her thoughts aloud, but she'd learned to guard her tongue.

"How sad," she said, following as the butler pulled her away. She looked back at the corpse on the beach, noticing the huge fallen tree farther off. Another discovery. She kept her thoughts to herself.

Sera ate her supper in silence while the guests of the manor chittered away. No one would have dared ask Sera a question. But she sipped the soup spoonful by spoonful, listening to the discussion of politics and fashion and events, gleaning what news she could about her empire. Lady Corinne rarely spoke, and when she did, it was to draw out a question from others. Sera was mostly familiar with the guests' faces now. Lady Corinne had many friends, and it was considered a high honor to be invited to her estate.

After the meal was done, Sera caught Sewell by the sleeve—discreetly—and asked, "Tell me of the man that was found on the beach. Did you find out who it was?"

"Yes, ma'am," he answered. He motioned for another servant to take his place and start removing the dishes from the meal. He eyed Lady Corinne a moment, nodded to her, and turned to face Sera. "As you know, we had an unexpected visitor several days ago. They departed that night in the storm, even though Lady Corinne had offered her hospitality. We found the wreckage of their zephyr farther down the coast. No sign of the pilot's body. He was probably struck by lightning, and the ship plummeted." He frowned at the thought. "Ghastly end, if you ask me."

"That's terrible," Sera said, her heart cringing. At school, Mr. Skrelling had been excessively fond of Cettie. "I knew him."

"I know, ma'am. That's why I'm telling you. He was a promising young advocate, or so I'm told. Pity."

Sera wrinkled her brow. "Do you know why he came, Sewell?"

His eyes became a little wary. "No idea, ma'am."

"It's a great pity, then. The poor man."

But in her heart she felt a sense of growing darkness. There was something in Sewell's eyes that worried her. Something he wasn't telling her.

She kept her true feelings locked in her heart. Her own expression would betray nothing. Not anymore. Not while she was trapped.

CHAPTER FIVE

MISS PATCHETT

One would think that after so much time, Sera would know her jailor better. But Lady Corinne was adept at drawing others out while keeping herself hidden. Sera had made a practice of studying her, both at her teas with the young ladies and at the rare family dinners when Admiral Lawton's military obligations had allowed him to return to his estate. Lady Corinne always listened to him while batting her expressive eyes and nodding encouragingly. She seemed fascinated by her husband's business and his military problems—like low morale, for example. Lord Lawton rarely asked his wife about her concerns, her interests, her thoughts, yet she obviously made them known in subtle ways—privately—because she was definitely the driving force behind their affairs.

From what Sera could observe, Lady Corinne had no confidantes. None whatsoever. It was strange to her, being a young woman. She was starved for companionship, for friendship. Not a day went by that she didn't think about Cettie and long to confide in her and share her feelings. Did Lady Corinne have no such needs? Perhaps she met them in some other way?

Yet Lady Corinne was always inviting groups of people to the manor, particularly young women. In her three years living at the estate, Sera had witnessed several of the woman's protégés make marriage alliances. Sometimes it was out of affection. Often it was more of a business alliance.

A few days after learning about the zephyr crash, Sera noticed a new young woman had arrived to be evaluated by the lady of Pavenham Sky at a ladies' tea. What struck her most about the visitor was the attention the girl paid to *her*. That Sera was being ostracized was perfectly clear—she was ignored in all the conversations, never even looked at. But this young woman kept glancing her way, either unaware of the prohibition or flouting it deliberately.

She was an elegant young woman of about twenty, approximately Sera's own age. She had dark blond hair, especially at the roots, and an inviting smile. She wasn't exceptionally beautiful like some of the other disdainful young ladies attending the tea, but she was pretty, and her lively expression was full of curiosity and intelligence. They were in the sitting room discussing the war—or rather the hostess and her young guests were doing so while Sera sipped her tea silently—when Lady Corinne put a question to the new guest.

"And what do you think, Miss Patchett, about the state of the war with Kingfountain? Do you think an armistice should be reached?"

All eyes turned to her, including Sera's.

"You ask me that, my lady," she answered without stammering, "knowing full well that my father has perished in the war"—there was just the touch of an accent to her voice. It sounded Pry-rian, if Sera were to guess its origin. The girl had confidence in her manner, and she looked Lady Corinne full in the face—"and that my brother was wounded in it. I should hate our enemies because of this. But I do not. Three years is a long time for bloodshed. I agree with Admiral Fitzroy. We should sue for peace."

Sera saw that it was not a popular opinion, and some of the other young ladies traded knowing smirks. The young woman had revealed her opinion too openly. It was a mistake.

"But should we not," asked another guest, Miss Ransom, "sue for peace after winning a decisive blow?"

"Indeed," added another young woman. Sera had forgotten her name and didn't care.

"Do you have a brother in the Ministry of War?" Miss Patchett asked pointedly.

"No, but my uncle is serving on a hurricane. War is a risk, like anything else. They knew what they were doing when they made their choice."

"War affects people differently," said Miss Patchett. She didn't rouse with anger or seem abashed by her unpopular opinion.

"Whatever do you mean?" asked Miss Flora, memorable only for her pale blue eyes and extraordinarily condescending air.

Sera noticed that Lady Corinne was enjoying the banter, her keen eyes roaming from face to face as she watched her guests attack each other. Sera had seen this many times and believed that Lady Corinne got a certain satisfaction from it.

Still, Miss Patchett didn't rise to the bait. Her demeanor remained calm, unruffled. "I love my brother. He has been in some of the worst of the fighting. He was wounded four times and still managed to blow up an enemy ship while all around him fell. But the experience of war has changed him, and he's been declared unfit for duty at present. I wish more than anything this war had not happened. I cannot get him back."

Master Sewell approached Lady Corinne and bent close to whisper something in her ear. She'd been watching the Patchett girl closely, but she nodded to Sewell and then rose and left the set. As soon as she departed the room, the tone of the conversation changed abruptly—as it always did. It became openly cruel.

"Well, Joanna," said Miss Flora snidely, "we know that *you* won't be invited back here again. You should really learn to be more guarded."

"I should say," agreed another girl. "My father has a contract to supply the Ministry of War with boots, holsters, and leather straps. We are making a fortune at present. He hopes the war goes on for three more years."

"My uncle supplies the ministry with wool blankets," another girl offered. "You can charge whatever you like, and they will pay it. He's raised the price every month, and it makes no difference!"

Miss Patchett remained aloof from the derision and sat placidly for a while, not bothering to respond to any of their comments. Then she rose and wandered over to a tray of food and took a square of cheese with a cracker. The other girls talked back and forth, bragging to each other about the money their families were making because of the conflict. Sera resented their foolishness, but she kept her expression vague and opened the book she'd left on the table to start reading.

She was a little startled when she heard Miss Patchett's queer, faint accent just at her shoulder. "What are you reading, Miss Fitzempress?"

Sera was so surprised she nearly dropped the book. In her three years at Pavenham Sky, she'd not been spoken to by any of Lady Corinne's guests. Glancing up, she met Miss Patchett's curious gaze.

"It's a history of the wars within Kingfountain," Sera explained. "Stories about the Fountain-blessed." She'd read extensively about them during her lengthy imprisonment. The Fountain-blessed were individuals equipped with incredible powers—though each seemed to have a particular area of expertise rather than a general ability to work magic. They attributed their unique skills to the Fountain, but surely it was the Knowing itself that had empowered them. Either way, she'd read story after story about these lauded heroes who'd made history.

"But do you believe in their religion?"

"No, of course not. Even so, the stories are quite fascinating." Why was Miss Patchett talking to her? Some of the other young women gave them annoyed looks.

"They are fascinating," said Miss Patchett. "I'm not a great reader, though. I prefer music."

"Do you play an instrument?"

"The harp," said Miss Patchett. "I studied at Tintern Abbey."

"You are from Pry-Ree, then. I thought I recognized your accent."

"Thank you, ma'am," replied the girl with a subtle nod.

Miss Flora rose from the group and came over, anger flashing in her eyes. "You shouldn't be speaking to her!" she whispered harshly to Miss Patchett.

"My name is Joanna," she said to Sera, ignoring Miss Flora completely.

"I'm Sera, but you already know that."

Joanna nodded to her. "It's nice to meet you."

"You are not coming back to Pavenham Sky," said Miss Flora angrily. "Mark my words. Just because you are *renting* a sky manor does not make you our equal. Learn your place quickly, Miss Patchett. Or you will suffer for it."

Sera was amazed by how calmly the young woman took the assault. "I'll take to heart what you've told me," she answered with a slight incline of her head.

Miss Flora sniffed and strode back to the others. Miss Patchett watched her go without flinching. She gazed down at Sera and sighed. "I think my brother and I are better off in Pry-Ree. We have a pretty farm there and raise grapes and sheep." A little smile curled on her mouth. "I'm going to have our steward raise the price of wool, I think." She gave Sera a conspiratorial grin. "It's nice to meet you, Miss Fitzempress."

"Likewise," replied Sera. She could see instantly why Lady Corinne had invited Miss Patchett. The newcomer was not cut from the same cloth as the others.

Master Sewell came over, appearing from one of the side doors, and Miss Patchett nodded to him meekly and went back to her seat. The butler had a little disturbed frown on his mouth.

"She came to me, Master Sewell. I was just reading a book." She held it up as a shield.

"I know, ma'am. I'm not here to scold you."

"Why do you look upset, then?"

He let out his breath and gave her an aggravated look. The other young women were still caught up in their own conversations, discussing teas and balls and money. No one was paying attention to Sera, as was usually the case.

"Come, Master Sewell. After three years, you're really the only person I'm allowed to talk to."

"There's a reason for that, ma'am," he reminded her.

"I'm not complaining. I noticed you came and told Lady Corinne something. Bad news?"

"To put it mildly, yes," he answered. He rubbed his temples. "Lady Corinne has leased a floating manor to Miss Patchett and her brother. I just received word that Mr. Patchett punched his steward in the face not long after his sister left to come here."

"He did what?" Sera asked with surprise.

"I do not have all the details, ma'am. But it does not bode well for the future."

"Indeed not," said Sera. "How did Lady Corinne come to know the Patchetts?" There was a good chance he would not answer her, of course, but the butler sometimes surprised her.

Sewell shrugged, looking disinterested. "Their father was an admiral from Pry-Ree. Very brave, very committed. A personal friend of Lord Lawton's. They served together in many campaigns. Randall Patchett, the eldest child, is a brave lad, but they say his father's death unhinged him. The boy has developed a reputation for being hotheaded."

"So this isn't the first time he's punched someone?"

"Sometimes the young men brawl with one another in the Ministry of War. It's normal. They say he's part of the betting pool and has knocked down men much bigger than himself. Bare-knuckle fighting."

"I see. And this brother and sister inherited a sky manor, you say?"

"Not inherited. Leased. They live in Gimmerton Sough in the north. It's by Fog Willows."

"Oh, I've heard of it. No one has lived there in years."

"True. Admiral Patchett died with a great amount of wealth. He kept an eye on Lawton's investments and tended to follow his friend's lead. It's not easy to acquire a sky manor these days. I think the Lawtons plan to sell it to the boy and his sister if they ripen in maturity. Seems to me that Lord Lawton asked his wife to bring them under her wing and tame them.

"They're an interesting pair—the brother is impulsive, and the sister is unflappable. Their steward has the right to control their wealth lest they squander it. Only the son can inherit, but the admiral didn't think him mature enough to handle the responsibility."

Sera had heard of such a thing happening before. It was going on in Lord Fitzroy's own family. It occurred to her that Cettie and Joanna would likely get along. Having these new neighbors might prove interesting for the Fitzroys. If she had another chance to talk to Joanna, she would tell her so. Part of her longed to ask the other girl to pass a missive along to Cettie, but she didn't dare. After all, Lady Corinne had brought Joanna into this circle. She didn't want to get the young woman in trouble with her benefactress—nor did she wish to be accused of not following the rules.

She looked at Sewell shrewdly. "Before the fog comes in, there's always a little change in the smell of the air. Have you noticed?"

"I have, ma'am. And you're astute to have noticed it. I see your little book of drawings. You like to observe things. And people."

She felt a flush of gratitude at his praise. Then she saw Lady Corinne reenter the sitting room. The conversation shifted in tone immediately in response to her arrival. The power the woman wielded was uncanny.

Lady Corinne approached her and Master Sewell directly. Her eyes narrowed as she looked at Sera. "You must come with me to Lockhaven, Sera," she said in a firm, unemotional voice. "The privy council wishes to speak with you again."

Master Sewell looked shocked by the news, but he quickly composed himself. "I'll make her bags ready, ma'am."

"Thank you," Lady Corinne answered. Before he left, she caught his sleeve and dropped her voice lower, but Sera was close enough to hear it. "Lady Flora is no longer welcome at Pavenham Sky. Send her away at once."

CHAPTER SIX

Lady Corinne

The next morning, Sera and the mistress of Pavenham Sky boarded the tempest together and soon were rushing toward the rising sun on their way to Lockhaven and the privy council. Sera was excited for the reprieve from her confinement and determined to tread carefully with her father. She wanted him to see a young woman subdued and broken, even though she wasn't.

Along the journey, Lady Corinne kept to her stateroom, giving Sera free roam of the deck, but eventually the lady ventured out to talk to the pilot about timing. The weather was fair, though there were storm clouds to the north. It almost seemed as if the tempest was racing the clouds to their destination.

After observing Lady Corinne and the pilot, Sera wandered toward the staterooms in the hopes of intercepting the lady—without seeming to do so—when she came down from the upper deck.

Moments later, Lady Corinne came down the stairs.

There were never many pleasantries between them, so Sera plunged in with her question directly. "Did Lady Flora do something to offend you, my lady?"

A tightening of her eyes was the only betrayal of emotion. Her mouth was still neutral, showing neither favor nor disfavor.

"Does it matter, Miss Fitzempress?"

"It matters to her," Sera said, keeping her own tone mild, trying to seem merely curious. "It will matter a great deal to her family, I suppose. Having lost your favor."

"So it will," Corinne replied.

"It's none of my concern, of course. I've never liked Flora, but from all I've observed, she's one of your most ardent imitators. Why cut her loose?"

"I don't have to tell you my reasons."

"I know," Sera said with a shrug. She thought she'd try another tactic. "I know it's none of my business, but I've learned a lot about power from watching you. You wield it very subtly. That's all."

"You overstate my influence," Lady Corinne replied blandly.

"Not at all," Sera said with a chuckle. "You're the most powerful woman in the empire. I'm in awe of you. Sorry for bothering you." Sera turned to leave, hoping she had added enough honey to the flattery to encourage the woman to talk.

"Miss Fitzempress."

Sera paused, resisting the urge to smile at her little triumph. She turned around, arching her eyebrows expectantly.

"No one is ever really secure in a position of power. Not even the prime minister. The ground is always shifting. The times changing. When a rival seeks to supplant you, sometimes it's best to knock them down when it's easiest to do so." She gave Sera a knowing look, one that revealed the tiniest glimpse of her character. Corinne said nothing else but strode down the remaining steps and disappeared into her stateroom. Sera stared at the closed door for a long while, savoring her small success. Lady Corinne had let down her guard, just a fraction. Yes, Sera had once been her rival. Now she was powerless. But it would not always be so.

Sera went to her own stateroom and quietly shut the door. Then she punched her pillow, once, twice, her face twisted with anger. Those two punches were the only release she allowed herself before she brought her emotions under control again. Screaming and raving would do no good. She must learn to be wise. But she swore in her heart that if she got a chance, she would see Lady Corinne finally come crashing down.

~

There was a timid knock on the door of Sera's stateroom. Sera left behind the book she had been reading and crossed the small space to see who was there. One of Lady Corinne's maids stood there, a girl no older than twelve. The household employed so many maids that Sera couldn't remember this one's name. The girl had a frightened look on her face and large brown eyes.

"Yes? Is something the matter?" Sera asked.

The girl cowered. She looked about to speak, but she shivered and shook her head no.

"What's wrong?" Sera asked, more tenderly than before.

The girl swallowed and shook her head again. She glanced back at the small corridor. "I beg your pardon, Miss. We're nearly there."

Sera gazed down at the young woman. What family had she come from to enable her to serve at Pavenham Sky?

"Thank you for telling me," Sera said, touching the young girl's dark hair. She remembered being that age. The girl shrank from her touch, as if frightened she'd get in trouble for the small kindness. She scurried away.

Sera went back to the main deck when the City came into sight. The usual fog was suppressed over the river, but the haze and smoke that rose from the crowded dwellings obscured the sky in brownish gray plumes. Her gaze was immediately drawn to several new structures that rose from the city proper like spikes. They were a new style of building, quite tall and narrow. Scaffolding was erected around each one, and as their tempest drew closer, she could see laborers working on them. She'd not seen such construction before. Sera mounted the steps to the helmsman's deck and asked the pilot about them.

"Those are siege towers, lass," he said with disdain in his voice.

"What?" Sera exclaimed in surprise.

"The populace is malcontented because of the war. They think they've borne the brunt of it, and they're seething in rebellion. Some of the richer ones, those who can't afford to live above, are combining to build those towers to fling rocks at Lockhaven. Course, the council sends zephyrs over to knock 'em down before they get too high. Some advocates have been stirring the rabble up. Durrant being one of the chief among them. You remember that one, don't you, lass?"

His look smoldered with anger. Oh, she knew that name. Mr. Durrant had been her advocate for years, right up until her banishment. He, too, had been banished, but only from Lockhaven. So much had happened while she was imprisoned in her dollhouse . . .

The only news she had learned was what she'd gleaned from overhearing others talk.

Lady Corinne joined them on deck as they descended to Lockhaven. They did not go to the Lawtons' manor but went directly to court. Sera's insides twisted with anticipation, but she kept her expression calm. She noticed the young servant girl slip back down the stairs toward the staterooms.

"Come with me," Lady Corinne said to Sera as the crew fixed the gangplank. They approached the court together. Sera had not been there in a while because of her past disgrace, and she noticed some vast changes since her last visit. Her father had spent a great deal on the ornamentation. Why he'd done this in the midst of a war, she had no idea. Some of the tower spikes at court seemed glazed with gold. It was late afternoon, and the sunlight glimmered. People bowed and curtsied to Lady Corinne. But not to Sera. She didn't care.

They reached the council chamber and found that the full council had not assembled. There was her father on his throne, which had been rebuilt into a more dazzling display of wealth. It was higher now, gilded and sparkling as much as the rings on his fingers. He wore sumptuous clothes that couldn't conceal his ever-expanding girth. His hair was covered by a large wig that looked, frankly, annoyingly silly. His eyes lingered on Lady Corinne as she entered the room, and when they finally shifted to Sera, she watched his lips twitch in agitation.

The prime minister was also there, Lord Welles, whom she despised because of what he'd done to her. There was also another man there, wearing a dark gray vest and the white cravat of a vicar. She didn't recognize him.

"My dear Miss Fitzempress," the prime minister said with a congenial smile. "You've bloomed into a handsome young woman. I almost didn't recognize you." He came forward to take her hand and squeezed it firmly. His gray hair was more feathered with white now, and he looked like a man under a huge weight of responsibility. But his eyes were still calculating and sharply intelligent.

"It is good to see you again, Prime Minister," Sera replied deferentially, bowing her head. She glanced at her father again, seeing his cool regard, and dipped her head submissively to him as she gave a low curtsy—a sign of respect accorded to his power and station. A satisfied look turned his face. Was he impressed by her little act? He had never once visited her during her confinement, though she suspected he saw quite a bit of Lady Corinne. Mother had come to see her, but not as often as had been promised.

"Seraphin, this is the high seer—Allanom Scott." Those were her father's first words to her. "He's the Minister of Thought. I don't believe you know him."

Sera shook her head no and then bowed to the new acquaintance. "It's my pleasure to meet you, sir."

"Thank you, Miss Fitzempress," he said in a formal, detached way. He said nothing else, but his aloofness indicated that she wasn't very highly regarded.

"I brought her as requested, Your Majesty," Lady Corinne said, bowing.

"Yes, yes, thank you," he said, giving her a ghastly grin. She was about to turn and leave, but he lifted a finger. "Stay, if you would, Lady Corinne."

Welles shot the emperor a sharp look. "My lord, we discussed—"

"I know, I know. But I've changed my mind now that I see the princess standing before me. Best to get it over with quickly, Prime Minister. It may come to nothing after all. You know how headstrong she's always been."

Sera prickled at the condescending rebuke, spoken as if she weren't standing directly in front of him. But she didn't bristle or anger. She imagined herself on the shore beneath Pavenham Sky, hearing the surf crash against the myriad of sea creatures there. No matter how hard the sea crashed, the creatures didn't budge. Neither would she.

Lord Welles sighed. The meeting wasn't going as he had planned. "Very well, Your Highness." He flashed a wary look at Lady Corinne. There was some history between them, of course. If nothing else, they had been allied in their efforts to keep Sera out of the way.

"My dear," Welles said to Sera, giving her an encouraging look. "There is a matter we wish to discuss with you. This war has claimed the lives of thousands of young men on either side of the mirror gates. It's been impossible to keep an accurate tally of all the dead. Our two worlds have been grinding at each other for three years now. The people are starting to revolt. They want us to sue for peace."

Her father was growing more agitated as Welles spoke. She could see the resentment and fury building up inside him. He hated to be told what to do—especially by those who lived below. He gripped the armrests of his majestic throne so tightly his knuckles went white.

"Lord Fitzroy, the lord high admiral, has put forth the suggestion of an armistice. We have deliberately permitted them to be the aggressors instead of attempting to invade their world. It has been a costly strategy, but not as costly as theirs. With each attack, they drain their resources more and more, especially since we have been able to predict their movements. But this cannot go on much longer. We need a cessation of violence as much as they do. They are summoning their forces for another offensive. If they manage to shatter our lines this time, we may lose the leverage we now have. But I'm confident we will hold them. It is a critical hour, Miss Fitzempress. Our spies have informed us that our best chance to broker a peace may be in the aftermath of this battle. Should they suffer a defeat, their ears will be open for an offer."

She believed him. There was conviction in his words and no small amount of worry. The last she knew, the world of Kingfountain had created a new kind of ship, one that could travel beneath the waves. Although the powers of the warring factions were quite different, they were evenly balanced and had remained so. Neither side could gain the upper hand. Victory seemed impossible for either side.

"I appreciate the severity of the situation, Prime Minister. How can I help?"

Lord Welles looked relieved by her response. He turned and gestured for the high seer to speak.

Allanom Scott had a deep scowl on his face. "It is my understanding, Miss Fitzempress, that you haven't taken the Test at Muirwood Abbey since your disgrace. I have not approved it happening at any rate, but I should like you to confirm it."

"I have not, my lord," Sera said simply.

The high seer nodded and sniffed. He tapped his lip and started to pace. "The Crown Prince of Kingfountain still has not chosen a wife. There is great pressure on him to do so, to sire an heir to the hollow crown. His own position is, shall we say, precarious. Their top general, the Duke of La Marche, has won great esteem on the battlefield. They say he harbors ambitions of his own to become a rival emperor. An armistice would serve in the interests of both worlds. The next battle may prove costly to both sides." His lips twitched. "Seraphin Fitzempress, could you find it in your conscience to renounce your religion, should that be required in a peace treaty between our realms?"

Now she understood. They wanted to use her as a political pawn just as they had before, only this time it was different. They wanted her to betray her own conscience. She couldn't imagine that Lord Fitzroy was behind this ploy. He would never have asked her to do such a thing. She couldn't imagine Thomas Abraham asking it of her either.

Everyone was watching her, studying her for a sign of her inclination. Would she be pliable and bend to their wishes? If not, no doubt she'd be sent directly back to Pavenham Sky. She needed time to think. To reason it through. But she had no time. What was the right answer?

She decided quickly. She would bend, but she would not break.

"It would be very difficult for me," Sera said in a submissive voice. There might still be time to stave off disaster another way. Maybe the prince would reject her anyway. Maybe she wouldn't have to actually go through with it . . .

She lowered her eyes and pressed on. "But I submit to the will of the council."

Our spies tell us the empire we face has a harbinger amongst them. This is what they call one who can see the future. Through some uncanny means, Lord Fitzroy has indeed predicted with great accuracy where we will attack next. Is this gift supernatural? I think not. I think his immense powers of concentration allow him to tap into the minds of others. And he does not panic in battle as most men do. You see, the battlefield is a scene of constant chaos. The winner will be the one who can best control that chaos, both his own and the enemy's.

There are those at the court of Kingfountain who are pressuring the throne to negotiate a limited peace. They know that if I am successful in crushing our foes, power will have shifted irrevocably into my hands. So I must tame my enemies before peace ruins all my plans. The stone is tipping. It will fall. All it needs is another strong push.

—Leon Montpensier, Duke of La Marche

CETTIE

CHAPTER SEVEN

HARBINGER

Cettie's visions came in her sleep. There was no warning beforehand. They differed from normal dreams both because of the strange perspective—she was never a part of the visions, only an unseen observer, sitting on what she could best describe as a whorl of golden light—and the clarity of detail available to her scrutiny. The visions also showed her, with perfect accuracy, places and things and people she'd never seen in real life. In her studies at school, she had learned about the court of Kingfountain. She had even seen etchings of it. But this was no etching.

Cettie hung in the air over a great waterfall that roared violently as the waters plummeted down the embankment. Several iron bridges crossed the mighty river at different intervals, each thick with carriages and foot traffic. A sunlit building sat on an island amidst the river, a sanctuary dedicated to the Fountain, with a gleaming silver spike rising from the highest turret. Though she had not devoted much study to other worlds, she instantly understood the significance of the place through her power as a harbinger. She could hear the magic emanating from it, a glorious cacophony of music that thrilled her to her core. The city was built up on either side of the river as well as a lower portion beneath the falls. But the lower portion looked just as beautiful as the residences above. They weren't tenements like the Fells. No, the city was proportioned with straight streets and hundreds of businesses. There was commerce, yes, but it wasn't the sole fixation of the populace. She saw people reading books as they walked, people pausing to greet one another.

Just like in her previous visions, she could focus in on small details, so much so she could even read the name of the book held by one of the men. And when he spoke, even though she didn't know the language, she understood every word.

"Good afternoon, Cregg, did you hear the news from up in the palace?"

"What news, man?"

"The emperor's daughter, Seraphin Fitzempress, has arrived. She's meeting the prince this very day."

"Do you think they will reach a peace, then?"

"I hope so. We can't afford another loss like the last one."

"True, my good man. But how long would the peace last?"

Cettie never heard the other man's answer, for the vision pulled her toward the palace. The castle that held the court of Kingfountain had stood for centuries. The shingles over the parapets were practically new, though, and the banner of the royal family flapped in the gusty breeze of the heights. She could see down into the middle of the castle, where circular walls surrounded various grounds and gardens. The golden whorl brought her over the first wall, and she saw a small company walking in one of the many resplendent gardens. A bubbling fountain caught her eye, and then, much to her excitement, she saw her friend Sera speaking to a handsome man. The two were in deep conversation, but Cettie was so taken by the sight of her friend, grown up and elegant in her stately gown, she didn't pay attention to the words. Her heart leaped again when she saw her guardian standing to the side in dress uniform, speaking to a small group of men. He was at the court of Kingfountain!

With that realization, the vision ended, and Cettie sat up in bed, breathing fast. She was back in her room again, thick with shadows. Her heart hammered wildly in her chest. After pulling aside the blankets, she got out of bed and hurried to one of the eastern windows and parted the curtains. There was a touch of blue on the horizon, but it was early still. Even so, she quickly put on her dress and shoes and tidied her hair. Once she was prepared for the day, she took her keys, the keys of the household, and fastened them to her belt before heading down to the kitchen. Not even the cook was awake.

Cettie walked through the empty corridors, keeping them dark except for what little natural light was let in by the gauzy curtains. The entire house was still, and she felt the assuring presence of the Leerings as she passed them. The house was aware of her. She felt its magic prodding her, trying to anticipate her next request. She trod lightly, not wanting to wake anyone else. Nervous agitation filled her chest the closer she got to the door leading to the Control Leering. The house was in order. The servants had done their work, and she was pleased with it. But she was still concerned about what she'd learned of Stephen from Mr. Sloan. Fitzroy needed to know, no matter how much she hated being the bearer of bad news. And he needed to know about her vision too.

Finally, she reached the door. After sorting through her keys, she inserted the proper one into the lock and twisted it. The door opened, and the short hallway beyond it grew brighter as she stepped inside. She strode down the corridor to another door, though this one did not require a key. She thought the command word, and the lock yielded to her.

Though she'd been in this room countless times, she was still in awe of it. This was the storage area for the Control Leering that kept Fog Willows afloat. If anything were to happen to it, the entire manor would come crashing down. Being the keeper of the house was a momentous responsibility, one Cettie felt keenly.

It was an octagonal room with dark wood wainscoting. There were no other doors leading in or out, no windows. The Leering was carved into a stone about as high as her chest, although it sat on a recessed platform and she had to go down two steps to reach it. The grave face was that of one of Fitzroy's ancestors. Whenever she looked at it, she imagined Fitzroy's stern father, even though she knew it wasn't him. This Leering had kept watch over many generations of Fitzroys.

Cettie steeled herself against her unease and reached out and touched the Leering. She closed her eyes and sank deeply into herself.

Father—are you there?

She waited, keeping her thoughts from drifting. Inside this room, she was connected to all the Leerings of the manor. This was the one that controlled them all, the top of the hierarchy. With it, she could see into every bedroom and discern whether the occupant was awake. It gave her considerable power and knowledge. It was a trusted responsibility.

Cettie, good morning.

The connection between them firmed, and it suddenly felt as if they were standing in the same room. Fitzroy was touching a Leering in the stateroom of his hurricane. But the two Leerings were connected, bringing the sound, smells, and vision of each place. His desk was covered in its usual spread of maps, and she saw the storm glass sitting covered on the table.

Now that they were connected, they spoke as they always did, although they could have communicated directly with their thoughts.

"I was afraid I'd wake you, but it doesn't look like you've been to bed yet," Cettie said, noticing he was still wearing his uniform, although the jacket buttons were loose.

"Ah, sleep. I miss it dearly," he said with humor. He was exhausted. She could see it in his eyes, his haggard expression, his unruly hair.

"I'm so sorry," she said, feeling sympathy for him and guilt that she'd had a good rest.

"There is much to do before a battle," he said firmly. "Orders to be given. Communiqués to dictate and then seal. The privy council wants to meet before the battle, but I fear I cannot get away." He shook his head. "But those are my concerns. You wouldn't have summoned me this early if it wasn't important. It's good to see you, Cettie."

"I miss you," she said, feeling the pangs of his absence. "And I miss you even more now. I had a vision last night. I just awoke from it and came hurrying."

His eyebrows narrowed with concern. "I thought so. What news, my girl? Anything that can help us win this fight?"

She shook her head. "I've already told you about the upcoming battle. It is going to happen in spite of the storm. That has not changed. No, the vision I just had was of Sera."

"Really?" Fitzroy said with interest. "What did you see?"

"I saw her at the court of Kingfountain. I've never seen Kingfountain before, of course, but somehow I knew. I saw the river, the sanctuary, the castle. I saw her walking in the garden with a man. And I saw *you* there."

He was stunned into silence.

"The first word that comes to mind is *impossible*," he said with a low chuckle. "This war feels unending . . . and Admiral Lawton told me recently that Sera is still in confinement at Pavenham Sky. But perhaps it is true. Perhaps we will reach an armistice after the battle." He sighed deeply, shaking his head. "Or perhaps it means that we must take the war to Kingfountain. Some enemies will not sue for peace unless they themselves are threatened. Our world has shouldered the greater burden in this conflict. They've attacked us. Maybe your vision means that must change."

Cettie bit her lip. "I don't think so, Father. I heard people speaking in the streets. They were talking excitedly about Sera's visit. They wanted the war to end too."

"I hope it is true," Fitzroy said with relief. "I am weary, Cettie. This responsibility would have been difficult even as a younger man, which I am no longer. It troubles me that we must keep this secret between ourselves. Any success we have won can be attributed to you and your abilities. Not mine. I get weary of the flattery and praise. And the mistrust. Oh, Cettie, I am not bred for war."

Tears stung Cettie's eyes. Through the Leering, she could feel his emotions, his agitation, his anxiety. Through the Leering, she lent her strength to him, giving him a portion of her power, sharing it with him.

"Cettie, no," he said sorrowfully as he realized what she was doing.

"Please let me," she asked, her throat catching. Weariness filled her soul as she took a portion of his exhaustion from him. But she would be able to rest. She would be able to sleep. It was a small thing.

As his limbs filled with strength, he gazed at her through the Leering. "You are too kind to me, Daughter."

She shook her head. "You gave me everything. I will always be faithful to you."

"I know," he said with a humble smile. He sighed again. "Give my love to Maren. I wish I had more time to speak with her."

"She loves getting your letters. I don't know where you find the time."

"Neither do I. I'm afraid they're incoherent at times."

Cettie grinned through her tears, shaking her head. "Be safe. General Montpensier doesn't know about the storm coming. Take advantage of it. I have no doubt you'll succeed."

"I will. How is everyone there at home? Is Anna well?"

He didn't know about Phinia and Malcolm's visit. He didn't know about Stephen or about his debt. She found she couldn't burden him with the information after all. He carried enough.

Lady Maren summoned Cettie to her room before breakfast. After receiving the summons through a Leering, Cettie went to her mother's room and gently knocked on the door before entering. Lady Maren was up and dressed, looking more agitated than normal.

"Thank you for coming, Cettie. I had a thought I wanted to share with you."

"What is it?"

Maren stood by the mirror, putting in a set of simple earrings. She was never ostentatious, although the family's wealth was prodigious. "I'm sure Stephen will be sulking today. He may not even come to breakfast, and if he does, he may cause another scene." She glanced at Cettie in the mirror. "I thought we might preempt it."

"How so?" Cettie asked with curiosity.

"He shouldn't have insisted on a ball and tried to usurp your authority. After meeting with Mr. Sloan yesterday, I begin to understand why he's been acting so poorly. When Stephen is agitated, the whole world knows. What if we invite the Patchetts over for dinner tonight? That way we can get to know them. They are our new neighbors, after all. It would give Stephen something to look forward to."

Cettie felt a hint of unease, but the plan was sensible. "What if he tries to create an informal ball?"

"That's very different than inviting all of our friends and acquaintances over for an event. You and Anna used to dance with Adam when you were younger. It wasn't a *ball*."

Cettie felt the need to squirm at the memory. She had danced with Adam many times. But not since the final celebration at Muirwood. Three long years had passed since she'd seen him in person, but at least they all heard from him from time to time. She treasured each letter he sent to her and kept them in her desk to reread whenever she was missing him.

"You don't like the idea?" Maren asked, her brow wrinkling. She had misinterpreted Cettie's reaction.

"I think dinner is a good idea," Cettie said. "I'll have Mr. Kinross send the invitations out directly."

"Thank you," Maren replied. "I think it will help ease the tension."

"I'm sure it will. I'll get on it straightaway."

"See you at breakfast shortly."

Cettie nodded and left the chamber. It was a good idea for them to meet their new neighbors. They would never live up to the jovial company of the Hardings, but she was relieved the house was finally lived in again. She found Mr. Kinross outside the sitting room and explained Lady Maren's request.

"Of course, ma'am," he said. "If they are not otherwise engaged, I'm sure they will attend."

"Good morning, Cettie!" Anna called out from inside the room. She had an eager expression on her face. "Mr. Kinross brought me a letter from Adam just now! I'm going to read it to everyone during breakfast. It's been so long since we've had news from him. Aren't you excited?"

Anna's words hurt like a dagger plunged into her heart. Another letter had come from Adam Creigh. Only he'd sent it to Anna, not to her. Her torture was acute.

"There's one come for you too, miss," said Mr. Kinross in a low voice, meeting Cettie's anguished eyes. He gave her a knowing smile as he slipped the other letter to her.

The paper burned her fingers when she touched it. And she felt her cheeks start to flame.

CHAPTER EIGHT

THE STEWARD OF GIMMERTON SOUGH

Cettie knew Fog Willows from one end of the estate to the other, but if she had to choose a favorite room, it was probably Fitzroy's study. It was this room where the Mysteries had first coaxed her into an understanding of quicksilver. The rain lashing on the window that overlooked the docking yard had inspired her to track it with her measurements. And it was also the place that reminded her most of the man she had chosen to be her father. So that was where she went to seek a quiet refuge to read Adam's letter.

She nestled on the window seat, running her hand over the folded letter as she thought about the breakfast they'd shared as a family. Anna had read her letter from Adam to everyone and had sworn he was the bravest man in the Ministry of War. Cettie had watched Stephen's look of envy build, but he was wise enough not to say anything derogatory about a man risking his life in the war between worlds. Phinia had been keenly interested as well—for she knew her sister's heart. Malcolm kept asking for more toast.

Cettie looked at how Adam had written her name—*Cettie Saeed of Fog Willows*—on the folded paper. It wasn't a hastily scribbled note. He'd taken his time to measure out the letters properly. She bit her lip, thinking herself a fool for delaying, and carefully broke the wax seal.

Dear Cettie,

I hope I do not smear any blood on this note. I had four surgeries this morning alone to remove bits of metal that were infecting wounds. It can safely be stated that I've seen more patients in one week here in this ministry than I would have in a month anywhere else. Although I was discouraged at first at being sent to serve in the war, it has provided invaluable experience. In short, it will make me a better doctor.

Thank you for the kind notes you have sent repeatedly. I cannot tell you how I treasure them and other news from Fog Willows. Remember when we went to see the crows together years ago? Sometimes it is only the memories of the past that sustain me.

The suffering is beyond anything I could have imagined. I do what I can. We all do. But it wears on the soul. So much needless death. I try to be positive in my letters to Anna and Lady Maren, but I've always felt that I can be my true self with you. That you will not think less of me for admitting that at times I'm quite discouraged this conflict will ever end. But, as we learned at the abbey, it begins with a thought. There are rumors that we might sue for peace. We could all use a season of peace.

I've heard that Gimmerton Sough has finally been let. Perhaps it is an idle rumor. Do tell me if it is true and what kind of people they are. I've enjoyed serving under Captain Harding as his ship's surgeon. We see a great deal of action. Please don't worry about me. I would rather be here than at one of the regimental hospitals. As you may know, we are preparing for another engagement. I cannot say more as our letters are sometimes intercepted. I hope this one makes it to you. When this conflict is over,

I hope I'm still welcome at Fog Willows to visit you and the Fitzroys before opening a practice down in the Fells.

With warm affection, Adam Creigh

She was about to read it over again when she felt the odd sensation of being watched. Glancing up from the paper, she noticed Stephen standing in the doorway, arms folded, staring at her intently.

"From Mr. Creigh?" he asked in a low voice.

Cettie's immediate inclination was to flush and get flustered, but she mastered herself and rose from the window seat. "It was, actually," she said pleasantly.

His brows needled together. "You didn't share it at breakfast like Anna did hers. You didn't even mention it. I wonder why."

She was on her guard immediately. "Is there something you want, Stephen?" she asked him, keeping her tone easy and unconcerned.

"I came to thank you, actually," he said, surprising her. Perhaps it showed, because he continued without letting her reply, "Don't look so surprised, Cettie. I know it was Mother's idea to invite the Patchetts over for dinner, but certainly the two of you spoke. She wouldn't have done it without your consent." His voice contained a hint of sulkiness.

"I have no objection to being good neighbors," Cettie said. "But a ball felt inappropriate under the circumstances."

"Of course you'd feel that way," he said, straightening. He brushed something from his fine sleeve. "You never cared for dancing."

That wasn't true. Cettie did like to dance. She was just never given much opportunity. But instead of countering his statement and provoking more hostility, she chose silence instead and folded and tucked the letter into her pocket.

Stephen's eyes narrowed again. "You and Adam aren't . . . courting, are you?"

Cettie felt another throb of unease. "No, Stephen. We are friends."

"Why the secrecy, then?" he challenged.

She was not going to put up with his interrogation any longer. "When have you ever tried to get to know me?" she said it in a calm, straightforward way.

"Ouch," he said in a wounded tone. "Sheathe your claws. I was only curious." He glanced around the chamber and quickly changed the subject. "Father always spent a lot of time in here. It smells of burnt metal." His nostrils flared. "I've never cared for it. Too musty. It always feels like you'll break a glass vial or something. Well, I came to thank you, not to argue. I'll depart."

Cettie nodded to him with civil composure. She had no doubt that Stephen would tell Anna about the letter. And she also knew that Anna would want to see it.

The Patchetts were not available for dinner that night, because the sister was away, but the steward accepted the invitation for the next evening. In the interim, there was dancing practice, and Cettie found herself making reasons to avoid the sitting room. The arrival of the older siblings had altered the mood at Fog Willows. She was anxious for them to leave, especially for Stephen to return to his responsibilities at Dolcoath. Surprisingly, Anna never asked about the letter. Cettie wondered whether she should preempt the awkward moment herself.

A tempest bearing the new residents of Gimmerton Sough arrived before sundown the following evening. Cettie had sensed its coming. She'd lowered the defenses after Mr. Sloan's visit, and there had been no new arrivals since then. With a thought, she communicated the arrival to Mr. Kinross through a Leering in the butler's domain. He went to welcome the new guests, whom Lady Maren and her children awaited in the sitting room. Cettie gave final instructions to the cook about dinner and left the kitchen to join Mr. Kinross in the entryway. Cettie observed through the Leerings as the group approached the house.

The steward was in his late fifties, not bald but with a fine ruff of gray hair spiked on his head. A fading brown bruise was prominent on his cheekbone. He looked surly and ill-tempered. The Patchett siblings walked before him. Not arm in arm, as one might expect in a formal situation. The sister wore a fine gown with a high, stiff bodice—the newest fashion that was all the rage. Cettie thought it looked about as comfortable as wearing a box. The brother, dressed in his regimentals, put her in mind of a caged beast—full of energy with no outlet. Something about him struck her as familiar, yet he didn't *look* familiar. His hair was a bronzed brown, and he had a haughty air. A scar ran across his cheekbone up to the bridge of his nose. She felt power and energy radiating from him, an intensity of thought that surprised her. As he walked, he gazed up at the ceiling, the tapestries, and the decorations with a judging eye. His sister, Joanna, saw Cettie approach and smiled in greeting and did a deep curtsy. Her air was calm and pleasant, the opposite of her brother's.

"You must be Miss Cettie," Joanna said with a probing look. "I've just come from Pavenham Sky. I met your friend there. Miss Fitzempress. She was charming."

Cettie was taken aback by the greeting. "Have you?"

"I wasn't invited," said the brother with a smirk. "Shall we get on with this, Sister?" he whispered to his companion, a trifle too loud.

"Be civil, Rand. Try, at least. This is our steward, Mr. Batewinch."

"A pleasure to meet you, sir," Cettie said, giving him a small curtsy.

He looked at her, as if startled to see someone so young in her position. "You are the keeper of the house?"

"I am," Cettie answered.

"May I discuss something with you before we enter for dinner?"

"If you *must*, Batewinch," said Randall with exasperation. He looked at Mr. Kinross and gestured impatiently. "Lead on. Lead on."

Cettie watched as Mr. Kinross escorted them down the hall to the sitting room. The feeling of familiarity faded as the young man continued down the hall, but Cettie couldn't shake the thought that she'd met him before.

"Miss Cettie, was it?" said Batewinch.

"Yes. Nice to meet you."

"You may not feel that way after tonight," he said with a gruff chuckle. "I will apologize in advance for my ward's behavior. Not Joanna, she's a pleasant young lady. But the young man can be rather . . . troublesome. In short, he's arrogant and rude. But I ask you to forgive him in advance. He's seen much action these last few years. And youth has never been known to be patient."

Cettie raised her eyebrows at that comment, for she was younger than Mr. Patchett.

The steward seemed oblivious to his own gauche comment. "Now then. I wondered if you might come to Gimmerton Sough on the morrow, or the next day if it suits you. I'm having a devil of a time getting the Leerings to obey. I've banished the foul creatures that lurked there in the years the estate stood empty, yet they keep coming back. It's like an infestation of rats. The keeper of the house quit after two days. I've started the search for a new keeper, but in the meantime, we're in a rather unpleasant situation. Would you do me that service, young lady? I hear you are especially gifted with the Mysteries. Rare for one so young, but I'm an old bachelor, and I say whatever I like and care not if it offends. It would be neighborly if you could give me your opinion."

Cettie swallowed, feeling at once uneasy and flattered. She'd not visited Gimmerton Sough since the Lawtons had taken ownership of the estate seven years ago.

"I will try, Mr. Batewinch."

His expression somewhere between a frown and a smile, he nodded. "Thank you, Miss Cettie. I'm much obliged." He snorted and looked down the hall, shaking his head. "Best follow them before more trouble starts."

His words were prophetic.

Mr. Batewinch and Cettie arrived in time to hear the end of the introductions. Joanna was doing most of the talking, while her brother was studying the room as if expecting it to burst into flames. Cettie felt it again—a strange connection to him, like a memory that wouldn't quite surface.

"You were so good to invite us," Joanna said. "Everyone has been so friendly."

"That's because most of them *want* something," her brother murmured under his breath. "Lady Fitzroy, I admire your husband. I've not seen anyone, even my own father, show more cool-headed responses during crises. He's a remarkable man."

Cettie noticed his gloves were stuffed into his belt. His hands, especially his knuckles, looked battered and scarred.

"Thank you, Mr. Patchett."

"It's commander, actually," he said with a shrug. "But please, those who know me better call me Rand. I hate formality in all its disguises. I'd just as soon call you Maren."

Mr. Batewinch scowled at his presumed intimacy, but Lady Maren merely nodded. "You may call me Maren."

"And you're Fitzroy's son," Rand said, giving Stephen a keen look.

"I am," Stephen replied, looking suddenly uncomfortable.

"When I heard you were looking after the family mines, I had presumed you'd be . . . bigger."

"Brother," Joanna said, putting her hand on his arm and looking at him with worried eyes. Though he flinched, he did not brush her hand away.

Stephen's face went pale with rage, his nostrils flaring. Malcolm, unable to help himself, snorted out a chuckle, which he quickly tried to play off as a cough. Phinia's eyes flared with shock and outrage as she dealt her husband's arm a discreet swat.

"I say my mind, Sister. I cannot do otherwise." Rand's eyes never left Stephen's face. "So you are *here*, wearing *that*, while we are out bleeding and dying to win this war?" The look of contempt on his face showed his feelings plainly. Stephen's cheeks went even paler, if that was possible.

Cettie glanced at Mr. Batewinch, who looked at once resigned and disappointed. It was obvious he had seen such behavior before. And that there was nothing he could do to control it. Now she had a better understanding of why the man had not yet redistributed Admiral Patchett's fortune.

"Perhaps we should return to Gimmerton Sough," said Mr. Batewinch sullenly, his eyes flashing.

"Already?" said Rand with bemusement. "No, I don't want to disappoint my sister. We can eat without becoming enemies, can't we? But if you start any music, I promise I will leave at once."

Lady Maren looked at Cettie with a surprised expression that nonetheless showed her willingness to press on despite the rude comments. "Shall we eat, then?" Maren said brightly.

Stephen glared at the other fellow. Cettie surmised they were probably the same age. So different in temperament and experience. She agreed with some of the neighbor's sentiments, but she would never have spoken such words aloud. It was a virtue to be soft-spoken. To be guarded and careful not to provoke enmity. Meekness was not weakness, at least not to her.

Rand's forthrightness had just earned him an enemy. She could see that in the smoldering look in Stephen's eyes.

But Cettie also sensed that Rand's outspokenness, his brashness and disdain for propriety, came from experiences he had endured in the war. This was a troubled soul, not a bully. There was something different about him, a spirit of independence and free thought. He would not have gone along with the wealthy set at Muirwood. No, this man wanted to *lead* others.

And that intrigued her.

CHAPTER NINE

Broken Leerings

The dinner did not go any better than the introductions in the sitting room. Cettie could not help but notice that Rand seemed incapable of sitting still for long. Joanna led most of the conversations, and sometimes her brother shot out a rude remark, but she didn't seem too upset by his behavior. She'd merely give him a pitying look before proceeding as if nothing had happened. Stephen was rankled and didn't involve himself in any of the exchanges.

Phinia could not be repressed, however, and she directed several cutting remarks at the visitor, which added to the awkwardness of the meal. Malcolm was more interested in the food than the conversation anyway, so it was left to Lady Maren to be a calming influence. By the time dessert was served, everyone was emotionally exhausted from the ordeal, and Mr. Batewinch remarked it was time to depart.

Cettie and Mr. Kinross escorted the guests back down the main corridor. She observed Joanna asking something of her brother but could only hear the brother's sharp response.

"Let it alone, Jo. You don't know what it's like."

Mr. Batewinch scowled at the young man and let out a frustrated sigh. Rand merely gave him a baleful look and shook his head. "I'll wait for you on the tempest. I need air." He then stormed ahead, and the servants posted at the doors quickly opened them before he could wrench them apart himself.

After he was gone, Joanna turned toward Cettie with a melancholy expression. "It was good of the family to invite us for dinner," she said, dropping a brief curtsy. "I'm sorry he was so difficult tonight. He's not always like this. Please don't think too ill of us."

Cettie was surprised by the comment. It would seem the Fitzroys weren't the only family Randall Patchett had offended. "It was nice to meet you, Miss Patchett," she said, inclining her head.

"Likewise." There was something in her eyes, a burden she was carrying. Cettie could sense it but did not think it the proper time to press her. "I did enjoy meeting your friend Miss Fitzempress," the girl added. "The others spurned her, but I thought she was charming. Three years is far too long in my view to shun someone. Especially someone of her rank. I could tell she was surprised that I spoke to her."

An ache bloomed in Cettie's heart. "I've sent her several letters," she said in a quiet voice, "but they have all been returned unopened. I don't think Lady Corinne will permit them. But I'm saving them for her still."

Joanna's expression softened into one of warmth. "You are a true friend, Miss Cettie. You may not know, but she was summoned to court. This happened while I was at Pavenham Sky."

"Indeed?" Cettie asked in surprise.

"You didn't know! Well, I'm pleased that I could be the one to tell you. When I have a reason to see her again, I will let her know about the letters."

"Please do." Cettie gave her a warm smile.

"Come, Batewinch," Joanna said to the steward. "Before Rand starts bullying the pilot to leave without us!"

Mr. Batewinch nodded to them and stepped closer to Cettie. "You will remember to come by Gimmerton Sough? On that favor I asked of you?"

"I will come tomorrow, if that is agreeable."

"It is. Thank you for your hospitality. And your . . . understanding." He looked pained and embarrassed by the entire ordeal. Normally someone of his station wouldn't have eaten with the family, but he had always been on hand—which Cettie had interpreted as a preventative measure.

After they were gone, Mr. Kinross shook his head and muttered, "Astonishing."

"Our new neighbors are quite different than the Hardings," Cettie observed wryly.

The butler flashed her a bemused smile and arched his eyebrows at her. "To say the least, ma'am. So you will be going to Gimmerton Sough tomorrow? I'll have the tempest prepared for you."

"I'll take the zephyr," Cettie said. She was confident in her piloting skills.

"As you please, ma'am." He chuckled to himself and departed to the dining room to oversee the servants as they cleaned up.

Cettie joined the rest of the family in the sitting room.

"Are they finally gone?" Phinia demanded angrily. She was pacing like an animal on the prowl.

Cettie nodded, for the Control Leering had alerted her to their tempest departing.

"Even though they're relations, I always thought the Hardings could be a bit ridiculous," she went on, "but at least they had courtesy. The commander is handsome, there's no denying it, but he's impossible. How ill-mannered."

Stephen was sulking in a chair, stroking his upper lip. "I don't know about you, but I think it was a show. They disdain those who *own* their property. They're only leasing, after all."

Cettie thought that a hypocritical comment coming from Stephen. He had been enamored with the Hardings' daughter—an infatuation that had ended as abruptly as the reversal of their fortunes. He was only interested in allying himself to someone he considered an equal.

"We are *not* inviting them back," Phinia said assuredly.

Lady Maren wrinkled her brow. "Is it now your decision whether or not to invite guests to Fog Willows?"

"Surely, Mother, you cannot approve of how they treated us?"

"I don't approve of rudeness in any of its forms, including my own children's," she said with a meaningful look at them. "We don't know all the circumstances. That young man is suffering from some sort of affliction."

"It's called arrogance," Stephen quipped.

"Because he wounded your pride?" she challenged. "Can you not summon a spark of empathy, Stephen? They lost their father in this accursed war. How would you all feel if that happened to our family?"

Her words caused a visceral reaction in all of them. Cettie's insides squirmed with dread, and Anna, who was sitting on a couch across the room, looked on the verge of tears. Even Stephen and Phinia appeared chagrined. Malcolm swallowed and set down the cup he'd been drinking from. He looked abashed too.

"So have a care," Lady Maren said, noting their reactions. "Don't pretend you understand the Patchetts until you've imagined being in their circumstances. There's a reason the Lawtons allowed them to lease Gimmerton Sough. They may have inherited more wealth than we realize. There may be some special consideration at work, which we don't understand. They are our neighbors, and I intend to learn more about them *before* I judge them."

Although Gimmerton Sough was the nearest manor to Fog Willows, it was still a journey by zephyr, but Cettie loved the thrill of speed when she was piloting the sky ship, which made the journey shorter.

The estate was an ancient castle that had been plucked out of a moat, and the stone on the lower portion still showed watermarks from centuries of high and low tides. There were two main sections connected by a double-arched stone bridge. While not as large and grand as Fog Willows, it was nonetheless a sizable manor. Even so, it bore the marks of years of emptiness—broken windows in need of repair, ivy that had crawled up the walls unchecked.

Once, there had been a small park before the entrance, and she saw a few laborers working hard to try to tame it again. The grass had withered, and many of the bushes were dead. As she landed and moored the zephyr, some of the groundskeepers glanced up at her before returning to their work. Several pots of lavender bushes had been brought up, and the ground was being prepared for the new plants. The sight of the lavender reminded her of the little cottage she and Sera had shared at Muirwood, the thought of which made her smile as she descended the rope ladder.

Cettie walked past the workmen to the front doors. No one opened them for her as she approached, so she lingered on the landing with a hint of confusion and unease. The wood around the edges of the door was weathered and peeling. There was a Leering at the threshold, but it felt dead.

"Go on in, miss!" called one of the workers, waving her forward. "No one will come."

That was a shock. She'd never visited such a manor before without a crowd of servants attending it. She looked at the iron handle and, after the encouragement from the laborer, twisted it and pushed.

The inside was dark and frigid and smelled of candle smoke. As soon as she saw the dark corridor, she sensed the presence of the Myriad Ones. She'd once thought them ghosts but had learned more about their true nature from the Test at Muirwood. They were not the ghosts of once-living folk but were instead beings of twisted evil. There was the usual telltale prickle on the back of her neck, the buzzing noise in her ears. She felt the malevolence of their thoughts as they saw her standing in the doorway, letting in the accursed light. A throb of fear started deep inside her gut, but she controlled it. The maston chain beneath her bodice lent her strength. She'd never taken it off, not once, since receiving it at Muirwood Abbey.

In her mind, she summoned light from the Leerings in the corridor. They resisted her thoughts, almost resentfully. But they did ultimately obey, and light began to glimmer in the carved stone eyes of the faces cut from the stone. The entire length of the corridor became illuminated, showing the dark splotches of mold stains on some of the walls. The light exposed cobwebs in the corners and even a scurrying rat, which promptly fled back into a crack in the wall. The light brought a hissing sound as the Myriad Ones retreated into the shadows.

"Hello?" Cettie called and heard her voice echo.

She left the door open behind her as she ventured in a few steps. The natural daylight streaming in behind her was comforting. Her apprehension intensified with each step. She was an intruder. She didn't belong. The dark thoughts hammered against her mind, but she recognized the source. The steward had downplayed the situation; the grounds were infested with Myriad Ones.

She made her way to the ballroom, which she remembered from her previous visit. After realizing she was shivering, and not just from fear, she invoked the manor's Heat Leerings, bringing waves of heat from the stones.

"Mr. Batewinch?" Cettie called out once she was deeper inside.

There was no answer, so she went to the nearest Leering and touched it, using it to search the rooms. She found Mr. Batewinch in the kitchen, slumped in a chair and snoring, some half-eaten food still on a plate in front of him. Knowing where to find the kitchen, she hurried in that direction. One of the door's hinges was broken, and when she entered the room, she saw his jaw was swollen and blood was coming from his mouth.

"Mr. Batewinch?" she asked in concern as she hurried to him.

He awoke with a start at her voice. A candle had burned out on the table, leaving a huge puddle of wax on the candlestick. It surprised Cettie that Miss Patchett would have left him in such a condition without assistance.

"Mmmfgh," he groaned, coming awake. He was still wearing the same clothes she'd seen him in the night before. He winced and touched the edge of his mouth gingerly.

Cettie crouched by his chair and looked up into his bloodshot eyes. "You are not well, Mr. Batewinch. Should I send for a doctor?"

He leaned forward in the chair, groaning. "No, that w-won't be necessary." He groaned again and massaged his injured cheek. Cettie noticed a bloody molar on the table next to the plate, and her eyes widened in shock.

"Did Mr. Patchett hit you?" she asked in a low voice.

"Miss Cettie, please. Do not concern yourself. I'm grateful you came." His words were a bit slurred, and he seemed to be testing the inside of his mouth with his tongue. "I see you got the Leerings working already. There's light and warmth again. Excellent."

"Where are your servants?" she asked him in concern.

"They already quit. It wasn't . . . the sort of job . . . anyway. It will all come to order. First, we must regain control of the house. I have the keeper's key." He touched his breast pocket in concern, and then a relieved look surfaced on his face. Dipping his fingers into the pocket, he pulled it out. Then he struggled to his feet, and Cettie hurried to help him rise.

"Thank you, ma'am." He winced with soreness and straightened himself. "All is well. All is well. Only the confounded Leerings keep shutting off. Especially at night, when they're needed most."

"Are Randall and Joanna mastons?" Cettie asked, following him as he left the kitchen.

"He is. She didn't pass the Test, and that was a condition in the father's will. We still have a household to maintain back in Pry-Ree. It's going to take some work and no small expense to get this place inhabitable again. But we'll do it. I've no doubt on that score. Thank you for coming. I'm sorry I wasn't in a state to receive you."

"Mr. Batewinch, it's against the law to strike a man except in extraordinary circumstances," Cettie said.

"I know . . . I know. Don't worry yourself. All will be made right."

Cettie wasn't sure that was true. But she followed him to the door that protected the estate's Control Leering. He slipped the key into the lock and turned it. After he pushed open the door, the Control Leering came into view—already lit up from Cettie's previous commands. They went inside, and she immediately felt the Leering reaching out to her. It seemed almost relieved she was there.

"I've invoked it before," Batewinch said. "And it cooperates. But then something always turns it off. The door is locked whenever I check on it, and I'm the only one with the key. I can't make any sense out of it, but then again, I'm not a keeper. Can you make sense of it, Miss Cettie?"

The Leering was in the shape of a smiling woman, which felt incongruous in the musty, haunted manor. Cettie laid one hand on it and one hand on Mr. Batewinch's shoulder. She would be the conduit between them. Immediately, all the Leerings in the manor came to life, and she heard the magic within them begin to thrum. It was like beautiful music to her. She listened closely to it, trying to detect a discordant tone. There was nothing off. The magic was working just as it should.

"Well," said Mr. Batewinch, glancing around the room in surprise. "I've not seen it react this strongly since I've been here. You have the right touch, ma'am. Is there anything wrong with it?"

Cettie let go of him and kept listening to the magic, trying to sense if there was anything amiss. She still felt nothing out of place.

"It seems proper to me," she replied, letting go of the Leering. "It *wants* to obey. And this is the right key. The connection between them is strong."

"Perhaps it is the many years of neglect," he said with a shrug. "Thank you for taking the time, Miss Cettie. I'm obliged to you. If you can recommend any keepers in need of work, I'd be further obliged. I'd offer to feed you a meal, but I'm no cook."

"I wouldn't want to impose," Cettie said, anxious to get back to Fog Willows.

As they departed the room, she was startled to find Randall Patchett leaning against the corridor wall. He looked haggard and morose. His collar was undone, his shirt partially open to the point that she saw the thin strand of his chain around his neck. His shirtsleeves were bunched up to his elbows, his muscular arms folded.

Their eyes met, and Cettie felt an instinctive stab of fear.

"Oh," he said, calmer than the night before. More melancholy. "I didn't know we had guests."

"I invited her," said Batewinch as he emerged next. He locked the door behind him. "She's gotten the Leerings working again."

Rand stepped away from the wall. "Thank you, Miss . . . ? I'm sorry, I don't remember from yesterday."

"It's Miss Cettie," said Batewinch with a grumble.

"That's right. Thank you for your help." Then he looked at Batewinch, and Cettie could see the naked shame and sorrow in his eyes. "Batewinch, I'm—"

"Not now," said the steward gruffly, cutting him off. There was another noise, the soft sound of footsteps, and Joanna appeared, still wearing a nightdress and shawl. She, too, looked like she hadn't slept much.

"I heard voices," she said worriedly, but when she saw Cettie, a look of relief came to her face. "Oh," she said with greater ease. "It's you. Thank you, Cettie. Thank you for coming. We're not in much state for visitors right now, are we? I'm sorry. If I'd known you were here, I would have dressed."

"It's quite all right," Cettie said, anxious to be gone.

"Rand?" Joanna said, her voice twisting with concern. She went up to him, her fingers grazing his neck. Cettie saw a series of purple marks she'd not noticed earlier; she'd looked away too quickly.

He seized his sister's wrists, not roughly, but he pulled her away and shook his head. Joanna's expression crumpled, and she started to weep.

Mr. Batewinch gestured for Cettie to follow him and took her down the hall toward the still-open front doors. Cettie fell in behind him, but she glanced back and saw Rand put a comforting arm around his sister's shoulder and press his chin against her hair. She shuddered as she cried.

Batewinch escorted Cettie to the door, his face grim with suppressed emotions. She was only too grateful to depart.

Before she left, however, Mr. Batewinch called her name. She paused on the threshold and turned around, feeling the cool wind brush through her hair. She hadn't realized how warm she'd become once the Leerings were working again.

"Don't judge us too harshly, ma'am," he said in an apologetic way. "The lad's always been . . . a brooding child. The Myriad Ones are attracted to him more than most. He . . . he sees them, miss. Even more so now. Have some pity. Don't call the Law in. If we need to, I will do it. I promise you that."

Cettie looked into his eyes, felt his sincerity and the misery of the situation. His words affected her more than he knew. And her sympathy for the Patchetts changed the way she looked at them.

CHAPTER TEN

DECEPTION ABOUNDS

Cettie read over the letter she'd written to Sera a final time and was satisfied. She had described her encounters with the Patchetts and asked if Sera had truly met Joanna at Pavenham Sky. She'd shared, as well, her experience at Gimmerton Sough and the news of how it had fallen so far into disrepair.

If only the Lawtons had allowed the Hardings back. Well, what was done was done, and Lady Corinne certainly wasn't known for a reputation of compassion.

Cettie folded the letter and placed a stub of wax on the folded side. She then pressed her small stone signet Leering against the wax and invoked it, causing a ripple of heat that melted the wax and sealed the letter with her fancy-scripted initials *CS*—Cettie Saeed. She turned the miniature Leering over and gazed at it with fondness. It was a gift from Fitzroy.

Cettie left the study and brought the letter to Mr. Kinross, who would see that it went out with the post later in the day. It would probably be returned, as they all had been, without being opened, but Cettie didn't give up hope that someday the lady of the manor would relent and allow Sera to read messages from her friends. Maybe the thaw was already starting to happen. She could hope so at least.

As the keeper of Fog Willows, Cettie had an array of tasks to complete each day. There were the storm-glass readings to assemble from the various stations, accounts to go through, and correspondence to reply to. Many times in the afternoons—such as this particular one—she'd go on walks with Anna, and they'd reminisce about the past or talk about Anna's favorite topic—her feelings about Adam Creigh. Cettie never brought up that particular subject herself, for she was always conflicted about her own feelings for him.

"I miss seeing Raj Sarin about," Anna said wistfully as they neared the old gazebo where Cettie had received her first lessons in the Way of Ice and Shadows. "Every time we come here, I expect to see him practicing his fighting style. I'm glad he's with Father, of course. I guess I miss them both."

"I miss him as well," Cettie said. "It's strange to think that he came from another world and chose to live in ours."

"Is it so strange?" Anna asked. "I couldn't imagine wanting to live anywhere else. Remember what we learned about Kingfountain at school? How if someone desecrates one of their fountains, they're thrown into the river by the falls? I shudder to think of it."

"That would be terrifying," Cettie agreed, "unless you were Raj Sarin. Being thrown into a waterfall isn't so terrifying if you can float. There are so many wonders in the universe. I doubt we'll ever learn them all."

"Sera met the Prince of Kingfountain, didn't she? Before the scandal, I mean."

"A scandal that was made too much of," Cettie answered, shaking her head. "Sera always thought that the Minister of War was on her side. Until he betrayed her. Her biggest mistake was trusting the wrong people. Sometimes I wonder if I should have gone with Sera to Lockhaven. If I could have helped prevent this from happening."

"Sera was always pretty headstrong. We all admired her for it. But it did get her into trouble in the end." Anna sighed. "I see the storm clouds to the north. You say they're going to move to the east? It's amazing what you can do with the storm glasses."

"I don't know what force causes them to move," Cettie said. "But we can see the results of it. And they are predictable. They follow laws with perfect obedience."

They walked past the gazebo, enjoying the breeze and the cool air and each other's companionship.

Cettie was about to suggest they head back to the manor when Anna said, "Cettie, can I ask you about something?"

Something about the tone of her voice made Cettie wary. "Of course you can."

Anna was quiet for a long while, staring down at the ground. "I hesitate to bring it up. I thought . . . I don't know. I suppose I wanted *you* to."

The wariness turned into a heavy rock in the pit of her stomach. Now she wished she had suggested going back.

"It's something Stephen told me," Anna went on, glancing at Cettie's face, trying to judge her reaction. Cettie felt her cheeks begin to flame. Yes, of course Stephen had said something. Hadn't she guessed he would?

A tree branch cracked behind them, and they both paused and turned back. Joses bounded up the trail toward them, his hurry immediately catching their attention.

"Something's wrong," Anna said in concern. The uncomfortable topic forgotten for the moment, they both hurried back down the path and met him as he rushed up to them, out of breath. He paused, hands on knees, to rest and gave Anna a furtive glance.

"What is it, Joses?" Cettie asked in alarm.

He was still trying to breathe, but he held out a note. In a moment of pure panic, Cettie worried Adam had written to her again and she'd have to read the note right in front of Anna.

"P-pardon," he gasped. "Don't m-mean to make you worry. Hello, Anna. It's just . . . the zephyr is w-waiting for a response. Mr. . . . Mr. Kinross said to get you right away, Cettie."

Cettie took the note from him at once. She recognized the writing as one of Father's stewards, the man who did his business in the City, Mr. James. She broke the seal of the note.

Miss Cettie,

I'm writing in haste to see if you've received word on the missing shipment of quicksilver from Dolcoath. The cargo was supposed to be delivered to the customer three days ago, and no word has come from Master Stephen. We have never had a late shipment before. I've sent word by zephyr to the mines and heard nothing back, so I thought I'd take the liberty of asking for your help and any news you may have. I've instructed the pilot to wait for your reply.

Sincerely,
Mr. James

"What is it?" Anna asked with a tone of fear. "You're so pale."

"I must go," Cettie said with grim determination.

"I'll walk her back," Joses volunteered.

"We can hurry back *together*," Cettie said firmly. "I need to check the business ledgers first."

Stephen was in the sitting room, as he usually was in the afternoons, playing a round of dominion with Phinia and Malcolm. He was lounging in his chair, the cards in his hand, and looked utterly bored. When Cettie arrived, he gave her a casual look and then focused back on the game.

"Stephen, may I speak with you?" Cettie asked, approaching him.

"If you're going to scold me about something, I'd rather you didn't." He set down three cards with a smug smile, and Phinia gasped. Malcolm chuckled, and his wife swatted his arm.

"We need to talk at once," Cettie insisted.

Stephen gave her an annoyed look. "Can't you see I'm in the middle of a game?"

Anna had followed them into the sitting room. "Stephen, it's important."

He slapped the cards down on the table and rose from the stuffed chair. "Very well! You have my attention. What is it?"

"Not in here," Cettie said, gesturing to the room. "Come to the study."

Stephen sighed again in exasperation and followed her into Fitzroy's study. He wrinkled his nose when they entered. "I hate the smell of this room," he muttered. Cettie had always thought the burnt-metal smell interesting. "Well? What is it? You want me to go? Is that what this is about? I've been here a few days, and you're ready to be rid of me?"

She handed Mr. James's note to him.

"What's this?" He opened the paper and quickly scanned the contents. His eyes bulged, and his cheeks flushed.

"Stephen, who did you leave in charge of the mines?"

He stared at the paper, his hand starting to quiver. "By the Mysteries, this can't be!"

"Who did you leave in charge of the mines? I checked the ledgers before seeing you, and the customer's payment hasn't been signed over yet. Now answer me. Who did you leave in charge of the mines?"

Stephen was trembling with fear and worry. "I can't believe he'd do this. Not to me."

"Who?" Cettie said.

"Mr. Savage," he replied in disbelief.

Cettie's blood went cold. "Mr. Savage? Mrs. Pullman's son?" The mere act of saying the woman's name made her heart race. The former keeper of Fog Willows had tormented her mercilessly. Her only son, Serge Pullman, had been the overseer of the Dolcoath mines back then.

"Of course him! He quit after Father fired his mother, but who knows the mines better than him? He came to me about a month ago. He offered to help, to share some of the burden. He respected our family, especially Grandfather. He felt he had to walk away all those years ago, but he still didn't think it was right, what his mother did. It has preyed on him." He started pacing the room, his hand crushing the letter. Cettie wrenched it away from him.

"You trusted Mr. Savage to oversee the mines again? After his mother betrayed our father?"

"*Our* father?" Stephen said, eyes flashing with fury. He stabbed himself in the chest with his finger. "*My* father. None of this would have happened if you hadn't come. Mrs. Pullman let us do whatever we wanted. She was always kind to me, whatever she did to you."

Cettie felt her anger rising, but she didn't wish to meet his emotions with her own. She didn't trust what she might say.

"I think one thing is very clear," she said in a measured tone. "You need to get back to Dolcoath immediately and find out what happened."

"It's a misunderstanding," Stephen said, shaking his head. "I don't think he betrayed us. He wouldn't have. Not me."

Cettie licked her lips. "Are you in debt to Mr. Savage?" She saw by his flinch that she'd hit the mark. "How much?"

"What does that have to do with—"

"Don't be a simpleton, Stephen. Mr. Sloan came here and told me that creditors have been nosing around about your inheritance. I know you have debts. Mr. Savage may have stolen the shipment to repay them. It's his aim, perhaps, to disgrace you and our family. Revenge, Stephen. It's a simple-enough motive—and a common one too. Now I may be wrong, and I hope that I am. But you need to return to your duty at Dolcoath and try to make this right. We have a customer who has not received shipment. Make arrangements to send another shipment from our business stores."

"But that will hurt *our* interests!" Stephen said, his voice shaking.

"What will hurt our interests most is not keeping our word," Cettie said firmly. "Now go back to Dolcoath immediately. Tell Phinia and Malcolm that you need to leave at once."

"I'll take the zephyr," Stephen said, but Cettie shook her head no.

"Impossible. I wouldn't trust you with a sky ship right now."

His eyes blazed with fury.

"Go," she ordered. "You go and make this right, Stephen Fitzroy."

Cettie told Lady Maren everything, of course. Lord Fitzroy would need to be told as well, especially since this was news that could damage the reputation of his family. Before Stephen left, Lady Maren took him to her private room. Cettie was tempted to eavesdrop through the Leerings, but she respected the privacy of mother and son. She also imagined that Stephen might rail against her, and she'd endured enough pain in her heart for one day. Stephen's defense of Mrs. Pullman had especially rankled her. The woman had subtly poisoned Lady Maren, making her weak and ill in order to strengthen her own influence over the household. She was still in prison, to Cettie's knowledge. In the Fells.

Cettie rubbed her temples, agonizing over the situation. Phinia and Malcolm were preparing their tempest to depart to Dolcoath, and of course the eldest Fitzroy daughter was in a near panic. Cettie saw the door to Lady Maren's bedchamber open, and a suitably chagrined Stephen came out. His red eyes showed he'd been crying. When he saw her, he didn't rail or accuse. Nor did he apologize.

"When I get to Dolcoath," he said in a subdued voice, "I will contact you through the Control Leering. We won't get there until late tonight, so I'll be in touch in the morning."

Cettie nodded, but then added, "I'll be up late tonight. You could contact me when you arrive. If you please."

He didn't resist her suggestion. "So I will. I'll have Milk push the tempest hard." He glanced back at the door. "I'd better go."

"All right," Cettie said. He nodded to her and marched away, striding quickly to the main doors.

Cettie watched through the Leerings' eyes as he left the estate and boarded the tempest. Phinia was gesticulating at him in accusation, and he looked even more shrunken. Moments later, the tempest lifted away and raced back toward the mines.

After seeing them off, Cettie knocked on Lady Maren's door and then entered the room. Her mother was seated on a chair, hand on her heart, stifling sobs. Cettie came up behind her and knelt to wrap her arms around her.

"I never thought being a mother could hurt this much," Lady Maren said through her tears. "I thought it was painful when they were children, but now that they're older, the worries have just grown bigger. And the pain worsens." She turned and gave Cettie a tear-filled smile. "You did a good thing, Cettie. You handled it so well." She gazed down at her hands. "I don't understand it, but that woman, Mrs. Pullman, twisted that boy up. I was so ill when they were little. And that was *her* fault too. But he cannot forget the kindnesses she did for him. The *mothering*. It breaks my heart, Cettie. It breaks it in half."

Cettie's own tears flowed, and she pressed her cheek against her mother's back. "She was grooming him to be like his grandfather. I've never met anyone as manipulative as that woman, but Father couldn't see it in her. Even with all his wisdom."

Lady Maren sniffled and smiled. "He always tries to see the good in people. Even those who hurt him." Her smile filled with pain. "I'm grateful he was patient with me. I was young once too, and I know that I hurt him deeply. There's a certain blindness most of the young are afflicted with. Except for you, my dear," she added, then kissed Cettie's hair.

"What did you tell Stephen? He seemed suitably humbled."

"I reminded him," Mother replied, "that if you hadn't discovered the secret of the storm glass, we would have lost Fog Willows *and* Dolcoath. We would have ended up just like the Hardings. He told me about his debts. He has many of them. He's been playing dominion too much, as well as other games of chance."

"And it's as Mr. Sloan said? They've lent him credit because he's bound to inherit something?"

"Precisely. He got used to having coins in his pockets, even though they belonged to someone else. He's imagined they were his, not that they were lent, not that they would cost him interest."

"How much does he owe?" Cettie wondered.

"A sizable amount," Mother replied with a pained sigh. "He began taking the money as soon as he arrived at Dolcoath. He's deep in the mire. He asked if his father will redeem his debt, and I told him that he probably won't."

Cettie's heart sank again.

"We learn by our consequences," Mother said with a shudder. "We have enough money to make it go away, but what lesson would that teach him? What debts would he accrue the next time? No, it will be a painful lesson, but he *will* learn. When his creditors see that Lord Fitzroy won't rescue him, then they'll stop lending to him. He earns sizable wages running the mine, just as you do as keeper. I think you've handled yours more wisely." She turned and gave Cettie a hug. "There's one more matter to discuss," she continued. "I received a note from Mr. Batewinch thanking me for allowing you to come restore order to Gimmerton Sough. He was very grateful. He asked if there are any servants we might send over, just for a time, to help bring the manor back to its former glory. Mr. Kinross suggested sending Joses for a month or two. How do you feel about it?"

Cettie pursed her lips. "He would do well. He's followed Kinross around enough to know how things work. But I'm a little worried about sending him."

"Why?"

"Because of the son," Cettie said. "He's . . . unstable." She quickly told her about what she'd witnessed at Gimmerton Sough. Lady Maren's expression filled with worry.

"I have pity for them, but that's certainly not a good sign," she said. "Family troubles are the most painful kind. Why don't you talk to Joses and explain the situation to him? He'll probably think it an adventure."

"Probably," Cettie agreed, laughing.

The two embraced again, and Cettie went back to her work. With the others gone, the estate was quiet and tranquil again. But beneath that semblance of peace, there were rumblings of chaos to come. Father was about to fight a major battle. Anna was going to ask her about Adam. Joses, who had practically begged her on his hands and knees to send him to Gimmerton Sough, would be flying off to danger . . . and so, she sensed, was Stephen.

Cettie stayed awake long after everyone else had gone to bed. She read from her favorite books and held vigil, as she'd learned to do at Muirwood, to calm her nerves and bring her closer to the thoughts and promptings from the Knowing. She needed additional wisdom, and there was no better way to get it than to go to the source.

It was around midnight that she felt the thought pulse from the Control Leering. She set down her book and went to the one by the fireplace. She touched it and felt an instant connection to Stephen's mind.

He was trembling with fear. She could see him at the manor of Dolcoath, the light of the fire from the hearth exposing the sweat on his face. He was terrified, his mind in a state of shock and panic.

What is wrong? she asked him worriedly.

It's loose, he thought back. She could hear the noises in his room as if she were standing there herself. And she heard a roar in the background, immediately recognizable to her ears. She'd heard that same roar on her first visit to the mines. The last time the monster trapped in the grotto had gone free.

The creature is loose again, Stephen wailed. *I think Mr. Savage did it.*

CHAPTER ELEVEN

Dolcoath Mines

The panic in Stephen's thoughts tried to leach into her own. It conjured memories of her childhood she'd sooner bury beneath a mountain. Mr. Savage had also been present for the monster's last rampage, and given his mother's duplicity and penchant for scheming, it hardly seemed like a coincidence.

Cettie strengthened the connection between the Leerings so they could speak to each other in their normal voices. The sounds made by the monster were fading. She saw Stephen's ravaged face more clearly.

"Stephen, the first thing that must be done is to ensure the safety of the workers."

"I know that," he said peevishly. "Believe me, they're terrified and have been for days. When night comes, everyone hunkers down and barricades the doors. No one's been hurt, but plenty of the villagers have seen it and tracked its movements. The beast—whatever it is—roams freely at night, then returns to the grotto before dawn. We have no idea how to kill or capture it. Those who've tried say an arquebus is useless. Savage is gone. And we all know this monster is deadly."

"I know, Stephen. I'll contact Father in the morning and—"

"No!" he nearly shouted. "No, you can't tell Father. Please, Cettie, what will he think? No, I beg you, do not tell him! Let me try and solve this problem. We can tell him afterward. I swear it. Just let me try to put this right . . . help me put it right. You don't have to, but if you would . . . Please, Cettie. I can't bear to disappoint him."

She closed her eyes, moved by the strength of his pleading. He'd never asked her for anything in his life. It was an opportunity to do him a favor, to win his good opinion. But at the same time, her father deserved to know about this situation. It was an emergency of the highest order.

"Please, Cettie. You're better at Leerings than me. You're better than any of us, Mother included. I've always been jealous of you because of it. Please . . . please help me."

She breathed through her nose, trying to judge the right thing to do. Her motives were tangled. Was he flattering her in an attempt to save face with his father? Or were his feelings sincere? Would her help truly mend the rift between them? She had no doubt that going to Fitzroy would alienate Stephen further.

"Let me think on it," she answered gravely. "I'll contact you again in the morning. If you must, have Phinia and Malcolm take the people away from the mines, especially the women and children and the infirm."

"Phinia's gone."

"What?"

"She fled as soon as she heard the monster roar. They wouldn't land the tempest."

Cettie wasn't surprised, but she was disappointed. Stephen was better prepared for this sort of challenge than his sister—he'd passed the Test—but he wasn't the kind of man who could be depended on. Maybe she would have to go out there herself.

"I think you should hold vigil tonight," Cettie told him. "Make sure the men are armed and just wait out the night. It will retreat in the morning."

"Very well. That's sound advice." His voice was calmer now. "Thank you, Cettie. Thank you."

The next morning, as the first spatters of rain started on the windows, Cettie knocked on Lady Maren's door and told her everything. She couldn't trust her own instincts at that moment to choose the best course of action. In her heart, she believed telling Fitzroy was the right thing to do, despite knowing Stephen would be humiliated and outraged. But a part of her still wished to appease her almost-brother.

Lady Maren understood her dilemma and was equally concerned by the additional bad news. Yes, Fitzroy would want to know, but his mind was pressed with the urgency of the upcoming battle. She advised that they wait to share the news, a decision she took responsibility for as lady of the manor. That eased Cettie's feelings enormously.

During the day, Cettie checked in with Stephen to see what else he had learned. With the sunrise, Stephen's confidence had increased. He said he would take some men armed with arquebuses down the river walk to the grotto, where he'd inspect the Leerings that should have kept the beast contained. It was a good plan, but Cettie doubted his ability to successfully execute it. There was danger in that place. It had affected her acutely on her one visit there, and if not for Adam's presence and coaxing, she might have been killed. Remembering him and his efforts to save her brought a flood of warmth into her heart.

There was so much to do and worry about that she forgot Joses had agreed to go to Gimmerton Sough until he approached her while she was doing ledger work at her desk.

"I'm sorry," she apologized, feeling the fatigue of her vigil pressing on her. "I should have made the arrangements before now. Maybe you can go tomorrow."

"I already asked old Kinross," Joses said with a grin. "He arranged it. Though I'd rather go with you to Dolcoath, to be honest. I've never been."

"Who told you?" Cettie demanded, upset that the staff might have found out about the family drama.

"Kinross told me," he said, calming her. "He tells me stuff he doesn't tell the others. Don't worry, Cettie. I'm not going to blab it about."

"You'd better not," she said, smiling at his choice of words.

"Well, this is good-bye . . . for now . . . at any rate. Thought I'd come see you before leaving."

"You be careful, Joses. I'm worried about you going there. If that young man strikes you for any reason, I'm bringing you back at once and calling the Law on him. I'll send a zephyr post to you every day. If things get ugly, you tell the pilot to bring you back here."

"Cettie," he complained, "don't you trust me? If he tries to pop me in the face, I'll throw him down on his. Raj Sarin taught us *both* the Way of Ice and Shadows, remember?"

His exuberance and self-confidence tickled her, and she smiled again. "All right, sir. Behave. Or at least try to."

"I will." As he started to back out of her study, he pointed at her. "And I'm coming back to go with you to Lockhaven when the next bidding is due. I hope someone chases us again."

"You're a rascal," she said.

"I know," he answered smugly, then turned and left.

Fresh reports from Dolcoath came later in the afternoon. Stephen and the men had visited the grotto, but none of them had dared venture close enough to see the actual Leerings. Stephen had sensed them, and they seemed to be working, but something was clearly amiss since they were no longer containing the creature. The miners were not soldiers, and they feared the creature in the grotto more than anything. Stephen said he'd try again the next day and bring braver men with him. Lady Maren, who had joined the conversation, suggested he offer additional wages. Stephen hadn't thought of that and promised he would do so the next day. Cettie went to bed early, exhausted, but her dreams brought her back to Dolcoath. She was running down the river walk, away from the grotto, hearing a snuffling and grunting noise chasing after her. It wasn't a vision. At least, it didn't feel like one. It was only a nightmare.

The following day resulted in similar news. During the night, the monster's howling could be heard all around the village. Stephen had promised additional pay for those willing to enter the waterfall with him, and while several had agreed, only two had summoned the courage to actually do so. Stephen had ventured into the grotto himself, not very far—his voice shook with fear as he recounted it—and inspected the first of the Leerings carved there. It readily responded to him when he invoked it, yet still the creature continued to escape its lair at night.

The situation at Dolcoath was getting worse, not better, and Cettie had a sinking feeling she would indeed need to go there to help restore order. The weather was foul as the storm continued eastward. She wrote a reply letter to Adam, seeking his advice, and explained that while she and Maren had decided not to tell Fitzroy yet, they'd appreciate his insights since he had lived in Dolcoath for so long. It felt better to do something about the situation. She signed and sealed the letter and brought it to Mr. Kinross to go out with the zephyr post.

She was surprised, an hour or so later, when the post arrived with Mr. Patchett as a passenger. A concerned frown pulled down her mouth as she observed the arrivals through a Leering, and she hurried to the front doors to meet the pilot and the soldier when they arrived. Mr. Kinross had beaten her to it and looked equally confused by the situation.

"Is Joses all right?" Cettie asked with concern. The last time she'd seen Mr. Patchett, he'd been in a terrible state. While he wasn't dressed formally today, his complexion looked quite a bit better. His waistcoat and jacket were varying shades of browns and greens, his boots battered and scuffed. He held his wide-brimmed hat in his hands, and both it and his cloak were damp with the rain.

"The young gentleman is fine," he said with a grunt. "Actually, he's quite impressive. And he makes me laugh, which isn't easy to do. No, ma'am, he's doing well with us. Even Batewinch likes him, and that's saying something." Just one side of his mouth twisted into a smile.

"Why are you here, then, Mr. Patchett?"

"Mr. Patchett? Please, call me Rand. I hate the formalities. Truly, I detest them." He was fidgeting with his hat with his bare fingers. She noticed the scarred knuckles again. "I'm here to offer my help. You were so kind, Cettie, to come to Gimmerton Sough. Whatever you did, it's worked magic. The air is much easier to breathe now. The place is starting to get cleaned up. And I haven't struck anyone in days." He gave her a knowing look. "I'm given to understand, from Joses, that there is a problem at the family mines. It took some wheedling to get it out of him, but my sister is an accomplished conversationalist. My sister and I wish to help."

Cettie felt a pulse of anger at Joses. "I thank you for your pains—" she started, but he forestalled her.

"Please," he said, shaking his head. "That won't do. The formality is . . . insufferable to me. I'll be quick, and if you still wish for me to leave after I've said my piece, I'll go back with the pilot. He agreed to wait for me, since I'm not permitted to fly alone. My family is from Pry-Ree, Cettie. There are things in the mountains there, beasts of terror called the Fear Liath. From the rumors Joses has heard—and he's decently well informed, I should say!—that is the trouble you're having at the mines. I know something about these creatures."

He glanced once at Kinross and then back at her. He looked into her eyes with great solemnity, his voice pitching lower. "You came and aided us when we needed you. We'd like to be decent neighbors. I don't know if I can ever truly be *good*," he added with a self-deprecating smile. "Those creatures prey on the fearful. They are powerful and dangerous, but they have a weakness. I'm still a dragoon. I've led men into battle. And I brought my arquebus in the zephyr. There, I've said my piece. I could have written a proper letter and sent it by post, but I can't abide inaction. I thought I'd come myself and try to convince you."

He paused, then his eyes wandered over her shoulder. Cettie turned and saw Lady Maren walking toward them.

"Good afternoon," he greeted her, but he did not bow as was the custom.

Cettie waited until Lady Maren reached them.

"What brings you back to Fog Willows so soon?"

Cettie answered for him. "He's offered to help hunt the creature in the grotto. He says it's called a Fear Liath."

"So it is," Lady Maren said, giving him an assessing look. "I've heard my husband speak of it by that name."

"They torment us in Pry-Ree as well," Rand said. "Up in the mountains, they lure the unwary to their deaths. I can only imagine what will happen now that this thing has gotten loose so near the Fells." He shrugged. "I was offering your family my assistance. To return the good service you did us."

"Do you not need to report back to your regiment soon?" Lady Maren asked.

He shook his head, the scar on his face twitching. "I'm still recovering from . . . a wound. A wound of the mind. I would rather be with Lord Fitzroy. I would rather face a thousand spears and shove them back through the mirror gate in flames. But thanks to Cettie, my thoughts are quieter of late. Well, I've taken enough of your time. I'm ready to leave in a moment if you need me." He turned and started to go.

Cettie and Lady Maren turned and gazed at each other.

"You are very kind to come and offer this in person," Maren said, her voice tinged with doubt. She looked at Cettie, clearly seeking her suggestion.

Mr. Kinross coughed into his hand. "I could send Maxfield Strong as an . . . *ahem* . . . escort?"

There was a little look of relief in Lady Maren's eyes at the suggestion. To Cettie, the path forward was clear. "I think the Medium has brought you here," she said. "We could use your help, if you give us some time to prepare."

Mr. Patchett paused in his retreat. "Fair enough," he said, hardly glancing back. "I'll wait outside." He returned his hat to his head and walked back into the rain.

The assault is ready. I've mustered the force necessary to crush Fitzroy's legions. Is he the harbinger that stands between me and victory? Our spies at court believe so. How else can he always know where we will strike next?

I have sent false messages throughout my ranks to mislead the enemy in case there are traitors on our side. Only the Fountain itself can divine where I will choose to attack.

We will strike hard and furious and leave nothing up to chance. Death means nothing to me. I would rather face a thousand deaths on the battlefield than spend an hour on a committee haggling for peace. To live defeated and inglorious is to die daily.

I must end this rivalry with Fitzroy. Only one of us can prevail over the other. If we keep fighting each other, he will learn all my arts of war.

—Leon Montpensier, Duke of La Marche

SERA

CHAPTER TWELVE

BECKA

The Lawtons' house in Lockhaven was of the same fashion as Pavenham Sky. It was supplied with an ample ballroom, a well-stocked library, and enough guest suites to house fifty families. Sera was given one of these suites, and Master Sewell advised her to stay out of sight while Lady Corinne entertained her guests. That suited her perfectly well.

Sera's baggage was stacked downstairs, but a single chest had been carried up to her room, and two maids were unpacking it and putting the clothes in a large, ceiling-high wardrobe. One of the girls was the young lass Sera had taken notice of on the sky ship. The other girl, who was perhaps two years older, continually scolded her. From the muttered words, Sera made out that her name was Becka.

"Hurry along, Becka, Lady Corinne needs us to prepare four other rooms after this one."

It was the fifth such complaint, and the frequent chiding gave Sera a headache, but she noticed the younger girl didn't respond—she just bowed her head meekly and hurried about her work. Young Becka kept glancing Sera's way, but she did her duties and finished hanging up the gowns.

"It's about time. Come on, Becka. To the next room."

Becka shut the chest and pushed it against the wall and then rose again. She looked at Sera once more, bobbed a little curtsy, and scurried out the door.

"Enough of your nonsense!" the older girl railed in exasperation as she shut the door behind her.

The younger maid's behavior seemed somewhat peculiar, but it wouldn't do to question her. The older girl would only make her more miserable.

Sera went to the desk where her books had been unloaded. Her favorite was a translation of a tome she'd brought with her from Muirwood. She read it often, remembering Lord Fitzroy's advice to her. Most students who failed the Test never retook it, he'd said. Sera hadn't yet had the opportunity to try. And now she was being used in a ploy to establish a peace with Kingfountain that might require her to renounce her religion. She didn't think that she could do that easily, even if the people of Kingfountain did believe in a variation of the same Knowing. But refusing outright would certainly harm her prospects. If she wanted her situation to change, she would have to *do* something to make it change. She was playing along for now, seeing what fate had in store for her. Lady Corinne hadn't won her power in a single day or a year. Sera had learned something of her methods during her long confinement.

Standing by the desk, she grazed her fingers across the book cover and picked it up—only to notice a folded piece of paper protruding from it. She hadn't left a marker herself. Squinting with curiosity, Sera opened the book and revealed a small folded rectangle covered in script. After removing the paper, she set the book down and quickly unfolded it.

He didn't fall. He was pushed.

Six words. They took up hardly any space at all, but Sera's stomach clenched, and her heart began to race. Someone had left her a note in a place where she was sure to find it. It was written in an unsteady, nervous hand, and the blot of ink in the corner told her it had been done in haste. Sera studied it carefully, trying to use logic to interpret what she saw.

He didn't fall. He was pushed. It could only be in reference to poor Mr. Skrelling, whose body she'd discovered on the beach at Pavenham Sky. Whoever had left her the note knew she had seen it. They also didn't want to be found out. There was no signature, nothing to identify the writer. Yet . . . Sera's mind immediately went to the young maid who had been paying her special attention. She felt a shiver of certainty go down her back, a feeling that could only come from the Mysteries. This was Becka's handwriting. That utter conviction went down to the depths of Sera's heart. The rightness of the insight struck her with the clarity of a bell.

Sera folded the note and slipped it into her pocket. The maid had witnessed something. And judging from the note, she had witnessed a murder. At Pavenham Sky. Though she'd long suspected Lady Corinne had played an integral role in her own downfall, this was much, much worse. No wonder the young maid had a frightened look in her eye. She had seen something horrible and now carried a burdensome secret. Who could she share it with? Her position at the manor was of the lowest kind. Who would believe her?

Sera would.

Sera the shunned. Sera the persecuted. Sera the patient.

Becka's staring had been a mute entreaty for her to pay attention. But how could she arrange a private conversation with the girl without putting them both at risk? Sera would have to be subtle. Extremely subtle. And she would need to watch for opportunities.

After dinner that night, Sera decided to take matters into her own hands. She found Master Sewell, who was directing the servants to clean up after the meal.

"Master Sewell?" she asked at his shoulder, approaching him from behind.

He turned, his brow furrowed. "Yes?"

She sighed. "I made a little mess in the library. I was trying to reach a book, and all the ones on the shelf next to it came tumbling down. One knocked over a plant, I'm afraid. I'm sorry, but I wanted you to know." She showed him the book in her hands. "I got the one I wanted."

She smiled sweetly at him.

Master Sewell rolled his eyes. "The next time you need help reaching a shelf, Miss Fitzempress, just ask."

"I will, I promise," she said, then turned and went back to her room, her heart giddy with excitement. If she had asked Lady Corinne to borrow a maid, it would have seemed suspicious and out of character. But make a mess, especially one involving soil, and they'd put the lowest servant on it. Sera anticipated they'd send Becka.

She was right.

In her room, Sera read from the book. Actually, she just flipped a few pages and adopted a feckless air. She didn't think she was being watched from a Leering in the room, but she couldn't tell for certain. After a time, she pretended to be bored with the book and went back to the library to fetch another.

And there was Becka on the floor, scrubbing the mess from the rug. The books had already been reassembled on the shelf. Handfuls of soil had been scooped back inside the pot. The girl glanced up at Sera, who was watching her closely to judge for a reaction. Her patience was rewarded.

Becka started with surprise and then quickly looked down and scrubbed harder. Some of her hair was pushed back over her ear, and Sera could see the skin of her ear turn bright pink.

Sera walked past her, ignoring her completely, and went to the shelves near her. She set down the book she'd returned and began to peruse the other books on the shelf, listening carefully to Becka's rapid breathing.

Sera moved a little closer to her, still focused on the books. Her own heart was pounding. She reached out and touched the spine of a book, tilting her head sideways.

"I found your note," Sera whispered. "Thank you."

She'd been thinking all day about what she might say. Would the girl deny it? It was impossible to predict.

"M-miss?" Becka stammered, still not looking up.

"The note you left in the book," Sera said again, very softly. She watched as the maid stopped scrubbing. Her hands clenched the rag tightly. Her little shoulders quivered.

"We can't talk here," Sera whispered, pulling a book out and turning it over in her hands. "But we need to talk soon. I'll leave a note for you in the same book and put it on the desk. Whatever you saw, I want to know about it."

The girl shuddered as if with cold. "Y-yes, m-miss."

"Thank you, Becka." Sera folded the book into her bosom and left the library, not looking directly at the girl once.

Sera knew the Leerings that controlled the light, heat, and sound in a manor could also be used to eavesdrop on any room in the manor at any time. And yet the household staff was kept busy, and it seemed unlikely the keeper would do such spying unless there was a direct concern.

Sera suspected that if she left her room at night, a Leering would notify the keeper, who would then watch where she went. Her actions were probably suspect, but she hoped that her complacency had lulled their vigilance. She couldn't wait forever for answers. A full day had already passed since she'd confirmed the note had come from the girl. The privy council would summon her again, and then she might not get the chance to corner Becka.

Sera had spent a large part of the day covertly studying the manor, looking for the Leerings. She channeled her thoughts to sense their presence, and while Cettie would have found the exercise simple, it was a struggle for Sera. Finally, she'd found a solution. There was a linen closet on the floor with the guest rooms, which, to Sera's best inspection, contained no Leerings at all. It was where the extra sheets for the beds were stored and shallow enough that light from the hall could reach it. It wasn't used in the evenings, and Sera had made it a point to walk by it multiple times.

So Sera left a note in the book that said *linen closet after supper*. She was taking a risk. It was clear to her that Becka wanted to share what she knew, but the girl was undoubtedly terrified. Witnessing a murder would do that to anyone.

During dinner, Master Sewell told Sera that the privy council would ask to see her the next day. She nodded in acquiescence. Would Fitzroy be there? Would she have an opportunity to tell him what little she knew? She decided it might be best to slip him a note. She trusted him above anyone else on the council.

"Thank you, Master Sewell. I'll be ready."

Sera glanced at Lady Corinne across the table, envying her poise and calm, but hating her all the more for it.

When dinner was finished, Sera was dismissed back to her rooms while the guests gathered in the sitting room to start a game of dominion. The servants would be focused on cleaning the mess and preparing for more refreshments later. It wasn't a ball, so there would be no dancing, but this was the moment Sera was waiting for. The commotion of the guests would keep everyone's attention off her. The Lawton household ran like a military operation, with designated times and routines for even the smallest events. A small discrepancy could pass unnoticed. Sera was counting on it.

She walked slowly back to the stairs and went up to the third floor where her rooms were situated. Most of the servants rushed to and fro below, but the upper floors were quiet and empty. Her heart tingled with excitement.

Sera dragged her fingers along the wall as she walked nonchalantly forward. The door to the closet was at the turn ahead. She paused when she got there, took a deep breath, and then twisted open the handle and pulled it open.

Disappointment struck a heavy blow.

Becka wasn't there.

She stood there for a moment, stunned, then shut the door as if she'd made a mistake and continued down the hall.

Back in her room, Sera examined the book. The note was still wedged inside it. But another word had been added to it.

No.

CHAPTER THIRTEEN

SECRETS

Sera awoke in the middle of the night. A sound had disturbed her sleep, and her eyes shot open, her heartbeat thrumming at the knowledge that she'd heard something. Festering disappointment had kept her up late, but she must have fallen asleep at some point. It was dark still, dark as a crypt. The sound came again, and this time she recognized it—the soft groan of the door handle turning. She lifted herself up slightly to see the door better.

Sera's mind became sharp and alert as she lay in the guest bed in her nightdress. There was a surfeit of pillows, and their quicksand softness made her feel especially vulnerable. A slit of black appeared at the front of the room—the door was being opened from without. She wanted to call out, but she hesitated. Was it better to feign sleep? A small figure in a white nightdress appeared in the black, dark hair falling over the crisp white fabric. Enough dim moonlight trickled in from the diaphanous curtains for her to make out that it was Becka. Sera slowly eased back down on the pillows to watch, the fear easing out of her.

The girl stole in quietly, walking with exaggerated slowness over to Sera's writing desk where she kept her books. There was something in Becka's hand—a folded note. Sera observed the girl tread softly, her bare feet not making a sound on the rug. Becka went to the table, carefully lifted one of the books, and slid the note underneath it. A little rasp from the paper was the only sound.

Sera slowly eased herself up to a sitting position, careful not to make a sound. After a moment of pondering what to do next, Sera waited until the girl was halfway to the door. The note had been left. If the girl ran, at least Sera had that.

"Becka," she whispered.

The maid stifled an audible *"Eeeep!"* with her hand and froze. Sera quickly rose from the bed and hurried to the door, blocking it. The maid trembled violently.

With her back to the door, Sera felt with her hands and shut it all the way. There was a muted thump and the clicking of the latch.

"I'm sorry, miss, I'm sorry, miss," Becka stammered worriedly. "I shouldn't have crept in like that. I'm so sorry."

"Don't be frightened," Sera said, trying to calm her. "I'm glad you came."

"Please let me go. If I'm caught in here . . ." Her voice broke as she started to cry.

Sera's heart ached for the girl. She wanted to relieve her suffering, but she also had to know what she had seen.

"It's very late, isn't it?" Sera said, coming closer. She put a hand on her thin shoulder. "No one else is awake?"

"No one, miss," Becka said through her tears. "I couldn't sleep. Not after I didn't come. I just couldn't do it, miss."

"I know you're scared, Becka. You've been carrying an awful secret, haven't you?"

The girl stared at Sera's face and nodded miserably.

Sera glanced around the dark room. With the room so dark, the Leerings wouldn't be able to see them very well. Still, there was a better place to hide. A safer place.

"Let's go inside the wardrobe. It's big enough to fit us both. Then we can talk. Would you do that for me?"

Becka bit her lip and looked nervously at the door. "I shouldn't be here."

"I know. Sometimes we must be brave, though. We're both prisoners here, Becka. But maybe we can be friends."

"Friends?" said the girl in astonishment.

"My best friend is from the Fells," Sera said. "You're not from there, are you?"

"No, Miss Fitzempress. I'm from the City. M-my mother serves Lady Kimball."

Sera knew the name and the woman's daughter. No wonder Becka was so terrified to lose her position. To do so would no doubt endanger her mother's livelihood as well.

"To the wardrobe, then? No one can hear us in there."

Becka looked nervously at the door again, wringing her hands. But she nodded and followed Sera to the massive wardrobe. Sera moved aside the dresses on the hangers and made a space for the two of them to sit on the floor, the fabric draping over their shoulders. She could hear the little maid's worried breathing in the darkness. The floor of the wardrobe was planked in cedar, providing a soothing smell.

"There, that's better," Sera said. "Why didn't you come after dinner?"

"I w-was too scared, miss," she replied with shame. "If someone saw us . . . We've all been strictly forbidden to talk to you. I'm-I'm breaking the rules right now."

"I know, Becka," Sera said, touching the girl's arm. "This is very important, though. Tell me what you saw."

"But if she found out," Becka moaned. "I don't want it to happen to me."

"What to happen?" The girl was utterly terrified. Sera could hear her teeth rattling as she trembled.

"He was pushed off, miss. *Off.* He was found on the beach, but he fell from the gardens, not from the zephyr like they told us."

"The young advocate?"

"Yes," Becka said with a shudder in her voice. "Mistress has a man who works for her. One who comes in secret. He looks so angry, so fierce. He's got a scar on his cheek. I've seen him before when I've gone to clean her room. He scares me, miss."

The news sent a flash of heat through Sera's chest. The girl's description sounded like the kishion who had tried to abduct Cettie at Muirwood. The one whose actions had led to the war. Could he really be working for Lady Corinne? This was damaging news, indeed. It would rock Pavenham Sky to its core. No, it would rock the *empire* to its core. Sera felt a throb of emotion, mostly revenge, but she tamped it down.

"I've heard of this man," Sera said. "I've not seen him at the manor."

"He comes and goes," Becka says. "There was a storm that night. I was in the garden watching . . . watching the lightning. It was so bright. I heard them coming and hid myself. I wasn't supposed to be out there. No one saw me. But the young man, he was being taken by force. The man . . . the man who came from darkness . . . he had him by the neck and arm. I watched them leave, watched them go past my dark patch of trees. I was so frightened, I couldn't move." She sniffed and started to weep softly again.

Sera rubbed her shoulder comfortingly, imagining the terror the young maid had experienced. She couldn't be more than twelve, an age Sera remembered well. That was the year she'd first met Will and had become entangled in the politics of the empire. Even then, Lady Corinne had been scheming against her.

"How do you know he was pushed?" Sera asked after the sobs had subsided.

Becka sniffled. "I'm sorry, miss. Sorry to cry. I've been so scared. There was no one I could tell. Who would believe me? I was still hiding when the dark man returned. He came back alone, and I heard him mutter that one problem had been solved and now it was time to get rid of the zephyr. I knew the young man had come by zephyr. She had them both killed, miss. The advocate *and* the pilot. I don't know why, and I don't know what to do. It's eating away at my heart, but if I tell anyone else, they'll throw me off the manor too, won't they? I-I don't think I could bear that."

"Sshhhh," Sera soothed, rubbing her shoulder. Not only did she want revenge for her own sake, but for the girl's as well. If the privy council learned of this deed, they would have to investigate it. But Lady Corinne was on the privy council, and Sera's father, the emperor, had some sort of sick fixation with her. Sera couldn't accuse her in front of everyone. And what would happen to Becka? If the mistress of Pavenham Sky had the merest inkling her maid had been a witness, there was no doubt in Sera's mind that Becka's life would not be worth salt.

Sera hooked her hand around Becka's neck and pulled her close, hugging her. The little maid sniffled and trembled in her arms. Sera's heart ached with compassion for the girl. After the tide of emotions relented, Sera took her hands.

"I promise you, Becka, that I won't do anything about this until I am certain you will be safe. I won't tell anyone unless they have my absolute trust. What she did was very wrong. It was wicked. That young man and I went to school together. He didn't deserve to die and especially not in that terrible way. We must part, but I will do my best to see you are brought to safety. I wish I could keep you with me as my maid, but that would make Lady Corinne suspicious."

"But you *can*, miss," said Becka hopefully. "That's why I came with the note. Before we left Pavenham Sky, Master Sewell asked the maids if one of us would volunteer to work with you. He said that you might be going to another world for a time. He said the lady would be very grateful to have one of us go with you and serve you. No one wanted to go. Even as a favor to the lady."

"Did you volunteer, sweet Becka?" Sera gasped in surprise, a feeling of relief flooding her.

"I . . . I did, Miss Fitzempress. I've been wanting to tell you. I'm not supposed to. Not yet anyway."

Sera squeezed the girl's hands again. This was beyond all odds, beyond coincidence. The Mysteries were more powerful than she had yet imagined. Her heart throbbed with gratitude.

"I would like that, Becka," Sera said, feeling tears in her own throat. "I would like that very much."

The note Becka had left on the desk revealed nothing of Mr. Skrelling's murder. It only informed her of the new arrangement. When the two girls served her the next morning, Becka shot her a grateful look, but she was solemn in her appearance, not giving away any indication that they'd spent part of the night together hidden in the cedar-lined wardrobe.

They helped Sera dress for her appointment with the privy council. Her hair was braided and coiffed and fastened with pins. Sera gazed at herself in the mirror, marveling at how calm and tranquil she looked on the outside. Her thoughts, on the other hand, were fierce and determined. She would bring about Lady Corinne's downfall. Whatever it took to achieve it.

At breakfast, Lady Corinne looked as she always did, resplendent in the latest fashions, her air mysterious and thoughtful. But Sera couldn't help but see her differently now. She'd always thought the lady a spider, yes, but now she saw her as a woman who would do anything to keep her power. What message had Mr. Skrelling brought that had cost him his life? What secret had been thrown off a floating manor to perish in the sea?

After the meal, she and the lady were given cloaks to protect them from the rain and escorted to the Lawtons' tempest, which would bring them to court. The wind raged against them, pelting them with rain as they walked. After boarding the tempest, Sera settled into her stateroom. She normally liked walking the deck and enjoying the view, but not in such foul weather.

Upon reaching their destination, Lady Corinne sauntered immediately into the meeting room, and Sera watched bitterly as her father stared at the stylish woman with undisguised hunger. The door shut behind them, and Master Sewell waited with Sera for her turn to speak to the privy council.

"You may as well stop pacing and sit down," Master Sewell said archly. "They will be in there a while before it's your turn."

"I'm nervous, Master Sewell, is that so surprising?"

"No, it's appropriate, ma'am. I was just advising you, that's all."

"Thank you for your advice. Do you really think that they will send me to Kingfountain?"

"I have no special insight, ma'am. But it would serve political expedience. Anything to stop this war. We are all weary of it."

Sera paused in her pacing to scrutinize him. "Would *you* give up your country and your beliefs, Master Sewell, to end it?"

He pursed his lips. "We all must make sacrifices, ma'am."

"The ancients used to sacrifice animals," Sera said with a tone of mockery. "Now I have compassion for the poor beasts. If I go, if I become their queen, then I will not be able to be my father's heir."

Sewell clasped his hands behind his back and leaned against the wall. "That may be the point, ma'am," he said.

There were things she liked about Master Sewell. He was charming, diligent, conscientious. Was he part of the plot or an unwitting servant?

Did it even matter? Sera was nineteen and eligible to be heir. But she was no longer naïve.

Lady Corinne's ambitions had not yet been satisfied. There was a reason she'd cultivated a relationship with Sera's father. Perhaps there was a larger game afoot—one that would only end when Lady Corinne ruled everyone.

It was several hours later when the doors to the privy council opened. There was much noise and conversation going on inside. She saw the prime minister, Lord Welles, on his perch of power, vain as a peacock. She abhorred the man. Her father looked pasty and ill, but he was in a jovial mood and sipped from a chalice. And Lady Corinne sat next to him, adjacent to the seat of power. There was no sign of Lord Fitzroy.

So, her three enemies were assembled against her.

Sera strode into the chamber, adopting an air of submission and meekness. But in her heart, she vowed to bring all three of them crashing down.

CHAPTER FOURTEEN

Anathema

It was the first time Sera had faced the full privy council since her disgrace. She knew they would judge her by her appearance, her demeanor, and most importantly, her words. She recognized most of the faces as she walked in and was led to a seat. It wasn't beside her father, a place she might go if she were the heir presumptive. Instead, she was brought to a stuffed chair near the Minister of Thought and the Minister of Law. Although she recognized some of the ladies on the council, others had changed, and they had the haughty looks of women who were Lady Corinne's set. Those women scrutinized her, concealing their disdain mostly—except for their eyes.

When Sera sat down, she felt her feet graze the floor and felt slightly better that she'd grown at least a little bit since her last encounter there. Inside she was seething with emotions, from the desire to repudiate the people who had entrapped her. Surely some of them expected this. She was on display for all to see. Well, let them.

"Thank you for joining us, Your Highness," said Lord Welles, the prime minister. Gone was the familiarity, the warmth that had made her trust him. He was civil, but cautious, as if she might suddenly bite him.

She nodded to him and said nothing. One of Lady Corinne's tricks.

"It has been several years since you have been before the privy council," Welles continued. "I think there is hope, from many of us, that you have learned the importance of propriety in our society."

He was giving her a chance to rebel. Tempting her even. She didn't rise to snatch at the bait.

"I have indeed," Sera replied in a humble voice. She even lowered her gaze. That would be a nice touch.

A few murmurs came from the assembled council. Was it approval? Surprise? It was difficult to tell.

"We trust that you have," Welles said. "A three-year exile may feel long to so young a person as yourself. But Lady Corinne has expressed her confidence to the council that you are . . . rehabilitated. You've caused no further scandal, and the people, well, the commoners are quite forgiving. It seems you're more popular than ever these days."

Sera almost flinched, but she remained cool and dispassionate. "I wouldn't know anything about that," she said in a soft voice. "I know very little about what is going on in the empire."

"As is understandable given your circumstances. But events are what brings you before us today. Your Majesty, if you would?"

It was Father's turn now. Sera found her insides twisting with anger, but she shielded all emotion from her face. Her father had gained even more weight, and his hair was thinning and gray. He looked awful, but he was still her father, and his eyes were still full of malice. He looked as uncomfortable as Sera felt.

"Yes, yes, Welles, I suppose we should get on with it. You are still quite popular with the masses, as Welles alluded to. Even after all you've done."

Sera felt her cheeks start to sizzle. She wouldn't meet his contempt with a surge of rebellion.

"Yes, after all you've done," he repeated for emphasis. "Well, the people aren't known for their wisdom or their discretion. We've been at war with Kingfountain for three years now. Surely you did know *that*?"

"Indeed," Sera replied simply.

"Good. It's run up a huge toll in lives. Thankfully, Lord Fitzroy has been able to deduce their attacks before they've come. It's uncanny really. They call him Fitzroy Harbinger. He's been able to hold off their encroachments, and we've managed to retake cities lost to the hollow crown. This conflict has bled both sides in coin and youth. Fitzroy feels that if the next attack doesn't prove decisive, there may be an opportunity to negotiate an armistice. Do you know what that means?"

"Yes, Your Majesty," Sera answered. She almost called him *Father*, but she knew how that provoked him.

"Good. Then I don't need to explain it to you. The privy council believes that the court of Kingfountain may still be open to a marriage alliance and a trade of technologies. Some think that this conflict stems from their distrust of what we've accomplished, especially in the realm of the Ministry of Wind. The council is considering whether to send *you* as a peace ambassador to the court of Kingfountain to negotiate the armistice. Our intelligence suggests that the prince was rather taken with you during his brief sojourn among us. You impressed him, Seraphin. If you could broker a peace between our worlds, it would do much to heal the rift between *us*."

Sera looked up at him, soaking in the hope in his expression. He seemed taken aback by her humbled demeanor. Did he trust his eyes? Inside, she was roiling.

"If I can be of service to the empire," she said.

Father's eyebrows arched at her response. "Surely, you must understand that the prince may require a marriage alliance as part of the negotiation," he said hesitantly. "Although our worlds share a common belief in the Knowing, our interpretation is much more . . . accommodating than theirs. You may be asked to submit to the water rite."

The Minister of Thought, Allanom Scott, reached out and patted her arm with his gloved hand. "We've spoken of this before, my dear, and you've had some time to reflect on it. The council would not wish you to act against your conscience. You may not be required to renounce your beliefs, but if the prince insists that you adopt the customs of his less civilized realm, would you be prepared, *ahem*, to do so?"

All eyes were on her. If she said no, then she would not be given the chance to be an ambassador. She didn't want to renounce her beliefs or her right to be considered an heir of the empire. But if she refused this mission, where would they put her next? Would they marry her off to some lord of their choosing? Perhaps even someone old and decrepit? She, too, had thought highly of the prince, and there was no denying she was curious about his world. This might be her best, or only, chance of influencing what happened to her. At the moment, she felt it was appropriate that her conscience should appear flexible.

"I would, High Seer," she answered firmly. "It would be a sacrifice. But so many have already sacrificed for the empire. So many have died. If there is a chance to stop more widows from grieving, more sisters weeping for dead brothers, then we must take that chance." She sighed and bowed her head. "I will do what I must."

There were more murmurs now, which caused Sera to look up in surprise. Many of the members of the privy council nodded in approval. They wanted to believe that she had succumbed to Lady Corinne's influence . . . and perhaps she had, only not in the way they thought. She had learned from the lady's subterfuge, her ability to equivocate convincingly when the need arose. Some of the council members began conversing in low tones, creating a swelling noise in the room.

Lord Welles coughed loudly. "Your sentiments are commendable, Princess. I applaud your willingness to sacrifice yourself to become a *queen*." His inflection was laced with sarcasm. "I know it's not what you wanted. And it may come to naught. Our spies tell us that Kingfountain is going to hit us hard in this attack. Their general is cunning and, we are told, anxious to overshadow the king he serves. If they defeat us in Hautland, they will not listen to an overture for peace. It would be taken as an indication that we're going to surrender. We'd sooner collapse all the arches rather than allow that to happen, but to do so would be to relinquish all of our trading partners. It would allow Kingfountain to win what is ours. No, we cannot allow that either."

"Hear, hear," said another council member sharply.

Welles held up his hand to forestall other similar agreements. "But, to put it bluntly, Seraphin, there are many people down below who might . . . misinterpret the situation. There are factions that might feel this council compelled you to sacrifice yourself." The murmurs in the chamber grew quiet again. "These individuals might rise in revolt if they were to learn about your peace mission. As I said, you are quite popular these days. After the negotiations end, you may need to assure the populace in a public statement that you did not act under coercion. What do you say to that?"

Sera felt a thrill go through her and almost smiled. What an opportunity that would be! To voice her beliefs and convictions in front of a crowd. Oh, she would relish it.

She did not answer straightaway. They could not know her thoughts, and yet she did not wish to lie. She would be truthful. Mostly. Let them judge her words however they wished.

Sera bowed her head. "I will do what is best for our people," she said simply. "Even if some of them don't understand why I do it."

Her words were met with applause from the privy council. The sudden noise startled her into looking up again, and she regarded those gathered around her with wonder. An involuntary smile came to her mouth. Their approbation did feel good, even though she didn't want it. She touched her heart as if their applause humbled her. Some of the privy council members rose while they clapped.

Sera looked around the room, bowing her head in submission. Then she glanced at Lady Corinne, seated by her father. The regal woman wasn't clapping. She was studying Sera with wary eyes.

You should fear me, Sera thought before turning away.

Her appearance at the council had been left to the end of the meeting. Following the adjournment, many members of the council approached her with praise and encouraging words. She even overheard a few of them praising Lady Corinne for the work she had done with the princess. Lady Corinne deflected all praise from herself.

Sera had started to wonder how long she'd be the target of such effusive attention when Lord Prentice, the Minister of Wind, greeted her with a brief bow. She had wanted to see him but dared not seek him out, knowing that she was being watched.

"Well done, Your Highness," he said with a sour expression. He looked about to leave, but she stepped in his path.

"Lord Prentice, I was hoping to see Admiral Fitzroy soon."

"Soon? Not likely, Your Highness. He's on a hurricane off the coast of Hautland waiting for the storm."

"You mean the battle?"

"No, I mean an actual storm. There's no denying the storm glasses' prediction. The winds are all blowing northeast. I spoke to him through the Command Leering earlier today. He's ready for the battle. Then all will change," he added grumpily.

"What do you mean, sir?" she asked.

"Well, there will be a season of peace, of course. And Lord Scott will no doubt become the prime minister. The Ministry of Thought is always predominant in times of peace." He said it with such resentment, as if his turn had been too brief for him. "Well, such is the way of life. We each get our turn. I'm sure the good admiral will get his chance after Scott is done with it. Well, he can have it. I don't want it."

Sera could sense he was patently lying. She'd never liked the man—and he'd made his distaste for her egalitarian sensibilities known to her.

"Thank you, Lord Prentice. Have there been any more cases of the cholera morbus? I really am ignorant of the current state of affairs."

"Oh, certainly," he said. "Especially among the troops. There's a young doctor, studied in my ministry at school . . . you probably know him, Mr. Creigh."

"I do indeed," Sera said with a smile.

"He wanted to study the disease ere he was done taking the Test. When the first cases began on the hurricane *Anathema*, he was sent for immediately. All the other War doctors wanted to flee for fear of infection. Not Creigh. Brave chap. Don't know what causes it, but it will be our ministry that cures it. Mark my words!"

"I will, Lord Prentice. Thank you for informing me."

"Not at all, young lady. I must be going."

Sera curtsied to him and glanced over at Lady Corinne. The mistress of Pavenham Sky was still watching her closely. Master Sewell was standing beside his mistress, and after she whispered something to him, he nodded and maneuvered his way across the room.

"I think it went well?" Sera said to him.

"We could hear the applause on the other side of the door, ma'am," Sewell answered, bowing. "Congratulations are in order."

"I don't think so. My part in all this has been very small."

"Yes, but your part is soon to become paramount. My lady informs me that you will likely be traveling to the court of Kingfountain. You'll be given a maid to attend to you while you're there. A companion of sorts."

"Do I get to pick her?" Sera asked hopefully, feigning her excitement.

"Sorry, ma'am. As you can imagine, none of Her Ladyship's maids were willing to part from Pavenham Sky. But they do obey when asked. Just as you did today. Your maid's name is Becka Monstrum, daughter of the maid of Lady Kimball from the towers in the City. She's a quiet lass. Rather shy. She's very nervous about going and may experience some pangs of homesickness."

"Poor dear," Sera said, shaking her head. "Tell her I'll be gentle."

Sewell smirked. “I wouldn’t expect otherwise, ma’am. If all goes to plan, you’ll be missed at Pavenham Sky, I’m sure.”

“I doubt it,” Sera replied, looking him straight in the eye. “But I will miss the beach and that fallen tree and the sound of the surf crashing on the rocks.”

“There’s quite a bit of that in Kingfountain,” he said with a bow. “They worship the waves of the sea there. Maybe you’ll meet a water sprite,” he added with a teasing tone.

“I hope so,” Sera said with exaggerated eagerness.

“Your attention, please!” said a commanding voice, silencing the chatter. Quiet descended on the room. Lord Welles stood at the entryway, his face grave. The room was completely silent, as if everyone was collectively holding their breath. “The attack has begun,” he said.

A few gasps came. Eyes tightened with dread, some with greed.

The speculation of the war was nearing its end. Some would rise. Some would fall. The machine continued its endless churn.

Again they were expecting us. Our fleets crossed the mirror gate into a storm. The waves tossed, and the skies were black and crackling. Then came the storm of bullets and fire from above. It was a catastrophe. It spelled ruin. Our first phalanx of ships was completely obliterated by the attack. The waters were thick with the dead and the drowning. But the Deep Fathoms were not to be overruled so quickly. The weather hampered their victory as much as it ensured our failure. I personally saw three hurricanes struck by lightning and crash into the sea.

Though we lost the battle by any objective measure, I told the court at Kingfountain that we won but took heavy losses. If the other side had pressed the attack and chased us back through the mirror gate, they would have found no opposition. It's a curiosity that they didn't, despite the reputation Fitzroy has for leadership and wisdom. They could have taken the war to us, but instead they suffered us to retreat—even to leave a token force to collect the corpses. But sometimes the dead can be a great advantage.

When they describe the Battle of Hautland, what will be said? History, after all, is the version of past events that people have decided to agree upon. We will each tell our own version of events. And who is to know the truth save the Fountain?

—Leon Montpensier, Duke of La Marche

CETTIE

CHAPTER FIFTEEN

INTO THE GROTTO

When Cettie had last taken the river walk to the grotto, she'd been a girl of twelve, accompanied by Anna and Adam. But the memories of that afternoon were so vivid that she still recognized the path, the wood bridges, the crystal-clear water, and the narrow chasm carved by the river itself. Tree roots were enmeshed with rock on either side of the river, and some little trickles of water came down the sides.

The last time had been a pleasant journey that had ended in fear. This time, she hiked the trail with Rand Patchett, Stephen Fitzroy, and ten other men. Her quiet, stoic escort, Maxfield Strong, had remained behind at the manor, awaiting their return. Her companions each carried an arquebus, but Cettie did not, for she'd never trained in shooting at school. Though she was a proficient archer and had considered bringing a longbow and arrows, her skills were better suited to controlling the Leerings. Besides, if twelve men could not defeat the creature with their weapons, what good would she be with her bow?

A loud slap startled her, and she turned to see Stephen examining a bloody mosquito on his palm. He scowled in disgust and brushed the remains against the chasm wall. His discontented look shifted to Rand, who led the journey, much to Stephen's disdain and embarrassment.

When he noticed Cettie was watching him, his expression turned to one of chagrin.

"Have you found anything about the missing shipment of quicksilver?" she asked him, breathing hard. They were not keeping a leisurely pace.

Stephen brushed his forearm against his mouth. "No, there's been no word at all. Not only is the shipment missing, but the tempest that carried it is also gone. Do you know how much those cost?"

"I do," Cettie answered, her heart sinking. With the war going on, the sky ship would be impossible to replace.

"I don't know what we're going to do," Stephen said darkly. "I've ruined everything."

"We'll make it right, piece by piece," Cettie answered. "Just as Father would."

The trail ended abruptly at a wooden ladder leading up to a trail of planks built against the side of the rock wall. Rand slung his weapon around his back with its strap and ambled up the incline. Stephen went next, his face flushed and sweating. Then Cettie climbed up and was surprised to find Rand waiting there, crouching, hand outstretched to help her up. Stephen stood nearby, hands on his hips, staring down the trail.

Cettie was taken aback, but she reached up and felt Rand's strong, calloused grip. It was a strange sort of familiarity, since neither of them wore the traditional gloves. With ease, he pulled her onto the planked walk.

"Thank you," she said, and he shrugged with unconcern.

"Lead the way," Rand told Stephen. There was only room to walk single file. The other men shuffled up the ladder rungs one by one.

Stephen did as he was told, though his expression was marred by resentment. The glassy water down below looked so refreshing. In the distance they could hear the waterfall. If Mr. Patchett was experiencing any dread, he didn't let it show. He looked as unconcerned as a man going for a walk in a garden, while Stephen grew edgier with each step he took toward the grotto. Rand looked back to count the men, then pursed his lips and nodded.

"None have forsaken us yet," he whispered to Cettie. "That's a good sign."

"Your little speech before we left gave them some confidence, I think," Cettie replied.

"Men are more apt to follow if they believe you know where you're going," he said, smiling. "Even if you're lost, you mustn't look like you are."

They passed a giant green leaf deflecting a small rivulet of water that seemed to come from the cracked bowels of the stone around them. Rand paused to admire it, then bent low and turned his head so that the water ran into his mouth. He drank a little and then straightened, wiping his mouth on his sleeve. He nodded to her in appreciation and continued. Cettie glanced back and noticed one of the miners copying him.

They had left Fog Willows immediately for Dolcoath and planned the excursion to allow for the maximum amount of daylight, which Rand believed would help their mission. The muted sunlight emanating through the screen of trees made everything seem green and lush—the beauty of the day a sharp contrast to the dangers of their mission. The thunder of the waterfall increased as they approached the grotto, and finally they reached the heap of boulders that marked the entrance. Memories preyed on her mind. The first time she'd visited this grotto she'd barely managed to get out.

Cettie sensed the Leerings inside the cave. The magic touched her like music, and the chords and strain were hollow and mournful. She looked around and saw the worry and fear on the miners' faces. Each man held his arquebus in a white-knuckled grip. There was only one exception.

Rand's weapon still hung from its shoulder strap as he hiked to a large boulder and stood atop it, gazing into the deep shadows of the grotto. He motioned for Cettie and Stephen to approach, and they did.

Planting his hands on his hips, he said, "This feels like the lair of a Fear Liath. Sunlight is the only thing that makes them vulnerable."

"There's no sunlight that can reach the end of that cave," Stephen said, shaking his head and pointing. His eyes glimmered with fear.

Rand looked at him and gave an exaggerated sigh. Then he gazed at Cettie. "That's why the Leerings are there, Stephen. Their light is comparable to sunlight. So long as they shine as bright as daylight, the beast will be vulnerable to our weapons. I think Miss Cettie here could make them glow rather brilliantly—enough so that the beast will be driven toward us. The biggest danger is the creature's ability to play with our heads . . . freeze us with fear and make us lose our resolve. Now, I'll scout ahead and check the boundaries. I want you to set up the miners around the grotto, each with a clear shot at the mouth of the cave. There is enough light out there for them to injure or kill it. Can you do that?"

Stephen, who was still gazing fearfully at the grotto, nodded brusquely.

"Good. I'll be back presently."

Cettie stopped Rand with a touch. "Will it attack you if you come near?"

He looked surprised by her question and perhaps her concern. "I don't think so. I'm not afraid of it." Then he stepped off the boulder and entered the headwaters of the river. The water went up to the top of his boots, which were cuffed above his knees. He maneuvered over the river rock until he found a shallower path to follow.

While Cettie watched Rand venture into the grotto, Stephen began to curtly order the men into position.

On Cettie's last encounter with the Fear Liath, its thoughts had twisted her mind into knots, paralyzing her with fear. She was a maston now, and she'd had years of practice calming her thoughts. There was reason to be concerned, but she wanted to project the same calm assurance she saw in Rand.

"No, that one. Yes, behind that boulder. You two, over to that one. Go," Stephen said, ordering the last of the men into a protected position.

Cettie folded her arms worriedly as Rand disappeared into the grotto. The miners had fanned out and stood with their weapons ready. She could see the concern in their eyes, but they were much more willing to defend the area outside the grotto than they were to venture inside it.

Rand returned, balancing well across the river rock until he reached them. Stephen approached, his lips pursed and grim.

"Well?" Stephen asked impatiently.

"I think you'd both better come with me," Rand replied. "The Leerings are there, but . . . something is wrong. I can't make it out."

"Cettie can go with you," Stephen said.

Rand gave him a sharp look but lowered his voice. "If she goes in and you do not, you'll lose all respect from the miners. Come, Stephen. I'm trying to help you regain their confidence."

Stephen's face turned white with fear. "W-what if one of the men shoots at us?"

Rand looked at him seriously. "All three of us are mastons. They can't harm us with their arquebuses. Come, Stephen. You can do this. I know you can."

Stephen was trembling slightly, but he nodded again and stepped off the rock. Rand gave him an approving smile. He reached up so Cettie would have something to grab onto before stepping into the river. She took his hand again and then stepped into the shockingly cold water. Her skirts immediately hugged her legs.

"Follow where I walk," he told her, keeping hold of her hand to help guide her. She was fearful she'd fall face-first into it and soak herself through.

Stephen gripped his arquebus and pointed the barrel toward the grotto as he moved forward, step by step. Cettie had always wondered what it looked like beyond the overhanging rock ceiling. Her heart beat fiercely in her chest, and she was conflicted by her feelings—the sensation of the cold water against her legs, Rand's firm grip on her hand, and the unknown facing them. They all entered the shadowy interior of the grotto, but they had not gone far enough yet for it to be completely dark.

The first Leering was just inside the shadows, carved into the rocky side of the cave. The face was that of an angry man with wrinkles and crags around the eyes. The water echoed strangely in her ears now that they'd ventured within the space. Then her shoe shifted on the slippery stone beneath it, and she would have plunged into the water had Rand not pulled her back just in time. He cocked a grin at her but then raised his brows, looking for assurance that she could go on. She nodded and continued.

"This is as far as I went," Stephen said, his voice sounding strange in the chamber.

"The first Leering is here, and there's another deeper in," Rand said. "Both are still active, but something's off. They create a shield of sorts, mostly to prevent anyone from venturing into the deeper caves. The Fear Liath naturally attract the fearful. We shouldn't have been able to come in this far without releasing the first Leering. Can you inspect it, Cettie?"

Her dress was soaking up more water, making her shiver. She moved toward the Leering carved into the wall and reached out to touch it.

"Be careful," Rand said before she did. "Sometimes they'll try to lock minds with you."

She nodded, acknowledging the risk, and set her palm on the rugged stone face. She felt the magic of the Leering swaying and pulsing, a warning song to repulse anyone from exploring the caves. Only it was unusually muted, not strong enough to affect someone's mind.

She did not sense the creature in its lair. If it was there, it was hiding from her. Cettie let herself drift more deeply into the magic, keeping on her guard. There was a distortion in it—a subtle weave that had been added. Her memory shot back to the night Anna had been abducted from Muirwood. The defenses of the abbey had been breached by just such a trick.

"Do you sense anything?" Rand asked, standing behind her.

"I do," she answered. "It's been tampered with."

"How can you tell?" Stephen asked, still squinting deeper into the shadows, fear emanating from him.

"Because she's bloody good with Leerings!" Rand scoffed. Then he turned to her. "Did you notice there weren't any Myriad Ones in here? I can't feel a single one."

"Why would there be?" Stephen asked, bristling.

"Because they are attracted to strong emotions. This place," he said, gazing up at the rocky ceiling and around the chamber, "is a feeding ground. Like a kirkyard," he added in a serious manner. "Come on. Let's check the next one."

The darkness grew more pronounced as they continued their exploration, and each step brought more worry into her chest.

"Can we have some more light, Cettie?" Rand asked. "Just a little. It will stay as far back as it must to remain in the dark."

She invoked both Leerings, and the space around them began to glow. Even Rand's face looked tense as he gazed at the walls of the interconnected caves. In the farthest corner of the space, there was a dark opening, a shaft leading into the throat of the mountain itself. The sight of it made Cettie's blood freeze.

"That's the place," Rand whispered. He brought his arquebus around. Stephen's weapon was trembling violently in his hands.

The other Leering was carved into the boulder facing the opening. Light shone from it into the gloom, but the cavern still looked inky and impenetrable. Cettie's mouth was dry, and her hands were chilled.

Rand stepped cautiously forward, aiming his arquebus at the opening. He motioned with one hand for Stephen to go around the other side.

"What do they look like?" Stephen whispered hoarsely. "I've only seen it on the move, and it's fast."

"Like an unholy vision," Rand replied. "Part bear, part nightmare. I still don't sense its thoughts, Cettie. Do you?"

It was difficult to even speak. Her own nerves were taut, like the bowstrings at the archery butts.

"No," she answered tremulously.

"Which is strange," he answered. "They have a strong instinct for survival." He continued ahead until he reached the second Leering. Stephen quaked and trembled, the arquebus rattling as he did so.

Then Rand lowered his weapon. He waved her over.

Cettie obeyed, her worries only growing as she took in his bleak expression. When she arrived, she saw that the Leering's face, although lightly glowing, was broken. As if someone had taken a hammer to it.

Who would have done such a thing? Would Mr. Savage have done it, knowing the fear it would cause in the people he used to help? Would he have braved such a monster in order to release it? Her mind returned to that long-ago night when Anna had been stolen. Could it be . . . ? And then her suspicions became vividly real when a noise rumbled from inside the blackness.

"Yes," said a voice that echoed inside the cave. A voice Cettie recognized. A man emerged from the tunnel, gripping a pistol. "Because I knew you'd come."

The kishion. The man who'd claimed to be her father.

CHAPTER SIXTEEN

Mystery

The dim light from the Leering revealed the man's familiar visage—the scar running down his cheekbone, his mass of dark hair, and his unshaven cheeks. His eyes bored into hers as they became silver, and a dark chord of magic swelled inside the grotto.

Out of the corner of her eye, Cettie saw Stephen raise the arquebus to his shoulder in a posture to fire. The kishion didn't give him a chance. He raised his own pistol first, and a deafening explosion ripped through the void along with a belch of fire from the tip of the weapon. Acrid smoke spread, and Stephen fell into the water, shrieking in pain. Cettie's heart spasmed with horror. A feeling of hopelessness and grief ravaged her senses, heightened by the dark magic swirling around the kishion. But Cettie refused to stand in the cold water and do nothing. She went to try to help Stephen, remembering how the Aldermaston's pilot had been killed in a similar attack. The water hampered her speed, and Stephen's groans and shouts of pain continued to echo off the walls. He thrashed in the water, which turned cloudy with blood.

Rand Patchett let out a cry of anger and fired his arquebus at the kishion. The shot missed, and the reverberation filled the space as the kishion and the dragoon engaged each other. Glancing at them, she saw

Rand use the butt of his arquebus to strike at the man who had ambushed them. He landed a blow before the kishion struck his face and knocked the weapon away.

Stephen's head went below the water, muffling his shouts, and he came up spluttering. Cettie grabbed him, lifting him up, afraid of the damage done. His shirt was soaked in blood, and his face was a mask of agony.

"Where, Stephen! Where did it hit you!" she cried, her thoughts scattering with fear.

"It hurts! Oh, shades! It hurts!" he wailed.

She gazed at his chest, where a direct hit was most likely to be fatal, but the blood wasn't thickest there. He thrashed in the water, full of terror and pain, and she struggled to steady him, to calm him.

"Where, Stephen?"

"My arm," he groaned.

His sleeve was drenched and nearly black with blood. His arm—that was a relief to her. He'd dropped his arquebus into the water, and his good hand was pressed against the wound.

Another explosion sounded, and the flash of fire gripped her attention. The kishion had let off another shot, but Rand had been struggling with the man's wrists when the weapon discharged. More stinging smoke billowed into the air. The kishion thumped his forehead into Rand's nose, then quickly wrapped his arm around the young man's neck and twisted, dragging his head underwater. Rand thrashed against the hold, but he wouldn't last long submerged. No one would.

Cettie saw Stephen's arquebus in the water and plunged her arms in to reach it.

"Cettie! Cettie, don't leave me!" Stephen begged.

The water covered her face, but she managed to retrieve the weapon. She brought it up and started toward the two fighters. Rand hammered his fist into the kishion's side repeatedly, causing grunts of pain, but he hadn't managed to break free. Cettie wiped water and hair from her face as she advanced on them, then held up the weapon, which was shaking. She didn't worry about hitting Rand. He was a maston, and the ball wouldn't kill him. But she only had a single shot before the arquebus would need to be reloaded—something she didn't know how to do.

The thrashing began to lessen as Rand ran out of air. Cettie raised the arquebus, gritting her teeth, and aimed.

The kishion turned his head, seeing her approach with the weapon.

"Would you kill your own father?" he said with anger. She felt a flash of emotion arc between them—a paralyzing uncertainty that sprang from his chest to hers. There was magic at play, and it was powerful.

Cettie steadied her arms as best she could. Her thoughts were iron against his. "You are *not* my father," she said coldly and pulled the trigger.

There was no explosion, just the jolt of the arquebus and the zip of the ball as it fled the chamber. She hit him in the shoulder, and the impact spun him around violently. When his face came into view again, it was contorted with pain. Releasing the dragoon, he clutched the wound and started toward the entrance of the grotto. The waters parted, rushing away from him as if repelled by his presence, his magic. The people of Kingfountain had power over water, she remembered. It was just as Aunt Juliana had described after seeing this man escape from the waters surrounding Muirwood.

She hurried over to Rand, setting down the empty arquebus on a protruding boulder, and helped pull him out of the water. He looked bewildered but determined. Wiping water from his eyes, he stared at the mouth of the grotto. Then, seizing the arquebus from where she'd put it, he reached into his pocket and quickly loaded another ball. He raised the stock to his shoulder, took aim, and fired just as the kishion reached the mouth of the grotto. The ball hit him somewhere in the back, making him arch and sag to his knees. Suddenly the waters came gushing in around him.

Cettie watched as the kishion's body was struck by multiple shots from outside. She'd forgotten about the miners they'd left guarding the entrance. The man fell face-first into the waters, disappearing beneath the surface.

"Did you get him? You got him!" Stephen said, his voice thick with pain.

Cettie realized she was panting and shivering at the same time. She was soaked through, racked by emotions that were too disjointed for her to understand.

Rand gripped her arm and pulled her with him toward the entrance. "Come on, Stephen," he ordered gruffly. As they advanced, he loaded another ball into the weapon and trained it on the spot where the kishion had fallen.

"I can't move," Stephen groaned. "My arm was hit."

"Use your legs, then," Rand said sternly. "Stand up, man."

Surprisingly, Stephen obeyed and staggered after them, his face pale and wretched. Rand approached the entrance and held his hand up to his mouth to shout, "Hold fire! Hold fire!"

There was splashing on the outside. Cettie was momentarily blinded by the difference in light, but she shielded her eyes until they adjusted. The three of them emerged from the cave and saw several of the miners approaching with their weapons raised. Rand handed Cettie the weapon and then ducked under the water.

He emerged with a dead man.

The kishion's eyes were still open, but the hate and the silver were both gone. His expression was vacant, his lips pressed together. Bloodstains from his arquebus wounds marred the front of his shirt. Through her tears, she caught a glimpse of metal flashing in the sunlight. An amulet beneath the kishion's shirt.

Rand hoisted him higher and felt the man's neck. He looked at Cettie and shook his head. His eyes asked her questions. But not his mouth.

The doctor at Dolcoath had served there for many years, fixing broken bones and treating the workers' various illnesses. Indeed, he was the one who'd trained Adam before her friend's time in Muirwood. An old man, Doctor Dunferm now had a fringe of silver hair and beard and walked with a stoop. He was almost seventy by the looks of him. He wiped the blood from his hands on a rag and looked up at Cettie over Stephen's comatose body.

"It's a good thing he fainted," said Doctor Dunferm wisely. "It probably helped. You were a great help yourself, lass. Not many a maiden would have watched a ball being dug out of a shoulder like that."

Cettie did feel nauseated, but she had endured the discomfort without fainting herself.

"Not one in a thousand," said Rand, standing nearby. He, too, had been a witness to the makeshift surgery performed in one of the rooms in the manor. "I've seen enough blood to fill a hurricane. So Stephen will recover?"

"He'll need rest, but yes," said the doctor. "And you all look like you've been swimming in the river." He shook his head. "You brought a dead man back with you and not one of ours. Strange occurrences happening in Dolcoath. Might I send word to Lady Maren?"

"Yes, Doctor Dunferm," Cettie said. "I wish you would."

"Very well, Miss Cettie. You look weary to the bone. You should get some rest yourself."

"Perhaps later," Cettie answered. "For now, I need to change."

"So do I," said Rand. He gave her a searching look but didn't press her for information. "I'll see you later."

Cettie nodded and went to the guest room that had been prepared for her at the manor. She had to work to get the wet dress off, and then she slung it over a chair near the Fire Leering, and increased the heat with a simple thought. Gooseflesh lined both of her arms, and she rubbed them while standing in her shift, thinking about what had happened. She hadn't killed the man who claimed to be her father. But she had been ready to. She'd *tried* to.

Cettie bowed her head, feeling a strange mix of grief and loneliness. Was that man truly her father? Did he ever have a name besides "kishion"? His hard, angry look had told her he'd endured much in his life. Those secrets had died with him. Was it better that way?

She didn't know how long she'd been standing there, brooding and shivering, but a knock on the door startled her from her reverie. "Who is it?" she asked.

"Rand Patchett," said the muffled voice.

"Give me a moment; I'm still changing."

She hurried to the bag she'd packed and withdrew another dress, this one dark green with gray stripes and a velvet collar—one of her favorites—and hastily put it on. The pearl buttons on the front gave her tired, clumsy fingers some trouble. She looked in the mirror and saw her hair still half-done, but she sighed and went to the door and unlocked it.

Rand stood leaning against the frame, wearing an open-collared shirt beneath a blue dragoon-uniform jacket with large iron buttons on each lapel.

"Sorry for the uniform," he said with a wry smile. "I only brought it in case I was called away on duty related to the upcoming battle. I didn't fancy I'd be taking a plunge in a pond."

"Neither did I," Cettie replied, folding her arms. "What is it?"

"I didn't think you'd want to study a corpse. It can be . . . unnerving. But I found some clues about his person and wanted to show them to you. May I come in?"

She gestured to a small table with two chairs, and he entered and stood beside them. She left the door open deliberately. There were servants bustling around the halls, so they weren't entirely secluded, which would be improper for a young lady. He looked more on edge than he had before, more aggravated, and it didn't surprise her that he remained standing. Rand was the kind of man who was always restless for action, and no doubt the encounter in the grotto had brought back difficult memories of his past duties. She was grateful he'd been there. Without him, something worse might have happened.

"What did you find?" she asked, coming to the table.

"He had coins on him," he said, scooping them from his pocket and laying them on the table. "A few from the mint of Kingfountain." His eyebrows arched. "Then there's this . . ." He gestured to something he'd fastened to his belt, then removed it and set it on the table. "It's called a powder horn." It was a capped leather flask, though not one for water. The leather wasn't even damp. It was waterproof.

"Smell it," he suggested with a gesture.

Cettie twisted off the cap and lifted it to her nose. It had a strange, pungent smell, an alchemical smell. It made her instantly curious.

As she did this, he set down another handful of small iron pieces fashioned into various shapes. "These are the balls from the pistols. He had two of the weapons. They're both in my room, drying out. I'd like to keep one, if you don't mind. I'm curious about their methods. I've been in many battles against our foes. They call that powder 'black ash,' and their pistols are equipped with stubs of flint that ignite it. The Ministry of Wind is still trying to understand how it works. It's not like ours. You put it to fire, and it burns quickly. The smoke it generates makes it more difficult for us to see them . . . and hit them . . . and it propels the ammunition. Sorry, but I'm just a dragoon at heart."

Cettie screwed the cap back on and set it down. "Was there anything else?" The words came out breathlessly, for she knew—and feared—the answer.

"I saved the best for last," he said, rubbing his bristled chin. From the pocket on his uniform, he withdrew a tarnished silver medallion quite unlike anything she'd ever seen. The edges were rippled from time, and there were bits of grime and stain on it. It didn't bear a symbol so much as a strange whorl-like pattern—a variety of flower perhaps. It was an intriguing thing, an artifact from another world. He handed it to her, and she took it and examined it closely.

"Do you have any idea what it is?" he asked her.

Cettie felt a strange tingling coming from it. There was some connection between this pendant and the Mysteries. A little burst of excitement swelled in her heart.

"I don't know," she answered truthfully. "I've never seen its like before."

"Well, it doesn't *feel* like any ordinary medallion. I thought you'd want to see it."

"Thank you." The longer she held it, the more intrigued she became by it. There was something almost . . . familiar about it. She slid it into her pocket.

Rand folded his arms and gave her a piercing look. But still he didn't ask.

Cettie glanced down. "You're wondering about that man," she said.

"Clearly."

"This was not my first encounter with him. He came to my school, to Muirwood, and tried to take me."

"Was that the time when Fitzroy's daughter was abducted? I heard about that. It's known as one of the incidents leading to the war."

She nodded. "It was a difficult time. I never would have imagined he was waiting for us. I'm sorry I put you in danger."

"Sorry? I volunteered, if you remember. And you stopped him from drowning me. I'm not unfamiliar with fighting, Cettie. And he twisted me into a Bhikhu hold I couldn't get out of. Without your intervention, I would have been done for. I'm glad the villain is dead. But I can see . . ." He paused, giving her a probing look. "You're unsettled by it."

"Not in the way you are thinking, Mr. Patchett."

"Mr. Patchett? I thought we were well past all that nonsense. I think you ought to be permitted to say a man's name if you just saved his life."

He gave her an encouraging smile, so she could tell he was jesting with her. "Now what did you mean by that?"

It was a secret only a few of the Fitzroys knew about. While Father and Mother and Anna knew, she'd never told Phinia or Stephen.

She did not trust easily, but a strong urge to unburden herself gripped her. She'd held so many secrets for so long. Besides, Rand was different from the other people she'd met in society—almost another outcast. Her natural reticence attempted to silence her, but he had secrets of his own, ones that she knew about. Surely he would understand.

"He said he was a kishion," she said softly, watching his eyes to see how he reacted. "They're hired killers, Rand. I never knew about them until meeting him. He . . . he claimed to be my father."

His lips pursed, and he nodded subtly. "I see. Well, that explains some things. You tried to kill your father today." He rocked back on his heels. "That would trouble anyone. Well. I don't know what to say. Other than . . . thank you. I can't say I cared for the man much."

His comment made her smile a little. "Neither did I, Rand."

"I guess that amulet is yours, then. But this brings new questions to light. Why was he after you? Why did he free the Fear Liath to trick you into coming? And where is the Fear Liath now? It's broken free of its cage. It must have gone somewhere."

Talking about her father had reminded her of the past. A memory struck her, followed fast by an idea. "I think I know a way we can find it," she said.

"I'm a soldier, not a hunter," he said. "They have scouts in the Ministry of War that can follow trails, but they are all deployed in the war at present."

"No, there's something else. I know a teacher at Billerbeck Abbey."

"That's where I studied," he said in surprise. "Who?"

"Caulton Forshee."

Rand's face revealed he knew the name. "I remember him well." A look of chagrin quickly followed. "I think he's disappointed that I never took his advice and switched to the Ministry of Thought. I always found his lectures fascinating. All my life I've struggled with the Myriad Ones." His lips twitched. "How could he help?"

"He has something that can find what is lost. I think it requires permission from the privy council, but we can ask him."

He folded his arms and gave her a serious look. "I'll go with you, if you'd like. But I have bitter memories of that place." He sighed. "Memories can be a torment. Best to let them lie."

CHAPTER SEVENTEEN

BLACK FOREST

Night descended on the mines of Dolcoath. Through the window, Cettie watched the light strain against the shadows before yielding to them at last. With dusk came the droning chorus of insects. The street Leerings had begun to glow in the small village. Cettie leaned against the open window, arms folded, breathing in the cool night air that smelled of thick green vegetation. A night bird called, and she could picture it in her mind from the drawing she'd seen in Adam's book. Intense feelings of loneliness and worry followed the remembrance, and she wondered where he was at this particular moment. Had the battle started? Was he safe?

Her melancholy thoughts were interrupted by the sound of steps and voices coming toward her. She recognized them as Rand's and Stephen's, and since her door was already open, she turned in time to see them enter. Maxfield Strong had followed them, but he remained outside.

Stephen's right arm was bandaged below his shoulder, cradled in a sling. He looked healthy—the pallor had left his cheeks and his gray eyes were bright with vigor. Rand's expression was strained, but the two were in conversation.

"Is the night watch posted?" Rand asked.

"They are. The first shift will patrol until midnight, and the second will patrol until dawn. The sun set a short while ago, but there have been no howls like in previous days."

Rand nodded solemnly. "The beast is no longer attached to its lair, so it could be leagues away by now. The night watch will give reassurance to the people living here."

"I agree," Stephen said. Then he turned to Cettie.

"You look much better," she told him.

"Doctor Dunferm did his work well," he said. "He gave me something for the pain, but the wound itself isn't too severe. The ball grazed my chest before embedding in my arm. I didn't even feel that part until the doctor saw it. It slowed the ball down enough that it didn't shatter the bone."

"I'm relieved," Cettie said.

Rand put his hand on Stephen's other shoulder. "I told him that the fellow might have shot *me* first if Stephen hadn't been so quick to react." He gave Cettie a nod. "And without your interference, Cettie, we both might have perished. Thank you. You did well today."

She felt her cheeks warm with his praise. "It took courage to go into the grotto, Mr. Patchett."

He arched his eyebrows at her accusingly.

"Hang propriety, Cettie," Stephen said with a chuckle. "This man is a solid dragoon. As solid as they come. I thank you for volunteering for this duty, sir. I didn't think very highly of you at first, but I do now."

Rand nodded humbly and leaned against the doorjamb. "I took the liberty of seeing the villain put in a box. I don't know what else we can learn from a corpse, and his body is starting to smell. The miners will bury it in the morning. Per Stephen's orders."

Stephen smiled and nodded vigorously. "I never realized a wound could make me this popular. I haven't had this much respect since my first days here. The men look at me differently now."

Rand clapped him on the back and made Stephen wince. "Don't let it go to your head. But yes, a little courage and fortitude go a long way toward earning a man some respect. Cettie and I are off to Billerbeck next. We need to find out where that beast has gone."

"What about the missing shipment of quicksilver?" Cettie asked Stephen. "Have there been any updates?"

"I sent word to Aunt Juliana to see if she'd help there," he answered. "I also had a zephyr sent to the customer with a notice that the shipment was lost and that a new one would be forthcoming . . . at a discount."

"Well done," Rand said with a supporting grin.

The younger Fitzroy shrugged off the praise. In that moment, he looked very much like his father, and Cettie felt a throb of appreciation and respect for him in her heart. The feeling extended to Rand as well, for it was his influence that had contributed to the change.

"You'll stay until morning, won't you?" Stephen asked.

A look of dread came into Rand's eyes. He shook his head. "No, I think we should leave by midnight, after the first watch is done. Just to be sure all went well. I truly believe the beast will seek a new lair. The sooner we find it, the better. Perhaps, *Miss Cettie*," he added with a coy smile, "you could get some rest now so you could pilot us later? Unless Mr. Strong is a pilot?" He turned and looked back at the thin young man standing just outside.

Cettie's escort from Fog Willows shook his head of blondish-red hair. "I'm afraid not, sir."

Rand didn't appear to be particularly afraid of the Fear Liath, so what had set him off? She didn't understand it, but she'd noticed it.

"Midnight," she agreed with a nod.

"I'll be sure to see you off," Stephen promised. "But I also wouldn't mind if you stayed." He gave her a look of acceptance, something she'd rarely—if ever—seen from him.

At midnight, Stephen walked Cettie, Rand, and their chaperone to the tempest, which hovered at the landing yard. Stars gleamed in the skies above. There were no clouds to mar them. It was cold enough that a little mist came from Cettie's mouth as they walked. The homes were dark and quiet, but there were watchmen patrolling the street. No disturbances had occurred, and for the first time in a while, the people rested peacefully. Stephen had a jacket hanging over his shoulders—the sling prevented him from wearing it—but he looked the part of a leader. Rand's clothes had been washed and mended, just as hers had been, and he wore the more casual outfit he'd arrived in.

When they reached the tempest, Strong climbed up first while Stephen extended his left hand to Rand, and the men exchanged a firm handshake.

"Thank you for coming, Patchett," Stephen said. "I shall call on you at Gimmerton Sough when the opportunity arises."

"Hopefully that will be soon," Rand replied. After they broke the clasp, Rand gave him a smart salute, looking very much like the officer he had been. Stephen nodded at him before Rand turned and ambled up the rope ladder.

"Good-bye, Sister," Stephen said, touching Cettie's arm with affection. He'd never before called her that.

Cettie felt like her heart might burst, and she hugged Stephen, her lashes wet with tears. Her throat was too tight to speak, but she turned and waved farewell before following Rand up the ladder.

Soon the tempest was rushing up past the trees and over the gorge, joining the night sky. Cettie was very comfortable at the helm and controlled the craft's speed and bearing as it raced to the north. She knew the constellations to navigate by and set the Leerings to follow the correct course. Mr. Strong stood on the deck, off to the side, staring at the sky.

"You should get some sleep, Rand," she said as he climbed up the rungs to the helmsman's deck.

"Sleep and I are old enemies," he said with a wary tone. After reaching the deck, he folded his arms and gazed up at the stars. "I'll never tire of seeing such wonders."

"Neither will I," Cettie answered, smoothing her hand on the wooden railing.

"Can I see that amulet again?" he asked her.

She wasn't sure why he asked, but she fished it from her pocket and held it out to him. The metal felt warm in her palm. She still sensed the strange magic coming from it, its connection to the Knowing.

He took it from her and held it close, gazing at the strange, whorled surface. "Such a strange thing," he muttered. "Another Mystery, no doubt. I wonder what this means. It feels like something I've seen in nature, only I cannot make it out." He gave it back to her. "You should put it on."

A strange, uneasy feeling tightened in her stomach. She took it back from him, seeing the moonlight glimmer on the metallic edge. "This pattern is found in nature," she answered. She stared at it, wondering how it would look as a medallion over her green and gray-striped dress. But that little tinge of doubt prevented her. She put it back in her pocket instead.

"You came from the Fells," he said, gazing at her face. "Do you still remember it?"

"Very well, unfortunately," she answered lightheartedly. "They are awful memories, really. I try not to dwell on them. I'm grateful to live in Fog Willows now."

"I'd always wanted to live in a sky manor," he said eagerly. "There is still a prejudice against people like us, alas. So many of the upper crust are vainglorious hypocrites. But not Fitzroy. You were given a rare gift."

"I know," she said. Uncomfortable with his scrutiny, she wanted to turn the conversation away from herself. "You're from Pry-Ree, yet you studied at Billerbeck and not Tintern?"

He nodded vigorously. "It has a better reputation for the disciplines of War. Some of the best dragoons come from there and from Naess."

"I've never been as far north as Naess," Cettie said.

"I have," he answered. "It's always dark up there. Well, part of the year. And cold." He turned away, his countenance darkening again. "I'd better start my duel with sleep. Sometimes my mind will not quiet down enough for me to rest. Especially after a day like today."

"Are you haunted by the war?" she asked.

He twisted his neck to look back at her. "Life is sacred. You can't spill a man's blood without feeling it, though you do grow numb to it after a while. But that's not it . . . not quite. I'm haunted by the thought that no matter what I do, I will never be half the man my father was. That's something I can relate to Stephen about." His lips curled with emotion. "That I will never be enough."

Cettie felt a surge of sympathy for him. "I'm sorry your father died."

His eyebrow arched in surprise. Then he surprised her by asking, "Are you sorry *yours* did?"

Cettie swallowed and met his gaze without flinching. "He wasn't my *true* father. I'll always have Lord Fitzroy."

She felt a strong, sudden gush of emotion, one almost like jealousy tinged with rage. It hit her strongly, powerfully. It made her grip the helm more tightly. What could be the source of the powerful feelings? She swallowed, anxious to regain control of herself.

"Good night, Cettie," Rand told her. "If I do manage to fall asleep tonight and don't awaken before we reach Billerbeck, do let me know."

She nodded and watched him disappear belowdecks. After he was gone, Mr. Strong gave her a curt nod and returned to his quarters. The feelings roiled her, despite her efforts to banish them. It felt almost like a Myriad One was on deck with her, infecting her with its evil thoughts. She'd always been able to sense—and even see—the Myriad Ones, but this was different, unfamiliar. There were some dark feelings brooding beneath the surface of her mind and heart. Something had let them loose, but what?

Whatever was causing her feelings of foreboding, she wanted them gone.

~

Although Cettie had never been to Billerbeck Abbey before, the tempest she flew knew the way. Like the other abbeys of the realm, it was secreted away from the prying eyes of the populace, surrounded by a huge forest of towering black pine that showed only a single road leading to the village encircling the abbey. The forest went on for leagues with no major rivers running through it. She saw the abbey coming up, a beacon of silver in the midst of the black, and ordered the tempest to slow its approach and angle toward the landing yard.

She climbed down the steps and went to Rand's room and knocked on the door. She was still attuned to the sky ship's Control Leering, however, and watched as they approached the tips of the trees. It was a stunning sight. The abbey was smaller than Muirwood but just as ancient. It had three square towers, two jutting from the longest end and one in the middle. The morning light had finally reached it above the vast wall of trees, coloring the shaded side of the walls a deep purple.

She knocked again and heard nothing. The door of Mr. Strong's quarters opened, and he emerged, giving her an inquisitive look.

A little pit of worry started in her stomach. Was he sleeping? He'd asked her to wake him. Her indecision lasted only a moment before she connected to the Heat Leering in the cabin so she could see through its eyes. Rand was sprawled on the bed, still in his clothes, the blankets rumpled, the curtain over the port window shut. He was fast asleep.

"I think he's still asleep," she told her escort.

Cettie opened the door and slowly entered the room, smelling the scent of him, one that she found a little heady.

"Rand?" she called. "We're almost there."

Still no response. She bit her lip, wondering what to do. Finding the dregs of her courage, she walked up to him.

As soon as her hand touched his arm, he jerked awake with startled surprise, as if he'd been holding his breath for hours. She recoiled, seeing the look of bewilderment in his eyes. His hand was suddenly poised in a fist, cocked back as if to strike at her. Cettie retreated farther.

Then he blinked, and his fist lowered. "Oh, it's you," he moaned. His neck and face were slick with sweat. He swung his legs to the floor, leaning forward on his knees and panting.

"I'm-I'm sorry for startling you," Cettie apologized.

"No, it's all right. Did you knock?"

"Twice."

He shook his head in disbelief. "It's my fault. We are almost there, then?"

"Yes, we'll be landing soon." Cettie's heart was still hammering in her chest.

He looked miserable, his nostrils flaring and a look of disgust on his mouth. "I'll be up soon. Forgive me for frightening you. I thought . . . never mind."

Cettie hastily retreated from his cabin and went back to the helm. The tempest had lowered to the landing yard, adjacent to two other tempests, one of which she recognized immediately as the *Serpentine*, Aunt Juliana's. A thrill of excitement shot through her. She hadn't expected to see her aunt at the abbey. Several zephyrs were also moored in the yard.

Cettie smoothed her skirts, wondering why she suddenly felt so skittish, and waited a few moments before Rand appeared. He gazed at the abbey in wonderment, shaking his head slightly.

"Hello, darling," he said to the structure, a half-mocking smile on his face. Then he turned to face her and nodded to the abbey.

Cettie looked up and grinned at the sight of Aunt Juliana striding energetically toward their sky ship, outpacing the men from the abbey, who'd likely been sent by the Aldermaston. Rand let Cettie go down first, and as soon as she reached the bottom, Aunt Juliana caught her in a powerful hug and lifted her off her feet.

"Cettie, what are you doing here! Look at you! What a treasure you are. Why have you come?" She beamed at her and kissed her on the cheek before looking up at Rand coming down the ropes. "Who's this?"

"Commander Patchett at your service, ma'am," he said, bowing to her.

The two older men arrived. "You know this young lady, Captain?" one of them asked Juliana.

"Of course I do. She's family." Turning away from them, she asked Cettie, "Why are you here?"

"We came to see Caulton. I didn't know you'd be here. Did you get Stephen's message?"

Juliana nodded. "I did. In fact, I was about to leave to go to Dolcoath. I've spent a fair bit of time at this abbey over the years." She gave Cettie a knowing look. "Well, if you need to see him, I know where to find him. It just so happens he hasn't had his first class quite yet. Come with me." Then she shooed the two men away.

"Do you want me to wait with the ship?" Mr. Strong asked Cettie.

"Yes, please. I don't see us staying here long."

As they started to walk, Juliana cast Cettie a probing look and slightly inclined her head toward Rand.

Cettie shook her head no.

Despite the early hour, there were already a few students wandering the grounds. The large clearing around the abbey was filled with gardens and lawns interspersed with small cottages. Cettie admired the view, trying to absorb all the sights. At Muirwood, she could see the hills in the distance, but this abbey was completely engulfed in black pine.

Caulton was in his classroom, preparing for the lessons of the day. He looked as she remembered him—a dark-haired man in his thirties, dressed in a simple waistcoat and white sleeves. When she entered, he gave her a surprised but welcoming look.

"Cettie," he greeted cheerfully. "I've always hoped you'd come for a visit." Then his eyes fell on Rand, and he looked even more taken aback. "Randall Patchett?"

"Good morning, sir," Rand replied softly, hands clasped behind his back. He had an almost guilty look on his face.

"A day for surprises," Caulton said. "What brings you all to Billerbeck? I had no notion you were coming."

Cettie noticed that Juliana had joined Caulton's side and brushed something from his arm. There was a look of intimacy between them. Of shared affection.

"We came seeking your help," Cettie said.

"Show him the medallion," Rand said.

She had the medallion in her pocket, so she reached in and pulled it out. At that moment, she felt uneasy showing it to him. Part of her feared he might take it from her. She dangled it from the chain and held it up for him to see.

Juliana squinted, but didn't appear to recognize the bauble. Caulton recoiled in surprised recognition, his expression instantly alarmed.

"Where on earth did you get that, Cettie?" he demanded.

CHAPTER EIGHTEEN

HETAERA

Seeing Caulton's reaction to the medallion, Cettie immediately closed her fist around it and pulled it back. He was no longer merely surprised—something about the amulet both terrified him and angered him. Juliana looked on in concern.

"The man who kidnapped Anna, who tried to kidnap me."

"Have you had it all these years?" Caulton asked in dread.

"No!" Cettie explained, "We just came from Dolcoath. The monster in the grotto is loose. When we went there, that man—the kishion—was waiting for us. Rand and the other guards killed him, and they found this around his neck. You clearly recognize it, Master Forshee. What is it?"

"It is called a *kystrel*. There has not been one in the empire for hundreds of years. They were all destroyed back during the time of the first empress. That one looks quite old."

"There is a lot of tarnish on it," Rand said.

"Yes, I noticed. This is terrible news, Cettie. I have a book in my study that shows what they looked like. Come with me."

Caulton's study was connected to his classroom by a door. They followed him inside and Cettie stared in wonderment at his collections from his travels. There were Leerings of varying sizes—small ones used to fix seals, larger ones the size of bread loaves. There were so many, each with its own unique power, and a feeling of sweet music ignited her senses. She longed to touch them all, to learn their secrets. A hexagon-shaped one was carved out of a deep-black rock. It looked naturally formed, and she remembered from her studies that basalt formed such a pattern. There was a three-leaf sigil carved into it instead of a face.

Caulton went behind his desk to examine the bookshelves suspended from the walls, loaded with volumes and some golden tomes that were clearly of ancient origin. He rifled through the books as the three of them gathered around his desk. The small room felt crowded and confined. Rand stood very close to her, but his gaze was on his old teacher.

After some searching, Caulton took one of the books away from the shelf and laid it flat on his desk. The desk was tidy, but it, too, held a collection of oddities—an hourglass filled with white sand, a small leather-bound book wedged in between a sculpted set of bookends carved to resemble mythical dragons, an assortment of stubbed quills and inkwells and stacks of paper, scriving tools, and a wax tablet. The room smelled interesting, of leather and burnt metal, and it reminded her a little of Fitzroy's study.

Caulton flipped through pages, gazing at the book intently.

"What exactly is a kystrel?" Juliana said, leaning over the desk to gaze at the book. "I thought they were a species of bird."

"They are," he answered and then tapped his finger on one of the pages. He beckoned Cettie over to examine the image. "Look. Isn't that the same design?"

Cettie opened her hand and compared the two. The medallion did appear to match the picture, especially the whorl-like pattern found throughout nature.

"Is this one of the Mysteries?" she asked him.

He nodded. "One that is reserved for the Ministry of Thought. Any vicar would know that symbol, but not many from the other disciplines do."

"Why keep it a secret?" Juliana asked. "You've never told me about them."

"The main reason we don't talk about it, with *anyone*, is to avoid the temptation that comes with curiosity. There are those, especially in our society today, who would seek out a power such as this without stopping to consider the potential cost of using it."

"Power?" Rand said with wariness. "What do you mean?"

"Perhaps a little history lesson is in order," Caulton replied. "Centuries ago, there was an order of women called the *hetaera*. The members of this order were skilled in the arts of deceit and manipulation, and they hungered for power. You all remember taking the maston oaths when you took the Test. Well, there were other oaths, secret promises, covenants of evil and usurpation. No record of them exists today—the documentation was all destroyed by order of the first empress. The hetaera had a Leering, one that could bind a Myriad One inside the body. It left a mark on the shoulder, as I understand it. It gave them great power, especially over the emotions of those around them." His eyes were intense as he spoke, his voice throbbing with worry. "The hetaera knew how to forge kystrels.

"There are two ways to gain power. One is by free will and surrender. The other is by force. Anyone in possession of a kystrel can achieve the latter. That is what makes them so dangerous. The hetaera expanded their power and influence by seducing others into wearing the amulets they made. Through the kystrels, they could sense the thoughts and intentions of their followers—they could manipulate their feelings and lend them power. Some manipulated their way into the nobility and held kings in thrall. These rulers they then persuaded to persecute and murder the mastons. These were terrible times for the empire."

Cettie felt a darkness spreading inside of her, a worrying sickness. She was grateful she didn't live in such evil days.

Caulton looked down at the pages before him and sighed. "The hetaera destroyed nearly every man, woman, and child who lived within the borders of the empire, back when it was composed of separate kingdoms. A great curse was brought down upon the people, a Blight unlike any other. Some were rescued from death by fleeing by sea to another land—Assinica—across the ocean. After the people here were destroyed, marauders from Naess came to inhabit these lands. Do you see that stone with six sides?" He pointed to the one Cettie had admired earlier. "That is a Naestor rune. They took over these lands and began to live in our empty cities. They also found the abandoned kystrels and used them to re-create a religion called the Dochte Mandar, which had originated centuries before in Kingfountain. When the ships from Assinica began to return, the civilizations comingled. Some Dochte Mandar even earned trusted positions in the realm. When Empress Maia came into power, she banned kystrels and destroyed the Hetaera Leering."

He rubbed his lips and stared at the drawing of the kystrel.

"So the hetaera are just a myth now?" Juliana said. "There are no more?"

Caulton shook his head. "Would that it were true," he sighed. "There are many in my ministry who believe that some hetaera survived and crossed worlds. Why does Kingfountain keep attacking us? They say because of trade. Because of dominance. They say we pervert the true faith, even though we both worship the same Knowing. The kishion who attacked you—twice—is of that world. And he wore a kystrel. This is solid evidence the hetaera may still exist! Or that someone intends to bring them back. The Dochte Mandar used kystrels centuries ago to control the people, so their order is dangerous enough in its own right. This also means the war we are engaged in may be even more dangerous than we believed. If Kingfountain defeats us, there is no doubt in my mind that either or both of those orders will try to infect us again. Our history is filled with the tragedies spawned by the medallion in your hand." He reached out. "I ask you, Cettie, to give it to me so I might share it with the Aldermaston here and inform the privy council. If there are any hetaera or Dochte Mandar already in this world, we need to hunt them down at once."

Cettie saw his outstretched hand and felt a sudden, blinding hatred for Caulton Forshee, accompanied by the urge to attack, maybe even kill him. The power of it startled her. She wavered a moment, engulfed by the brutal and horrific emotions. Why did he want it so much? Was he seeking to use it for himself?

Although her thoughts tortured her, she overruled them and quickly dumped the medallion into his palm. He immediately stuffed it into his vest pocket, and the feelings she had experienced left her. Relief followed.

"Thank you, Cettie," he said with respect. "I felt the struggle in you. That was quite terrifying."

"We came here for another reason," she answered, trying to slow her wild heart. "The monster that escaped the grotto needs to be found. We hoped to use the Cruciger orb to locate it. Rand knows how to kill it."

Caulton nodded. "Tell me about this monster."

"It's called a Fear Liath," said Rand. "Some think they are only legend."

Caulton pursed his lips. "Far from it."

"You know of them?" Juliana asked. "I've never liked Dolcoath because of it. The river walk to the grotto always made me wary. I spent too many years there not to notice it."

"No, a Fear Liath is a creature of incredible power and danger. The population on our island alone is three or four times what it was centuries ago, and most of our people live in close-packed cities on the surface. They would do much harm to the populace. I will notify the Aldermaston of the threat, but I cannot imagine the privy council refusing permission to hunt it. The Cruciger orb is right on the mantel . . ."

His voice trailed off, and his eyes narrowed with concern. He rushed around the desk and walked over to the mantelpiece. An ornate gold stand sat there, the size and shape of which indicated it once held an orb. But it was empty.

"Where is it?" Caulton asked in astonishment. "I . . . it's always been right there!"

A sickening feeling of dread went into Cettie's heart. She blinked quickly, feeling a queer sensation of satisfaction inside. Why would she feel that?

"When was the last time you saw it?" Juliana asked.

"I don't know," he said, shaking his head. "Yesterday maybe? I don't think about it." His distress was palpable. "It has been handed down in my family for centuries. I don't . . . no, he couldn't have."

"What?" Cettie asked worriedly.

He shook his head. "I had a visitor some weeks ago. An advocate from some office in the Fells. Skippling? I don't remember."

"Mr. Skrelling?" Cettie pressed.

"Yes, that's the one!" Caulton declared. "He came seeking information from me and asked if I could use it." He looked at Cettie, his countenance changing. "He wanted me to use it to find your mother."

That news jolted her. Mr. Skrelling?

"W-what did you tell him?"

"I told him no. They are not to be used for personal matters. Only by command from the privy council. Very few people have the strength of will to even summon its power. Most don't *believe* it will work for them, and so it doesn't. I know you can use it, Cettie—I saw you use it the night we searched for Anna. But humility must be foremost in the person who uses it. Otherwise, there's a danger they'll be tempted to look for something they would be better off not finding. Sometimes the Medium will give us what we are craving, even if it hurts us." He turned back to the mantel, his distress growing. "But I *know* he didn't take it. I thought I saw him touch it, but I noticed it was still there later that day and the next. No one can get into this office without me opening the door."

Juliana put her hand on his shoulder. "You are certain you didn't take it off that pedestal for any reason?"

"I know I did not," he answered in bafflement. "I rarely touch it. Skrelling was the last one who mentioned it."

And he was missing . . . unless Mr. Sloan had found him . . .

Cettie's heart began to sink even more. Her shoulders sagged.

"What's wrong?" Rand asked her, noticing her reaction.

"Mr. Skrelling works for Sloan and Teitelbaum," she said huskily. "Mr. Sloan came to visit recently to tell us about . . . about a personal matter. He asked if I'd seen Mr. Skrelling. Said that he had come to this abbey to visit about a private concern. He hasn't been seen since."

"I must tell the Aldermaston about both predicaments at once," Caulton said firmly.

Cettie wanted to leave immediately, but Caulton asked if they would wait for him. He locked his office door after they departed and even invoked a sigil on it to further secure it. Alas, it felt a little like locking the factory door after all the materials had been stolen.

Juliana went with him, leaving Cettie and Rand alone. Perhaps recognizing how badly she needed a distraction, he offered to show her the grounds while they waited.

There were fewer students than there were at Muirwood, but the feeling of the abbey was similar, even though the trees looked foreboding. The small student cottages reminded her of her time at Vicar's Close, and she felt a familiar stab of longing for Sera. Everything was so green and vibrant, and the air had a wet smell to it.

Rand took her to a stone bridge that crossed a small stream at the foot of a tiny waterfall. The ground on either side of the bridge was covered with moss, as were most of the stones that formed the bridge. Tall pines and weak saplings filled the ground. Even though the sun was firmly established now, the path lay in shadow.

"I've always like this old bridge," Rand said, sighing, stopping part of the way across. "My mind is still reeling from what he told us, though. Did you know any of that lore before?"

Cettie shook her head and rubbed her arms. "I knew that Empress Maia hunted down all the kishion. If they murdered for the hetaera or the Dochte Mandar, then I believe we know why." Had her father worked for a hetaera? That thought made her wince.

"What?" Rand asked again, sensitive to her mood.

"It's nothing," she said.

"You still don't trust me," he said. "Well, I can't blame you. I don't trust myself." He stooped and picked up a stick and flung it upstream.

"Please don't think that, Rand," she said. "It's not that at all."

"Then why won't you tell me?" he asked, watching as the stick freed itself from some of the waterfall rocks and drifted toward them.

She bit her lip. "Because it's painful."

He still wouldn't look at her, but she could tell he was not convinced. "I always thought this forest was full of secrets. It reminds me a little of Pry-Ree." He gave her a sidelong glance. "Why is it that we keep the abbeys such a secret? They're all hidden amidst forests or surrounded by water." He shook his head. "What Master Forshee told us . . . Should we not have *learned* that while we studied? Knowledge is so guarded and controlled in our empire." He frowned deeply. "I don't think it's fair."

"Neither do I," Cettie agreed.

Then he turned to look at her. "Secrets can be so damaging. Can't they?"

The sound of approaching footsteps called them to attention. Caulton and Juliana moved swiftly toward them, and Rand and Cettie left the bridge to meet them halfway. Juliana looked as if she'd been struck across the face. Her eyes watered.

Caulton's gaze was hard and intense. "I'm going to Lockhaven at once. The Aldermaston contacted the privy council."

"We can take you," Cettie offered, then realized Juliana would likely be the preferred choice. The two were clearly more than friends, which gave Cettie a bit of joy amidst all the doubt and uncertainty. Her aunt deserved happiness.

Caulton shook his head. "I can be in Lockhaven within the hour. There is no need to trouble yourself."

"How?" Cettie asked in surprise, then remembered that Fitzroy had managed to travel equally quickly in the past.

"The abbeys are all linked together," he said. "I can enter one and emerge from another. Yes, it's one of the Mysteries." He smiled, but it was a pained one.

"Cettie," Juliana said, her voice thick. "The Aldermaston said that a battle was fought over Hautland yesterday. A terrible battle. There was a storm." She swallowed. "Fitzroy's hurricane went down. Thousands are dead on both sides." She shook her head, and the tears began to streak down her cheeks. "Neither side won. But F-Fitzroy is gone. He wouldn't evacuate the ship until all the men were out. There wasn't time before it crashed into the sea." Caulton put his arm around Juliana's shoulder. "They just ordered a zephyr to tell Maren. Hurry home, Cettie. Hurry."

Cettie felt as if the world lurched beneath her feet.

Peace is such a tepid word. It fails to rouse the imagination. A much better term for it is an armistice. A cessation of hostilities. A truce from war, temporary by nature and design. Such a pleasant ring to it. In reality, it will be our opportunity to lull them into complacency. To let Comoros's machine of industry begin to revive. They are sick of war. I am not.

When the empire of Gahalatine fell, his people fled on enormous treasure ships to seek a land of safety. They were offered refuge in Kingfountain. One of the great Wizrs of the past had summoned a once formidable, vanquished land back from the depths of the Deep Fathoms. The drowned kingdom of Leoneyis was reborn and occupied once more. My mother named me after that ancient land. The glory of the past can be reborn as well. It is my name, my birthright.

Let our enemies sue for a temporary peace with their disgraced princess. I'll have none of it. I want more than just a throne. For after all, a throne is only a bench covered with velvet.

—Leon Montpensier, Duke of La Marche

SERA

CHAPTER NINETEEN

Mirror Gate

The news was delivered by the prime minister himself. The knock at the bedroom door could have been anyone, but Sera heard Becka's gasp and turned suddenly to find Lord Welles standing in the entryway, his face a grimace of bad tidings. He looked wrecked, broken, and he'd aged since her meeting with him and her father only days before.

"What has happened?" Sera asked him worriedly, leaving her book on the desk and striding across the room.

"I think I'll take a chair first," Welles said with exhaustion.

Sera obliged, and the two were soon sitting adjacent to each other, Welles's head resting against a propped arm, his fingers massaging his eyes. Had the man been weeping? Sera hadn't thought such a thing possible.

Becka shot a questioning look at Sera, a silent query as to whether she should linger. Sera nodded subtly yes, and the maid retreated out of sight.

"You look as if you are carrying the weight of the world, Prime Minister," Sera offered gently. "The battle is over, I take it? Your news isn't good. Please tell me."

A weary sigh expelled from Welles's mouth. "It is over, my dear. If they attack us again, our defenses will fail. The empire is more vulnerable than it has ever been. They have been hit hard too, however, and we must sue for peace before they realize our desperate situation." He lowered his hand, his bloodshot eyes meeting her concerned ones in an entreaty. "It is all up to you now, Sera."

She felt a flush start to rise in her cheeks. Oh, how she wanted to throw his failure in his face. But she resisted that dark impulse and carefully kept her expression under control.

"Tell me what happened, Lord Welles," she asked quietly.

He snorted. "Our worlds collided. And the Knowing fought against us both. Our superiority in the air was diminished by a raging thunderhead. And their superiority in the sea was disrupted by enormous waves. They lost many ships. I can't imagine how many. But we lost our ships as well. Three admirals and their hurricanes went down. Including Lord Fitzroy, our harbinger."

Sera gasped and felt a real stab of pain.

"Indeed," Welles said tightly. "Our harbinger has been lost. If they realize this, if they discover we can no longer foresee where they'll attack next, we will be overrun by their ships. They don't know he's dead, not yet. We've kept that knowledge a state secret."

"Have you told his family?" Sera pressed.

"Of course!" he snapped in frustration. "But they cannot tell a soul. Not yet anyway. I just finished telling Lady Corinne that her husband was also killed." His lips trembled. "And she took it so composedly," he muttered under his breath.

"What was that?" Sera asked, unprepared for the shock of the news.

"It's no secret that your father fancies her," Welles said disdainfully. "It's all rather sickening. She and Lady Maren are now the wealthiest people in the empire. All the better reason to send you to broker a peace, Sera. Richard will not want you to corrupt his chances of siring another heir. He gets what he wants after all." The last words were spoken with bitterness.

Sera's mind roiled with fury, but she kept her reaction muted. "The other admiral? You said there was a third?"

"Admiral Rushworth," he said flippantly. "Three capable men. Three strong leaders. The privy council is in a panic. I've been sent to enlist your aid in this situation. I've been charged to ensure that you will do all in your power to broker an armistice between our peoples. Even if that means forsaking your religion and homeland to appease their sensibilities. We just spoke of this, Miss Fitzempress. Are you prepared to make that sacrifice now that the moment is thrust upon you?"

Sera was *not* ready to do such a thing, but she would never admit it to him. If she gave him any reason to doubt she'd do his bidding, they wouldn't permit her to go. They'd find someone else more . . . amenable.

"Of course, Lord Welles. If I can forestall another invasion, I will. What must be done?"

Her words satisfied him. He *wanted* to believe her, and so he did. "Good. Good. Our ambassador is at the court of Kingfountain at this moment negotiating the terms so that you can cross through one of the mirror gates."

"I'll admit that I'm rather ignorant of what all is involved. If I recall correctly from my studies, there needs to be an exchange of hostages, does there not?"

"Precisely," said Lord Welles. "The Law requires that anyone seeking to exchange worlds permanently must have a willing person to go the other way. A balance is required, one for one. We do this for visiting as well. Hostages are exchanged, people of comparable value. We wouldn't accept a peasant for a princess. The length of stay is determined in advance and brokered with a covenant. If either party does not return on or before the agreed-upon time, then the magic binding the selected mirror gate will rupture, and the arch bridge will collapse. It is within the interest of both worlds to preserve these gates. But when there is a war, all the usual covenants are meaningless. We do this now as a sign of good faith." He sniffed and leaned back in his chair. "You will have a fortnight to negotiate the armistice before you're compelled to return and report the terms to the privy council. The privy council insists that the peace terms be at least three years, but you are to negotiate more if you can. See if you can also get reparations from them for the death and damage inflicted on us over the years. Anything would be acceptable, but I advise you to ask for a startling amount to begin the negotiations in earnest. Eight million? Also see if you can reclaim any of the treasures they stole from us in previous centuries."

Sera nodded at each of his requests to show him she understood. "Who will be coming with me?" she asked after he fell silent.

"Our ambassador will be there to meet you, of course. And your maid to attend you. A representative from each of the four ministries will also accompany you to offer advice and protection. But you are the one the privy council has authorized to negotiate on behalf of the empire. Remember that the people of Kingfountain are not as enlightened as we are, Sera. Their monarchy still holds absolute power, whereas Empress Maia created a shared responsibility in the empire. She believed each of the ministries deserved its turn in power."

She gave him a curious look, inclining her head slightly. "Does that mean you will not be prime minister for much longer, then?"

Her words were clearly nettles in his ears, and he squirmed in his chair. "No. Well, not for a few more years at any rate. The Ministry of Thought will probably get its turn," he added with a sneer.

Sera nodded sagely. "I am ready to go when called upon," she answered.

"Good. You will be leaving today."

Sera's mother came from Castlebury to see her off from Lockhaven. In the three years Sera had lived in Pavenham Sky, her mother had visited her once every other month, but they had little in common, and their relationship was still strained by their very real differences in opinion. Sera pretended even in front of her that her contrition was real. Her mother was weepy as she clung to her and hugged her good-bye. The bitterness she felt toward Lady Corinne seemed to emanate from her in waves. The lady of Pavenham Sky had elected not to greet her guest and had instead sent Master Sewell to the living room in her place. The insult was pointed.

"Mother, can you post this to Fog Willows for me?" Sera asked, handing her mother a letter she'd written to Cettie. She'd kept it concealed until that moment, hoping for an opportunity to post it. Given that Lady Corinne was not present, she decided it was worth the risk.

"I want you to write to *me* too, Seraphin," Mother said through her sniffles, taking the sealed paper with an offended air. "I shall worry about you every day. If you do choose to wed the prince"—she struggled again—"I will not be able to visit you very often. There are so many legal difficulties. Your father has been trying to persuade the privy council to reduce my allotment. I must fight him from every side. It is odious how he makes me suffer so."

"I'll be back in a fortnight regardless," Sera said, anxious for the awkward moment to be over. She kissed her mother's cheek. "Thank you."

Mother dabbed her eye with a silk handkerchief. "Be strong, Seraphin. You must be, for all our sakes."

Sera hugged her again and watched her leave. After her mother was gone, she turned and glanced at Master Sewell, whom she caught trying to stifle a wry smile.

"You don't approve of my mother, do you?"

Sewell shrugged and said nothing. Had he noticed the letter? Probably. Very little escaped the man.

"I will miss your companionship," Sera said to him. "My stylish jailor."

"There are worse prisons than Pavenham Sky, ma'am." He quirked an eyebrow as he said it.

"Yes. I'm not complaining. You've run a splendid prison, sir. I thank you for your hospitality."

"I hope it has changed you," he replied.

"It has," she agreed with a nod. *Just not in the way you think.* "Will Lady Corinne say farewell?"

His brow furrowed. "No. She's still grieving for the loss of her husband."

Truly? Sera wanted to ask, but she knew better. "Well, give her my regards as well."

With those parting words, Sera and Becka boarded the tempest that was waiting for them in the landing yard. Becka followed her up the gangway to the craft. On deck, Sera met the pilot and the four others who would be joining her. There was Mr. Pond, a vicar from the Ministry of Thought, with his reddish hair and overlarge nose. Colonel Worthington was her middle-aged escort from the Ministry of War. He wore a blue dragoon jacket bedecked with medals that were a welcome distraction from his scowling expression. Mr. Ricks, from the Ministry of Wind, was also middle-aged and had curly dark hair dashed with a little gray. He bowed respectfully to her when she noticed him. And the Ministry of Law had sent Master Baggles, who had once been a private tutor of hers years before. His partner, Master Eakett, had obviously elected to remain behind. Surely each of these men were in favor with her father and had been sent to spy on her.

After greeting them all brightly, she retired to her stateroom, where Becka was arranging her things. The tempest departed Lockhaven, heading toward a heavily guarded mirror gate on the coast.

They arrived a few hours later. Sera did not confide in Becka during that time, knowing they were undoubtedly being watched from the

Leerings hidden around the sky ship. She gave her maid small orders but showed her no special favor, as they'd agreed on.

They arrived at the mirror gate. The buildings of a small town dotted the coast, and there were probably fifty tempests posted there as well as a hurricane hovering in the sky. The town center had several dozen small buildings, the roofs speckled white from the multitude of seagulls infesting the area. Sera enjoyed the scent of the ocean on the breeze as the tempest docked.

The sun was beginning its decline in the western sky, and the sea looked choppy and gray. It was blissfully empty but for a few fishing boats. Sera joined her guardians and her maid as they made their way down the plank and headed to the magistrate's office in town. A snowy-haired bearded fellow awaited them, along with officers from the Ministry of War, in a cramped bureaucratic room that smelled of dust and rotting fish. He perused the documents provided and administered an oath to each one to certify that they were willing to exchange places in another world for the agreed-upon time. Sera was the last to swear the oath.

That done, the group was escorted down to the docks, where they boarded a rowboat that would carry them to the mirror gate. Their baggage was already stowed in the back. Sera had never been on such a vessel before, and the boat's swaying on the waters made her slightly nervous. Her stomach was a bit queasy as the oarsmen began to pull. But when she noticed Becka's terrified look, she swallowed her own fear.

Sera wanted to squeeze the girl's leg comfortingly, but her movement was hampered by her dress. Her gown was restrictive, the bone bodice and corset too tight, as was Lady Corinne's preference. And the heavy jewelry that had been provided for the occasion was swaying ponderously with the movement of the vessel.

Colonel Worthington sat to her right, scowling in a rather uninviting manner, his arms folded over his chest.

Ignoring his high-handed demeanor, she asked, "Why didn't we use an airship, Colonel?"

He didn't look at her. "Because we don't want to give them the chance to study our technology," he answered gruffly. "They haven't earned it."

As soon as they were a good distance from the pier, four zephyrs glided down to form a protective position around their boat. The oarsmen labored hard, and the water was choppy enough that it made Sera increasingly nauseated. So did the prospect that lay ahead of her. She was eager for the opportunity to see another world, but it was still daunting. There were so many places in her own world she hadn't seen. That she might never see. As the boat rocked and swayed, she watched the cliffs approach. The jagged walls were thick with moss and nesting seabirds, their squawks getting noisier and noisier.

Then she saw it. The mirror gate.

It was a high arch of gray rock, taller than a palace, made from the sea's erosion of a mountain. Greenery still grew atop it, and a small beach, unapproachable except by sky ship, lay just before it. There were tempests moored above the arch, hanging still despite the breeze. The cliffs were almost vertical. The opening was perhaps twice as tall as it was wide.

As they approached, Sera saw that an enormous face was carved into the rock at the top of the arch. It was a Leering—one that issued warnings. It also empowered them to use the mirror gate as a portal to innumerable worlds.

Seeing it, she was reminded sharply of her time at Muirwood. Of how she still had not taken the Maston Test. Regret and wariness brooded inside her heart. Their boat got closer and closer, and each moment she feared a disruption, something that would block the portal ahead, stealing her one chance at freedom. The scenery reminded her a little of Pavenham Sky, where she had met the prince of Kingfountain for the first time. She alone had recognized that he was disguised as a servant. She'd not seen him in three years. How had he changed in that time? Though their interaction had been brief, it had made a deep impression on her. She genuinely believed he was someone she could talk to. Someone who might be sympathetic to her situation. An ally? Maybe that was too strong a word for someone on the other side of this great divide.

She twisted a fold of her dress in her clenched fists, watching the gate loom closer. The huge mountain rose above them with crushing force. What power could topple such a structure forged by nature over thousands of years? Would it truly happen if they failed to keep their covenant?

As they reached the gate, one of the zephyrs dipped lower.

"All is clear, my lords!" shouted a soldier. "Send up the oarsmen!"

A rope ladder was dropped down to the bobbing boat, and the oarsmen climbed it one by one, leaving the rest to their fate.

Colonel Worthington reached for one of the oars, and Mr. Ricks took up another.

"It's not far, lads," said the colonel gruffly. "They'll be waiting for us on the other side."

Sera's breath quickened as the boat began to move steadily toward the arch again. She gazed up as the eyes of the Leering started to glow. There was a zephyr parked in the air just before the Leering. She could sense that they were controlling the Leering from it.

Becka wriggled nervously, breathing fast and hard and blinking back tears. Amidst all the turmoil, a feeling of calmness pierced the energy flooding Sera's bones. She recognized the feeling from Muirwood Abbey. She closed her eyes, offering a silent plea to the Knowing.

"Here we go," said Worthington.

Sera's eyes snapped open just as the boat lurched down, as if plunging off a waterfall.

CHAPTER TWENTY

THE COURT OF KINGFOUNTAIN

With the plummeting fall came a shroud of blackness that completely engulfed the boat. Becka screamed, and some of the men grunted. Sera gripped the wooden edges of her seat, trying not to panic.

When the drop abruptly ended, Sera still could not see anything, but the air smelled different, and the climate was more humid. Water splashed against the hull, some of it washing over the gunwale and soaking the floor. The boat rocked for a while before steadying.

As Sera's eyes adjusted to the sudden change, she looked up and behind them and saw a maelstrom of stars overhead. That was when she realized that it was night in Kingfountain.

The boat thumped against something solid, startling her, and a man's voice called out from above them.

"All is well. The exchange is complete. Board the frigate, please."

Sera turned in the direction of the voice and saw that their small boat had butted against the side of a massive sailing ship. Sailors with hooked poles fixed the prow of their boat and brought it alongside the much larger ship. Colonel Worthington rose first and clumsily made his way to the side, where some rungs had been fastened to the frigate awaiting them. He clambered up and spoke to the officer on duty above. Then the passengers climbed up to the deck one by one, Sera making her ascent in the middle of the group.

A hazy smoke emanated from the lamps on deck, so different from the Light Leerings she was used to at home. The sailors' dark green uniforms slashed with gold ribbons across the chests looked familiar, for she'd seen them in the gazettes. Their hats were taller and more angular than the broad, arched variety favored by the Ministry of War. Sera rubbed her arms, experiencing a shocking spell of dizziness.

Worthington was speaking to a man who, from his more formal uniform, appeared to be the vessel's captain. A few moments later, he brought him over to Sera.

"Your Highness, this is Captain Farrow," he explained. The captain had a salt-and-pepper mustache that drooped well past his chin. He bowed respectfully to Sera.

"Welcome, Your Majesty," he offered with a pleasant voice tinged with an accent. She could understand him, though she wasn't sure if he was actually speaking her language or if it was a feat of this world's magic. "We are your escort to the court of Kingfountain. The wind is fair, and we should arrive before morning. There is a stateroom prepared for you and your maid. If you will follow my adjutant?"

Sera nodded in compliance, and soon she and Becka were settled away in the stateroom. The room was simple yet elegant, just two small beds, a table nailed to the floor, and a lantern hanging from an iron chain. The blankets on the beds looked soft and sumptuous, and they bore a colorful pattern. There would be no scenery to look at on the voyage, however, for there was no moon. Becka began to address the luggage when it arrived, but Sera stopped her and took her hands. It was an intimate gesture, and one she made deliberately.

"Here we are," she said softly. There were no Leerings at all in the room. They could speak frankly here.

"I'm frightened, Your Highness," Becka said, her voice trembling.

"I am too," Sera admitted. "Please call me Sera. I'm glad you are here with me. I'll need your help now more than ever. Together, we will try and make things right."

Becka looked confused. "What can I do?"

"You are very quiet and unobtrusive."

Becka looked even more confused.

"That means you don't attract attention." Sera pulled the girl to one of the beds, and they sat down next to each other. "I need you to watch and listen for me. Not only to those who came with us, but to those from the court we are visiting. Listen to what they say when I'm not there. And then tell me what you learn. That will be of great service. We are both of us away from Lady Corinne now," Sera added with a relieved sigh. "We must negotiate a peace treaty with Kingfountain. And we must stop Lady Corinne's grasping for power. I learned from the prime minister that Admiral Lawton is dead."

"Dead?" Becka gasped in horror.

"Was it an accident? Was it part of Lady Corinne's plans? I don't know. I think she's going to establish herself with my father soon. I have to stop it. If she becomes his wife, and if they have any children, it will ruin my chance of ever becoming empress."

Becka looked at her in confusion. "B-but I thought . . . ? I thought you were going to become the Queen of Kingfountain?"

Sera patted Becka's hand. "I'm not done making my maneuvers yet. This is only the beginning. And you're going to help me win it all back."

They did arrive by sunrise. Sera had been too nervous and excited to sleep very much. She chose a fresh gown, one in the style preferred by Lady Corinne, both because that was all she'd been given and because she wished to appear docile. As the frigate docked at the quay, Sera watched through the porthole with astonishment. So many ships crowded the wharf, the masts looked like a forest of denuded trees. Were there thousands? The city of Kingfountain was vast but built at varying heights. She saw both the famous waterfall and the huge cathedral that sat on an island in the middle of the river right before the plunge of the falls. There were multiple bridges spanning the river behind it, each one crowded with people. The old palace still adorned the hilltop opposite that island, but rings of defensive walls and military barricades surrounded it in concentric circles. The great building itself had many towers with gleaming silver spikes.

Smoke from tens of thousands of chimneys filled the skies, but the homes were decorative and constructed with expert craftsmanship. She saw no evidence of slums or tenements. The air filled with the distant roar of pounding water.

After disembarking, they were loaded into ornate carriages manned by uniformed servants, six passengers per carriage. The horses were as white as pearls. On the other side of the river, cheers and shouts could be heard, but the noise was muted by the distance, especially since the clop of hooves on the cobblestones made for a noisy ride. Royal officers were posted to escort the carriages.

Sera was used to seeing zephyrs coming this way and that. There were none. Her world existed in the sky; everything in this land was rooted in the earth and in the sea. Her excitement at the novelty increased as the carriages took them up some winding roads leading to the palace. Becka, too, gazed out of the carriage in wonderment, her eyes focused on the colorful costumes of the royal officers. They passed several military buildings, and Sera took note of the soldiers marching with muskets.

At last they reached the upper heights, and the carriages, in single file, crossed the huge wooden drawbridge that led into the castle.

The clattering wheels of the carriages came to a stop in front of phalanxes of servants who stood at attention to greet the new arrivals. The palace had an air of antiquity, but it had certainly been refurbished many times, and the grounds were immaculately kept. Not a stray leaf littered the ground. Sera gazed up at the splendor of the place, feeling its strangeness acutely. The dresses the maids wore were so different from her own, the bodices more open and frilly. Long, luxurious hair, worn up in elaborate styles, seemed to be the fashion. The male servants wore trifold hats, their uniforms a pale gray with silver trim on the arms and legs. And instead of tall boots, they wore shoes with shiny buckles on the front. It was a warmer climate, and the clothing spoke to that.

The door of her carriage opened, and Sera was surprised to find herself staring into a face she recognized instantly despite the years that had passed since she'd last seen it. Prince Trevon extended a gloved hand to help her out.

She had not expected to see him so soon, and her heart pounded with surprise. He wasn't disguised as a servant this time and looked every bit the part of a prince. His jacket was green and gold with a short collar and no necktie. The cuffs of the sleeves were threaded in gold all the way up to his elbows. Over his pants, he wore a braided sash with tassels.

His initial expression was one of wariness as he helped her down from the carriage, but a welcoming smile soon replaced it. "I still recognize you," he said, and even his voice was familiar. His hair was longer than it had been, though it was still the rich nutty-brown color she remembered. He had a common but appealing face, and there was a scar on his chin that hadn't been there before.

"Please tell me I've grown a little taller since we last met," she said with a mischievous smile.

Her pursed his lips and eyed her. "No, I can't say that you have."

"Is it a custom to tease your guests upon their arrival?" she asked archly.

"If I thought you would prefer flattery, I would have tried that. Welcome to Kingfountain, Miss Fitzempress."

"I am grateful to have arrived safely. Will we conduct our business in the courtyard, or are we going to enter the palace?"

"The palace, of course," he said brightly. But before escorting her away, he reached up for Becka's hand and helped her down as well. The girl flushed and bowed her head.

"This is my maid, Becka."

"Welcome, my dear," the prince said, bowing to her.

Sera wasn't surprised Becka couldn't speak.

Then Prince Trevon offered his arm to Sera, who responded with her own courtly gesture by putting her hand on it. The two started walking toward the main doors, where it seemed the rest of the royal family had gathered. There were several young men standing there and two younger girls along with the prince's parents, the King and Queen of Kingfountain.

Before they reached the group, the two girls came fluttering up and hugged the prince, who seemed a little surprised by their attention. One of the girls eyed Sera with interest.

"These are my little sisters," he said, wrapping his free arm around the shoulders of one of the girls. "Could you not wait until we reached the steps?"

One of the girls replied to him in a language Sera had tried to study. She caught some of the words, but they'd been spoken too fast for her to understand. Both girls seemed to be vying for his attention, and the prince sighed and gave Sera a helpless look. She thought his doting on them was rather sweet, and it made her more tenderhearted. They mounted the steps together, and he introduced Sera to his siblings, all of them younger than him.

"Prince Kasdan, Prince Lucas, Prince Renowen, and Prince Gannon. And these are my sisters, Princess Lyneah and Princess Elaine."

"It's a pleasure to meet you," Sera said, dropping to a curtsy. They looked at her with open curiosity. Some of the brothers clearly didn't approve of her presence and barely concealed their scowls. There was a strong familial resemblance, and each of the siblings was within a year or two of each other in age, the youngest being at least ten.

"These are my parents," Trevon said, gesturing to the king and queen. Sera saw the famous hollow crown on the king's head. She'd heard it described before and recognized it at once. It was the source of authority of the kings of this land and had been handed down from ancient times. "My father, King Henricus, and my mother, Queen Christiana."

The king had a long, narrow face with tired-looking eyes and a formidable goatee and expression. Only a slight fuzz of hair covered his head and the area beneath his crown. He wore medallions and chains around his neck and a fur-lined cape over his fancy tunic. The look he gave Sera reminded her of her father, and she felt a premonition of dread. This was a hard man, a strict man, and no ally. The queen, Christiana, was a little younger than her husband but still middle-aged. She had rich auburn hair with some gray in it and, if Sera wasn't mistaken, an arrogant look. When her daughters returned to the platform, she gave them both a stern rebuke with her eyes.

"Welcome to the court of Kingfountain," said the king dispassionately, "Seraphin Fitzempress." His accent was a little stilted, but still accurate.

"Thank you, Your Majesty," Sera said, dropping low again.

"I see you brought four henchmen with you," the king said. "Are they prepared to negotiate in good faith on behalf of the prime minister?"

"No, Your Highness," Sera answered. "I represent my people."

The king pursed his lips and nodded. "Good. We won't treat with underlings. Neither my wife nor I will participate in the negotiations, my dear. They have been entrusted solely to my son and heir, Prince Trevon. I am not in favor of this armistice. But if the young man is to become a king, he must learn to use judgment and discernment. We will be bound to whatever agreement he makes with you. That is my promise, as a sovereign lord." His lips twitched into a sneer. "Do not have the impudence to suggest that a *contract* is needed to affirm this."

Sera could see the resentment in his eyes, the result of centuries of bad blood between their realms. There was no trust. Though she knew he was interested in the technologies Comoros could share, she understood that Kingfountain regarded the empire as inferior, their ways offensive. And she could also tell that he didn't think too highly of her, for all his fine talk and "dears."

"Thank you for making your position clear, Your Majesty," Sera replied coolly.

"You will join us for dinner?" the queen asked in a suspicious manner.

"I have no other present engagements," Sera replied.

"Do you not?" asked the queen, raising her brows. Was this a reference to the scandal that had resulted in her imprisonment in Pavenham Sky? Sera felt her blood growing hotter, but if she'd learned one thing these past years, it was how to control her expression.

"Mother," said the prince in a low warning tone.

"You are, of course, welcome," said the queen. Then Sera noticed that she was holding a garland made of white flowers. She gave it to her eldest daughter, Lyneah, who brought it to Sera and gestured for her to bow. Sera did so, and the young woman gave her a wink as she put it around her neck.

The scent from the flowers was lovely. The garland wasn't heavy, but in that moment, it might as well have been an iron collar. She could tell they expected her to stay, a prize won for peace, which would make Kingfountain as much a prison as Pavenham Sky had been. She straightened and inclined her head to the family once more.

"Walk with me," Prince Trevon said, extending his arm to Sera. She was only too grateful to escape his family. She put her hand on his arm again, and he escorted her away toward the gardens.

An iron gate blocked the entry, but a servant opened it ahead of them, exposing a wondrous garden as lush and beautiful as any she'd seen at Pavenham Sky. There were birds flittering, and tall trees with rich green leaves providing plentiful shade. They were different breeds than what she was used to seeing, and it piqued her curiosity to explore. This was what she'd dreamed of as a young girl who'd had to resort to climbing trees to see the world outside her palace.

"I'll admit I was surprised that you agreed to come after all," the prince said as they walked on the soft lawn. "That you would be so willing to give up your beliefs . . . everything you've ever known."

She gazed at the beautiful hedges, admiring the bubbling fountains interspersed throughout the garden. They were beautiful, and she knew they were also sacred to his people.

"Oh, I only said that to mollify Lord Welles and the privy council," she said. "I don't think I could give up my beliefs." She said it simply and sincerely and then turned and looked him in the eye. "Could you?"

CHAPTER TWENTY-ONE

Overtures

The effect of her words was immediate. His brows knitted in confusion and consternation, and he frowned—not out of anger but in reaction to an unpleasant surprise. Whatever Trevon had been expecting of their first outing together had been dashed.

"You look confused," Sera said consolingly.

"Shouldn't I be? I was given to understand that you were open to this change."

Sera began walking toward the nearest fountain. A quick perusal of the gardens confirmed that there were servants on the grounds watching them from a discreet distance. He noticed her change in direction and quickly followed.

"For the last three years," Sera continued, "I have been a sort of political prisoner. A pariah. This is my first opportunity for freedom since you made your state visit. It is also our first real opportunity to talk. To be candid with each other. If our situations were reversed, would you abandon the one thing that has given you the strength to endure the hardships you've faced? Please be honest with me, Trevon. Would you do it?"

He was taken aback by her question. His expression was serious. "To be honest, no. Asking someone to abandon their conscience is too hefty a price to pay. So why are you here, then? Why did you come?"

She gave him a smile. "To negotiate a peace treaty between our worlds. We have to stop killing each other."

He clasped his hands behind his back. "Yes, but you came here under false pretenses."

"And you *didn't* when you came to Lockhaven three years ago?"

That comment roused him. A look of anger darkened his eyes. "I did not, Miss Fitzempress."

"We are well past such formalities, Trevon."

"Very well. No, I came to the court to seek a wife. I found myself caught up in the political schemes of a disingenuous people."

"You compared our system of government to a machine, as I recall. It's an apt metaphor. I think we want the same thing. We both want to break that machine. My father, the emperor, seeks to maintain the status quo. But it's unsustainable."

He began to rub his mouth thoughtfully, but there was still a look of deep concern in his eyes. "This is not going the way I expected."

"And you're disappointed, I can tell. But I ask you again, Trevon. Reverse our positions. What would you do in my place?"

"I don't know," he answered. "I don't know what to believe right now. I thought you were coming as a . . . under different . . ." He trailed off, at a loss for words, his hands held up in confusion.

Sera gave him a chance to find his words as they continued to walk, but he looked increasingly vexed, and she didn't want him to become angrier with her. "What do you remember of our first meeting at Pavenham Sky?"

Her question caught him off guard again, and his eyes narrowed. "You mean after I dropped the platter or before?" They had reached the fountain and now stood near it.

The memory brought another smile to her face. "What do you remember about *me*?"

"You stood apart from the other young ladies," he replied seriously. "And you frankly surprised me when you came to offer assistance after I bumbled that disguise and broke a glass. Tell me true, had someone told you who I was? Before or after?"

Sera shook her head. "No one told me. Well, that's not entirely true. The Knowing told me."

His eyebrows arched.

She gazed at his face. "I knew it as assuredly as I'm standing before you now. I thought your disguise a clever one if a bit disingenuous."

"I didn't have much time to choose a wife," he replied evasively. "It was a ploy, for certain, but with the intention of securing happiness. I'm sure any of those in attendance would have dissembled well enough had they known I was there."

"I agree. You do get to know someone better if there aren't any pretenses. Which is why I am being so candid with you. I felt then, and still do, that you are motivated by honorable intentions. You are doing what you feel is right and true. So am I. There has been this ill blood between our realms for so many years, caused in part by envy and perhaps a mutual failure to understand each other's beliefs. I crossed the mirror gate today in the hopes you and I might begin to bridge that gulf. Like you, I don't have much time. But I hoped that if we put our minds together, we might come up with a solution to benefit both our sides."

His eyes were an interesting warm brown, with a small band of green flecks around the pupil. She had noticed them when they were crouching over the shards of a broken glass together that day in Pavenham Sky. But she'd been more caught up in the embarrassment of the moment and the subsequent understanding of his true identity.

"I'm beginning to discern where I stand in your eyes," he said, his voice tinged with disappointment.

She didn't like the change in his tone, his growing wariness. "What do you mean?"

His nostrils flared just slightly. "You came here seeking an ally. Not a husband. A solution that benefits both sides. If you had your way, you'd be empress. You're still grasping for it. And you need my help to achieve your ends."

The look of anger darkened, and he turned and walked away from her, leaving her alone by the fountain.

After wandering alone in the gardens for a while, Sera approached a servant and asked to be taken to her room. The palace was elegant and decorated with the finest works of art and craftsmanship from the court as well as the riches of foreign worlds. The soldiers lining the main corridors wore breastplates and helmets over their colored tunics, each of them holding a flag bearing the insignia of Kingfountain. The floor was made of polished marble tiles with alternating colors, arranged to form different geometric designs. There were statues in the small alcoves instead of Leerings.

When she arrived at her chambers, she found her four escorts awaiting her there. Colonel Worthington was pacing and scowling, but the others were lounging on the furniture and taking part in the refreshment. Master Baggles was stifling an enormous yawn, which reminded Sera that while it was not yet noon in Kingfountain, it was late in the evening back in the empire. Catching himself in the yawn, Baggles hastily sat up and stifled it.

"There you are, Your Majesty," said the colonel accusingly. "So you've met with the prince already. How did it go?"

Mr. Pond turned from the window and approached her inquisitively.

"Don't you all have your own staterooms?" Sera asked as she strode in. Becka stood by the study table, arranging Sera's books there. If the men had discussed anything she needed to know, her maid would be able to inform her.

"Of course we do, but we wanted to know the moment you arrived," Worthington said.

"Why don't you all return to your own rooms," Sera suggested. "When I am ready to seek your advice, I will send my maid for you."

Worthington glowered at her dismissal. "Your Highness, I don't think you recognize—"

"I'm tired, Colonel," she said, cutting him off. "When I need your help, I will ask for it."

His scowl only deepened. No doubt Lord Welles had given him special orders concerning his role in the peace negotiations. He flashed her a look of fury and then strode to the door. The other three left as well, Baggles yawning again while Mr. Pond snatched another treat from the tray on the serving table.

When the door was shut, Sera let out her breath.

The stateroom was enormous, the ceilings high and upheld by tall pillars. The ceiling had been painted and decorated with intriguing scenes awash in color. She walked to the nearest window and pushed aside the thin veil. She was on an upper level overlooking another set of gardens, but the windows also overlooked the river and the sanctuary and the enormous waterfall. It was a stunning view, one chosen to please her. The floor was made of alternating black and white tiles, like the Wizr boards she'd learned about.

"Can I get you anything? Are you hungry?" Becka asked, having quietly approached her from behind.

Sera smiled at the girl's thoughtfulness. "It's quite a view, isn't it?"

"Oh yes," Becka agreed eagerly. "Everything is so different here." Becka touched the glass with a faraway look in her eye as she stared outside. "The colonel has everyone else under orders. He said they should report anything suspicious to him. Oh, and he also said the palace is full of spies, so they should all be wary of what they say."

"That is very helpful, Becka. Thank you for being watchful."

Kingfountain was an enormous realm, all unified under a single king. She knew there were other kings who paid homage to the hollow crown. There was no parliament, no assembly of experts elected for their skills and abilities. Kingfountain was still a hereditary monarchy. The rule would go to the eldest son, regardless of his qualifications or aptitude. Still, she could hardly deny that Trevon seemed capable. He'd been groomed for the burden of leadership.

"Are you tired, Becka? Do you want to rest?"

"No, ma'am. I can still work."

Sera turned away from the window, looking at the huge room again, the enormous bed piled with blankets and an assortment of pillows. There were three grates filled with a small lump of burning coals, but the room was already a comfortable temperature. Not a single Leering. Ah, well. She'd never been all that good with them anyway.

"The fashions here are quite different," Sera said.

"They are, ma'am."

Sera thought for a moment. The king and queen had invited her to dinner that evening. She would be on display. Her insides still twisted with worry at the prince's final words to her before stalking off. Had he already revealed all to his parents? Would they send her back to Lockhaven in disgrace? She wished she knew what it would take for her to win Trevon's trust and support. A peace treaty would benefit them both. And were there not certain technologies that Kingfountain craved? Surely a matrimonial alliance couldn't be the only acceptable outcome?

Sera pursed her lips, thinking hard. She needed to keep things moving forward. To give them reason to believe that she wanted to broker an armistice.

"Becka, I need you to do something for me. I'll be joining the prince and his family for dinner. I don't want to wear one of the gowns we brought. I want you to find one from this land. Something pretty but not too fancy or revealing. If you can, bring me several to choose from and try on."

"I will," Becka said. "One of the servants told me to find her if you need anything. She's the maid for the prince's sisters."

"Good," Sera said, pleased. "See what you can manage."

Becka left, and Sera began to pace the large room, replaying the scene in the garden again and again in her mind. She thought back to Trevon's reactions, his facial expressions, and how he'd held himself. She'd flustered him, probably more than once. If he were younger, he might indeed have gone to his parents to complain. But they had left it to him to negotiate the treaty. If he wanted to display his wisdom and judgment, he'd hesitate to consult them. He'd seek out another advisor, someone else he trusted. Sera entwined her fingers and then tapped her lips with them. As she paced, brooding about the encounter, she explored the stateroom. There was a darker antechamber with a huge stone-tile bath, surrounded by opened curtains, and a number of various closets and side rooms.

After some time passed, a knock sounded on the door. It opened, admitting a man dressed in the style of her realm, except his outfit included a military sash and several medals pinned to his coat.

"Welcome, Miss Fitzempress," the man said with a bright smile. He was blond with a darker beard. His look was oily and obsequious, and she took an instant dislike to him. "My name is Lord Datchin. I'm the ambassador who has been negotiating the terms of your passage here." He rubbed his earlobe as he entered, looking around for others and not finding anyone. "You're alone?"

"At present, Lord Datchin. Do come in, but leave the door wide open, please."

"Is that wise? Would not some privacy help against prying ears?"

"After what I've been through of late, I'm sure you understand."

He gingerly rubbed the skin of his cheekbone as he sauntered into the room. "I'm given to understand that you are not as amenable . . .

how shall I put this? To a *union* with the court of Kingfountain as presupposed?"

"I'm not certain I understand you, Lord Datchin. Can you please be more clear?"

"I'm given to understand . . . what I mean is . . . do you intend to marry the crown prince?"

She gave him a perplexed look. "Isn't that why I came here?"

He looked surprised by her answer. "Well, Your Majesty, I'm quite sorry to have interrupted you."

The sound of footfalls from the corridor made them both look up. Becka had entered the room along with another young maid, each of them carrying two gowns. Lord Datchin turned in surprise as the girls brought the gowns over to the bed and began to arrange them next to each other.

"Those look lovely," Sera crooned, smiling with exaggerated delight as she made her way to them, bending to examine the fabric and style. Lord Datchin's brow needled together in confusion as he watched the display unfold.

"What are these for?" Lord Datchin asked in bewilderment.

"I'm having dinner with the royal family tonight," Sera explained brightly. "I want to make a good impression on them, naturally. To show that I'm willing to adopt their customs, their manners." She touched one of the gowns, a gold-and-cream confection that would do wonders for her complexion.

"So you are not going to wear something you brought? Something showing our fashions and sensibilities?"

She gave a little laugh. "This is Kingfountain, not Lockhaven, Ambassador. Must we not try to fit in?"

"I'm . . . I see I was mistaken."

"Thank you. If I need you, Ambassador, I will call for you. Now if you'll let me change."

He bobbed his head and bowed deeply before hastening from the room. As the door closed, Sera smiled in triumph. She'd rather enjoyed outfoxing him.

"What is your name?" she asked Becka's companion.

"My name is Liselle," the girl answered in a thick accent, dropping to a curtsy.

"Thank you for helping Becka," she said. "These four all look very fine."

"If you pick which one you wish, ma'am, the seamstress can make sure it fits the best for dinner," Liselle said.

Sera tried them all on, one by one. There was an ornate mirror near the window, so she could study each dress in turn. Sera kept her opinions to herself. It felt strange—and strangely freeing—not to wear gloves or a hard bone bodice.

Sera chose the gold-and-cream gown as her favorite and put it back on. The maids helped her prepare for dinner, providing an array of tasteful, understated embellishments to apply to her lips and cheeks and eyes. Sera decided in the end to wear her hair down instead of trying to mimic all the fashions of the new land, but she did wear the flower garland she'd been given earlier. Weariness settled on her. She'd been up all night and felt it keenly. But she was determined to make it through dinner before sleeping.

When another servant came to announce dinner, Sera was ready and followed him out of the room, giving a wink of approval to Becka and Liselle before leaving. Her stomach churned again as she prepared herself for another encounter with the prince's family. Some of the servants in the hall noticed her and blinked in surprise at her transformation.

The dining hall was very different from what she was used to. No long tables at all, but a number of small round ones, probably twelve in all, each surrounded by six stuffed chairs. The tables were quite decorative, and each one had another round contrivance in the middle. Chandeliers hung from iron chains above each table, and they were lit with slender white candles. The royal family had already gathered, but no one was sitting yet. They were all watching her as she entered the room.

There were looks of distrust on their faces still, and the queen examined Sera's choice of gown with open curiosity. Prince Trevon approached, wearing a different costume than the one he'd had on earlier. He held out his arm for her. She noticed he was again wearing gloves, adopting her customs as she was adopting his.

"We'll be sitting together," he said courteously, but his eyes were still full of misgivings.

"I was hoping to," she answered, looking up at him. She noticed the other emissaries from Lockhaven stood out from the rest in their traditional dress. They appeared quite uncomfortable in the strange circumstances. She felt unsettled as well, but she smiled and bowed her head before surveying the room.

"We'll be joined by two distinguished guests tonight," the prince said as he escorted her to one of the tables. "General Montpensier has just arrived. And he brought with him a prisoner of war from the battle we recently fought. Someone you might recognize." Sera gasped as they came closer to the table. Two men stood by it, and she recognized the haggard face of one of them instantly. Her expression widened with surprise and delight at the sight of him, and she covered her mouth and felt a rush of joy.

"Lord Fitzroy!" she gasped aloud.

CHAPTER TWENTY-TWO

FALSE HARBINGER

There was no mistaking the pleasure in Lord Fitzroy's eyes upon seeing a familiar face at the court of Kingfountain. Sera rushed to him and took his hands in hers, her emotions shifting from wonder to gratitude to hope, all within seconds. News of his survival had not reached Lockhaven. Was that deliberate?

"Hello, Sera," Fitzroy said, looking at her with relief. He gave her hands a firm squeeze.

"So this is the young Miss Fitzempress," said the other man, sidling up next to them. He was much younger than Fitzroy, perhaps not much older than herself. He had a prominent forehead, paired with a small, rounded chin, and his visage rather reminded her of an upside-down pear. His hair was sandy brown, and he wore the military uniform of his kingdom, with large strips of buttons and shoulder epaulets. His eyes were cunning and inquisitive, and he regarded her with open curiosity.

"We've not met," Sera replied guardedly, "General Montpensier."

"Please, call me Leon," he replied with a deep bow. "So you are the emperor's illegitimate daughter," he said with a brassy smile.

His words shocked her, and she started, squeezing Fitzroy's hands in return.

"Please, General," said the prince in a scolding tone. "She won't be used to your teasing."

The general grinned at her. "They say the lord high admiral here is a *harbinger*." His accent made the word sound a little ridiculous. "I am only exercising my prerogative to be one as well. If you guess enough times, you're bound to pick it right once in a while, and that is all the people will remember, eh? No doubt your father will divorce his wife, marry another, and then find it convenient to declare you . . . illegitimate, just as was done to your ancestor, Empress Maia. Remember, Your Highness, you heard me say it first!"

"General," Trevon said with strained patience.

"So you are the one who has been leading the armies against us," Sera responded coolly.

"Winning against you, you mean," he said with a mocking tone. "Why else would they send you to negotiate a surrender?"

Sera realized he was goading her deliberately. Testing her. There was an obvious strain between him and the prince. A rivalry of sorts. But Lady Corinne had taught her well. She wouldn't rise to such open provocations.

"Prince Trevon," Sera said, turning her attention to him. "I love the flower garland. I've studied many plants, but I cannot recognize this variety."

"Those are magnolia blooms," he replied. "They grow here at the palace. The leaves are woven into the garlands as well."

"That was very thoughtful of you. And thank you for bringing Lord Fitzroy to dinner."

"*I* brought him to dinner," said the general.

There was the tinkling sound of a bell, and all eyes turned to the head table. The king and queen had just seated themselves. The rest of the party followed, and Sera found herself sitting next to the prince. Fitzroy was across the table from her. She longed to speak to him, to share everything she'd discovered, but it wouldn't do to show him too much attention and snub the prince. She would try to find time later.

The prince introduced her to the other dinner guests at the table, and she promptly forgot their names and titles.

The general made a flourish with his napkin, and the servants began to place dishes on the middle circle of the table. It rotated so that each person could be served a portion.

"Don't worry about being *poisoned*, Miss Fitzempress," the general said, reaching up and using the large silver spoons to ladle food onto his plate. "We serve all our dishes in this manner. Every person takes their own portion. A simple precaution . . . in case you were worried."

She turned away from him and looked at Prince Trevon. "Can you explain the dishes to me?"

The general's eyes flashed with anger. His personality was excessively strong, and it was clear he was not accustomed to being snubbed.

"The best delicacies come from the sea," Trevon said, gesturing to the various dishes and calling out an assortment of shrimp, pike, lobster, oyster, and salmon. Each had a colorful sauce and appealing little garnishes. "The berries are from Brythonica, a treat of themselves. I think you'll fancy them. May I?" He offered to serve her, and she nodded her acceptance. He gave her small portions of each dish while General Montpensier began devouring his food like a soldier who'd been on the march for too long.

"You've come to negotiate the armistice?" Fitzroy asked her, his eyes holding hers. If only they could talk in private . . . if only she could consult with him privately.

"The *surrender*," Montpensier grumbled with a mouthful.

"I have indeed, Lord Fitzroy. Where is your bodyguard? I would have thought to see him with you."

Fitzroy shook his head. "We were separated when the hurricane went down."

"The Bhikhu, yes?" the general interrupted.

Fitzroy glanced at him. "Yes."

"You saved him from a poppy addiction on another world," said the general slyly, "if my intelligence officer informed me correctly?"

"You have capable men, General." Fitzroy looked not the slightest bit flustered.

Montpensier took his wine goblet and twirled the contents. "I do indeed. Which is why I know a surrender is in order. My prince, I am a soldier first and foremost. Some say I am Fountain-blessed." He shrugged as if it meant nothing, but Sera could almost hear his jacket buttons straining to pop off. "I have a gift for strategy and leading men. I'm especially adept at playing Wizr. Which brings me to a suitable analogy. We just captured your most valuable piece, Miss Fitzempress. The rest of the game is a foregone conclusion. We both know that. Without your *harbinger*, you will not be able to predict where we will strike next." He slammed his palm on the table suddenly, jostling the dishes and silverware. He had tried to startle her into flinching, but she didn't. She gave him an icy stare instead. "You're defeated," he continued. "Your Highness, let's save further bloodshed and negotiate terms in this light. Surrender is your most viable and promising option. You must forsake your religion before it is ripped away from you. Marry His Royal Highness, Prince Trevon, and someday *you* will become Queen of Kingfountain and ruler of Comoros too. You'll get what you've always wanted."

Sera picked up her napkin and dabbed her mouth with it, buying herself time to think. She glanced quickly at Fitzroy, who sat stern but imperturbable, and then turned toward the prince.

"I think the salmon is my favorite," she said. "The lemon and pepper adds such a delightful contrast."

Trevon looked surprised at her coolheadedness. He'd no doubt anticipated a more hotheaded response to the general's tactics.

Montpensier hissed in resentment, pushed his plate away, and signaled for a servant to refill his wine goblet.

"The lobster is my favorite," Trevon said. "I was always frightened of them as a boy. They look like monsters."

"I've never seen one," Sera answered.

"If you wish to frighten yourself, I can take you to the kitchen afterward," he said with a small smile.

"General," said Fitzroy in a low, thoughtful voice.

"Yes?" the younger man replied peevishly.

"The scenario you disclosed just now would be quite compelling. If it were true."

Montpensier scowled and sat up. "What do you mean, Admiral?"

Sera fixed her attention on Fitzroy, her heart beating hard in her chest. He was looking at the general, but she had a feeling that his words were meant for her. He was sliding a dominion card across the table to her to help her hand.

"We know about your spy network, General. The Espion. And we've allowed it to operate unmolested. It helps us more than it hurts us."

"Fancy words, Fitzroy," said the general petulantly. "You are bluffing."

"For example, the identity of the harbinger is a deliberate ruse. You were led to believe, wrongly, that I am the one with that rare gift. I am not, but I know who it is. And so does Miss Fitzempress. That is why your threat holds no concern for us. You strike through a mirror gate again, and there will be a fleet of sky ships waiting for you. If you don't believe me, by all means, throw the lives of your men away in testing it."

Cettie. It could only be Cettie. Sera felt a thrill go through her heart. Yes, Fitzroy was giving her a dominion card, the most powerful one in the deck. She had not known the truth until that very moment. But Fitzroy did not lie, ever—according to him, she knew the harbinger, and she did. He was trusting her intuition to figure it out. The dinner was just another phase of the negotiations. They'd thought they could leverage her into acquiescence by demonstrating Fitzroy was their hostage. But he had given her a bit of knowledge that had foiled their plan. She was so grateful to the Mysteries for arranging the dinner.

"I would like to try some of the berries, General," Sera said sweetly.

A hand touched Sera's arm and gently shook her. She came awake drowsily amidst the enormous stuffed bed that was so soft it felt like sleeping on a cloud. Her eyes fluttered open, and she saw Becka next to her, shaking her.

"Look, Sera! Look!"

It was morning already. It felt like she had laid her head on the pillow only moments ago, but brilliant light filled the room. There was a pleasant odor in the air, a flowery scent. Becka tugged at her nightdress, and Sera sat up and rubbed her eyes.

"Look!" The maid pointed toward the anteroom with the bath. A look of fearful interest shone in her eyes. "It just started filling itself."

There was a hazy steam coming from the bath, and Sera scooted off the edge of the bed before walking that way. Near the bath, the tiles were damp with mist under her bare feet. As they approached the massive tub together, Sera saw that it was indeed filling itself. Had the magic been done by Leering, water would have gushed from stone mouths carved into rock. Instead, it appeared as if water was rising from beneath.

"Magic," breathed Becka in wonder. The flowery scent came from the water, and heat emanated from the pillars around it. She could feel the gentle tingle that always accompanied the Leerings. It was similar magic, just applied differently. Sera went to the edge and scooped up a palmful of water, which was milky in color rather than clear. It was very warm. She shook it off.

"I suppose it's time for a bath," Sera said. She disrobed and stepped into the tub and felt her muscles immediately relax.

"Which gown would you like for today, Sera? The red one?"

"Yes, the red one." The temperature was perfect, and she felt little tingles from the bath as if the water itself contained some revitalizing magic. At the edge of the tub were various vials and cakes of soap. The weariness of her journey seemed to melt away in the bath. Her mind became sharp and alert. She wanted to speak to Fitzroy, to tell him what she'd learned about Lady Corinne. But he was here as a prisoner, not an ambassador. She would need to negotiate for his freedom as well.

After the satisfying bath, she emerged and fetched a towel to dry herself. Becka helped her put on her undergarments and the red gown. It was a luxurious satin with a glossy sheen and a wreath-like girdle that went on the outside instead of the confining corsets she was used to wearing beneath her gowns. The cut was elegant, the bodice decorated by a golden choker and pendant. Sera asked Becka to braid part of her hair back, and she did it quickly and deftly.

After she was done, a knock sounded on the door, and servants entered with trays of food for their breakfast, mostly consisting of slices of various-colored melons, quince, and more of the delicious berries she'd tried the night before. Before she'd finished eating, the door opened and the prince's sisters, Lyneah and Elaine, came in excitedly. They spoke to each other in giddy tones as they approached and dropped into deep curtsies before her.

"Good morning," Sera greeted them, rising. She mimicked their curtsies, which were different in style than the form of greeting in vogue at Lockhaven.

"Did you sleep well?" Elaine asked.

"Of course she did, doesn't she look rested?" Lyneah answered for her.

"Are you going to marry Trevon?" Elaine asked, earning a sharp elbow from her sister.

"You can't ask her that," Lyneah scolded. "I'm sorry, Miss Fitzempress."

"You can call me Sera," she replied. Her mouth tilted into a smile. It was impossible not to smile around these two. "I don't have any siblings. I didn't realize Trevon had so many."

"They're mostly *brothers*," Lyneah said sourly. "We're the only girls."

"I wish I had a sister," Sera sighed. No sooner had the words left her mouth than Elaine hurried forward and hugged her. The show of affection surprised her, but the hug felt pleasant. The girl's emotions were ever on the surface.

"My brother is ready to see you," Lyneah said. "We're supposed to take you to him."

"I will come, then," Sera replied.

"Are you finished with your breakfast?"

"I've had enough. Shall we?" She linked arms with each of them and let them lead her out of the room. As she left, she glanced back at Becka, who was already starting to make the bed.

The girls led her through the twisting corridors of the palace, past sentries armed with pikes, and through a set of double doors leading outside to a different garden. There were pavilions erected on the grounds to provide shade. Trevon was at the archery butts, his jacket folded over a chair. He had a longbow in one hand and was nocking an arrow when he turned and saw her approach. Several targets were lined up in front of him at varying distances. She saw several arrows sticking from each of them.

"Do you shoot, Sera?" he asked her, easing the tension on the bowstring.

She'd been more of the dancing sort at school, but she remembered how talented Cettie had been. She wished her friend were there to show up Trevon.

"Is this another attempt to make me feel inferior at something?" Sera asked archly. The two sisters giggled and then pranced over to one of the other pavilions to watch them from a discreet distance.

Trevon turned to face her. "So you don't shoot?"

"I don't shoot well," Sera said. "But I'm not afraid to handle a bow."

"There is a Fountain-blessed lass from Legault," he said, raising an eyebrow. "She shot an apple off her father's head. She is quite amazing."

"Are you suggesting I go over and stand by the target?" Sera said with a laugh.

"No, not at all." The arrow was still fixed on the string, and he raised the bow, drew it back at an upward angle, and loosed it. The bow twanged, and the shaft flew to the farthest target, embedding itself within one of the inner rings. "It clears my head when I need to focus. It is easy to get distracted by what's beyond the mark."

There was a square wooden table nearby with leather shooting gloves and several other bows propped against it. Sera took one of the gloves and began securing it but couldn't get it quite right. Trevon offered to help her, but she shook her head and persisted until she managed it herself. She examined the different bows and took the smallest one. It had been a while since she'd practiced, so she took her time preparing the arrow and then brought the feathers back to her cheek. The need to hit the closest target roiled inside her. She didn't want to embarrass herself. It would be easy to avoid the challenge completely, but she wanted to portray self-confidence to him. Even if she missed, it was better to have tried than to be afraid of trying.

She loosed the arrow, which struck the center of the target by some miracle. Sera laughed in surprise and noticed Trevon's upturned eyebrows.

"Again you deceive me," he muttered.

"Maybe you'll believe me if the next one goes into the woods. I don't think I have ever hit the center before unless I was standing next to it." She lowered the bow but held it with both hands.

The prince studied her closely. "So Fitzroy isn't the harbinger after all."

"I think you know him enough by reputation to realize he wouldn't lie deliberately."

Trevon nodded. "Your father, when he was prince regent, asked him to become prime minister. And he refused because of a little girl." He nodded to her. "Your friend."

"A friend I haven't seen in three years."

Trevon looked down at the grass. "You've been at Pavenham Sky all this time. How did you find Lady Corinne's company?"

"Considering that she and Lord Welles plotted with my father to undermine my rights . . . well, you could say she's not my favorite person."

"She's formidable," said Trevon.

Sera looked at him. "So am I."

"I already knew that!" he joked. "Before we continue our negotiations, I wanted to ask you something that I'm afraid might be uncomfortable."

She'd expected this might come up. She lifted her eyebrows and looked at him questioningly.

He took another arrow, set it in place, and turned back to the targets. "Tell me about the dragoon."

She was tempted to ask what sordid rumors he'd heard about her, but truth and transparency were her best allies here. "Will Russell was a friend who betrayed me. Before I was sent to Muirwood, my father had me tutored at home. One of my tutors was Will's mentor, which meant he used to come along for our lessons. He and I became friends and wrote innocent letters to each other. I've always been concerned about the plight of the poor. That's something else you and I have in common, I think."

Trevon loosed the arrow, and it struck the target right next to hers. "It is."

"His father was cheated by someone living in a sky manor. It ruined him, and he was forced to sign away his son's deed to the military. My father was angered by Will's attentions to me and practically exiled him. Years later, we met down in the City, where he promised to return the letters to me lest my father find some way to use them against me." The memory of that night still made Sera burn with fury. She didn't know how she could talk about it so dispassionately, but she managed it. "I realized too late that he'd made an agreement with Lord Welles to humiliate me. To shame me. We did kiss that night, but it ended there. I fled out of a window as soon as I discovered his intentions. I was lucky to find safe shelter until my advocate arrived, but we were caught by Welles's stooges shortly after that. The privy council never gave me a chance to explain myself. I told Lord Fitzroy the truth, so you can ask him if you don't believe me."

Trevon took another arrow. "I did ask him."

"And?"

"He said to speak to you. He said you'd be honest with me."

"And I was. Shall we see if honesty works both ways? Have you loved another? Would you break your beloved's heart to make this truce between our worlds?"

Trevon picked up another arrow and examined it closely. He pursed his lips as he set it on the string. "I had an older brother . . . Dallis . . . who drowned many years ago. He and two of my younger brothers, Renowen and Gannon, were exploring the shoreline in Averanche. They wandered too far along some rocks at low tide, something they didn't realize until the waves started coming back. The waves kept beating them against the rocks. Dallis helped Gannon climb up to a boulder above the coming tide, but he and Renowen kept slipping each time the waves came." He stared at the target but didn't lift the bow. "They tried calling for help, but they were too far from the others. The waves kept getting higher and higher, and he knew that they were both going to drown. My older brother lifted Renowen up on his shoulders. The waves kept smashing them against the rocks, but he held our brother up for as long as he could. He drowned before help arrived. It was a terrible day. I was fifteen when I became the crown prince."

He raised the bow and loosed the arrow, which struck on the other side of hers. "Since that day, I imagined that someday I might marry a lady from Comoros to try and heal the breach between our worlds. To stop this never-ending cycle of violence and death. It would not be easy. There are people in both our worlds who do not want it to happen." He lowered the bow and gave her a serious look. "But since I met you three years ago, I have not been able to imagine marrying anyone else."

I begin to think that this troublesome princess may be more thorn than rose.

—Leon Montpensier, Duke of La Marche

CETTIE

CHAPTER TWENTY-THREE

SECRETS

As the tempest descended toward Fog Willows, Cettie's mind was in a state of turmoil that only increased when she saw the military sky ship already moored there. It, too, was a tempest, and the dread in her heart deepened at the sight of it. She had pushed her own vessel to its limits, and Rand had insisted they go to her home first. He'd suggested that he could take the zephyr post later to return to his sister and Mr. Batewinch.

Although she had not felt like talking, Rand had coaxed from her memories of Fitzroy and how he had rescued her from the Fells. What she didn't understand was why she had seen a vision of him and Sera together in Kingfountain, something she absolutely could not share with Rand. He had to be alive, didn't he? Worry mingled with doubt and heightened her anxiety. She could not bear to lose him, not so soon. It was the one thing she knew she lacked the strength to endure.

She landed the tempest in the docking yard, only to find Raj Sarin floating down from the upper balcony. Cettie flung herself down the rope ladder with Rand following a few steps behind. There was a haunted look in the Bhikhu's face, his eyes bloodshot and his mouth pressed down in a frown of misery.

When she reached him, she embraced him and heard him mumble "Cettie Saeed" with a strain of anguish in his voice. He certainly thought Fitzroy was dead.

No, it wasn't possible. It couldn't be true.

Before she could answer his forlorn greeting, the main doors of the manor opened, and she saw Lady Maren emerge with Sir Jordan Harding. And then her heart lurched at the sight of Adam Creigh following them in his dress uniform. Just the sight of him brought her up short, the long absence making her ache. She yearned to throw propriety aside and run to him . . . and then she noticed a tear-stricken Anna clinging to his arm.

The sight of them together was like a physical blow to her heart. She covered her mouth, still not comprehending, still not willing to believe it. The core of who Cettie was began to wobble. Could she be wrong? What if her vision had not come to pass because some circumstance, however small, had changed?

No, no, no! She froze in that instant, trying to rally her courage, her conviction.

Lady Maren arrived first, sweeping Cettie into a tight hug. She clung to her mother, feeling tears burn in her eyes. But crying was akin to mourning, and she would not do it. She clenched her teeth and pulled away, shaking her head.

"I'm sorry, lass," said Sir Jordan, his normal humor extinguished by the ill news he'd brought. "I wish there was something I could do to bring him back."

A gust of wind blew across the yard, sending Cettie's hair flying. She flung it back defiantly with a shake of her head.

"Father is not dead," she said with determination.

Sir Jordan's face was grave. "I saw his hurricane go down myself, Cettie. Raj Sarin saw him go under the waves. We searched for him, but there was no sign. The life of his crew meant more to him than his own life. He's not the only one who perished. Lord Lawton is dead, and so is another admiral. The empire has never been this vulnerable."

"Cettie," Lady Maren said in despair, shaking her head.

"He is not dead!" Cettie insisted, unable to hold the words back any longer. She gripped Maren's arms. "Remember? I saw him, at the court of Kingfountain. I saw him with Sera. It was a vision, just like the others. They all came to pass, so this will too."

"What are you saying? What visions?" Adam pressed, his face a mixture of surprise and sorrow. Anna nestled closer to him, her eyes brightening with hope.

They all stared at her. Her secret had come out at last.

They all retreated to the sitting room for Cettie to tell her story. The wind howled outside as she told them that she was a harbinger. That her visions had helped Fitzroy predict the movements and tactics of General Montpensier's army. She recounted the visions in turn and explained that they'd begun after she'd taken the Test at Muirwood Abbey.

Adam seemed especially struck by the news, and his look told her that he was disappointed she hadn't confided in him sooner.

"You *have* to tell the Ministry of War," Rand said, his expression serious as he paced slowly in the room.

"Absolutely," Sir Jordan concurred. "The privy council must be informed as well. The prime minister."

"No," Cettie said, shaking her head. "I don't want to get drawn in to all of that."

"We have no choice!" Sir Jordan said passionately. "Have you had any other visions since the last one? I know for a fact that Miss Fitzempress has already departed for Kingfountain to negotiate a cessation of hostilities. She left yesterday."

"So you believe me?" Cettie asked. "If what I saw is true, then Father is still alive." And it was comforting to think that he was with her dear friend in that foreign place.

"Of course we believe you," Adam said, shaking his head. "There could be no doubt on that point."

"Even knowing what you'd told me," Mother said, "I'm afraid I doubted. The news was too horrible. Everyone seemed so certain. I still . . . I don't know what to think. Your other vision didn't show that we would lose so much in the battle—it only told us where they would strike."

"I know," Cettie agreed. "If I had seen the devastation, I would have tried to prevent it."

"Can you *change* the future?" Rand asked. "Or only see it?"

"I don't know," Cettie answered. They were all still looking to her. But the mood had changed. Hope was emerging again, like the sun from behind a cloud.

Sir Jordan approached her. "The prime minister needs to know this, Cettie. Surely you see that."

She bit her lip and gave him a miserable look. "The prime minister doesn't like me very much."

"Nevertheless, he must be told," Sir Jordan continued. "Why did Fitzroy keep this a secret?"

Lady Maren spoke up. "The three of us made this decision years ago, Jordan. There is already a strong prejudice against those from the Fells. The privy council would be slower to act on the instincts of a young girl than a trusted member of the council. We also didn't know how frequently the visions would come. My husband never claimed to be a harbinger. That reputation has blossomed on its own. But I agree, Cettie, that we cannot keep the truth away from them any longer. Not when there is so much at risk."

It pained Cettie's heart to hear it, even though she secretly agreed. The time had come for her to stop hiding.

"This is what I propose, Maren," Sir Jordan said seriously. "I will return to Lockhaven this moment and notify the prime minister. If he asks to see her, then I will contact you, and she can come."

"I don't trust Lord Welles," Cettie said, wringing her hands. "Not after what he did to Sera."

"What did he do?" Rand asked in confusion.

Cettie shook her head. Her feelings were too twisted and confused for her to talk about it just yet.

Sir Jordan's countenance was grim. He put his hand on her shoulder. "Young lady, despite your feelings, we must do this. I have a duty to protect and defend the empire. Even now, the privy council is summoning its final reserves to defend Lockhaven, leaving the mirror gates unprotected. If Montpensier attacks right now, he can conquer our empire almost without opposition. And there are doubts"—he lowered his voice more confidentially—"that the emperor is suitably strong in the Mysteries to control the defenses." He shook his head. "These are perilous times. I've never seen our world at so much risk. Welles *must* be told. Do you know what our enemies would do if they conquered us? They would destroy our society and steal our advancements, just as they have stolen from us in the past. They would compel us to adopt their ways and their religion under pain of death. It would be a massacre, Cettie." He put his hand on his chest and tapped it. "And I've sworn a covenant to defend my beliefs, my people."

Cettie knew he was right and lowered her head. She nodded glumly.

"Well, at least we depart Fog Willows with better news than we came here with," Sir Jordan added with a lighthearted chuckle. They all rose from their seats. "I'll send word immediately. Come along, good doctor. Your next patient is the empire. Let us go save her."

Anna looked crestfallen that he'd be departing so soon. She immediately wrapped her arms around his waist and hugged him tightly, pressing her cheek against his chest. Adam looked surprised by the show—his cheeks flushed with embarrassment, and his arms bent at awkward angles in an attempt to keep the hug from being inappropriate.

"Be safe," Anna said, squeezing him even harder, then pulled away.

Lady Maren gave her daughter a stern look.

Adam gave Cettie a helpless look. He wanted to talk to her, she could see it in his eyes, but Sir Jordan was already heading to the door.

"I'll walk you to your ship, Sir Jordan," Cettie offered. Adam looked relieved.

"Very well. We should arrive at Lockhaven by midnight. Expect a zephyr by afternoon."

Cettie accompanied them down the main corridor toward the front doors. Kinross approached quickly and asked her if the gentlemen were leaving or staying for dinner.

"They are leaving straightaway," Cettie told him.

The footmen at the door opened it for them. Cettie didn't have a cloak to protect her from the howling wind, but she braved the inclement weather and followed the two men to their sky ship.

"I'll see you next in Lockhaven, I have no doubt!" Sir Jordan shouted over the bluster. He started up the rope ladder.

Cettie stood at the base, arms folded, shivering, and Adam retrieved his own cloak and set it on her shoulders.

"You'll need it," she objected.

He stood at the base of the sky ship, hands on his hips, the wind tousling his dark hair. Oh, how she wished to reach out and touch it, to touch *him*. "I hope this war ends soon," he said, half shouting to be heard. "It is not worth the cost we've paid." He glanced back at the manor, a conflicted look on his face. "Cettie, I . . ." His voice trailed off.

Part of her feared what he might say. The other part longed to hear it. Sir Jordan was nearing the railing above.

Suddenly, an overwhelming feeling of powerful emotion flooded her chest. The intensity of it took her breath away. Her love for him nearly made her burst apart inside. Oh, that he might want to be with her, in the Fells or anywhere in the world. It wouldn't matter so long as they were together. She nearly confessed her feelings, saying words that could not be unsaid. But she was just shy enough that she didn't dare. She wanted *him* to say those words first, to end her suspense and torment, to end the uncertainty about his connection with Anna.

"I pray it ends soon," he said, the wind nearly extinguishing his voice.

"Get up here, Creigh!" Sir Jordan hollered.

Adam gave her a final miserable look, as if parting from her was ripping him in half. Then he turned and reached for the ladder rungs. Cettie took off the cloak and put it around his shoulders instead. Just touching him sent a spasm of feeling down her arms.

He hung his head, then turned and smiled at her as she fastened the clasp at his throat.

"Be safe," she told him.

Cettie watched, shivering in the wind, as he hoisted himself up the ladder, and she didn't move until the tempest was out of sight.

The wind raged all through the night. Rand Patchett had taken the afternoon zephyr post back to Gimmerton Sough, but he said his good-byes to the family first. They'd explained the circumstances of their journey to Dolcoath and Billerbeck Abbey, and Lady Maren had thanked him profusely for his help. She was especially pleased to hear that Stephen's injury was not too serious, and his leadership had increased his standing at the mines.

Rand had given Cettie a tender look before departing, which caused her some small feeling of alarm. He was a good man, and their friendship had brought them closer together during the journey. But she was still utterly devoted to Adam. If only Anna would fall in love with Rand.

The following morning, she was anticipating the arrival of a military zephyr with news, but she had so many duties to attend to she barely noticed the Control Leering's alert when a tempest approached the manor. She paused in her perusal of the account books. Something was familiar about this ship. Cettie tried to activate the defenses of Fog Willows, but it was too late—the tempest was already landing in the docking yard.

She hurried out of the study and walked down the steps. Kinross was already striding down the hall ahead of her.

"I thought you said we were expecting a military zephyr," he told her as she caught up to him.

"This isn't the ship we're waiting for. This is one of those merchant tempests that tried to force a landing here earlier. Captain Francis."

Kinross's eyes widened with shock. "I don't think Lady Maren—"

"Can you get Raj Sarin, please?" Cettie interrupted.

Kinross smiled. "At once."

When she reached the front door, she arrived just in time to see Captain Francis striding up to the entryway. He'd not wasted any time in disembarking. He wore a heavy gray wool coat over a fine jerkin and impressive buckled boots. His dark hair was windswept and had a touch of gray. He was Lady Maren's own age, much younger than Fitzroy.

"Ah, you must be the keeper," he said, rubbing his gloved hands together. "The wind has been ferocious."

"What are you doing here, Captain Francis?" she demanded, blocking the doors and folding her arms.

"I'm here to comfort a grieving widow," he said. "Stand aside."

"You didn't waste much time," Cettie countered.

"I've wasted too much already," he said peevishly. "Stand aside." He tried to move around her, but she blocked him again.

"You are not welcome at Fog Willows."

He arched his eyebrows at her and snorted. "What business is it of yours who Maren sees? I'm her friend from past days. She'll want to see me."

"I don't think so," Cettie replied. "I believe her last words to you were never to return."

His look smoldered with anger. "But things have changed, you little chit of girl. Her husband is dead. There is nothing improper about it now. She has the right to see anyone she chooses and to welcome me into *her* manor." He glanced up at the doors. "When I become its new master, you will be the first one to go."

Behind him, she watched Raj Sarin slowly descend from the air. She couldn't conceal a smirk.

The visitor saw her look and whirled around, startled by the sudden arrival.

"How did you—?"

"I believe the keeper of Fog Willows bid you to leave, sir," Raj Sarin said respectfully.

The captain glowered at them. "You are both *servants*!" he roared.

His anger and disrespect made Cettie shudder inside, but she would not quail before him. "That may be true," she answered, "but we serve the family's interests. Not yours."

The captain's face twisted with fury. She saw him fling aside his coat, revealing a pistol in his belt.

That was when Raj Sarin humbled him the Bhikhu way.

CHAPTER TWENTY-FOUR

DIVULGING

A day went by, then two, but the memory of Clive Francis's bloodied nose, twisted wrist, and his anguished cries of pain did not fade from Cettie's mind. In fact, it often made her smile. Lady Maren had shaken her head at the news of what Raj Sarin had done to her former paramour, reiterating that she wanted nothing to do with the man. But she had failed to mask her own pleased smile. Surely Clive had deserved to be taken down a notch. As the days progressed, however, Cettie's anxiety grew steadily. She watched the skies and kept the manor ready. She was sickened by the thought of what would come of her revelation to Sir Jordan, but her responsibilities kept her busy.

Since word of Father's supposed death had spread throughout the realm, they received sympathy notes, bouquets of flowers, ribboned garlands, and other things from those who admired and respected Fitzroy. Kinross was perplexed by the influx of tributes, but ultimately he arranged them on tables for the family to peruse at their leisure. Cettie was encouraged by the volume of well-wishes, most of which were from people she didn't know. It shouldn't have surprised her, though, especially since she esteemed Fitzroy so highly herself.

She was in the middle of a discussion with Kinross about the accounts when the zephyr post arrived. She saw the ship land through the Leering's eyes, and much to her startlement, Joses disembarked and rushed toward the front doors of the manor.

"Is something troubling you?" Kinross asked her, noticing her altered mood.

"Joses has returned," she said. They exchanged a look and hastened to the main doors.

Her friend had let himself in, his hair wild from the windy ride, his expression grave.

"What's happened?" Cettie asked in concern.

"Mr. Batewinch sent me," Joses said. "He wondered if you could come again."

"Is it serious?"

Joses nodded. "Mr. Patchett is much altered since your journey. He's angry, shouts at everyone. He's a different man than he was before."

What had happened to change him so? She wondered if the Control Leering in Gimmerton Sough was still working as it should.

"Has he turned violent? Did he strike Mr. Batewinch?"

Joses shook his head. "No, Cettie. Not yet, but it wouldn't surprise me if he did. Something set him off, and I fear he has truly gone mad. Batewinch thinks you might be able to help. Rand has had nothing but kind things to say about you, about the journey you took together. But the day after you returned, I couldn't wake him, and then he snarled and threatened me. Something is not right with him."

Kinross looked at Cettie with blatant worry. "What can *you* do, Miss Cettie? I think perhaps it is time the Law were called upon to intervene."

She sighed. "I can try at the least."

Kinross pursed his lips. "If you go, then I want you to take Raj Sarin as well."

Cettie frowned. "I am capable of defending myself."

"And I'll be there too," Joses said.

But Kinross would have none of it. "No, I think Joses should stay and Raj Sarin should go. It would make me feel better if he went with you. Mr. Patchett is a dragoon, after all."

"I'll confer with Lady Maren first," Cettie said. She gave Joses a warm smile. "You did the right thing coming here."

"I know," he said. Then he shuddered. "Cettie, it reminded me of what it felt like in the Fells. Be careful."

Lady Maren agreed with Kinross's suggestion, and Raj Sarin went with her to Gimmerton Sough. They left that afternoon on the family tempest and rode the jostling air to the neighboring manor. The Bhikhu stood on the prow, eyes shut in deep thought as Cettie piloted the sky ship. She was grateful that Joses was safe and sound back at Fog Willows. What would she find at the other estate? Worry and dread filled her heart, but she kept the tempest straight on its course.

When they arrived at the manor, she saw that some plants had been added to the landscaping, and the weeds were sparser. She docked the tempest and watched as Raj Sarin leaped over the side, a jump that would have injured anyone other than a Bhikhu, and floated down on a single exhale. She envied his gift as she climbed down the ladder. The air was cold with a bite to it, and she chafed her bare hands as she and Raj Sarin approached the main doors.

They were met by Mr. Batewinch, whose collar was loose and whose cheeks were flushed. Inside, they could hear Miss Patchett weeping.

"Welcome to Gimmerton Sough, Miss Cettie," Batewinch said dejectedly. "Unfortunately, you find us under difficult circumstances yet again."

When Cettie entered, she felt the unease of being watched. A stab of dark emotion struck her breast at once. Though the corridor Leerings still glowed, their light seemed dimmer. A pall hung over the manor. Raj Sarin narrowed his eyes and sniffed the air, casting his gaze at the dark corners.

Joanna Patchett hurried down the hall, still crying, and flung her arms around Cettie's neck. Cettie held her as she sobbed. After some time, the young woman pulled back, cheeks blotchy and pink.

"T-thank you," Joanna said with a shuddering voice. "Thank you for coming."

"Where's your brother?" Cettie asked, smoothing some hair from the woman's face.

She sniffled and dabbed her nose with a silk handkerchief. "In his room. *Again.* I'm afraid . . . I'm so afraid, Cettie."

"Of what?"

Joanna looked haunted. "That he will do himself harm again. He doesn't want to live. I don't know what made him lose hope this time. Maybe it's the rumors that the war might soon be over. I don't know. He won't talk to me. He won't tell me." She sniffed again. "I think he'd tell you, though. He really admires you. I've never heard him speak about anyone else the way he does about you."

Though she had clearly intended to be kind, her words increased the burden Cettie already felt. "I will try. Can you show me where his room is?"

Joanna took her by the hand and escorted her up the steps. Raj Sarin quietly followed, his eyes narrowed with suspicion. Sweat gleamed across his bald dome.

The upper corridor was thick with shadows, despite the daylight outside. Their shoes made little thumping noises on the carpet as they walked down it. Then they reached the door, and Joanna stifled another sob. "In there," she whispered.

Cettie wasn't sure what she could say to comfort the girl. Her own unease was great, and the darkness of the hall did indeed remind her of her past life in the Fells. She didn't sense any Myriad Ones, but something was undeniably wrong. A feeling of trepidation rose in her as she reached for the door handle.

Steeling herself, Cettie clenched the handle and turned it. The door opened. The curtains were closed, blotting out more light, and all the Leerings were dark. Cettie bit her lip and willed them to life, if only to chase away some of the darkness. A groan sounded from the bed, and she saw Rand sitting at the edge, using his arm to block the light. He was soaked in sweat, his hair wild, his cheeks still unshaven since their journey together. His shirtsleeves were rolled up, revealing muscled arms that seemed as taut as ropes.

"Who is it?" he said angrily and with some confusion. "Joanna?"

"It's Cettie," she replied, coming into the room. She left the door ajar.

A quick sucked-in breath showed Rand's surprise. He lowered his hand, seeing her at last, although he was still squinting.

His hand dropped down to his leg, and he let out an anguished sigh. "You shouldn't have come."

"I came because I wanted to help," she said, taking a cautious step forward. He didn't look agitated or angry.

"What I meant is I didn't want you to see me. Not like this."

"I'm sorry you are in distress, Rand. But did you not come to our aid when we were so?"

He glanced up at her, a thick chuckle in his throat. "It's not the same at all." He rose from the bed and folded his arms over his chest, suppressing a shudder, then started pacing. She watched him warily, trying to understand.

"It shouldn't be so difficult," he muttered, shaking his head. "It's all in the mind. Just the mind. Why cannot I subdue it?"

She stared at him, not knowing what to say. Not sure of how best to help.

He looked up at her in anguish. "Go. Just go. Forget you saw me like this. Try to remember what I was like before. I cannot *bear* it."

Cettie swallowed. "If I go, will you do yourself harm?"

"Undoubtedly," he answered with a hint of vengeance in his tone.

"Then I will stay," Cettie said. Why was her voice trembling? "Why do you keep yourself in darkness? Open the curtains. Even a window might be helpful. It is stifling in here."

"Because I cannot abide the light sometimes," he answered sadly. "I cannot even stand to look at myself. To face my shame."

"What are you ashamed of?" she pressed.

"Myself. I disgust myself in every possible way."

"What do you mean? We all want to help you."

He gave her a pointed look. "I don't deserve help. I don't deserve your pity. If you only knew." He looked away, gritting his teeth.

She glanced around the room, her eyes lingering on a scattering of books around a nearby table. As if he'd tried to still himself by reading and then flung several of them away in anger. They were books translated from maston tomes. Some she had never read.

"If you knew what I truly was, you would hate me," he said.

"Are you so sure?" she asked.

"I know it." He squeezed his eyes shut. "I am so wretched. I cannot live like this. I cannot endure it. My skin is on fire!"

"Why?" Cettie pressed. The desperation in his eyes showed the extent of his torment.

"Because it's here! It's still here in this room. I hear it. Why should it have so much power?"

Cettie looked around the room. "There are no Myriad Ones here," she said.

"Not yet," he groaned. "If you pity me, then leave now!"

"You have a secret," she said, coming closer. "It's ripping you apart."

"Of course it is! I cannot stand it. I don't care what happens anymore. I don't care what you think of me. Just take it away, Cettie. I should never have gone to Dolcoath with you. I stole it from there. Here, take it!"

He fumbled in his vest pocket and withdrew a small vial of dark liquid, which he then thrust at her. She recognized the tincture. It was poppy oil.

His hand shook violently as he held it out to her, his eyes half-crazed. Cettie took it away from him and slipped it into her pocket.

Rand sank down to his knees, his fingers pulling at his hair again. He started to weep as he trembled. Now she understood. Raj Sarin had told her of his addiction to the oil, the darkness of the cravings he still felt after years of abstinence. The problem was not an infrequent one for soldiers—some of the men who were given poppy extracts for their injuries became enslaved to it. Rand had been wounded many times during the war. Had he deliberately sought out injuries so that he might receive another dose? Compassion for him welled up in her heart, and she stepped even closer, touching his shoulder gently.

He looked up, his visage raw with pain and pleading. His voice was hoarse as he whispered, "I have tried to rid myself. I can't . . . do it . . . alone."

Cettie knelt next to him and pulled him to her. "You don't have to do this alone, Rand," she whispered thickly. "Does Batewinch know?"

He nodded against her neck.

"Does Joanna?"

He shook his head no, and his arms slumped down to his sides.

She reached for his hands with both of hers. "Tell her, Rand. It is possible to overcome this. I know someone who has."

He looked startled. "Truly?"

She nodded, feeling strangely comfortable kneeling on the floor with him. It reassured her to know the reason for his torment. Perhaps now they could help him.

"I've never told anyone," he said thickly. "I thought . . . I thought they would hate me if they knew. I cannot be trusted, Cettie. I have no self-discipline if I come near it."

"Not now, anyway," she said gently. "But if you forsake it, I promise you, it will lose its power over you."

His lip twitched. "My sister looks up to me."

She squeezed his shoulder. "She still will. Tell her, Rand. I implore you."

His nostrils flared, but he nodded. "If you commanded me in anything, I think I would find the strength to do it. Take that wicked vial far away. You do not spurn me . . . for my weakness. I thought for sure you would."

"It will take several days for the poppy to ebb from your blood. It will not feel very pleasant, I'm afraid."

He chuckled darkly. "I know. It is easier to resist the allure if there is none that I can take."

Which was likely why he and Joanna had moved to the secluded sky manor. It would be far easier to come across poppy somewhere else.

"Your mind will heal itself if you stop taking it," she promised. "I believe that you can do it, Rand Patchett. You can be the man your father believed you were."

He looked down, a fresh gust of misery blowing through him. "Take it away, Cettie. Take it far away. Destroy it. Part of me wants to force you to give it back. I don't like these thoughts. You are . . . too special to me. I will tell Joanna. She will help me."

Cettie nodded and rose. Then Rand suddenly wrapped his arms around her, pressing his cheek against her middle. The embrace was surprising, and he squeezed her hard, but then he released her and rose shakily to his feet.

"You are my angel," he said.

Cettie went to the door and saw Joanna waiting in anticipation in the hall. She nodded for her to enter, and she did, rushing up to Rand and pleading with him to tell her what was wrong. Their murmured voices reassured Cettie, as did the changing mood of the manor. It seemed lighter, as if the shadows had retreated into the corners and walls. The secret was out at long last. Cettie sucked in a breath as she reached into her pocket. The oil was still there—he hadn't stolen it back. She released the air in a huff.

"I know what it is," Raj Sarin murmured to her. His eyes were sharp and alert, as if he could smell the oil in the air.

"We should go," Cettie said, taking him by the arm. "But you are right."

"At least he is young," Raj Sarin said, looking through the door at the brother and sister embracing. "And he is not alone."

They bid farewell to Mr. Batewinch and took the tempest back to Fog Willows. As soon as they were a good distance from the manor, Cettie flung the evil vial overboard, knowing it would shatter as soon as it struck the boulders below. Even so, her mind lingered on Rand on the journey back to Fog Willows. His father had died recently. The drug would have helped him cope with that pain as well.

What she'd learned had not damaged her opinion of him. There was much she admired about him: his bravery and confidence, his hostility toward the rules of society. She believed he deserved another chance. Hopefully, he would prevail against the demon that had enslaved him. That admiration mixed with the emotions he'd caused by their intimate encounter—a potent and dangerous combination. She willed her mind to think of Adam instead. *He* had never embraced her like that before. He had never let himself become so vulnerable.

Darkness met them before reaching Fog Willows. Which was why she didn't see the prime minister's sky ship until they were landing in the yard.

CHAPTER TWENTY-FIVE

RISKS

Lord Welles and the rest of the Fitzroy family awaited Cettie in the solar. The prime minister looked at ease, lounging in one of the many stuffed chairs and enjoying the subtle strains of music piped in from the City by the Leering in the wall. Anna looked subdued, but Mother spoke to the statesman with energy and animation.

As Cettie shut the door behind her, Welles's eyes lifted to her face. She saw cool calculation there. They had met before, of course, but this time was different. He was looking at her with much more interest. He rubbed his upper lip thoughtfully.

"The keeper of Fog Willows has returned," he said.

Lady Maren rose and greeted her with a kiss. "I told the prime minster that you were helping our new neighbors."

"And how fare the young Patchett siblings now?" Lord Welles asked, rising from his chair. "Is Commander Patchett still suffering from his . . . condition?"

His look and tone revealed to Cettie that he already knew. He was the prime minister, but he had been the Minister of War, and he knew his men. Cettie felt herself bristling.

"I think he's doing much better now," Cettie said plainly. "You honor us with your presence, Prime Minister. I wonder that you came all this way."

"Do you?" he asked with a bland smile. "I travel far and wide when necessary, young lady. Especially on matters that affect so many people. I know the Patchetts well. You could do worse. Now, Maren, I'd like to speak to Miss Cettie alone, if you please."

"Alone?" The word carried no small amount of surprise. He clearly had not stated his purpose earlier.

"This situation goes well beyond the norms of propriety," Welles said. "If the reports I have heard are true, and I must judge for myself that they are, then the situation warrants a minor breach in social protocol."

"But she's still a young woman—and our keeper, no less. I don't think it would be fair for you to interrogate her without representation. Had I known you intended such a thing, I would have summoned our advocates."

"I know," Welles answered flatly. "Which is why I didn't let on. Come, Maren. Be sensible. This is a grave matter, a state secret. If I must, I will have my officers arrest her and bring her to Lockhaven. We are still at war, and my powers permit the detainment of anyone I deem suitable. Nothing has been said about the secret you and Brant kept from me, which was surely against the interests of the empire. I think you can accommodate me in this small request."

The threat in his voice was real, and Cettie felt herself tingle with fear. She knew from experience the prime minister was capable of great cunning.

Maren took a step closer to him, her expression guarded. "May I remind you that your powers are *temporary*, Lord Welles."

"Indeed they are. And I will put them aside once this war is over. We dangle over a precipice, Maren. All of us." He nodded to the door.

Her eyes flashed with anger, but she beckoned for Anna to join her, and they both left the room, giving Cettie final encouraging looks before doing so. Cettie positioned herself by a table, putting it between her and the prime minister. He looked satisfied by the outcome, and his demeanor softened.

"Some people are excessively stubborn," he said lightheartedly.

Aren't they indeed, Cettie thought to herself.

"Well, my dear, now we can have our little interview. I suppose that is the proper word. How old are you? Nineteen?"

"Yes," Cettie answered, resting her palms on the table.

He pursed his lips and gave her a studying look. "I have no reason to disbelieve Sir Jordan. He is convinced you are our harbinger. I could have brought you in to see the privy council, but I have concerns that there may be some members of it who . . . shall I say this delicately . . . have not completely earned my trust. I'm not certain dragging an urchin from the Fells before them would be a wise decision."

Cettie frowned at his disrespectful tone.

"Surely you must understand, my dear, that there is a great prejudice against those of your station. In my many years of service to the admiralty, I have seen firsthand the differences between the common soldiers and trained officers."

"Differences due to circumstances?" Cettie asked.

"Differences due to character, temperament, and breeding. Which brings me to my next question." His eyes narrowed with suspicion. "Where do *you* come from?"

"Father has spent the last seven years trying to find out," Cettie said.

"I know. And he's poured substantial resources into it. They say you are the natural daughter of George Pratt and some paramour. Not a birth of high distinction in any case. But you look nothing like Mr. Pratt." He shook his head. "And my understanding is that Pratt's current wife is wheedling him not to settle for anything less than an equal portion of your due inheritance. Which is absurd. Even if it were given to them, they'd be swindled of it in their first speculation. No, I cannot believe that he is your father. Any more than I can believe some adulteress highborn lady is your secret mother. Now tell me plainly, young lady, do you know who your parents are? I will remind you that lying to the prime minister is a crime." He set his hands on the table opposite hers, his gaze intense and hostile.

"Why should I answer your question without an advocate present?" she asked in a half whisper.

His lip curled. "You may not know this, but your advocates are rather wrapped up in problems of their own. One of their young men, a Mr. Skrelling, recently died in a zephyr accident."

Cettie swallowed, surprised and grief-stricken by the news. "I went to school with Mr. Skrelling."

"That makes no difference to me. I came here to seek answers of my own. Do you want me to bring this family under investigation?" he asked coldly. "If Fitzroy is alive, as you've claimed, he is a prisoner of war. He'll not be returning anytime soon. I can shut down your businesses, suspend your operations, and choke the family's source of income if you fail to cooperate with me. Do you wish to see Fog Willows come crashing down?"

He was trying to intimidate her. And he was doing an excellent job of it. Despite herself, she felt cowed by his presence and his display of power.

"No," she mumbled, unable to conceal the trembling in her legs.

"Well then, young lady, I *suggest* that you cooperate with me. Enough secrets. Our empire hangs on the brink of destruction. A primeval monster is still on the loose. An irreplaceable artifact has been stolen from Billerbeck Abbey. You know of this because you were *there*. Did you take it?"

"No!" Cettie protested.

"Do you know who did?"

She suspected, yes, but that was not what he'd asked. "I don't," she stammered. She tried to calm herself and her thoughts, but she was thoroughly rattled. She remembered Caulton telling her of Mr. Skrelling's visit. But surely, *surely*, he wouldn't have stolen the orb? She'd always known him to be a straightforward man.

Besides, if he had stolen it, wouldn't it have been found? She determined to send a zephyr post to Billerbeck to inform Caulton. Perhaps he'd discovered the news already for himself. Clearly the prime minister had been told of the Fear Liath escaping as well.

"You hesitate. You cannot refuse to answer my question. Do you know who your parents are? Or who stole the Cruciger orb?"

"I-I don't know . . . for certain."

"Yes? Say on."

She squeezed her eyes shut. His thoughts were incredibly powerful, his will indomitable, but she didn't trust him in the least. What would Fitzroy have done in this situation?

He would have stood up to the man.

"I don't understand why this is so important," Cettie hedged.

Lord Welles's eyes blazed with anger. "Who you are is *very* important. Do you not realize that there has not been a harbinger in centuries? One must be very strong in the Mysteries. One must be chosen by the Knowing. Who are you, a little chit from the Fells? Or did you have more august parentage?"

"Isn't it possible the Knowing chose me *because* I am of lesser birth?" Cettie argued. "Isn't the pride of the empire leading to its downfall?"

Scowling at her, he pushed away from the table and started pacing. "I don't have time for this nonsense," he muttered. "You claim to be a harbinger? Is that so?"

"I have visions of the future. Yes. They have all come to pass."

"What was the last one that you had?"

"I saw Sera Fitzempress at the court of Kingfountain. Father was there too."

"How did you know it was the court of Kingfountain? Have you been there?"

"Of course not! One cannot cross a mirror gate without permission and the proper covenants."

"So then how do you know?"

"The visions I experience are very vivid, Prime Minister. They are not the same as dreams. I can learn things without being told them. It's difficult to explain. The previous visions showed me where General Montpensier would attack next. I warned Father so he could defend us."

Welles bared his teeth. "Our defense has been in your hands all along."

"I didn't choose my role, Lord Welles. You were given that choice—I was not."

His feelings were ruffled by her comment. "I serve at the pleasure of the emperor. He's a weak-willed man."

"I know. That is why you preferred him to Sera. She would have been the better choice."

That her words were true probably galled him all the more. "We don't always get what we desire," he answered curtly. "Now, will you answer my question? Do you *suspect* anyone of being your parent?" He paused, his eyes fixed on her, then asked, "Does Fitzroy shield you so much because *he* is your true father? Is there a scandal beneath all this?"

"No," Cettie said, shaking her head. "How can you even accuse him of it?"

"Long study in the school of human nature," he replied mockingly. "Sometimes the most devout are the most depraved."

"If you can even suspect him, then you do not know him at all," Cettie answered. "He has protected me and shielded me because of men like you. I am finished answering your questions."

Lord Welles screwed up his mouth into a frown. He had tried to bully her—and failed. The sour expression on his face revealed as much. "As I said, I hoped to spare you the scrutiny of certain members of the privy council. The emperor already doesn't like you."

"I think you hoped to control me," Cettie answered simply. "If you shut down Dolcoath, then you will only be hurting your own ministry. The weather always changes, Prime Minister. You might have forgotten that."

He was taken aback by her comment, his look softening. "You are a shrewd negotiator, young lady."

"Not at all," she answered, straightening. "I don't know why the Knowing chose me. Only that I *was* chosen. If I have another vision, what should I do?"

"You can't control them?"

"One doesn't control the Mysteries, Prime Minister."

"True. Mr. Forshee said you were exceptionally gifted. Well, I suggest that we continue to keep this a secret. The Cruciger orb was stolen. Our high admiral is a prisoner of war. And Miss Fitzempress is on a peace mission in Kingfountain." His brows narrowed. "I have a suspicion there may be a traitor in the government. Were it to become public knowledge that *you* are the harbinger, your life would be at risk as well." He shook his head. "I can't afford that risk."

Cettie looked at him, dumbfounded. "So you never intended to bring me to the privy council?"

"Not unless I absolutely had to," he replied flippantly. "Stay here for now. You will be coming to Lockhaven soon with another report to sell?"

She nodded. "I have already begun preparing it."

"Very well. If you get another vision, then send a zephyr post at once to Sir Jordan. I will contact you through a Leering to hear the details."

"What Leering?"

"Why . . . any one that I choose." He gave her an enigmatic smile and bowed to her before leaving.

Two days after Lord Welles departed, they had another visitor—Joanna Patchett from Gimmerton Sough. Her hair and dress were fashioned in the latest style, and she even carried a parasol trimmed with lace and silk. So altered was she from her previous visit that Cettie hardly recognized her as she watched her approach through the Control Leering's eyes. Since Cettie was busy with the latest reports, Kinross greeted Joanna at the door and brought her to see Lady Maren and Anna in the sitting room. But he came to see Cettie immediately afterward.

"Yes?" she said, looking up from the notes.

"Miss Patchett is asking where you are. She had hoped you would be with the family as well. She wishes to speak with you."

Cettie set down her quill and followed Kinross to the sitting room. As soon as she entered the room, Joanna brightened immediately and rose to greet her.

"You are my friend forever," Joanna said, hurrying forward to kiss her on the cheek.

Cettie wrinkled her brow. "I don't understand."

"Well, you do not dote on Stephen as much as I do Rand, so you might not understand." She took Cettie's hands in hers and squeezed them. "Lady Maren, I am so hopelessly in debt to Cettie that I cannot possibly repay her. She has transformed my brother." Her smile was beaming. "He's helping Mr. Batewinch supervise the renovation of the manor. It's not so dark and oppressive anymore. He's so much like his old self again." She sighed with wonder. "I owe it all to you."

Cettie was embarrassed by the praise, but she hugged Joanna back and then joined the gathering by sitting on a nearby couch. Joanna shared it with her, choosing her above the others.

"I'm glad to hear your brother is so improved," Mother said. "There was a time when I was very sick. She helped restore me as well." The loving, grateful look she gave Cettie filled her with warmth and reassurance.

"I don't think we can overestimate her worth," Joanna said. "What do you think of your almost-sister, Anna?"

"I adore her," Anna said with a pretty smile.

"And we all know she is wisdom itself," Joanna continued. She took Cettie's hands in hers again. "I received notice this morning from Miss Ransom, inviting us to a ball at her manor in Lockhaven. The event will be in honor of the fallen soldiers, and there will be donations, of course, going to the soldiers' families. I think it a very fine idea. Miss Ransom specifically requested Rand to come. She knows he's a wounded soldier and feels that his presence would encourage others to be generous. I would like to go, but I confess some unease. You know how outspoken my brother can be in social situations. I wondered if I might cajole you to come with us? All of you," she added, but she squeezed Cettie's hand plaintively.

Lady Maren tilted her head. "I don't think the Ransoms would invite us, Miss Patchett."

What she was too well-mannered to say was that Lady Corinne would never have encouraged her young admirer to invite them. Indeed, it was curious the Patchetts were so kind to them given how little patience their high-ranking friend had for the Fitzroy family.

Joanna gazed at her with confidence. "They will if *I* ask them to."

CHAPTER TWENTY-SIX

THE RANSOM BALL

Cettie had never imagined being invited to a ball in Lockhaven. But Joanna Patchett had some uncanny influence, and an invitation to the charity event had arrived with particular mention of Miss Cettie of Fog Willows. She piloted the tempest into the landing yard of the spacious manor, which was already crowded with ships. Servants with Leering lanterns helped direct the incoming arrivals.

"That's Welles's tempest," Mother said from the edge of the vessel, gazing down at the courtyard as they slowly approached.

"I'm surprised the prime minister came," Anna said worriedly.

"The Ransoms are well connected," Mother answered. She flashed Cettie a determined look. They'd discussed Lord Welles's visit several times since it had happened days before. "We all must be on our guard. He may try to bully us again."

Cettie nodded with a grim-faced expression. Lady Maren and Anna were both dressed in their best formal gowns, but Cettie had chosen instead to wear her favorite velvet dress. She looked more matriarchal than a young woman at a ball should, which was her intention. She did not believe that Joanna's ability to secure an invitation for her meant she would actually be *welcomed*. She had been snubbed at too many dances at Muirwood Abbey to wish to repeat the experience. They had prepared a sizable donation for the occasion, and Cettie planned to stay in the background while Anna enjoyed herself.

Cettie was directed to land the tempest before the main doors in the ample courtyard, which she did. The gangway was lowered, and servants arrived to assist the family down. One of the men took the invitation, read the names, and then looked up at Cettie quizzically.

"Where's the pilot? I don't see him."

"I am the pilot," she answered bluntly.

His surprise increased. "I beg your pardon, ma'am. I'll have to ask you to moor your tempest yourself, then. If you please. The pilots are all drinking cider in the gaming room." He bowed apologetically.

Lady Maren looked back at her in concern, but Cettie waved her on. "I'll join you after I'm done. Go on ahead."

The lantern light gleamed off Anna's golden hair, and Cettie wondered at the reception she would receive. Anna was also nineteen and unmarried, but she was the legitimate heiress to a sizable fortune. Her reticence to become attached was due solely to her feelings for Adam Creigh. Cettie's mood darkened at the thought. If only Anna were more changeable . . . if only she'd find someone else to fancy tonight . . . Yet she knew her sister's feelings had remained as steadfast as her own.

Cettie followed the servant's directions and brought the tempest down alongside the others. Those who lived in Lockhaven came by zephyr, but there were many larger tempests moored in the yard. After securing the Leerings and ordering them to warn her if anyone tried to board the ship, she climbed down the rope ladder and made her way through the crowd of sky ships.

The prime minister's tempest was not the only one she recognized.

Her stomach lurched at the sight of the *Glennam*, Captain Francis's ship. Cettie pursed her lips, realizing that Lady Maren was walking into a dangerous situation. She quickened her pace.

When she reached the main doors, the servant greeted her pleasantly and said she would introduce her, but Cettie declined and made her way into the bustling throng. Immediately, she felt out of place. Her gown was dark green with black and silver stripes. She wore no hat or gloves or fancy shawl. The women gathered at the ball were all sumptuously dressed in the latest fashions, with stiff bone bodices and frilled collars, nearly every inch of skin covered save for their faces. Their hats were bedecked with flowers and feathers and beaded pearls.

The men, of course, were also dressed to bedazzle. There was an abundance of military officers and many men in blue dragoon jackets. So many that Cettie found herself going face by face looking for Rand. She didn't see him in the company, nor did she see Lady Maren or Anna.

As Cettie wove her way through the room, she heard the light strains of music coming from the walls, but she also spotted a small ensemble with their instruments out and ready, preparing for the dancing. And she couldn't help but notice the looks that came her way from the other young women and some of the officers. They seemed to agree with her self-assessment—she did not belong.

A young officer suddenly stepped in front of her, forcing her to stop. "You are Miss Cettie from Fog Willows, are you not?" He gave a curt bow.

"I-I am," she stuttered, still straining to spy the rest of her family.

"I'm Bryson Esplin," he said, bowing again. "We went to school together at Muirwood."

His face did look suddenly familiar, but she remembered no previous interactions with him.

"I served under Admiral Fitzroy," he said. "He was a fine man. An honest one. He will be missed. I wanted to offer my condolences. Thank you for coming, Miss Cettie."

Emotion gathered in her throat. She had not expected such a greeting, but she genuinely appreciated the sentiment. Even more so because the young man did not ask anything of her in return. He simply bowed once more and stepped away.

There was an abrupt end to the Leering music, and the strains of real violins began to fill the air. Shortly thereafter, a song began, and the middle of the enormous hall cleared, making room for the couples coming to start the first dance. Cettie spied Anna among them, across from a young man who was a stranger.

That left Lady Maren alone. Cettie continued to work her way around the perimeter of the room, eager to find her. The dancing started, and the couples began the formal steps in precise rhythm. It was considered a disaster if a turn was missed or a clap done out of sequence. Joanna was one of the dancers, and Cettie admired her pretty gown and the beautiful smile lighting her face.

"Would you like a drink, miss?" asked a uniformed servant holding a silver tray with several small goblets on it.

"No, thank you," Cettie refused, still searching.

Seating lined the walls, and many of the older women had congregated around the chairs and sofas to gossip. Several of them gave Cettie cold looks as she passed by, increasing her discomfort. The song ended, and another began, but Anna had already been swept up by another young man, an officer this time. Working her way slowly around the sides of the ballroom, Cettie finally spied Lady Maren in the far corner.

Just as she'd feared, her mother had been trapped by a man in conversation.

Frowning in displeasure, Cettie wove her way closer to them, watching the dancers out of her peripheral vision and feeling more and more discomfited by the looks she was getting. Somehow Father had always managed to look unaffected by the slights given him. *You must take your lesson from him,* she told herself. She walked firmly and deliberately, trying not to care what anyone else thought of her.

As Cettie drew nearer, she recognized it was Captain Francis who spoke to her mother in urgent low tones. She arrived in time to hear some of his words.

"I will divorce her, Maren, regardless of what you say. I regret what I did to you all those years ago. Can we not have another chance?"

He must have heard Cettie's footsteps, for he turned as if he expected to bark at a servant. When he saw her, his eyes widened with surprise and then narrowed in wariness.

Lady Maren replied with animosity, "This is neither the time nor the place to have such a conversation, Clive. If you had any regard for my feelings whatsoever, you would leave me alone."

"But I cannot speak to you because of your pet dragon who guards the gate," he said savagely, giving Cettie a spiteful look.

"That is my *daughter* you are treating with such disrespect, Clive. Now go."

The captain chuffed with a snort. "Oh, so you've managed to secure the adoption after all? I think I would have heard. You *must* let me talk to you. Can I come to Fog Willows again without being driven off like a criminal by your Bhikhu?"

"If I'd wanted to see you, Clive, you would have been admitted. Now please. Go."

"Maren," he said in a low, familiar way. "Don't send me away. You have every right to be angry for how I treated you. How I shamed you. I have been a miserable creature ever since. Have pity on me. You chose better for yourself than I did for myself. But you cannot deny that what we shared was *real*." He shook his head slowly. "I have not forgotten it. Nor will I."

Cettie wanted to repel him like Raj Sarin had. It was at just such a ball that this man had driven Lady Maren to act against propriety, which had hurt her standing in society for a number of years. Father had already loved her back then, although it had not yet been reciprocated. She could only imagine the pain this moment was causing Mother.

Lady Maren's cheeks were flushed with heat. "I will not speak with you any longer." She reached for Cettie's arm, and the two of them left Captain Francis alone in the corner.

She squeezed Cettie's arm and let out a painful sigh.

"I do not trust that man," Cettie said in a low, angry voice.

"No one in their right mind would trust someone like him," Lady Maren replied. "Now I'm regretting that we came."

"I saw his tempest in the yard," Cettie said. Then she spied Rand Patchett in his dragoon uniform, surrounded by no less than seven young ladies fawning over him. Was he pleased by the attention? She couldn't tell.

"If I'd known, I would have remained behind on the ship," Lady Maren said. "How awkward and painful. He thinks my husband is dead, so he's throwing himself at my feet to get his hands on a portion of my wealth."

Cettie remembered that he had started his attentions even before the reports came of Fitzroy's death. She didn't mention this, however. Captain Francis was a scoundrel of the darkest sort. How much did he owe in debts? Cettie believed that was the true cause of his misbehavior, not any remaining tenderness for Lady Maren.

"Would you like to sit down, Mother?"

"Very much so."

The two found some padded seats and sat down together, still hand in hand. Cettie was grateful she was there to support her. But she still watched the dancers with a growing sense of envy.

Partway through the ball, Joanna approached them with a young woman of fashion, whom she announced as Miss Ransom. She had a pinched nose, and her blond hair was done up in little curls, half-hidden by the elaborate headdress she wore.

"I am so thankful you came," Miss Ransom said in a nasally voice. "The gala has been a tremendous success. Why, I just finished telling the prime minister that we've raised six hundred thousand just this evening. For the poor and the wounded," she added with an exaggerated pout. "He thinks we should do this again soon, that the need far outweighs the resources. Miss Patchett suggested we visit one of the hospitals tomorrow."

"One of the hospitals *below*," Joanna said, arching her eyebrows at Cettie.

Miss Ransom blanched. "I . . . I thought you meant one of the ones for the officers."

"No, dearest," Joanna said, shaking her head. "Would it not be a more powerful statement to visit one of the hospitals where the common soldiers are treated?"

"B-but, b-but the cholera morbus," Miss Ransom said. "They say it breeds in the air down there."

"No one knows what causes it," Joanna replied soothingly. "Think of what it would do for the morale of the men. Even if we just stayed for only a little while. We should try."

Miss Ransom seemed terrified by the notion. "Thank you for coming," she said to Lady Maren with a bow. She nodded curtly to Cettie before walking away.

Joanna watched her go. "Six hundred thousand. That's all. But it's a start." She came closer, smiling fetchingly, and pulled Cettie up from the chair by her hands. "Why didn't you wear a ball gown, dearest? Don't tell me the family can't afford one."

Cettie smiled. "I would rather not pretend to be someone else for the evening," she replied. "I know what I am. Who I am. I don't belong in a place like this."

"Tosh," said Joanna with a wrinkle in her nose. "You're every bit as cultured as any of these vain girls. You went to the same school. You're brilliant and charming."

"But I'm from the Fells," Cettie said, tilting her head and shrugging. "They'll never forget it."

"One day that won't matter," Joanna said, her gaze softening as her brother approached them from the crowd.

Rand looked restless. "I thought I'd never get away from that gaggle of geese," he snorted. "I nearly suffocated on their perfume."

Cettie stifled a laugh.

Rand raised his eyebrows. "Do I amuse you, Cettie?"

Lady Maren said, "You speak what most of us only think in our hearts but would never dare admit."

Rand folded his arms. "I abhor this excuse of a celebration. Six hundred thousand, did you hear that?"

"We did, Rand," Joanna said warily. "Now don't ruin it."

"That's how much it cost to appease their guilt," he went on, ignoring his sister's subtle warning. "They've wanted a ball anyway, and the soldiers' suffering became the pretext. Look at them." He shook his head, barely masking his disgust. "At least in war you can tell your enemy by their uniform. You know that their weapon is aimed at your heart. Here, it's all a mask. A deception."

"Have you been drinking?" Joanna asked, her look full of worry.

"I haven't had time," he said. "And no, Sister, I've not even caught a whiff of the other stuff. But it brings back memories from before the war. Thoughts of who I used to be." He shook his head, gazing at the crowd.

"Have you danced yet, Rand?"

He looked at Joanna and shook his head. "Not for a lack of offers, though! The young women here are brazen!"

The opening strains of "Sky Ship's Cook" started. It was one of Cettie's favorites, and she couldn't help but smile. There was a sporadic bubble of applause, and then three rows began to assemble for the dance. Anna hadn't yet been allowed a rest, and sure enough, Cettie spotted her across from a new partner.

"You like this song?" Rand said to her in surprise. "I saw you brighten just now. It's one of my favorites. Dance with me, Cettie. Let's cause a scandal." He held out his hand to her and flashed a mischievous grin. He wasn't wearing gloves either.

"Rand," Joanna sighed, shaking her head.

"I'm serious," he pressed, looking at Cettie. "Not about the scandal part, that was a joke, but I'd be honored if you would dance with me."

There was only a moment to decide. The rows were about to start dancing. If anyone else had asked her, she would have declined outright. She hadn't come there expecting to dance. The dress she'd worn would have dissuaded all but the most desperate. Or the most friendly. And yet she found she did not wish to deny him.

She nodded and took Rand's hand, feeling a little jolt of energy from his fingers. He beamed at her and led her to the end of one of the rows. Seeing them together, their hands uncovered and touching, some of the guests couldn't conceal their scandalized expressions. Cettie didn't care.

When the first beat sounded, she didn't miss it. She knew this song by heart and danced to it with great enjoyment, probably to the astonishment of most everyone around her. There was no misstep. No infraction. It pleased her to show them what she could do.

When the song and applause ended, she turned to go back to Lady Maren.

Rand caught her hand. "Not yet," he said with resolve, his eyes gazing into hers as if she were the only one in the crowded ballroom. "One more," he asked. The new song began, and she acquiesced, recognizing the tune and knowing the steps.

And after that song came another. And then another.

Until the ball ended.

CHAPTER TWENTY-SEVEN

Sisters

Phinia and her husband arrived on the afternoon following the Ransoms' ball. Cettie thought the timing of their unscheduled trip was odd, for there had been no communication from them. They had already informed both Phinia and Stephen that the reports of Fitzroy's death were inaccurate, but one look at Phinia's flushed cheeks and pouty lips suggested this had nothing to do with Fitzroy. After they all convened in the sitting room, Phinia insisted that Cettie stay to hear her out.

"I cannot believe what I'm hearing!" she said, pacing. Malcolm, completely unaffected by whatever had angered his wife, helped himself to some tarts left over from the previous meal.

Mother sighed and gave her eldest daughter an arch look. "And what is it you're hearing, Phinia?"

"About the Ransoms' ball, of course! And how the entire Fitzroy family was invited except for Milk and I. Did you even consider that I might want to go?"

The Control Leering alerted Cettie to the arrival of another sky ship, which she recognized to be the Patchetts', and so she rose from the couch to greet the visitors.

Phinia pointed at her fiercely. “Don’t you go yet, Cettie. You must stay for the duration.”

Cettie maintained her composure. “There is much I have to do, Phinia.”

“I’m not here just to complain about not being invited to the ball. What I have to say concerns you.”

That took Cettie by surprise. “What do you mean?”

“All of Lockhaven is talking about your conduct at the ball.”

“My conduct?” Cettie asked, perplexed.

“Indeed.”

“Phinia,” Mother said, rubbing her eyes, “what in the world are you talking about?”

“And you as well, *Mother*,” Phinia said accusingly. “I heard you had a tête-à-tête with Clive Francis of all people! I wouldn’t have thought it possible, but I heard it from three separate people. Mother!”

Lady Maren’s nostrils flared, but she tried to rein in her patience. “I was accosted by Captain Francis and got away from him directly.”

“But the rumors, Mama. They’re already starting. They say you went back to your old love as soon as Father was reported dead. The gossip I’ve heard . . . Why, it’s becoming another scandal.” She turned back to Cettie, who felt her heart pumping with anger. “And then there are the rumors that you are secretly engaged to Randall Patchett. Why else would the two of you dance together all night? I never suspected that you could be so indiscreet. There are other whispers that the two of you have been spending much time together. *Alone.*”

“I am not engaged to anyone,” Cettie said in bewilderment.

“Whether you are or not, they’re saying it’s a good match. You are both from down below, after all.”

“Phinia,” Anna said, rising from the couch. “We are your family. Why are you turning on us like this?”

“Can’t you see how your behavior affects me?” Phinia said, stamping her foot. “Affects Milk and I? There was no ill rumor about *you*,

Anna, but if one of us gets shunned, the rest of us will be ruined too. But I came here at once to set things right. There are proprieties that must be followed. Isn't that right, Milk?"

He was caught midbite and started to choke, before spluttering out, "Yes, dear. Whatever you say."

Mother was clearly outraged by Phinia's lecture, but she managed to bridle her temper. "Phinia, you are my daughter, and I love you. But truly, it is not your place to accuse any of us of impropriety. I'm sure the rumors are putting things in the worst possible light. Or perhaps there is an orchestrated effort to discredit our family. But we need to be firm. We need to remain loyal to one another."

"But is it true, Mother? Would you remarry if Father is truly dead?"

Lady Maren pursed her lips. "He is *not* dead, and even if he were, do you truly think I would dishonor his memory by going back to a man who jilted me so cruelly? Captain Francis is in debt, no doubt. Believe me, it's more than affection that has brought him back. We've barred him from coming to Fog Willows. And will continue to do so."

There was a knock on the door, and Kinross entered. "The Patchetts are arriving, ma'am. Did you invite them?"

"I did not," Lady Maren sighed. "Suddenly we have a surfeit of visitors."

"They come here frequently, do they?" Phinia snorted.

"Daughter, if you can't be civil, I will ask you to leave."

"I can be civil. If I had been there, none of this would have happened. It seems I know more about the ways of the world than all of you put together."

Mother shook her head in wonderment, and soon after, Rand and Joanna were led into the room with Mr. Batewinch. Joanna greeted them all with a bright smile and warm demeanor.

"My goodness," she said, looking at all the faces. "Is there a storm at Fog Willows? Look at all of you. The ball last night was a complete success."

"That's not what I've heard," Phinia said in an undertone.

Joanna's eyes narrowed a bit. "Hello, Phinia. Are you cross that you weren't invited?"

"Why should I not be?" said the other girl defensively. "Though I must say, I've heard nothing but scandalous rumors about the ball."

Joanna gave her a knowing smile. "You're listening to the wrong people, Phinia. The jealous. The vain. The ball was such a success that there will be another one, held at Gimmerton Sough. You are all invited." She gave Phinia a small nod.

That changed Phinia's outlook completely, and she brightened like the dawn. "Truly?"

"Of course!" Joanna said. "The prime minister himself said that it would be a welcome thing. There are reports that we may be close to a peace treaty or at least a cease-fire. A possible marriage between Miss Fitzempress and Prince Trevon of Kingfountain. Would not that news call for a ball in celebration? We could hear word any day."

"That *is* news," Lady Maren said. "Where did you learn of it?"

Joanna shrugged. "You forget that Lady Lawton is our landlord. She approved of the ball and gave her compliments to Miss Ransom for holding it. She couldn't attend it herself, of course, not with her husband being so recently deceased."

"Lady Corinne?" Phinia said in surprise. "She approved?"

"Of course. She recently had to eject some ladies from her set. No doubt they're the ones who have been spreading spurious rumors."

"I don't know, Sister," Rand said, folding his arms and shaking his head. "The rumors might be true." He flashed Cettie a mischievous smile. "You didn't tell anyone about our secret engagement, did you?"

Phinia gasped, and Rand laughed at her.

"There isn't one!" he said, holding up his hands. "The things people will believe. I am weary of all the protocols and forms and nonsense that beleaguer our society. Now, don't get me wrong. I think Cettie is well worth having, and I'm not ashamed to admit it here in front of her family, but I do believe she and I had the same thing in mind. We danced in front of them to prove that we don't care about their approbation or approval." He gave Cettie a short bow. "And you were an excellent partner and knew all your steps as well as or better than any highborn lady there. Well done."

Cettie felt a flush rise on her throat at his compliment.

Joanna looked at her brother fondly. "There will be many invitations going out for our ball by zephyr, starting this afternoon. We wanted to deliver yours in person. Your entire family is welcome. Even Stephen, if you can spare him from the mines and if his wound is healing well."

Phinia's eyes glittered with excitement. "Milk and I can get him!"

"Of course, dear," Malcolm said. He set down a second tart, seemingly enthusiastic about the ball.

"Who else will be coming?" Lady Maren asked.

Joanna shrugged. "Many friends that I met at Pavenham Sky. They'll all attend. There will also be plenty of officers from the Ministry of War. But we don't want to limit it to just one ministry. I think we all ought to become more . . . unified. Do let us know if there is anyone you think we should invite. I considered asking the Hardings, but it might prove awkward for them to come back to their old home as visitors. What do you think, Lady Maren?"

Cettie was pleased by Joanna's outlook. She didn't understand how this young woman had risen so high so quickly in the esteem of their society. She was clearly a young lady of influence.

"I think they'd appreciate being invited nonetheless," Mother answered.

"Done," Joanna said with a bright smile.

"Might we take a walk around the grounds?" Rand asked. "I'd be interested in seeing the outside of this place, and the weather is quite fine. Can we?"

"If you'd like," Mother replied with a gracious nod.

It was a pleasant afternoon walk. The wind was mild, and the sun bright and warm. Rand kept at Cettie's side and showed particular interest in the grounds. Anna told him about the rooks and their nests, and he demanded that they see them, and so they went off the trail a bit to the place where Adam had once shown them the birds' nesting area. Returning to the place brought back memories Cettie had always relished. She thought it strange how the past had its own form of magic that could play chords on the heart. Rand was gallant and kind to all of them—he even teased Phinia and Malcolm—and there was little sign of the angry, tortured soul she'd seen before.

After the hour-long stroll, the guests all returned to their sky ships and left, and Cettie hurried to the study to catch up on her duties. From the desk, she found herself watching the two ships heading in two different directions. Phinia's outlook had been completely altered by the events of the afternoon. She was giddy with excitement at the prospect of attending the Patchetts' ball. And she'd come to realize that Joanna's influence far outpaced her own.

Cettie felt her brow wrinkle as she looked down at the desk. The ledger book was open, but she felt certain she'd closed it. One of the drawers in the desk was also ajar. Nothing appeared amiss when she pulled it open, and yet . . . She frowned, wondering if her memory was playing tricks on her. Reaching out to the Leerings in her mind, she tested them and saw that the defenses were still engaged. With another thought, she summoned Kinross.

He arrived shortly afterward, a curious look on his face. "Yes, ma'am?"

"Did anyone come in here to tidy while we were walking the grounds?"

He looked surprised. "No one, ma'am. No one comes in here unless you ask them to. Is anything wrong?"

A strange, uneasy feeling crept over her, raising gooseflesh on her skin. "No, I don't think so." She looked back at the table again, and the arrangement of things just felt . . . wrong.

"You got the letter, did you not?" Kinross asked.

"What letter?"

"It arrived while you were gone, and I left it on the desk. It came from a village on the coast. It arrived with several business deeds, I believe." He walked up behind her and riffled through some of the correspondence she'd not yet answered. "Ah, this one."

It was smaller than the rest, and she hadn't noticed it at the bottom of the pile. Possibly it was from Adam.

She picked it up and noticed at once that the wax was broken. The sight of the handwriting made her heart race in her chest. It was from Sera.

"Thank you," Cettie said, and the butler turned and left her alone.

Why had the seal been broken? Who else had read it?

Cettie opened the paper carefully, treating the letter like the precious gift it was. It was a short missive, but she savored each word.

Dearest Cettie,

I write this short message en route to a mirror gate. I am going to the court of Kingfountain to see if I can persuade them to stop this war for a season. I don't know if I will be successful, because I'm not sure I can give what is expected of me. I will try. Regardless, it is nice to be free of my gilded prison. I never want to visit Pavenham Sky again. I'd sooner live in the Fells! How I miss you, my dearest friend. If only I'd persuaded you to come with me to Lockhaven before the Test. I think you would have helped me avoid the pitfalls that brought me here. Still, I've learned my lesson. I hope, someday, that we can see each other again. My mission may be brief. Or perhaps

I will be there longer than I'd like. Either way, I wanted to send you word. I saw our mutual friend recently. Sad news. I wish I had your strength and determination. I will need it shortly.

With love and affection, your friend always, Sera

Tears thickened in her lashes. Sera had not been forthright about what "sad news" she'd heard, but of course she hadn't. Someone had clearly managed to read the letter. It could only be about Mr. Skrelling. When had they seen each other? Did Sera know more than she did?

She and her friend had been apart for three years, but this letter made it feel like no time had passed at all. It *felt* like Sera. She sniffed and read it again, then folded it and examined the smudges on the outside. It had traveled a distance to get to Fog Willows. Sera was in another world having adventures of her own. Cettie dabbed the tears on her sleeve, feeling a tug of longing in her heart.

"Was it from Adam?"

The question made her cringe.

Though she recognized the voice, she turned to look at Anna. The other girl stood just outside the doorway, as if she were reluctant to enter.

Cettie shook her head. "Why don't you come in?"

Anna approached her with a mixed look on her face.

"Who is it from?"

"Sera, actually," Cettie replied, still trying to settle herself.

"I thought she was gone?"

"She is. She sent this by zephyr post before she left for Kingfountain."

Anna stood by the desk and put her hand on Cettie's shoulder. "I hope she's successful," she whispered, sighing. "I wish that this war would finally end."

"We all do," Cettie said, growing more uncomfortable.

Anna was quiet for a moment. "I'm sorry, Cettie. I thought maybe Adam had been injured or something. That there was news he didn't want to share with anyone but *you*."

Cettie squirmed in silence, knowing that this was the moment for her to speak honestly about her feelings, come what may.

"Rand Patchett is a nice young man," Anna said, gazing out the window. "When I saw the two of you dancing last night, I thought you'd make a nice couple. He needs someone steady, I think. You could do much worse."

There it was, spoken but still unspoken. It was Anna's mute entreaty. *Must one of us suffer a broken heart? Let me have Adam Creigh. You can have Rand Patchett. Can we not both be happy that way?*

Cettie didn't know if she could hear Anna's actual thoughts, or if the words had sprung from her own imagination. She bit her lip, wishing she had someone she could confide in. She and Anna were close, but there was this insurmountable issue before them.

"Rand has many admirable qualities," she said evasively.

"He does," Anna agreed, probably too readily. "Well, this war has to end first, doesn't it? I'm wretched wondering if Papa is a prisoner and how he's being treated. Do you think he's in a dungeon?"

"No, he isn't," Cettie answered.

"Well, I should let you get back to your work," Anna said. She squeezed Cettie's shoulder and then kissed her hair. "I love you like my own sister."

Cettie stood, moved by the sentiment, and the two embraced. After Anna left, she sat back down in the chair, feeling listless, troubled, and unmotivated to finish her work. She opened the drawer at the front of the desk to retrieve the book Adam had given her. It was her only connection to him.

It was gone.

Her throat went dry. She knew she'd left it there. She opened the drawer farther and ducked lower, searching. Where could it be? Had she brought it somewhere else to read? Try as she might, she couldn't remember.

It bothered her for the rest of the day. She searched her room, under the bed, and in each closet and chest.

She went to bed that night worried sick about it, wondering where she'd misplaced it. Adam lingered in her thoughts all evening, and she kept imagining, again and again, what she would tell him when he returned and asked for it. Had Anna rifled through the desk earlier and found it? The possibility made her wince. The Leering would have told her if a stranger had tried to enter the room. But Anna was family and a maston herself. She could have disarmed it.

Well, if Anna had the book, so be it. She would never confront her about such a thing.

After hours of cyclical thoughts, she fell asleep and dreamed that night. And then the next vision came.

I am so close to success and to failure. My chief Espion in Lockhaven believes the prime minister knows something he's not telling. Lord Welles is a crafty man. I like him very much. He's a worthy foe.

If this armistice happens, it will catapult the Fitzempress brat to great heights of popularity. I cannot let that happen. The Wizr board hangs in the balance. One false move, and I could ruin the game.

There are a few rules to remember in Wizr. Do not let the pieces topple too early. If your enemy discerns your plan, they can counter it. Exercise patience until all the pieces are in place, save one. At the crucial moment, be sure not to draw attention to your real move. Feint. Draw the eye from the danger. That is how you win the game. That is how you win an empire.

The Fitzempress girl must be removed from the board.

—Leon Montpensier, Duke of La Marche

SERA

CHAPTER TWENTY-EIGHT

Our Lady

The rushing of the falls was still audible inside the massive stone structure of the sanctuary of Our Lady. Sera gazed in wonderment at the huge vaulted ceiling held up by impressive buttresses. The sides of the building boasted marbled stained-glass windows that let in streams of brilliant light. Even the floor beneath their feet was an impressive checkerboard of black and white marble tiles. Surely that had been replaced, given how many visitors came and went each day.

The main chapel and entry had been cleared for her visit with Prince Trevon, but various nobles of the court were in attendance. The sanctuary keepers were sequestered elsewhere for the day.

"That is a statue dedicated to Our Lady," he explained with a gesture. The impressive statue looked centuries old. Were Leerings just another manifestation of the same art, she wondered, the innate desire to craft objects of beauty from stone? There were no Leerings in the sanctuary, but she still felt the power of the Mysteries there. It reminded her of Muirwood Abbey.

They stopped near one of the many wishing pools, filled with shiny coins. Citizens came each day to toss coins into the pools and fountains, their way of petitioning the Fountain for blessings. She couldn't imagine such a tradition happening in the City. The people would claw each other to grab the coins from the water. The waters gurgled as the fountain in the middle gusted out fresh streams of clean water.

"And do you believe the Fountain grants these petitions?" she asked him. They'd had several long conversations over the previous days of her visit. But this was the day they had set aside to discuss their different religions. It was a moment she'd been dreading.

"I've thrown in coins, if that's what you mean," he replied, looking at her curiously.

"People do many things out of tradition. It is tradition that stops people from stealing the coins too, no doubt. Do people really get thrown into the river for doing so?"

"It has happened in the past," he said with a nod. "But not recently."

She spied the deconeus watching them from one of the shadowed alcoves of the sanctuary. Trevon had explained his robes and vestments to her already. *So much like an Aldermaston,* she thought. The similarities between their cultures were striking—to her mind, only the trappings were different.

Sera turned and faced him. "But do you *believe* it, Trevon? Or do you follow it because it is tradition? Because your parents taught you, or that deconeus frowned at you, or for a thousand other reasons? Do you believe it in your heart?"

He didn't return her look. He was gazing at the main statue, his expression pensive. It wasn't an awkward silence. He was genuinely interested in her line of questioning, in answering her as honestly as he could.

"I do," he finally said. "And that is the most troubling thing about this situation."

"Why do you say that?"

He did look at her then, all seriousness and conviction. "You look like you belong here, Sera. That dress you wear is Occitanian, and it flatters you. You've proven to be quite skilled in negotiation, knowledgeable about our customs and ways. And you've been more honest than I was expecting, frankly. I had hoped that you might . . . in time . . . come to see the Fountain as I see it. As the true wellspring from which your customs have strayed."

Sera bit her lip at that last part. "Is it not possible, Trevon, that we are both right? Perhaps the difference between our beliefs is that ours are more open and accommodating of others. What you call the Fountain, we call the Knowing."

"I've been educated in your principles," he said stiffly.

"But have you opened your mind to the possibility that your understanding might be more limited?"

He arched his eyebrows, and she regretted she hadn't chosen a different word.

"What I cannot understand," he said, his voice betraying his unease, "is why your people shroud their beliefs in the so-called Mysteries. Why you shun the common people from a deeper knowledge of your . . . Knowing. Some of our most famous Fountain-blessed were not noble born. The Fountain can touch and has touched even the lowliest of maids."

"And so it is in our world," she answered. "I agree with you that we do not always live up to our own ideals. That is something I wish to change. But change takes time." She pursed her lips before she could finish the thought. *I could not change it if I lived here.*

"But surely such secrecy is dangerous," he pressed. "You yourself did not pass the Maston Test. There are secrets even you do not know. Secrets that are kept from all except an elite few."

"True, but I lived for many years at Muirwood Abbey. I tell you, Trevon, it feels like *this*." She held up her hands and gazed around. His look darkened, and again she thought she'd offended him. "What did I say?"

"Nothing," he said, but it felt as if a wall had come down between them.

"Please, I'm trying to be open with you. I'm not trying to offend you."

His shoulders bunched up with frustration. "I know, Sera. But you have to understand . . . from my point of view, your beliefs are a heresy."

"And why is that? Who taught you that they were? And why did they teach that? You believe in the Fountain, the power of water. You revere pools and waterfalls and legends of the Wizrs of old. You believe in water sprites and treasure immersed in the sea and many such things that would be considered fantastical where I come from. Why should it seem so strange to you that we worship the water in the sky? Are not clouds made of water? Is it not all part of the same story of creation, that the waters beneath were divided from the waters above?" She was grateful that she'd been taught that in her studies, even though the origin story of the worlds hadn't interested her as much as her lessons about contracts and covenants.

"Yes, there are similarities," he conceded, the anger ebbing from his eyes. "There have been connections between our worlds in the past. The first King Andrew was taken to an abbey in your world to be healed. But the differences remain troubling. I cannot hold you accountable for beliefs or practices done centuries ago, but many of them are still vexing to consider."

"Neither can I hold you accountable for what *your* people have done," she said. "They plundered our shores during our darkest hours. Many artifacts were taken."

He held up his hands. "As we both said, we cannot undo the past."

She looked at his hand and felt the sudden urge to take hold of it. There were no gloves in this world. No prohibitions on dress or manners, at least none that she could tell. Their cultures were so different. How could she hope to bridge them? To help make them understand each other?

"What is it, Trevon, that concerns you the most? We don't have time to resolve everything. Is there something about our beliefs that makes you distrust us more than others?"

He lowered his hands and frowned, thinking hard. Sera could feel the scrutiny of the other nobles present, from the deconeus who still watched them. Was he worried that she would corrupt Trevon? If only they could speak privately, without any listening ears. Though she'd enjoyed her time in Kingfountain much more than expected, she could not shake the feeling they were running out of time. If she went back to Lockhaven without a peace treaty, her prospects would be dashed, especially if the privy council learned she hadn't even offered herself in marriage.

Still he brooded without answering. He was a thoughtful man, not one to rush with his words.

Sera sighed. "I wish there were a place we could go to talk privately. We're always being watched."

He turned and looked at her in surprise. "I had not thought of that."

"Thought of what? I was just making an observation."

"I know, but it is a good idea. If you could go anywhere in my world, where would you want to go?"

"We don't have time for sightseeing," she said with a laugh.

He arched his eyebrows. "What if we did? Where would you want to go?"

She was taken aback. "Dundrennan, probably," she said. "I've heard it has the most majestic falls, even more so than this city. But it would take days to get there."

"For most people, yes," he answered. Then she saw him reach into his pocket and withdraw a brass cylinder. She recognized it as the one she'd seen him use at the privy council before the war. He'd used the device to vanish out of sight.

"What is that?"

"Something I'm not supposed to show you," he replied with a grin and then offered her his other hand. He was asking her to trust him. In her world, being alone with a man had almost ruined her. Was she willing to risk that it would happen again? The norms were quite different in this world.

That part of her that had always rebelled flared up. She trusted Trevon, trusted he was not like Will. Would he protect her reputation by keeping their jaunt a secret from her cohorts? She felt certain he would.

Slowly, she reached out and took his hand. And then it felt as if the floor vanished and they were plummeting to their deaths.

They were no longer in the sanctuary of Our Lady. The sun was high overhead, and the roar of falling water filled her ears, no longer muted. Gasping, she realized she and Trevon now stood atop a bridge straddling a massive waterfall plunging from the lower peaks of the snowcapped mountains beneath them. The bridge was perfectly wide enough, but the sudden change had made her dizzy. She flailed for a moment, as if fearing she was about to plunge off the mountain. Trevon gripped her hand harder and steadied her, bringing her closer to him.

"T-this is Dundrennan?" she gasped, her knees weak. The air was much colder. She saw little puffs of mist come from her mouth.

"There is the fortress below," he said, pointing with the brass cylinder. She marveled at the view of the mighty stone building nestled amidst the rich green pines beneath them. "It was rebuilt after a battle with an emperor centuries ago. There is a city farther south that bears the same name, but these woods are protected in the king's name. The forest is a preserve."

"It's stunning," Sera said in awe, her eyes barely able to take in such a scene. "How did we get here?"

"Not by sky ship," he said with a teasing tone. "This is just one of the magics we have. I suppose you would call it one of the Mysteries. I can visit anywhere in the kingdom I wish to go. As long as I've been there before, my thought will take me back."

It begins with a thought, Sera remembered. The Aldermaston of Muirwood had told her that. "Can you go to Lockhaven?"

He shook his head. "It doesn't work between worlds. There are . . . rules and limits. That's probably not a good term. There was a Wizr from ancient times, Myrddin, who traveled between the worlds. He taught us what he knew."

"I thought he was a myth," Sera said. She'd heard of the legendary being who had brought the Ring Table to Kingfountain and had helped organize the kingdom.

Trevon shook his head. He was still holding her hand, which felt nice in the cold air. "No, he was real."

Sera started to shiver.

"You're cold. There are nicer climates to visit. Would you like to see Marq?"

"Can we?" she asked in surprise.

"We can. But we will need this," he said, releasing her hand and showing her a ring on his finger. Suddenly, he was wearing a dragoon uniform. She blinked in surprise. His form shifted again, and he was wearing another outfit, something of a different fashion and style, something likely popular in Marq. "When I left Pavenham Sky, I was wearing a servant's livery Lady Corinne had given me. I used this ring to disguise myself as one of Lord Welles's officers upon reaching Lockhaven—that's when you noticed me. This," he mentioned, wagging the cylinder, "was how I beat you back to the emperor's palace. I'd already been there, you see."

"But how did you cross back to Kingfountain? You said that couldn't take you."

He shrugged. "Mirror gates are not the only way to cross between the worlds."

"Will you tell me?" she asked, keenly interested.

"It depends on how forthcoming you are with *your* secrets. Shall we lunch in Marq, then? If you hold my hand, then the ring will also affect what you wear. It would look suspicious if you showed up there wearing an Occitanian gown, but I respect your sensibilities. I understand that there is a lot of formality between the sexes in your world."

"I would rather not stand out," she answered. And though she didn't wish to say so, she also liked the idea of holding his hand again.

"Thank you," he said, offering it to her. She took it, savoring the warmth, and in another blink they were in Marq.

They spent the afternoon together, visiting a few of the places she had previously only heard about. Each invocation from the cylinder took them to another wondrous place, and each place required new disguises. The sun kept shifting position in the sky as they traveled, indicating they were indeed traveling vast distances instantaneously. The magic of Kingfountain was shockingly powerful.

No one recognized them or gave them any notice at all. Sera had never felt so free, so unbound by rules or traditions. The several places they visited were all different, but they had one thing in common—Trevon's people remembered the past and honored it. The beautiful architecture from the past had been preserved and maintained. There were parks to walk in, bridges to cross, and markets to wander in. Her favorite place of all was probably the berry market in Ploemeur where they got in a laughing fit and tossed berries at each other. The tastes and smells were as delicious as the fun they had.

Their final destination was a sanctuary in a burg near the huge city of Pree. Now she was back in her Occitanian dress, the illusion gone. The sanctuary was much smaller than the one in Kingfountain, but it, too, felt ancient. There was a bronze statue of a knight there, the metal dimmed by time. As they drew near it, Sera asked who it represented.

"The Maid of Donremy," Trevon said, looking up at it in admiration. "The sword belted on her armor is the sword Firebos. It's real, Sera," he said softly. "It's been in my family for generations."

"Why did you bring me here last of all?" she asked.

The sun was sinking low, and the stained-glass windows were in shadow now. The chapel was nearly empty, save for a few local patrons speaking in a pretty language she didn't understand. She had not been able to understand the languages used in the places they'd visited that day, yet there was something in the people's tones and mannerisms that connected them, even if they didn't share a common tongue.

"She was one of the most famous Fountain-blessed of all," he said. "Though she came from nothing, she helped crown a prince a king. He betrayed her in the end, but her story is a symbol that sometimes the Fountain chooses the most unexpected people to be agents for uncommon good. I've read her story. I've read the transcripts of the trial." He sighed. "It was wrong of them to put her to death. Now, all these years later, we can see that. But at the time, they thought *she* was a heretic." He glanced at Sera. "I don't want to make the same mistake they did."

Sera smiled impishly at him. "I hope you don't feel tempted to chain me to an icy rock." She knew how the Maid's story ended, something she'd learned in her own reading.

Trevon grinned at her humor. He was not a traditionally handsome man, but she liked his face, the sound of his voice. His quiet, deliberate ways.

"Not yet," he teased back. Then he looked at the statue and became subdued again. "There are many secrets between our worlds. How could it be otherwise? General Montpensier is convinced he can defeat your empire. He doesn't want an armistice. He certainly doesn't want peace. It is easier to take something than to buy it," he added with a grim voice. "Or trade for it. Our people see yours as an enemy."

"But what do you see, Trevon?"

His mouth firmed. "I see a faint possibility that we might join forces someday to create something grander than either of us could build separately. But there is so much river to bridge, as we like to say. So many past conflicts." He turned and looked at her. "When you came here, I thought I would court a wife. Maybe that cannot happen. Maybe it shouldn't. But I respect you, and if you ruled the empire in your father's stead, I suspect things would be different."

Sera's excitement was growing at his words, but she also felt a pang of loss. She admired him too. Indeed, she wished their separate worlds did not stand between them. If only everything could be so easy as traveling with that brass cylinder.

"I don't know what will happen, Trevon," she said. "I don't think either of our sides wishes to admit defeat." She reached for his hand and squeezed it. "I asked you a question earlier that you didn't answer. What about my beliefs troubles you the most?"

He looked back at the statue. "I didn't forget . . . it's the reason I saved this chapel for last. We were wrong to persecute the Maid as we did. Our history is full of mistakes." He then gave her a probing look. "I think what disturbs me most about the history of your world is how it has persecuted women. You yourself have felt the sting of such persecution. For one thing, your women are subjected to strict fashions that I frankly find appalling."

Sera smiled at that. "Most uncomfortable, yes."

Trevon shrugged. "But in all seriousness, what I'm about to tell you is a matter of grave concern."

"Please go on," Sera said, anxious to know what he would say.

"I told you that Myrddin was real. There is another Wizr from our history, one whose power rivaled even his. Her name was Sinia Montfort, the Duchess of Brythonica. She was a special lady for many reasons."

"Didn't she marry Owen Kiskaddon?" Sera asked. If the Maid of Donremy was the most famous Fountain-blessed in the history of Kingfountain, Kiskaddon was a close second.

"Indeed. There are many legends about their daughter as well. But what I have to say concerns Sinia."

"How so?" Sera had read about Sinia Montfort, but most of the stories focused on her life with Owen, during the reign of the last King Andrew.

"Later in her life, she went to your world to try and make peace between us."

Sera looked at him in shock. "Really?"

"It doesn't surprise me that you don't know. I imagine it is a state secret. She never returned, Sera. We believe she was imprisoned in your world. Wizrs have unnaturally long lives, so it's possible she may still be living there, trapped. Why this was done, or how this was done, I don't understand. But considering your world's treatment of women . . . well, it would not surprise me to learn she was executed long ago." He glanced back at the statue of the Maid. "Sinia Montfort was a peaceful and caring ruler, who kept her principles despite difficult circumstances. She was quick to respond to pleas for aid, and she was powerful in the Fountain magic. Very powerful. I don't think I could live in the kind of place that would knowingly destroy her. There is much about your own world you do not know."

CHAPTER TWENTY-NINE

WARNING

They returned to the sanctuary of Our Lady in Kingfountain and were immediately accosted by members of the king's Espion, who had been alarmed by their sudden and prolonged disappearance. Prince Trevon refused to answer them on their way to the docks behind the building. The crowds of onlookers that had gathered to see Sera had long since dispersed. There was a strange boat in the docks, made of what looked like stone. And there was an unmanned door that opened as they approached it. They climbed down the ladder down from the docks, and servants then helped them into the vessel.

"This will take us back to the palace," Trevon told her. He gazed up at the setting sun and sighed. "My parents may not be pleased with our jaunt. But I don't regret it."

"Thank you for taking me."

The hatch was closed behind them, and Sera examined the cockpit before seating herself on a comfortable chair in the interior. Trevon sat down beside her. The outside could be seen in a mirror mounted across from their seats, and she gazed in wonder as the craft began to enter the strong surge of the river. They were so near the falls that she squeezed the armrests, but the vessel glided effortlessly upstream. She could feel a tingle in the air, a bit of magic that sent a thrill down her spine.

Soon they reached the palace docks and disembarked. The family was already seated at dinner when they arrived, and it was plain to see the king and queen were angry with their eldest son. Some sharp looks were exchanged, and the king motioned one of his attendants over and whispered something into his ear. The man nodded and left.

General Montpensier, on the other hand, looked smug. He raised a goblet. "To the errant prince!" he called with a grand voice. "The prodigals return."

Trevon escorted Sera to her seat before taking the one next to her. She glanced around the room for Fitzroy but didn't see him.

"We toured the realm," he said with composure. He offered no excuses, admitted to no wrongdoing.

"And you exposed her to more of our secrets, no doubt," the general said in an almost gloating way. "How daring."

"General," the king said, displeased.

"Did I offend?" replied Montpensier. "I beg your pardon, Your Majesty."

Everyone ignored him. Trevon was facing his parents' silent rebukes bravely, but she didn't want him to bear the burden of it alone. She looked across the table at the queen. "I was especially taken by Marq. That is where you are from, is it not?"

The queen had a sour look. "Indeed, Miss Fitzempress. It was the home of my childhood."

"There is much to admire about it. I was curious about the history here. One can only learn so much through a book."

Montpensier grinned. "So true." He took another slow drink from his goblet, his eyes piercing hers.

The tension in the room ebbed, and at the end of the dinner, Sera went back to her room and related her adventures to Becka, who listened eagerly and with interest.

"I wish I could have seen it too," the young girl said. "Everyone speaks so highly of the prince. He's not as hard as his father. All the servants are afraid of his mother, though. She can be very strict."

"I can see that," Sera replied with a knowing smile. Becka helped her remove the silk gown she'd worn that day. Such a gown would not be considered fashionable—or even suitable—in her world, but the feel and comfort of it pleased her. Becka fetched Sera's nightdress and a shawl, and the two stayed awake talking about what they had seen and heard. Sera asked if she could find out where Lord Fitzroy was being kept. Sera wanted to speak to him privately about Lady Corinne. She intended to ask for a confidential meeting with him the next day, but there was a chance she'd be denied.

After quenching the lights, Sera lay down on the immaculate and comfortable bed, although her mind was too preoccupied to sleep. She thought about her discussions with Trevon. Would he truly be willing to accept an armistice without a marriage? His parents would not support that, she was certain. But they had given him autonomy to make the decision. Would they honor it?

And what about his revelation about the missing duchess of Brythonica? Sera had never heard about such a thing, not even in rumor. If Trevon was to be believed, and she did believe him, it was yet another reason the court of Kingfountain regarded them so poorly. What other obstacles remained between them? How could she learn more about the concerns he had shared about the duchess? Well, she could try to speak to the Aldermaston of Muirwood upon returning home. He was an honest man, one who had been a help to her while she had studied there. If she could find out the truth, might there be a way to appease the court of Kingfountain and achieve a longer-lasting peace?

She didn't realize she'd fallen asleep until something startled her awake.

Sera sat up in bed, her heart pounding in her chest. An oppressive feeling of danger filled her soul. She stared at the dark room, unable to remember what had triggered the feelings. Again she felt a premonition that she should leave immediately. Something was coming.

She blinked quickly, trying to understand the source of her feelings. It was the Mysteries, she realized. It was warning her to escape.

Sera swung her bare legs off the bed and hurried over to the small couch where Becka slept.

"Becka! Becka!" she whispered, shaking the girl's shoulder.

The girl lifted up, looking confused and worried. "What's wrong?"

"I don't know. Come with me."

Becka rubbed sleep from her eyes. "It's the middle of the night."

"I know. Come with me."

The feelings grew even more emphatic. Sera clutched Becka's hand and half dragged her off the couch. Becka obeyed, following her to the door. Sera paused, listening at the crack, and then opened it. The corridor outside was dark except for some moonlight coming in from the upper windows.

The tile was cold against her bare feet. Sera had no idea where to go, but she started down the corridor, walking as quietly and stealthily as she could.

"Where are we going?" Becka whispered fearfully.

"I have no idea," Sera said. They reached the end of the corridor. There were stairs going up and down and then the corridor turned sharply to the right. Where should she go next? The feeling of danger hadn't abated yet, and she knew she had to heed it.

The impression to go down whispered to her.

Pulling Becka after her, she started down the steps, holding the railing with her free hand. The glimmer of torches could be seen on the lower floor, and Sera knew that hiding would soon become difficult. The oppressive feelings urged her onward nonetheless.

There was no one in the corridor when they reached the bottom of the stairs. There were two possible directions. She stopped again and tried to understand what she was supposed to do. The need to do something, anything, pressed on her, but she remembered how impatient she used to get at Muirwood when the Leerings didn't obey her. Slowing her breath, she opened herself to the Mysteries' will. Becka looked at her in confusion and worry.

"This way," Sera said.

They walked down the middle of the corridor, feet padding on the lush carpet cutting through the center. Sera looked at the paintings on the walls. Though she'd seen them previously, even admired them, they looked dark and frightening now. As if hundreds of eyes were silently scolding her.

The end of the corridor showed a massive set of doors. It looked vaguely familiar, but she couldn't be sure.

As they neared it, Becka gasped in surprise.

"What?" Sera asked.

"Someone's following us," the girl whispered.

Sera glanced back and saw a man striding down the corridor behind them, his boots not making a sound as he walked. The shadows of the corridor concealed his face. How had he gotten there?

"What do we do?" Becka whimpered.

Sera increased her pace, sensing the man quickening his as well. She reached the heavy doors and pulled on one of the handles. It was huge and massive and did not yield easily, but Becka helped her, and their combined effort opened the door. Light and voices emanated through the opening. Sera saw the man was almost upon them, looking determined to catch them both before they entered.

Sera pushed Becka in first and came in after her. Only then did she realize they'd entered the throne room. She'd heard legends of the Ring Table, and now the massive round table stood before her. There were carved wooden thrones around the table, each one decorated differently. They had stood through the ages.

"What are you doing here?" demanded a voice, which Sera recognized instantly as the king's. The king sat at the opposite end of the table, along with Trevon and one of his other brothers. Another man stood by him, one she recognized from earlier. An advisor perhaps?

Sera, anxious to be away from her pursuer, marched into the room, feeling very vulnerable in front of these men in her nightdress. She stepped in front of Becka to shield her.

"Sera?" Trevon asked in surprise, coming around the table and approaching her with obvious concern.

"Someone was chasing us," Sera told him when he neared. "In the corridor."

Trevon scowled and then marched to the door and flung it open. He stood there a moment, gazing outside, and then turned back. "There's no one there now."

"Answer my question," said the king angrily. "What are you doing up at this time of night?"

Sera wasn't sure if she'd done the right thing, but there was no going back. "Why are you here meeting without the rest of your council? You seem angry, Your Majesty."

The king's nostrils flared with anger. "We are dealing with a crisis, Miss Fitzempress. One you brought upon us."

"Father," Trevon said defensively.

"Perhaps she didn't know," conceded the king. "But that doesn't hold her guiltless."

"What is happening?" Sera demanded, coming forward until she reached the table. The Ring Table was made from the trunk of a massive tree—undoubtedly a *Shui-sa* tree like the fallen one at the beach beneath Pavenham Sky. It would have taken twenty grown men linking arms to encompass it. This tree was indeed the stuff of fables.

"You have no right to demand answers of a king," said the king gruffly.

"Father, please. How could she have known? We aren't even sure."

"Please," Sera implored. "Tell me."

The king threw up his hands in disgust, no doubt seeing the determination in Trevon's eyes.

Trevon's brother nodded firmly. "Tell her."

"Sera, there has been an outbreak of disease among the prisoners we rescued from the battle. They are dying quickly and experiencing violent symptoms. Some of our healers have been struck down as well. This happened today, while you and I were away."

"A disease, you say?" Sera asked.

"Yes. It's highly contagious and fatal, unlike any our healers have faced before. We think it's the cholera morbus."

That *was* news, and it would no doubt cause a frenzy of panic. She looked at Trevon in concern. "I knew nothing of this."

"But that doesn't mean," said the king, "that your privy council did not. Perhaps they seek to infect us to end this war."

"No!" Sera said, shaking her head vehemently. "This was not planned, but we've battled this disease for many years. There is no cure."

"We must shatter the mirror gates!" the king snarled. "Surely this is a punishment from the Fountain."

Sera looked at the king. "My lord, send for Lord Fitzroy. He was the Minister of Wind prior to the war, and he studied this disease and looked for a cure. He could tell you, definitively, if it is the cholera morbus and how best to quarantine the infected. Perhaps we can discover a cure if we work together. I implore you, send for him!"

The king looked at Trevon sharply.

"Would he help us?" Trevon asked.

"I *know* he would," Sera said. "With no conditions."

The king turned to the man Sera thought was his advisor. "Bring Fitzroy here at once."

"Yes, my lord," said the man with a curt bow. He gave Sera a wary look.

She rubbed her hands together, feeling the chill of the room.

"Come by the fire," Trevon urged, walking her and Becka over to the hearth where they could warm themselves. As they stood there, Trevon glanced back at his father.

"Why did you come in the middle of the night? How did you know we were here?"

"The same way I knew who you were at Lady Corinne's manor," Sera said, chafing her hands.

Trevon fell quiet.

⁓

They did everything possible to keep the crisis a secret. The palace staff were kept unaware, and Sera was asked not to tell the advisors she had brought with her. Because of the seriousness of the situation, she was confined to her rooms. There was no doubt in her mind the Mysteries had guided her to the throne room, though she wasn't sure if the danger it had alerted her to was the man who'd pursued her or the spread of the disease. Trevon had had her room searched, and he'd personally questioned the guards in the hall. Neither effort had yielded anything.

In late afternoon, Prince Trevon arrived with Lord Fitzroy. She was relieved to see both of them.

"Is it what we feared?" she asked him with concern.

Fitzroy nodded. "It is the cholera morbus. Some of the soldiers must have had it during the battle. This outbreak is in the early stages. Many more will die before it runs its course."

She'd feared as much, but the spark of hope in her heart refused to burn out. "What can be done?"

Trevon rubbed his mouth. "Lord Fitzroy lacks the tools to study it here. There are individuals better suited to this type of study back in your world."

"Like Adam Creigh," Sera said firmly. "He *wanted* to study it."

"I told them as much," Fitzroy said. "We could send some doctors over here to study it. I think some would be willing. Maybe pooling our knowledge is the answer. Perhaps that is what the Knowing intended all along." He gave Sera an arch look.

She felt a glimmer of excitement. His thoughts so perfectly aligned with her own.

"I don't think your privy council," Trevon said, "would be so willing to assist us. If they find out we're vulnerable, they might launch a strike against us."

"But not if a peace were negotiated first," Sera said to him, her eyes boring into his. "An armistice. Surely you must see this for what it is. An opportunity to reconcile the hostilities between our worlds."

"An armistice would certainly be to our advantage now," Trevon said. He sighed. "I was hoping that I might persuade you to stay longer."

"As your bride?" Sera asked directly. Her heart leaped in anticipation of his answer.

Trevon shrugged, looking conflicted.

"Trevon, can we not secure peace for the short term? I'm not saying that I'm unwilling to give you what you want. But does it have to be now? Can we not agree that it would benefit both of our worlds if we became allies instead of foes? You are authorized still to negotiate the terms of the peace treaty, are you not?"

"I am," he said.

"Then let me suggest some terms. You desire peace between our worlds, but measures must be implemented to guarantee that peace stands the test of time. Require that Lord Fitzroy be chosen as the next prime minister so we might exchange ideas on science and technology. Give us a chance to teach one another. Lord Fitzroy is highly respected and, most importantly, is a man of his word. We can name the peace for a period of two or three years. At which time," Sera added, lowering her lashes, "we will see where things stand between our worlds."

Trevon gazed at her closely, his expression a mixture of conflicting emotions. "You're not saying no entirely."

"I'm not," she answered. She liked him very much, but there was so much at stake. She wasn't sure what she wanted in the end, or even if a match between them would be possible. "Perhaps I can find some answers to the matters we discussed yesterday."

Trevon nodded. "What do you think, Lord Fitzroy? Would you accept peace on such terms?"

Fitzroy sighed. "I could be persuaded."

Sera wanted to hug the prince. He was not what she had feared he might be. Her admiration of him increased each day. She honored his reasonableness and ability to see both sides of an argument. "Thank you!"

Trevon smiled. "Let me talk to Father and my advisors. I will return soon."

"Can Lord Fitzroy stay with me a while longer?" she asked. "I'd like to discuss certain matters with him privately."

"I discharge our prisoner to your custody," Trevon said with a wink.

CHAPTER THIRTY

A CHARGE OF MURDER

Sera did not know how much time they would have. She took Fitzroy to one of the benches in her rooms and sat down with him, leaning in closely as she disclosed the details of how she had come to learn about Mr. Skrelling's murder. She informed him of the situation with Becka—what the girl had seen and how she'd been sent to Kingfountain as Sera's maid. She kept her voice calm and steady, but she was relieved to finally be telling someone, especially now that it was possible that Fitzroy would become the prime minister. He would do something about it. He would see justice done.

Lord Fitzroy was seemingly shocked by the news, and he absorbed her words without speaking, his expression shifting as he reasoned it all through. He rubbed his bottom lip with agitation, his brows furrowed and disturbed.

"And Becka was truly an eyewitness?" he eventually asked, his expression looking even more troubled.

"Yes, you can ask her yourself. She's here in the castle."

"I have no doubt about what you told me," he said, shaking his head. "I would never have suspected Corinne capable of murdering someone. What dark truth did she wish to hide? Mr. Skrelling worked for *my* advocates, so I have a personal interest in this matter. Believe me when I say that this is the most serious of accusations and will be dealt with in the most prudent way. If Lady Corinne is indeed guilty of murder, she will pay the price for it. Her husband will be shocked. Utterly shocked."

Sera leaned forward. "Didn't you know? Lord Lawton is dead."

"I did not," he said, looking even more surprised.

"And from what Lord Welles told me, Lady Corinne took it rather in stride. It's no secret that my father fancies her, and now with her husband out of the way, she may attempt to rise."

Lord Fitzroy grunted. "Well, as the ancient maston tomes say, how the mighty fall. You've warned me in the past about Lady Corinne. I believed you then, but now we have evidence. The word of a child may not seem to mean very much. But in this instance, it may rule the day. Thank you, Sera. What a burden you've been carrying."

Her sense of relief was overwhelming. "You *must* become the prime minister, Lord Fitzroy. The empire needs you at this moment. Our society has become too corrupt. It's time to instigate change."

He gave her a knowing smile. "I think, Sera, your help in that area would be paramount."

Sera glanced at the door, still unsure of how much time they had to speak frankly. "There's one more thing. I've learned a great deal about Trevon's people and the history of our rivalry with them. While I don't wish to give up my faith in order to win peace between us, Trevon is a good man, and I think highly of him. We've spent a good deal of time together, and he shared with me a controversy that I hadn't known about."

"Go on," Fitzroy said encouragingly.

"You are much more learned than I am. Was there a time in the past when Kingfountain sent an envoy to us? Someone by the name of Sinia Montfort?"

Fitzroy frowned. "I know the name from history, but I'm not entirely familiar with the story. I don't recall ever hearing about such a visit. But this would be centuries ago, would it not?"

"Indeed," Sera affirmed. "They believe our people abducted and imprisoned her because of our rancor against women. She may even be alive, he said, imprisoned somehow by magic. A Leering perhaps?"

Fitzroy's eyebrows lifted, and a strange look came over his face.

"What?" Sera pressed. "What is it?"

He tapped his cheek thoughtfully, his mind clearly conjuring something of interest. "Give me a moment," he said.

Sera was restless, anxious to learn more. Her eyes kept darting to the closed door, but she stayed silent until he spoke.

"You remember after you left Muirwood," he said, his voice low and guarded, "how Cettie was attacked?"

"Yes," Sera answered promptly.

"She mentioned to me that the man who attacked her had some power over Leerings. Her assailant was the man my sister-in-law saw using one of Kingfountain's special ships." He paused, rubbing his forehead, before continuing. "There is some knowledge that I cannot share with you because you have not faced the Maston Test, but there used to be an order that sought out and murdered mastons. This order was run by women who possessed incredible power. They brought about the destruction of thousands, even millions, but Empress Maia hunted down the remnants of their group and abolished it. It is possible, Sera, that some of them escaped. Perhaps they found a home here in Kingfountain, where no one knew the true nature of the order and the dark role it played in our history. There is more that I cannot say, but it's possible this may shed light on Lady Corinne's actions as well. I don't know for certain. I will be careful and cautious and wary about whom I trust with this information you've shared with me. I encourage you to do the same. If Corinne was willing to murder someone to keep a secret, she would have no qualms about doing so again."

"I agree," Sera said. "Is this something I can share with Cettie? We both knew poor Mr. Skrelling at school, and he was always quite fond of her."

Fitzroy frowned at the request. "His death isn't a secret. But Lady Corinne's involvement should be." He was silent for a long moment, and his features tightened as he gave it further consideration. "I don't want Cettie to get involved in this. At least not yet. I have some suspicions I'd like to confirm first."

Sera nodded. "It will pain me to keep it from her, but I'll respect your wishes, of course." She was normally so open with Cettie, yet she'd learned how to keep silent when necessary. That thought put her in mind of Lady Corinne, the woman who'd taught her that lesson. "I've observed Lady Corinne very closely for the last three years. She is subtle and incredibly cunning. I had always assumed it was because she wanted to secure her position and influence. Before what happened to poor Mr. Skrelling, I thought her motives rather petty but at least mostly harmless. One thing I noticed about her is that she reveals nothing about herself and always draws information out of others. She brokers power like an advocate does in contracts. Who was she before she married Lord Lawton?"

Fitzroy pursed his lips, lost in thought for a moment. "Goodness, you're going to tax my memory. She and her sister were from the Pared family. I believe Corinne was the younger of the two but the first to get married. She was much younger than her husband, though I am not one who can cast stones about *that*, since Lady Maren is significantly younger than I am. Corinne was determined to secure her position back then, even at the expense of others. My wife suffered for it."

Sera heard the story with growing contempt. "I've seen how she treats other women, Lord Fitzroy. She can be very cruel."

"Our world can be very cruel," Fitzroy said with a sigh. "But do we not all have a duty to make the world as we wish it to be?"

Sera smiled and patted his arm. "Indeed we do, sir. Indeed we do."

That afternoon, the delegation from Lockhaven assembled in a large sitting room decorated with intricate murals. Huge silver chafing dishes were loaded with an assortment of treats and delights, and a small group of musicians played softly in one corner. Most of the men appeared bored and resentful, and little wonder—Sera had not used any of them during her negotiations. Colonel Worthington was speaking in low tones to Lord Fitzroy, however, and seemed less sullen than he had the last time she'd seen him.

While they waited for the royal family to arrive, Becka approached Sera with a small plate full of berries and offered them to her with a smile and a curtsy. The young girl had been relieved to learn they had Lord Fitzroy's support. Sera wasn't hungry, even for the delicious berries from Ploemeur, but she accepted the plate and, remembering their playfulness in Ploemeur, was sorely tempted to toss one of them at Trevon when he finally arrived. Moments later, she set it down and started pacing. Would the terms she'd proposed be accepted by Trevon's parents? Would they countermand him in the end? She wished she could have been invisible, watching the proceedings.

"Will they never come?" Colonel Worthington muttered in an excessively loud voice.

As if his rude comment had summoned them, a butler arrived at the door soon afterward and announced the arrival of the royal family. The musicians stopped playing, and everyone who wasn't already standing rose and bowed in greeting. Sera wrung her hands behind her back. The king came in with a measured look that revealed nothing. The queen seemed cross and held her head in a haughty manner, but neither was unusual for her. Finally, Sera watched Trevon enter the room with his brothers and sisters. He searched the crowd until he saw her.

Sera stared at his face, hoping for some sign from him that his efforts had not been wasted. He gave her a neutral look, which sent a shock of disappointment through her, but then he winked at her.

"Welcome, one and all," the king said graciously. He looked as if he'd swallowed something sour. "You will be departing soon for the mirror gate and returning to your own world. We hope our efforts at hospitality have been acceptable."

A few murmurs of assent were accompanied by a smattering of applause.

The king waited until it was quiet again. Sera noticed that General Montpensier and some of his commanders had also arrived in their colorful dress uniforms. The general's face was not pleased. Indeed, he looked especially agitated.

"The queen and I gave the crown prince the right to negotiate the terms of an armistice. Some thought this unwise," he added, glancing at the general. "But we learn from our mistakes as well as our best efforts. If the word of a monarch cannot be trusted, then he does not deserve to be one. Therefore, Prince Trevon will announce the terms of the armistice, which you will carry back to the privy council. We will not barter with you. We will not haggle over terms. If the privy council does not honor in good faith the negotiations made by Miss Fitzempress, then all is null and void." The king raised his finger almost accusingly. "Mark these words, ambassadors. The fate of our worlds hangs in the balance."

The king then gestured for Trevon to speak.

Trevon nodded to his father. "You do me great honor, Father. I have tried, to the best of my ability, to faithfully discharge the duty you put on me. Princess Fitzempress and I would both see this conflict end. More can be gained by our cooperation than by our conflict. We propose a sharing of knowledge between our worlds. We will send scholars to you, and you will do the same. The amount and frequency of these exchanges will be decided by a joint council. As a sign of good faith, the emperor's privy council must elect Lord Brant Fitzroy as the new prime minister, not because of his military successes but because of his interests in the fields of study we care about. He holds secrets we wish to learn."

Sera couldn't help but smile when she saw the startled looks on the faces of the members of the delegation. Colonel Worthington looked very surprised. Lord Welles would lose his place. The machine was being rattled.

"We propose that this armistice last for the span of two years," Trevon continued in a straightforward way. "Any disputes will be resolved by Princess Sera and myself. She will agree to spend three months of every year here in Kingfountain." This was a surprise to Sera, and she gazed at him in shock but listened as he continued, "and I will spend three months of each year in your world. We will better learn each other's customs and beliefs in the hope of securing an even more lasting peace between us."

Although Sera was surprised by the proposal, she didn't object to it. It was fair, and it would require both of them to leave their homeland for an equal amount of time. It provided an opportunity for them to personally nurture the new peace . . . and it would also give them more time to get to know one another.

"What say you, Miss Fitzempress?" Trevon asked, gazing at her with a wry smile. "Are these not the terms we discussed?"

She walked up to him and made an elegant curtsy. "They are indeed, Prince Trevon. This is excellent news."

The occupants in the room began to applaud. The dignitaries were clearly surprised, but now that the news had settled in, she was grateful to see most of them also looked relieved. Sera caught sight of Lord Fitzroy talking to Becka in a gentle, kindly way. But her attention was soon fully encompassed by the prince.

Sera felt her cheeks flush from the way he was looking at her. He bowed his head to her formally.

"I don't know about you," she murmured under her breath, "but I wish someone would drop a tray right now and cause a commotion."

"I could arrange that," he said, smiling.

"How did your parents take it?" she asked as the noise in the room became louder and louder.

"It was a bitter pill to swallow," Trevon replied. "My father doesn't believe the empire will accept the terms. No government wants to be told what to do or who to accept as a leader. He thinks it will not be ratified."

"Then that's my job to see to it," Sera said boldly.

"If anyone can, it would be you."

He looked like he had more to say, but his two sisters rushed up just then. They hugged Sera and enthused about how excited they were that she'd soon return to Kingfountain. The brothers' reactions were more muted.

A feeling of warmth spread in Sera's heart. A new day was coming. She would not be sent back to Pavenham Sky after this. She imagined the privy council would give her an allowance that would allow her to fund her own household. Such independence would enable her to keep Becka close. And to start seeing Cettie again.

Prince Trevon was distracted by one of his brothers for a moment, and Sera heard a voice pitched low for only her ears to hear.

"Well played, Princess," said General Montpensier. She turned and saw him facing away from her so that it wouldn't look like they were talking. "But just remember. A lot can happen in two years."

"I'm sorry if you're disappointed," Sera said, but she wasn't sorry at all.

"Don't worry about me, Your Highness," he said. "You should be worried about yourself. There's a saying here in Kingfountain." He turned his head slightly so that their eyes met. The look he gave her was dangerous. "The walls have ears."

I sent a poisoner to her room so I could learn information from her that she would not be willing to openly divulge. There are certain powders, you see, that can make anyone talk without retaining any memory of having done so. But she fled to the throne room at a moment of critical importance.

But the Espion on duty later witnessed her conversation with Fitzroy. They spoke too quietly to eavesdrop, but thankfully all Espion are trained in lip reading. Our most precious asset in Lockhaven has been compromised. A spy who has ascended to heights unimaginable.

Well, I could not predict this would happen. But there is no such thing as accident. It is fate misnamed.

—Leon Montpensier, Duke of La Marche

CETTIE

CHAPTER THIRTY-ONE

PARLIAMENT SQUARE

Cettie gazed at Admiral Peckton as he frowned at her. The report showed a calming in the weather, which meant it would be easier for Kingfountain to launch another invasion. It was her regular meeting, and she'd anticipated Lord Welles's attendance. He was watching her shrewdly.

"This is grim news, young lady," Admiral Peckton chuffed. "It makes us even more vulnerable by sea than we were before. The fortnight of the negotiations is nearly over. If it failed, a new attack could begin in days."

"I don't make the weather, Admiral," Cettie replied. "I just tell you what is going to happen."

"That is true. Well, the funds will be transferred," Peckton said. "As you see, we did not haggle as fiercely as we've heretofore done. It is, after all, the first time we've met since Admiral Fitzroy . . . *ahem* . . . was lost."

"That was very considerate of you, but I expected no such accommodation."

"All business, are you? And so young. Very well. Your payment terms have been accepted, and the contract will be provided." He gazed at the chart again, studying the various symbols she had drawn showing the storm glasses' weather predictions for the various regions. "That is all."

Cettie nodded and rolled up the map. She glanced at Lord Welles. "May I have a word with you, Prime Minister?"

His eyes widened, and he leaned forward. "Is there news?"

"There is, sir," she answered.

"Why don't we go to my private study, then?" he replied, rising.

"I don't think that's necessary," Cettie answered. She had discussed her vision with Lady Maren, and they'd decided it would be best to give Lord Welles the least possible amount of time to react to it. "It will happen today."

The prime minister's face blanched. "Today?"

"What is this?" Admiral Peckton asked.

"Lord Welles and I have an understanding," Cettie said. "There is some news he was expecting. It comes today."

"And?" Welles asked, growing more impatient.

"There will be an armistice," Cettie said, gazing at him. "Sera will bring the treaty today."

Peckton looked confused. "How do you know this, young lady?"

"Silence, Peckton," Welles snapped. "Anything else?"

Cettie slid the rolled-up map into the leather tube before handing it over. "Just one more thing. Your time as prime minister has ended."

In her vision, Cettie had seen Sera addressing a large crowd assembled at Parliament Square in the City. Her vision had informed her of what the speech would entail and where it would be delivered, so she and her family were some of the first to assemble when the announcement came that an armistice had been signed and Miss Seraphin Fitzempress would be addressing the people . . . not from Lockhaven but from Parliament Square.

Their tempest was docked at a hotel, which was suddenly overcrowded with people anxious to participate in the momentous event. The open square could fit perhaps thirty thousand people, but there were people leaning from windows and gathered on rooftops. The crowd brought back memories of the stifling streets of the Fells, but this crowd had a thrilling energy. The Fitzroy family had taken a position that would yield a good view.

As Cettie gazed over the sea of faces, she imagined someone making a painting of the event someday. This was the kind of momentous occasion that would be remembered for centuries.

"How did Lord Welles handle his disappointment?" Lady Maren asked over the tumult.

Anna took her hand and squeezed it. Raj Sarin kept his gaze on the crowd nearby, always vigilant for signs of danger.

"I didn't tell him *who* is going to replace him," Cettie answered with a smile. "But he wasn't pleased."

The old parliament building had been standing for at least two centuries, but it was the hulking underbelly of Lockhaven that caught her eye. This was her first trip to the City, so she'd never seen the underside of the great island in the sky. The peaks of the mountains supporting Lockhaven loomed above them, upside-down. There were no zephyrs rising to and fro from the City at the moment, and several huge hurricanes had lowered to form a defensive posture. The government had probably forbidden flight until the speech was over. As Cettie gazed up at the shadowy crags, she spied a tempest descending and realized it was time for the summit to begin.

A cheer swelled in the square as the people gathered there witnessed the descent of the sky ship. Soon the excited screams became deafening, and Cettie and Anna both covered their ears. Even the vendors who sold their buns and beverages to the people gathered in the square had stopped trying to earn a few coins and joined in the enthusiasm.

The tempest lowered right near where they stood. A podium covered in drapes had been erected on the outer steps of the parliament building. The Fitzroys were close enough to see the curtains fluttering. The tempest lowered to the area before the podium, and Cettie thrilled when she recognized her friend stepping down the gangway.

"It's Father!" Anna gasped, clutching Cettie's arm again. Indeed, she was right, and the sight of him filled Cettie with such relief she felt a tear prick her eye. No longer dressed in his regimentals, he wore his normal attire of jacket, waistcoat, and breeches. Lady Maren hugged both girls.

The cheering grew even louder as both Sera and Fitzroy ascended to the top of the platform. Then, almost at once, the crowd fell silent.

Cettie felt a prickle of gooseflesh go up her arms. She could sense the activation of Leerings throughout the huge square. The Leerings would amplify the speakers' voices, allowing even people far away at their manors to hear the words. She felt the power of the Leerings radiating down from Lockhaven as well.

Fitzroy stood at the podium first. When he spoke, his voice came from every side, echoing from the thousands of Leerings all united in one purpose.

"Thank you for gathering on this momentous occasion," he said. "My name is Brant Fitzroy, and I greet you today as your new prime minister."

A roar of approval rippled through the air, and Cettie felt the ground shuddering. She clapped with all her might. Fitzroy waited for the crowd to quiet again before continuing.

"We fought a terrible battle off the coast of Hautland recently, and it was reported that I was lost at sea. I was rescued by our enemies and taken as a prisoner of war. I would have remained in bondage were it not for the negotiations of Miss Fitzempress, who led the embassy to the court of Kingfountain. She has persuaded the court at Kingfountain to cease all hostilities. Now I would like you to hear from her directly. She is a brave young woman who has been much maligned. But as you grow to know her, as I have, you will see she is a capable and valiant defender of the empire."

The cheers began again as Fitzroy stepped aside. Cettie was close enough that she had a perfect view of Sera. Her friend was still shorter than her, but she had grown and matured and had a look of wisdom and experience. She wore a splendid gray gown that contributed to her regal air, and she emanated a poise and self-confidence that was endearing. When the crowd's cheers finally subsided again, Cettie waited anxiously to hear Sera's voice. This moment was so unusual. Royalty never spoke directly to the masses, certainly not in person. News was always brought down from above and revealed in the gazettes. This announcement was happening below first. It was a remarkable change, a sign of things to come.

"I am so grateful for the opportunity to speak to you today," Sera said, her voice trembling at first. No doubt she was nervous. "Thank you, Prime Minister, for your wisdom and willingness to serve my father and the people of our great empire. Your compassion and integrity do you credit. You have always cared for the lives of those born without the privileges of rank. You will be an excellent leader and an example to us all.

"I come to you all today to declare that we have agreed to terms with the court of Kingfountain to suspend the war between our empires. I do this with the knowledge that there are parties, on both sides of the mirror gate, who will not find this welcome news. Some have profited from the conflict. Some have risen to power because of it. Some have even speculated great sums on what I will say today. For shame."

Sera took a deep breath. "Many of our brave young men have died because of distrust and fear. I was sent to Kingfountain as a bribe, to marry their prince and make peace through a marriage alliance. I was willing to do this if it would stop more of you from losing sons, brothers, and friends. The greatest victims of war are the families who lose the most. However, Prince Trevon and I have struck up a different deal. Instead of a marriage alliance, we will start to trade secrets and knowledge we have each acquired. I have been to Kingfountain. Their people do not live in poverty like we do. There is much we can learn from them, and them from us. I have agreed to live in their world for three months out of each year. And their prince has agreed to live among us for the same amount of time. We will learn from each other, and we will teach each other to be friends. There is room for both of us to prosper without the other side suffering."

Her words stirred another round of applause and cheering. Cettie imagined that Sera's father wasn't pleased by her remarks thus far. She was speaking to the common people and didn't attempt to pretend otherwise.

After the noise subsided again, Sera continued. "I would also like to announce that now that I am of age, I will be forming my own household. The privy council has granted me an allowance, and I have chosen to live here, in the City, among you."

Cettie had known she would say that. She had heard the speech already in her vision. Had there been any doubt as to Sera's popularity, the explosion of cheering and noise would have shredded it instantly. Suddenly the crowd was moving, rushing against the barrier of dragoons in an involuntary spasm of wonderment. The soldiers struggled to keep the press back. People wanted to get closer to Sera, to touch her, to claim her as their own.

Fitzroy escorted her off the podium and back to the tempest before the crowd started to riot. Had Sera even told the privy council her plans? Probably not. Certainly she would not have told them about her plan to live in the City.

Cettie beamed at her friend's triumph. The world was about to change forever.

The role of prime minister came with its own manor, supplied by the government. The upheaval was so sudden that there wasn't even time to neatly pack. When Cettie and her family arrived at the new manor, all was in commotion as servants bundled the belongings of Lord Welles into trunks and carried them away. The manor staff greeted them warmly.

Anna gazed up at the vaulted ceilings, looking anxious about the change of environment. It was far grander than Fog Willows, but Fitzroy would be the only one to keep a permanent residence there. The rest of the family would travel back and forth between this mansion and Fog Willows. Lady Maren clutched both girls to her as the butler escorted them to the study, where they found Fitzroy, Lord Welles, and Sera.

As soon as they were introduced, Lord Welles's eyes narrowed on Cettie for a moment, but he quickly cleared his countenance, ever the consummate politician.

"Ah, your family has arrived," Lord Welles said. "We can discuss matters further on the morrow if you wish, Prime Minister. I am, as always, at your disposal. If you'd like any recommendations for the new Minister of War, I will be happy to offer a few suggestions."

Fitzroy smiled blandly. "I'm rather familiar with all your cronies. We'll talk tomorrow. I'll send for you."

Lord Welles bowed and left them, keeping his poise until the end.

Sera rushed forward and hugged Cettie fiercely.

"My dearest, dearest, dearest friend!" Sera said, squeezing Cettie. "Did you get the letter I sent you before I left? Please say that you did!"

"I did," Cettie answered. "I was so grateful for it. You haven't gotten mine, I know. They've all been returned. But I saved them for you anyway and brought them with me."

Sera beamed with delight. "I will read each one as a treasure. That odious Lady Corinne must have kept them from me. She'll pay for that."

Cettie observed the tearful reunion going on between Fitzroy and his wife and daughter, and all felt right with the world again.

"Look at you," Sera said, pulling back and admiring Cettie. "You are very striking. I would try to persuade our new prime minister to let you go, but I'm afraid he'll need you even more now. But at least now you can come and visit me. And there will be no one barring the gate."

"I look forward to it. So much has happened since we were parted."

"You don't know the half of it," Sera said, shaking her head. She gave Fitzroy a discreet look but didn't offer more.

"Did the privy council know what you were going to say about living in the City?" Cettie asked.

Sera grinned. "Of course not! Well, Lord Fitzroy knew because I told him. I just asked for an allowance, and the one they gave me would have been perfectly adequate for leasing any number of luxurious properties in Lockhaven. But instead, I am going to lease a home in the City and save the rest so I can begin funding things I care about. I need to stay nearby to continue the negotiations with Kingfountain." Sera looked over at Fitzroy and beamed. "I think someone else wishes to greet you as much as I did!"

Cettie felt her heart fill with warmth as Fitzroy stepped up and pulled her into a hug. It felt so good to have him back again. To know without a doubt that he lived.

She looked up, wiping tears from her eyes.

He had tears in his eyes too. "I can't thank you enough, Cettie," he whispered huskily.

"For what?" she asked, confused. She was so proud of him. He had finally achieved the status that he deserved. And knowing him, it wouldn't make him proud or ambitious.

He gestured for Lady Maren and Anna to join the embrace. With his thumb, he wiped a tear trailing down Cettie's cheek. "It was your vision that kept me from drowning," he said. "When my ship went down, I had to swim beyond the point of exhaustion. I kept going under, and it felt like I was going to die. But I remembered what you had said, that you'd seen me in Kingfountain with Sera. I believed in it and kept going, even when I ran out of strength. I know I fell unconscious. When I awoke, I was holding a piece of timber. I don't know how it happened. But I didn't give up, because I trusted your vision. You saved me, Cettie. Thank you."

CHAPTER THIRTY-TWO

Fog of Peace

Cettie had always wanted to share Fog Willows with Sera, and that dream was finally a reality. Since Sera was no longer under the control of her parents—and could come and go as she pleased—Fitzroy had offered her the opportunity to stay at Fog Willows as long as she needed while she selected a home in the City. The process would take some time since the ministries would need to be able to protect the residence.

The two girls walked arm in arm through the gardens, talking about everything in their hearts. Cettie had already given Sera a tour of the interior of the manor, and Sera's little maid was unpacking their belongings, preparing for an extended stay. Cettie rather liked the young girl and her serious eyes.

"It is so peaceful here," Sera sighed. "It may not be as posh as Pavenham Sky, but I feel like I can finally breathe again." Turning to look at Cettie, she added, "you were so sweet to have written all those letters, Cettie. Each one is so precious because it came from you. It would have made the confinement so much easier to bear."

"How did you manage to stay unbroken?" Cettie asked in wonderment. "You have changed so much, but the essence of who you were is still there."

"'It begins with a thought,'" Sera said with a grin, bumping into Cettie deliberately. "I made the best of a difficult time. But I hoped for something better. I fixed on that hope and on my determination to claw my way out of prison."

They neared the gazebo and increased their pace until they reached it. After walking through the sizable grounds, they were ready for a rest.

"I do wish I could persuade you to join my household," Sera said.

"Would you want to leave this place?" Cettie asked with a smile.

"No. But you must come and visit me."

"I shall, and often."

Sera gazed out at the beautiful afternoon sky. "In Lockhaven there are always sky ships fluttering about like so many butterflies. So busy. Fitzroy will grow to hate it, I'm afraid. But how we need him." Her expression became graver. She cocked her head to one side. "Can I ask my old advocate Mr. Durrant to come see me here? I don't want to impose."

"Mr. Durrant? Of course. I didn't know the two of you were still connected."

"We haven't been in touch. Not since my disgrace. He was cast out of Lockhaven and humiliated. But he was always a very capable advisor. A shrewd man. I need people like him more than ever. I plan to ask him to find me a decent house and keeper in the City. I don't need my parents' funds to pay for him anymore. I finally have my own resources. At *last*."

They sat together in comfortable silence for a moment, looking out at the gardens, thinking through all the abrupt changes that had shaken their lives.

"I divined from your letter," Cettie said, breaking the silence, "that you saw Mr. Skrelling before his death?"

"I did," Sera answered. "He came to Pavenham Sky on a zephyr and without an appointment. There was a storm when he left, and they say his pilot lost control of the zephyr." She looked away, suddenly unable to meet Cettie's eyes. For a moment Cettie got the impression there was something Sera was conflicted about, something she wasn't saying, but then her friend shook her head and added, "I'm the one who discovered his body on the beach."

"How awful," Cettie said with a groan. No wonder Sera seemed so out of sorts. "It's strange timing too, because I also learned he went to Billerbeck Abbey. He may have stolen something from there. Something that is needed now."

Sera wrinkled her nose. "He did like to skulk around for secrets, at least at Muirwood, but I can't imagine him stealing. That's strange. Well, if he did, then I'm sure it will be found."

"It's all very odd and disturbing."

"Things were much simpler back at school, weren't they? I've told you everything about Prince Trevon," Sera said, giving her a look that meant she was about to pry. "I haven't heard you mention the name of a certain young doctor. Or have your feelings changed? Is there someone else?"

"My feelings?" Cettie said, beginning to squirm inside. "I don't even know where to start."

Sera didn't push, but she was looking at Cettie with such a tender smile that the words started rushing out.

"I'm tormented actually," Cettie admitted. "I still love him. He is exactly the sort of man I wish to marry. But Anna loves him too. She always has. And I love her and don't want to hurt her. Adam has written to us both since the war started, but he's shared things with me that he hasn't told the rest of the family. He gave me a book to keep for him—a book which I've gone and lost," she added with a tone of despair. "And then there are our new neighbors."

"The Patchetts," Sera said, nodding.

Cettie bit her lip. "Joanna's brother is a dragoon. He's had his share of troubles and challenges, but he seems to be correcting them. He has helped our family so much recently. I hardly recognize Stephen anymore. You saw him at Father's new manor—hasn't he changed?"

"Very much so," Sera agreed. "Less self-centered. More agreeable. Phinia hasn't changed at all, though."

Cettie laughed, enjoying Sera's candor. "Well, we shouldn't always expect miracles."

Sera studied Cettie's face closely. "And how do you feel about Mr. Patchett?"

"I admire him," Cettie said, looking down. "He's pleasant to talk to. He doesn't care a fig about all of society's fastidious rules. He's brave, and while he can be sharp, he is also kindhearted. When his father died, he could not inherit the fortune directly because of some of his problems. His sister can't inherit either since she didn't pass the Maston Test. Their steward, Mr. Batewinch, is a decent man who holds the authority in trust."

Sera reached out and stroked Cettie's arm. "I see your struggle, and I don't envy it. Mr. Patchett no doubt admires you for your strength and knows you'd be a good match for him. Anna probably wants you to marry him, which would remove you as competition for Adam Creigh. And you have just enough guilt to be the perfect martyr."

That last part surprised Cettie. "What do you mean?"

Sera took Cettie's hands and patted them. "You've always loved Adam. Even if you've only just admitted it to yourself. And I've always believed he returns your feelings. He's served the Ministry of War well, even though he had a different plan for his future. And he may yet be called upon to sacrifice more for the empire."

"In what way?"

"I shouldn't be the one to say it. I'd rather leave the two of you to talk directly. But suffice it to say that he is still a man of honor and integrity. And he doesn't love Anna. He loves *you*."

Cettie tried to suppress the shivering in her heart. "He's never told me."

"Of course not; he's too honorable! He's been serving as a doctor in the thick of a war. No worthy man would declare himself under such circumstances. But that war is now over for a season, hopefully forever. Give him a chance. Then make your choice. Anna is beautiful and sweet and a rich heiress . . . and the unwed daughter of the prime minister. She will not struggle finding a husband."

The comforting words soothed the disquiet in Cettie's soul. She reached out and hugged her friend, grateful for this moment and the many more that would come. Everything felt more balanced now that Sera was back in her life. A preternatural awareness struck her mind as she sensed the approach of a zephyr and recognized it as the Patchetts' sky ship.

"You flinched. What is it?" Sera asked.

"We have more guests," Cettie said with a sad smile. "The Patchetts are coming."

"Isn't their ball tomorrow night?"

"Yes. I know they've been very busy in preparation."

"Well, let's go see this young beau together," Sera said, hooking arms with her as they rose from the bench.

The guests had already been admitted into the house by the time they reached the docking yard. They headed to the sitting room, where Rand and Joanna were visiting with the family, all except for Father, who was still in Lockhaven. The mood in the room was cheerful and pleasant, and Lady Maren looked particularly pleased.

When Cettie and Sera entered, Rand immediately took notice. He was always attentive, but a strange look surfaced on his face when he saw Sera. His eyes crinkled with wariness—was that the emotion? It was difficult to make out. He broke away from his sister and approached the two of them.

"If Phinia tells us one more thing about the new gown she bought for the ball," he said in an undertone, "I might jump off Fog Willows and trust my chances." He grinned at them both. "It's a pleasure to meet you, Miss Fitzempress."

"Thank you, Mr. Patchett."

"Please call me Rand."

Joanna was quick to join them. She greeted Sera with a familiar smile and gave her a small hug. "We've not seen each other in a while, but I do hope we gave you enough time to settle in. We came because of you, Sera." Joanna then hugged Cettie next.

"*You* came because of Sera," Rand pointed out. "I came because of Cettie."

"Don't be troublesome, Rand. You've been unfailingly polite lately. You mustn't ruin it before the ball."

"Very well, then I will ruin it *at* the ball," he teased.

Joanna sighed and gave him a stern look. "Behave yourself, Brother. Now, Sera, we just learned you will be staying at Fog Willows for a time. The family was already invited to our ball at Gimmerton Sough. I wanted to personally invite you to join the festivities. We heard about what you did at Parliament Square. Everyone is going to be demanding your company. But we'd be overjoyed if you'd do us the honor of coming tomorrow night."

"I will consider it, of course," Sera replied with a nod. "Thank you for the invitation."

"You are still coming?" Rand asked Cettie, putting his hand on her elbow.

His touch sent a jolt of feeling up her arm, and his abrupt familiarity startled her.

"Yes," Cettie answered, feeling a little uncomfortable, especially after her conversation with Sera.

The rest of the afternoon would be spent in idle chatter, for which Cettie had little time or inclination, so when Sera said she would go to her room and rest awhile, Cettie took advantage of the opportunity to withdraw as well and walk her there.

"Are you going to the ball, then?" Cettie asked. "I was surprised you didn't accept right away."

Sera looked back down the hall, not gazing at anything in particular. She had a wary look on her face. "I don't know." She looked at Cettie next, her eyes serious. "It concerns me that they're friends with Lady Corinne and her set. I'm still thinking about it."

"Why should that matter?" Cettie asked, confused.

Sera's look was enigmatic. "It does."

The servants had transformed Gimmerton Sough in the weeks preceding the Patchetts' ball. To Cettie it felt as if time had wound itself backward. As she entered the ballroom, festive and lavishly decorated, she could hear the distinctive loud guffaws of Sir Jordan Harding—now *Vice Admiral* Harding—and it felt like things were back to the way they once were. It must have been strange for the Hardings to return to their old home in such a manner, but Joanna was true to her word and had invited them regardless.

Sera had also chosen to come, her decision made to be close to her friend and to be on hand if needed. Several of the young women she'd met at Pavenham Sky were in attendance, but their attitudes toward her seemed to have transformed overnight. Cettie was surprised when so many came up and reintroduced themselves, speaking courteously and praising Sera's hair and the cut of her gown.

After they left, Sera looked at Cettie with raised eyebrows. "See what I mean? I don't trust any of them."

Servants carried trays arrayed with small silver goblets, and lovely music streamed in from the Leerings.

One of the servants came and stood before Cettie and didn't leave when she waved him away.

"Don't tell me you don't recognize me," Joses said with a sigh.

"Joses!" Cettie said with a gasp. "I didn't. I'm so sorry."

"We all look the same in these matching coats," he said, wagging his elbows. "Who's your friend?"

"This is the emperor's daughter," Cettie said, gesturing to Sera, who smiled sweetly.

Joses chuckled as if it were a joke, but he stopped himself before he could make a quip. "Oh! Miss Fitzempress! I-I'm . . . I'm so sorry. I didn't recognize you."

"That happens a lot," Sera said with a look of ease. "I'm very short."

Cettie smiled at the look on Joses's flummoxed face. He bowed to her friend, as if trying to remember the appropriate protocol when dealing with royalty, and then backed away. But he came around behind Cettie and pitched his voice low. "*Ahem.* He's going to propose tonight. He's been practicing the speech all afternoon."

Cettie looked at Joses in horror, but he clearly thought he'd delivered good news because he simply winked and walked away with his tray. Instead, feelings of worry and painful anticipation flooded her heart.

Sera's brow furrowed. "You've gone pale. Are you feeling well?"

The news shook Cettie to her core. She had not expected something like this to happen so soon. Was this why Rand had come to visit them the day before?

"I might need to sit down."

"Come this way."

As they walked toward some stuffed chairs, the sound of "Sky Ship's Cook" started up, causing some clapping and cheering from among the guests. Of course Rand had chosen it. It was the first song they had danced together.

Before they could make it to their seats, Stephen and Rand intercepted them. Stephen was wearing one of his finest suits. He'd gone to great lengths in his grooming and attire. Rand looked freshly shaved, his smile sincere and tender . . . but he swallowed with nervousness.

"Miss Fitzempress," Stephen said with a bow and flourish. "If you'd be so kind to dance with me?"

Rand didn't make an offer. He merely held out his hand. A bare hand.

Both girls accepted—what else could they do?—and the ballroom around them filled with dancers and partners. Cettie had never been invited to dance in the first set before.

"I love your dress," Rand said with a slight bow as they began to perform the familiar steps. "So much less formal than all of the others. It suits you."

"Thank you," she said shyly.

Her nerves felt like bolting horses. But as she danced with him, his touch brought her an overwhelming sensation of peacefulness, of being comfortable in his presence. She wasn't trying to coax her feelings into something more, but it was happening anyway. There was something in the music . . . it felt like the Mysteries were at work in the room, and not just in the form of the music.

When the song finished, he bowed to her, and then he and Stephen left, which surprised her. At the previous ball, he had danced with her multiple times. As the next song began, she saw that he had invited Lady Maren for a dance, and her heart melted even more.

"He's very charming," Sera said at her side. "There's something familiar about him. I can't make it out, though."

The song after that, he danced with Anna. She noticed they were talking as they danced, and Anna's smile looked like a beam of sunshine. Suddenly a bolt of hot jealousy stabbed into Cettie's heart. It was so overpowering and raw that she had to turn away to stop looking at them. Her emotions were all off-kilter, barely recognizable as her own.

"You're distressed," Sera said. "What's wrong?"

"I . . . I don't know."

"Do you need some air?"

"No, we haven't been here that long. I'm just not feeling myself." She looked back at the dancers, saw Rand and Anna together again, and *again* was struck by a feeling of jealousy that made her want to hurt her sister.

"Come sit down," Sera offered, taking her by the arm and bringing her to some stuffed chairs. They seated themselves, and Sera looked at her in concern. "What's wrong, Cettie?"

Tears pricked Cettie's eyes. "Look at me. I'm crying."

"I know. It's not like you."

"When Joses came by, he whispered to me that Rand was going to . . . to propose tonight."

Sera nodded sagely. "Ah."

"And I'm not used to this," Cettie said, looking around. "Being *invited.* Being *wanted.* At Muirwood I was treated like a pariah. But it's all changing."

Sera squeezed her hand. "You've been persecuted for so long you can't imagine anything else. But you are an amazing woman, Cettie. And it's a sign of Mr. Patchett's good judgment that he wants you. You'd make him a better man." She shook her head slowly. "But even if he asks, you do not have to say yes. You have a choice. Choose with your heart."

Cettie despaired. "It will hurt either way."

Sera smiled sadly. "Probably."

They sat together until the song ended and another song began. "Genny's Market." It was Mother and Father's favorite, and she'd always been fond of it too. It was so romantic and slow and included a part where you gazed into the eyes of your partner.

And there was Rand, marching up to fetch her from the sidelines. He looked vulnerable, as if he felt unsure of himself. His fists were clenched in nervousness. But he arrived, bowed, and extended his hand to her again.

"Will you dance with me again?"

Cettie both wanted to and didn't want to. The feelings of jealousy were gone. He was asking *her* now. He wanted to be with her, not Anna.

"Yes," she answered huskily.

She took his proffered hand, and they walked back to the line and took their positions. She knew this number so well it was easy to surrender to the music.

"I'm sorry I'm so quiet," he muttered. "There has been a lot on my mind this evening."

I know, she wanted to say. "Really?"

They began the steps, flowing and gliding in rhythm together.

"Yes. It's quite distracting. Is Sera enjoying herself?"

Cettie wondered at his familiar use of her name, but then again, he was never one for formalities.

"Yes. The decorations are so lovely. Thank you for inviting the Hardings."

"Sir Jordan is a good man. Well, most military men *are*," he added with a grin.

It came time for them to turn, and they crossed their arms over their heads in preparation. His other hand dropped to her hip, his arm against her bosom, as the movement required. She wore no bone bodice and could feel how close they were together, could feel his warm breath on her cheek. She looked into his eyes and saw his yearning for her. It was an almost pleading look, one that showed he was afraid of what he was going to ask her but was daring enough to face that fear. Her connection to him grew deeper as she peered into his vulnerable eyes.

They broke the pose and retreated around in a circle to begin the routine a second time. Her heart was hammering wildly in her chest. The feelings in her heart were love. She recognized them, and they frightened her. She'd always been so careful about her feelings. But in the past weeks she had spent so much time with Rand, had experienced his weaknesses and helped him overcome them. Could a heart change so quickly? She was deeply confused, and when they began the second set, hands bridging above their heads, bodies pressed closely together for a second time, she felt the room begin to spin.

"Can I talk to you?" he whispered.

She was afraid to. Afraid of what she might say, of what she might do. Every resolution she'd formed before coming here tonight was turning to water. She might say yes. She might not be able to help herself.

She stared into his eyes again, his pleading, tormented eyes. She wanted to kiss him, to comfort him, to make his hurts go away.

In all her life, she had never felt so vulnerable. Or so hopeful. Or so confused.

This isn't you.

"No," she answered, breaking their grip. She pushed away from him and walked away, tears of mortification burning her eyes. There were gasps of shock as she fled the floor, interrupting a dance—shaming herself in the eyes of everyone present. There would be gossip for certain. There might even be shunning.

Is this what Lady Maren had felt like all those years before?

She was half-blind from tears as she rushed toward the tempest. She had to leave, to escape the night's disaster.

She wouldn't be able to face him again.

As she walked, she felt another strange feeling. An almost gleeful cackle in her mind.

CHAPTER THIRTY-THREE

CHOLERA MORBUS

Cettie was not alone when she left Gimmerton Sough. Both Sera and Lady Maren deserted the ball in order to comfort her and keep her company. Cettie had paced the deck of the tempest, anxious to be away, while Mother made arrangements with Phinia and Stephen to bring Anna home. Then all three returned to Fog Willows together.

As they departed, the feelings of mortification began to subside, but she still felt terrible about what had happened. What had Rand done to deserve such treatment from her? He would be upset by her actions—he deserved to be. She'd wounded his pride for no rightful cause, all because Joses hadn't been able to keep the news to himself. Cettie covered her face in her hands and then felt Sera's comforting palm smooth her back before her arms enfolded Cettie.

Looking up at her mother and her friend, Cettie felt calm reassurance. She was still loved by those who mattered most to her.

"I can't believe I did that," Cettie whispered.

Lady Maren sat on the other side of her. "The heart is a strange and fickle thing. There's no need to talk about what happened tonight. Tomorrow will be soon enough."

When they returned to Fog Willows, Cettie wanted to go to sleep, but she waited until the other Fitzroy siblings had returned, needing to know they were all safely in their beds. She did not listen to their conversations. She didn't trust herself to at that moment. It was well after midnight when the estate finally went dark and quiet. All was silent and still. All except her heart.

Deep into the night, Cettie sat in her chamber, gazing out at the star-swept sky.

The next day at a late breakfast, Cettie learned there would be no repercussions from the previous night. Though there had been some nasty gossip about Cettie after her abrupt departure, Joanna had refused to accept such talk. She'd quickly scolded all the naysayers, reminding them that Cettie of Fog Willows was one of her greatest friends. If the lady of the manor had no harsh words for Cettie, then no one else would be permitted. That was such a relief to her.

The household business needed to be conducted, a welcome distraction, and Cettie spent most of the day answering correspondence and giving directions. The Control Leering alerted her to the arrival of a zephyr, and when she gazed through its eyes, she recognized Mr. Durrant as the visitor. She closed the books and went to the front door. Kinross had arrived ahead of her, and she asked him to inform Sera, who was in her guest room, of the man's arrival.

"Yes, ma'am," Kinross said with a bow and went to perform her request.

Cettie opened the door as Mr. Durrant reached the threshold. He'd changed in the last few years. His hair was grayer and sparser, but he had the same look of cunning in his eyes, the glint of always being privy to a secret.

"Ah, Miss Cettie," he said, doffing his hat and bowing to her. "The keeper of Fog Willows. It's a pleasure to see you again, my dear."

"Hello again, Mr. Durrant. Welcome."

"Am I welcome?" he asked with a self-deprecating grin. "Miss Fitzempress sent for me?"

"She did. Please, come in."

Mr. Durrant nodded and kept his broad hat tucked in the crook of his arm. He gazed around the entryway. "I've not been to a sky manor in quite some time. If I start to wheeze, it is because the air is thinner up here, and I'm not used to it."

Cettie smiled as they walked to the sitting room, which she knew was already empty. The others were outside strolling the grounds. When they reached it, Cettie directed Mr. Durrant to a chair, but he replied, "No, I'll stand, thank you. As you can imagine, I have some trepidations about this interview. I may not be staying long." He fingered a small decorative globe on the nearby mantel, then lifted it up with one hand to gaze at it before putting it back down. "Do you know why she summoned me?"

"I do," Cettie answered. "But it's not my place to say."

"And your expression is guarded, as befits a true friend." He pursed his lips in resignation.

Mr. Kinross came through the open door and announced Sera.

Mr. Durrant set down his hat and clasped his hands behind his back. A sheen of nervous sweat had risen on his brow.

Sera entered and brightened when she saw him. "Mr. Durrant! I didn't get a return letter from you. You came right away."

"You summoned me, ma'am," he replied, bowing. "Of course I came."

She gave him a warm, welcoming smile and then hurried to shake his hand. "Well met, sir. I have need of your services in many matters. I was hoping to engage you as my advocate."

"Y-your advocate?" he said in astonishment.

"That is what you are, Mr. Durrant, is it not? You still run your firm on Kayson Street in the City?"

"W-well, I do. Of course I do. I do not have many clients at the present. Mostly small jobs. Criminal work has been the majority since your father banished me from Lockhaven."

"I'm certain that can be remedied," Sera said with a wave of her hand. "There's a new prime minister now. He and I see things along the same lines."

Mr. Durrant smiled and rubbed his eyebrow. "I imagine that you do. Forgive me, but I'm still rather astonished to be here. That you are even speaking to me."

Sera looked at him in surprise. "Why should you be surprised, Mr. Durrant?"

"The last words we spoke together were not . . . kind. At least on my part. I've been fairly confident, up until now, that you hated me."

"Oh, Mr. Durrant," Sera said, shaking her head. "I was the one who blundered, not you. You have always given me sincere and excellent advice. And I need that, now that I don't live with either of my parents. I have an allowance, and—"

"I know," he said, interrupting. His voice was thickening. "I was there at Parliament Square, my dear. I heard your little speech." He shook his head. "I was thunderstruck by it. The people . . . you don't understand . . . the people were ready to seize you and proclaim you as empress then and there."

Sera smiled at his words and shrugged. "Well, they don't have the authority to do that. Only the privy council does. And with your help, Mr. Durrant, I would like to change their minds about me."

He seemed impressed by her answer. Cettie saw his mind begin to crank as the reality of his new situation settled into place. "I have some ideas on that front, Miss Sera."

She beamed. "I knew you would. But first, I need you to find me a suitable place to live in the City. Not too grand. But very visible."

"I'd be honored to arrange that for you," he answered. "And anything else you may require."

"Oh, I am *counting* on that, Mr. Durrant. You and I are not finished yet."

Another storm was beginning to brew in the west. Cettie consulted the readings again to be sure and saw that all the storm glasses situated in Pry-Ree indicated the change. The severity of the storm would depend on how drastically the quicksilver dropped, but the overnight readings alone had been remarkable. She unrolled one of her maps so she could study the tiny area where the readings had come from. She'd never been to Pry-Ree before, but it put her in mind of Rand. It had been two days since she'd snubbed him at the ball. He still hadn't come to visit yet, to see what was wrong. She would not be able to put off seeing him forever. But she wasn't looking forward to it.

The sound of approaching steps on the rugs in the hallway told her someone was coming, but Fitzroy was in Lockhaven, and few people ever ventured into his study. She waited for the steps to walk past, but they did not. She felt someone standing in the open doorway and turned, expecting to see Mr. Kinross or one of his underlings. She was not prepared to find Adam Creigh standing there.

There had been no warning. She hadn't even noticed an incoming sky ship, other than the one that had brought Mr. Durrant.

"Adam!" she gasped, rising from the chair. He still wore a uniform, and the faded stains she saw on it were likely blood. His face looked weary, but it still emanated his usual self-confidence and courtesy. And he was smiling at her.

He glanced at the implements in the room, the books and glass vials and various instruments Fitzroy had gathered over the years.

"May I come in?" he asked.

"Of course you may," she answered. "Did you just arrive? I'm so surprised to see you!"

"Old Kinross was surprised you didn't beat him to the door," Adam said with a smile. "I came on the zephyr post. I wondered if I might stay a few days before I must leave."

"Of course you can," she said.

He entered the room and examined a series of stoppered vials. "I've always loved the smell of this place," he murmured. "It brings back many memories."

She could hardly speak through the thrill of seeing him. There were no questions left for her. Though she couldn't deny she'd felt something for Rand, it would never be comparable to this. Her admiration for Adam was not changeable. Neither time nor weather would alter it—she could not say the same about the feelings Rand had stirred. She rose from the chair but leaned back against it, feeling some measure of comfort in its bulk. On his previous visit, he'd come bearing news of Fitzroy's death. That had all changed, and he'd learned that she was the true harbinger and not her guardian.

"And w-what brings you here?" she stammered, feeling flushed. "You said you were leaving?"

He nodded, picking up one of the vials, examining it, and then putting it back. "I'm heading to the court of Kingfountain."

Her wildly beating heart suddenly shoved itself into her throat. "Truly?" she asked, feeling a sense of dread.

"I'm afraid so," he answered. There was a resigned look on his face, another dashed hope. "It's not with the Ministry of War. I'm back in my own place again, the Ministry of Wind. I plan to change out of this uniform promptly. Lord Fitzroy told me that some of our soldiers brought the cholera morbus there. They have no idea how to treat such an epidemic. I'll be joining some other doctors to study it and hopefully find a cure."

It made sense that he'd been chosen. He'd always hoped to study it. So why wasn't he more excited?

"You don't seem very pleased by the new assignment?" Cettie offered.

He shook his head. "I had hoped that by the end of the war, I would be able to open a practice in the Fells. I've learned so much about being a doctor these last three years. Why not put it to good use? But duty calls . . . again." He gave her a dejected look. "And Kingfountain is so far away. It's on another world."

Cettie nodded, feeling her hopes begin to fade. "I'm sorry for your sake. But I know you will do well wherever you are."

He stepped closer to her. "Am I too late, Cettie?"

She wrinkled her brow. "What do you mean?"

"My prospects are still pretty bleak, but I've been promised a substantial reward for willingly going to Kingfountain. I . . . I don't want to lose you. I'm afraid I already have, that I came too late."

The bleakness in her heart began to stir with more excited emotions. "Lose me? Am I lost, Adam?"

A look of hope kindled in his eyes. "You aren't engaged? You aren't promised to that young man from Gimmerton Sough?"

Cettie flinched and bit her lip, unable to believe this was happening. "No, I am not, Adam. I've made no promises to anyone."

He looked as if a great burden had been lifted from his shoulders. His eyes closed in relief and he sighed, the sound loud and prolonged. "I'm not too late," he whispered.

Cettie felt tingles shoot down to her feet. She stood by the edge of the desk still, only then realizing she was gripping the edge of it hard enough to hurt.

"What is your intention, Mr. Creigh?" she asked, feeling the giddiness swell inside her.

"I don't know how I should ask it of you, but it seems I can hardly help myself," he said, shaking his head. "I want to marry you. I want to spend the rest of my life with you. I cannot bring you with me, but I could not leave without telling you how much I love and care for you. I did not declare myself before the war because we were both still so young. We were practically children. But I've thought about you every day since I left. And you kept writing back to me and sharing the details no one else thought to share. Your letters meant so much to me. I've saved each one. If you could wait for me, for this assignment to end, you will make me the happiest of men ever to live." He clenched his fist. "I know it's not fair to ask this of you, to implore you to wait again, but I had to ask, even if the answer is no."

"Yes," Cettie answered, feeling as if her heart would burst.

"What?" he asked in confusion.

"Yes, Adam. Yes to all of it. However long it takes. No matter what happens. I will be faithful to you. I want to be your wife."

His smile was like a ray of sunlight bursting from a cloud. He'd obviously come because he'd heard rumors about her and Rand. But he'd come nonetheless—and he'd bared his heart to her. While she knew Anna would be heartbroken and disappointed, she could not let that stop her from choosing the man she'd always loved. Not when he loved her too.

He stood sheepishly, suddenly uncertain. And then he came forward and embraced her, pulling her into a hug that was possessive and tender. She held him back, claiming him in return. It felt so good to finally be held by him. Perhaps it lasted minutes. Maybe it was only moments. She only knew that she had never felt so sure about something or so safe.

He finally pulled back slightly, but only enough to look into her face.

"So we are engaged? Just to be clear?"

"Yes!" Cettie said with a laugh. And then she rested her cheek against his chest and felt the tears start to fall. She couldn't believe her good fortune. Or that the Knowing had granted her heart's dearest wish. Had she done anything to deserve this happiness?

They had to tell the others. But for that moment, she wasn't ready for everyone else to know. Especially knowing the pain it would cause Anna. It was a secret just between the two of them. And it was the most delicious secret in all the world.

EPILOGUE

PAVENHAM SKY

The zephyr glided down to the landing yard well after sunset. The moon hadn't risen yet, but Rand could see the glimmering ocean beneath the majestic manor and its multilevel gardens. He was in no mood for finery or walks on flower-strung paths. He wanted to punch something. He felt like a miserable failure.

The yard was empty. There were no other visitors at Pavenham Sky, which was quite unusual. He dropped the rope ladder over the edge and watched it swiftly unravel down the side of the craft. Then he climbed overboard but quickly got bored of it and jumped, plummeting the rest of the distance. His face burned and itched, and he frowned in annoyance as he walked down the path, not pausing to look back at the zephyr. He passed beneath the arches into the courtyard. Master Sewell approached him before he even reached the door.

Sewell was an interesting chap. How much did he really know?

"Lady Corinne is expecting you," Sewell said.

"She summoned me, didn't she?" Rand said petulantly.

The steward frowned at the rude comment, but Rand was in no mood to be civil. His failure at the ball still chafed.

"Are we feeling a bit irascible this evening?" Sewell said.

"What does that word even mean?" Rand shot back. "Can we get this over with, man?"

Sewell frowned and shrugged. "I have a feeling your interview will be quite short. She had some questions for you about the ball that was just held."

"Well, she should have come herself, then," Rand answered. "Lead on. I don't like standing in doorways."

"Follow me," Sewell said, exhaling dramatically.

Rand had the urge to punch him in the kidneys just to see how he reacted to it. But he resisted the petty nonsense and followed Sewell down a dark corridor to Lady Corinne's private study, the one that opened to the gardens on the other side of the grounds. Sewell rapped on the door and then opened it.

"Randall Patchett, ma'am," he announced.

"Thank you, Sewell. Please let him in."

Her voice was always so calm and collected. She was the epitome of ice. Nothing enraged her. Well, maybe he had finally managed to break her reserve.

Sewell shut the door, and Rand stood there, arms folded, trying to find her in the dark room. There were no Leerings in this room. None at all.

"Where are you?" he called out.

"You can't see me because I don't want you to see me," she answered.

Then suddenly she was standing right in front of him. The web of illusion had fallen away. How close had she been standing? For how long? It unnerved him that she could creep up on a person like a spider.

"Let's just get this over with. I failed," he said with a disgusted sigh. "I did the best I could, but her mind is the strongest I've ever tried to bend. I almost had her at the ball . . . but she ran away."

Lady Corinne didn't react. "I know, Will. I was there."

"Of course you were," he said, chuckling. He hated when she used his *real* name. He wanted to forget that one forever. To never be reminded of it. "Then why summon me tonight? You saw it all happen in person. What else do you need to know?"

"How do you think it went?" she asked, turning away from him. Had she asked him the question? No, she was speaking to someone else.

There, in the shadows. The kishion.

"It will take something big, but she'll fall," he said in his dark voice. "She'll turn. I have no doubt."

"No, of course you don't," Corinne said with a throb of satisfaction. "Even killing *you* didn't rattle her too hard. But mothers are different, aren't they?" She turned back to Will Russell and gave him a penetrating look. "You've done what you were supposed to do. Now focus your attention on wooing the sister. Make it seem like a fit of jealousy. It will add to the guilt she already feels. I will finish what you started with my daughter. She'll be one of us soon."

"You think you can do it?" he quipped back, then realized he shouldn't have questioned her.

Her eyes narrowed dangerously. "I'm very good at what I do," she answered coldly. "Last night, Richard Fitzempress pleaded with me to marry him. 'Too soon,' I whispered. 'The rumors would spread vicious lies about us.' He's groveling now. Desperate. The divorce writs have been drafted for weeks. He hates his daughter even more, if that's possible. She's stronger than she's ever been. But we're very close to learning the secret, the one they've hidden so well. Richard knows it. Once it is ours, Lockhaven will come crashing down." Her smile was devious. "We have the orb now. We'll blind their harbinger. This peace of theirs won't last very long."

"What about Montpensier?" Will demanded.

She smiled. "He's nothing but a pawn in all this. He'll get the velvet bench he wants. And rue the day"—the look in her eyes terrified him—"when all of it comes crashing down."

The scars on Will's face started to itch again.

AUTHOR'S NOTE

Inspiration comes to authors from many sources. Sometimes it's a view of a majestic scene. Sometimes it's standing by a waterfall in Yosemite. Sometimes it's a line written by another author in another book.

The opening scene of this book was inspired by such a thing. I'm an unabashed fan of period dramas, and one of my favorites is *Bleak House* by Charles Dickens. I've seen the miniseries many times, but the line that set my wheels turning is in the book. In the story, a young lawyer named Guppy confronts Lady Dedlock about her past. Dickens does an aside at that moment that jumped out to me: "Young man of the name of Guppy! There have been times, when ladies lived in strongholds and had unscrupulous attendants within call, when that poor life of yours would not have been worth a minute's purchase, with those beautiful eyes looking at you as they look at this moment."

That passage leaped into my mind. It's true that Lady Dedlock wouldn't have killed Guppy. But in another world, such a character as Guppy would not be safe. There would be henchmen nearby who would solve the problem with murder. That was the moment when I invented Lady Corinne's character and determined she would be the villain of the story. Sometimes characters just leap fully formed into my mind and are ready for their close-up. As we proceed in this five-part tale, get ready for some more surprises.

Until we meet again in Book 4 of the Harbinger Series.

ACKNOWLEDGMENTS

As I write these words, my oldest is submitting papers to become a full-time missionary for our church. As this book is released, and you are now reading them, she'll have been gone for many months. I'd like to acknowledge my daughter, Isabelle, for her insights, her enthusiasm, and her energy for this series. She has been a great sounding board for ideas. I'd also like to recognize my sister, Emily, who, like my daughter, has the fortitude to suffer through three chapters a week in their rawest form.

And to Angela, my awesome developmental editor, congratulations on the new baby! This book was edited in thirds, which we'd never done during our long partnership, and it worked its magic. Getting her feedback before it was completed was especially helpful in the creative process. I'd also like to thank my entire team at 47North for hosting us in Seattle in the spring. I had a personal dream come true, appearing on a panel with my mentor and inspiration, Terry Brooks, as we discussed with Robin Hobb and Tamora Pierce how to keep it PG in the age of *Game of Thrones*.

Last but not least, to my able group of first readers who keep it real: Shannon, Robin, Gina, Travis, Sunil, and Dan. Thank you!

ABOUT THE AUTHOR

Photo © 2016 Mica Sloan

Jeff Wheeler is the *Wall Street Journal* bestselling author of the Kingfountain Series, as well as the Muirwood and Mirrowen novels. He took an early retirement from his career at Intel in 2014 to write full-time. He is a husband, father of five, and devout member of his church. He lives in the Rocky Mountains and is the founder of *Deep Magic: The E-zine of Clean Fantasy and Science Fiction*. Find out more about Deep Magic at www.deepmagic.co, and visit Jeff's many worlds at jeff-wheeler.com.